I0461029

DUAL

by **Tipton Froy**

Copyright 2013 Published by Tipton Froy

ISBN: 978-0-9575588-4-7

2nd Edition *(2020)*

Cover Illustration by Samuel Lucas Fraser

This book is licensed for your personal enjoyment only. This book may not be re-sold or given away to other people. If you would like to share this book with another person, please purchase an additional copy for each recipient. Thank you for respecting the hard work of this author.

This is a work of fiction. Characters and incidents are products of the author's imagination and used fictitiously. Any resemblance to actual events or persons (living or dead) is entirely coincidental.

Main Cover image (Black Hole): This work is licensed under the Creative Commons Attribution-ShareAlike 3.0 Unported License. To view a copy of this license, visit http://creativecommons.org/licenses/by-sa/3.0/ or send a letter to Creative Commons, 444 Castro Street, Suite 900, Mountain View, California, 94041, USA.

Contents

ACKNOWLEDGEMENTS

My gratitude goes to my mother, Mary, for proofing versions of the book and advising on the use of language. My thanks also to my friends – including Paul, George, Ieva, Alice, and Mark - for their comments on initial chapters. Outpourings to Sam Fraser for his creative flair in the making of the cover.

Finally, thanks to my lovely family for their enduring love and support.

PREFACE

Dual is a thriller about the entangled lives of those with the power to change our future. There is a basic premise underlying the story; an inevitable and radical breakthrough in our understanding of the inter-relationship between quantum mechanics and the physical limitations of the human species will offer mankind the opportunity of avoiding our otherwise certain extinction from the Universe.

Note: There are various musical references – a playlist if you like – embedded in the story. I chose these songs because they somehow seem to encapsulate particular moments, and it might enrich the experience to listen to them as they come up.

CHAPTER 1: BEGINNING WITH AN END

"My fellow Americans…"

Ellis Garfield's mouth is so dry that his words sound hollow and distant. The Vice President is addressing the nation from deep within the White House. His ashen complexion blends with the tone of his bland grey suit, allowing his black tie and white shirt to take centre stage. The image conjures a previous era.

Behind him is a large screen playing a video loop of the American flag, gently flapping in the wind. Superimposed on the bottom right of screen is a small, oblong digital clock displaying year, month, day, hour, minute and second. In the hurry to get on air, a glass of water placed in front of a picture of Abraham Lincoln diffracts the light and distorts the former President's face. Garfield reaches slowly for the glass and takes a sip of water, an action that reveals the real Lincoln, dignified and strong. A slight gargling sound escapes before he returns the glass so that it once again warps, much like a trick mirror might do.

The camera gently zooms in so that Garfield's face begins to fill the screen. He is perfectly still, yet his features begin to appear exaggerated; deep set eyes and pinpoint pupils balance on a sharp nose above pursed lips and a heavy jawline, all carrying the burden of communicating terrible news.

"It is with deep regret and a great sense of sorrow that I can now confirm that our President, John Montgomery, was pronounced dead today at 1:17 p.m. local time."

In the heavy pause that follows, a nation struggles for breath. The U.S. flag silently flutters in the wind. As the seconds pass, Garfield seems to be struggling for words even though they are right in front of him on the auto-cue.

As the camera reaches yet further in, taking millions closer to Garfield's features, something strange takes place. The image flickers negative, reversing black and white, before switching back. The negative after-image makes his skin tone appear noticeably darker, so that the rather sharp features sink back into more rounded contours. The lighting in the studio seems to follow this occlusion of form, to the point where it is not obvious any more who we are looking at. The increasingly heavy sway of the American flag and the sluggish slowing of the second hand on the clock darken the moment before both come to rest. The only perceptible movement remaining is the dilation of Garfield's pupils as all light is gradually trapped within and they turn menacingly black. The eerie silence tensions the air like a vice, building an uneasy and expectant anxiety. The pressure becomes unbearably intense.

An agonizing howl slices through the turgid atmosphere. A hybrid distorted face metamorphoses on screen, as if the dead President is somehow screaming out from within Ellis Garfield. The effect is deeply haunting; like watching someone trapped and terrified behind a grotesque translucent mask. The warped, anguished contortions of the person behind it chill to the bone.

And suddenly the deformation of features is shattered by a violent camera-judder. Or Garfield - one of the two. Montgomery's features become unstuck and are shaken off Garfield's face with the sudden movement. The net effect of this bizarre sequence is like a reset button – Garfield returns to default mode. The clock has started to tick again, as if time begins to matter once more.

The TV on the wall of the small canteen on the second floor of the Heisenberg building buzzes and flickers for a second. There are few people around, most having gone home on hearing the earlier reports about the President's demise. After a long session, Catherine Jumeau and fellow students Malcolm Baines and Wendy Xiu seem mesmerized by the TV screen, having just emerged from Lab Seven, secure and isolated underneath the building.

"Did you..." Catherine begins, hesitantly.

Jumeau gets to her feet and looks innocently upward like a child watching a magic trick; but she is turning pale, a knot taking hold of her stomach and adrenalin causing her pulse to race out of control. She stares at the screen, waiting for a further revelation, but it doesn't come. Faintness takes over and suddenly she feels unsteady. Sensing this, Baines, a burly young man, lets go of Xiu's hand and quickly moves over to make sure his fellow student doesn't collapse.

"Hey, Catherine..." is all he can get out before Wendy interrupts.

"Get a damp cloth Mal," she says to Baines. He goes over to the canteen counter to get a cloth while Xiu helps Jumeau back to her seat.

Garfield is talking in the background. His face fills the entire area of the large screen on the wall.

"Uh, right now we are unsure how the President died, but I can tell you that the relevant authorities are initiating an immediate and thorough investigation. Know also that these agencies will be relentless in their search for the truth behind the events that took place earlier today." Garfield takes a moment to gather himself. "As you will be aware, I worked closely with the President. I am deeply shocked and saddened to have lost both a committed colleague and long-time friend. Our nation's deepest sympathies and condolences go to his wife Sylvia and his three children. We mourn your loss, and pray for you today."

The initial shaky tone in Garfield's voice has gone, and as the camera pans back some color flows into the Vice President's cheeks as he adopts an altogether more relaxed demeanor. It looks like he has things back under control.

"Now, in circumstances like these it falls to me to take charge of matters of governance, and I'd like to take this opportunity to commit myself publicly to following in the footsteps of John Montgomery and carrying his good work and many progressive initiatives forward with vigor. I believe that this will be his legacy.....his lasting memory.....his history." He pauses slightly, but this time he re-engages quickly. "I will be making announcements regarding the Presidency, ongoing investigations and our collective future over the coming hours, days and weeks. For now, though, I would make a plea for calm and reflection among all of us. We have lost Presidents in the past, it's true. Yet it is always difficult to lose someone you love. We hope and pray for John, that he has gone to a place where he can rest in peace. God bless America."

Garfield's departing words are accompanied by the hint of a smile, meant to reassure but somehow unconvincing.

Xiu and Jumeau are fixated on the screen. The image of Garfield is replaced by the local anchor man for Boston News. The sudden change in image seems to bring reality back to earth with a bang.

Malcolm Baines returns with a damp cloth and gives it to his girlfriend Xiu who gently wipes Jumeau's forehead.

"Jeez," says Baines, "I hate this fuckin' country sometimes."

"Mal," Xiu says sharply to her boyfriend, as she gives him a look to indicate that this isn't helpful. Xiu is petite and just five foot three inches in height but is in charge, and trying to help her friend. She turns to Jumeau. "It's frightening alright. I can't believe what I just heard."

Catherine studies her friend's face, seeing how the neon light from the canteen illuminates one half, leaving the other dark. What just happened has had a profound effect on her, but she is struggling to work out what is going on.

"You didn't see it?" Catherine asks Wendy anxiously.

"Yeh, I saw alright!" Xiu says.

"You did?"

"Yeh, it's just awful honey, the whole country will be in shock," says Xiu.

"I mean his face – did you see how his face changed?" She looks at her friend desperately for acknowledgement.

"Uh, what do you mean, honey, 'his face'? I'm not with you..."

Jumeau's shoulders drop and she turns her head away, partially hiding her face from her friend. She realises that neither Xiu nor Baines witnessed what she did.

"Catherine?" Xiu prompts.

Jumeau turns back and smiles uncertainly at her friend. "Oh, it's OK Wendy, I must have just been seeing things..." There is a long pause, during which Xiu takes in just how shaken her friend is.

"Jeez, something really has spooked you, girl...let's get you home."

"You going to be alright?" asks Baines.

Catherine Jumeau nods unconvincingly.

The three walk gingerly out of the canteen and approach the lift in silence. Normally they would take the stairs. Outside, Malcolm makes for the Union building while the two girls head off campus and take the bus over to Allston.

——-

Wendy and Catherine share an apartment in the upper West side of Boston, where living is modest and a bit more bohemian. The pair decided to share a flat after being in Dudley House at the University as undergraduates. Now postgraduates, there is less need to live on campus, but it still makes sense to be where you can live frugally. A patchwork fabric of newsagents, mini-markets, arts and craft specialists, cafés, bars and restaurants predominate here. The shop fronts are brightly painted, if only to distract from the somewhat makeshift nature of the ageing wooden shutters and awnings that reach out to passers-by on the street.

It is April, and winter has given in to the ambition of spring. It's a fine day, and late in the afternoon a gentle breeze makes the awnings and coffee shop parasols flutter lazily. Routine here seems unaffected by faraway events, or at least that is how it seems.

As the pair get off the bus, things don't seem that different to when they left for University this morning, yet in reality they are. Both girls strain to see in the bright sunlight. Catherine reaches for her sunglasses. The mood on the street seems muted, the busker singing a haunting version of 'Blue Mind' by Alexi Murdoch. It is a beautiful rendition, conveying a sense of wonderment and discovery. Usually, Catherine Jumeau would enjoy the atmosphere, lingering in little shops or sitting in the sun with a coffee when the weather was good, just so that she could take it in. Not this time though.

They climb the stairs to the flat above the record store where they live, and breathe a sigh of relief to be home.

"I'll put the kettle on," says Xiu, and disappears into the small kitchen to make some of their favorite green tea. Catherine heads over to the sofa, only to squint as a beam of sunlight bounces off the mirror and hits her square in the eye.

"Damn it," she mutters, as she shifts to avoid the light. Her vision is impaired momentarily as her eyes come to terms with the temporary damage. Drawn to the mirror, she peers at her reflection, the blurry image of her face making her think back to Garfield. She shivers. She is transfixed for a moment.

"Mirror, Mirror," she whispers as things begin to become clear.

She would rarely wear makeup, and probably didn't need it, having a very healthy hue and a few freckles in the summer. She has striking features; soft yet strong. Her large eyes radiate openness and dignity, and depending on the light can appear green or turquoise. The brighter it gets the more likely they are to appear toward blue. High cheek bones, a fine nose, broad mouth and defined jawline complement these to create an overall effect of simple, classic beauty. Her last boyfriend once told her that she was like a perfect cross between Grace Kelly and Liv Tyler, but she never knew how to react to that, being somewhat embarrassed by compliments, and latterly just not believing a word he said.

She flops onto the sofa and puts her left hand up to shade her eyes from the light coming in through the window. She looks like she is saluting some higher authority.

Wendy returns with the tea. "Do you want to tell me about what happened earlier? It's OK if you don't – I'm just worried and don't know what I can do to help."

Xiu splits an apple in two and offers half to Jumeau, almost as an apology, a peace offering.

"Hmmmm...." Jumeau takes the half-apple. She tries to explain how she saw the Vice President's face on the TV. "I don't really know how to describe it. It's like...well, have you ever just been looking in the mirror or at a photograph of someone for a while and your eyes can't see the face any more?" She is getting a little more excited now. "You know, like, what happens sometimes is that all of a sudden the picture might just go dark and you see, uh, just forms or maybe weird movement because your eyes lose focus?"

She looks expectantly at Xiu, who is concentrating hard, and frowning.

Jumeau continues. "I mean, well...imagine if you look at a face in a picture for long enough, it can begin to change. Do you know what I am talking about?"

Xiu looks away and shifts in her seat, beginning to feel slightly worried that her friend is still emotionally distraught.

"Kind of, honey...I guess," she says.
"Come on, Wendy, you *must* know what I mean – like, remember as a kid seeing all sorts of shapes and movement when you lay there with your eyes open in the dark?" Jumeau remarks, beginning to sound a little desperate.
Xiu interjects, partly to stop a conversation that is not going in a good direction. "Look, Catherine, I know it's been a difficult day, and we are all tired, believe me, and I kind of know what you are talking about but I don't know what that's got to do with what Garfield was saying on the TV this afternoon – why did you max out like that?"

Catherine looks down at her hand which she realises she has clenched so hard that her knuckle is turning white. As she thinks back she begins to wonder if *anyone* else saw what she saw. It scares her, and for a second she can't find any words. Instead the sense of being alone in her vision manifests itself in the slightest appearance of tears in her eyes. Immediately she resists the urge to cry, and gathers herself.

"Wendy, you know me well enough to know that I am not going to make stuff up or get freaked by stupid things, right?"

Xiu nods her head in agreement, hanging on her friend's words. "Sure," she says.

"Well, I think I saw something today which could be important. Don't ask me why but when I looked at Garfield's face on that big screen it really changed, but in a very scary way. I felt fear deep in my bones and I just knew that something was wrong. I saw Montgomery's face come through Garfield's as if he were trying to come back or say something to us."

As the surprise takes hold on Xiu, the frown gives way to a wide-eyed stare. She is desperately trying to reconcile what her friend is saying with the fact that she herself saw nothing. "You're saying that you saw John Montgomery on the TV today?"

Jumeau is about to speak, but Xiu needs to explore. "Well, isn't that simply the thing that you just told me about, where your mind makes stuff up. I've heard about when you really feel the loss of someone or just want to see the old person there in front of you – like some of those stories about people whose long-term loved ones die and they see them the same night at the bottom of the bed – that sort of thing?" Xiu is trying to be helpful, but struggling to keep her scientist hat on.

"No, it's not that," Jumeau comes back. "That's what it was *like*, but this was different. If you and Mal didn't see anything when you were, like, looking *directly* at his face, then I don't know why I saw what I saw, but I *saw* it." Jumeau takes her friend's hand. "Oh Wendy, I know I can be a bit weird at times, but something has happened with Garfield and Montgomery and it's just not right. It felt to me like Garfield wasn't even there – like it was Montgomery trying to tell us something."

"Catherine, that can't be, unless you mean that Montgomery is, like, the undead or something...is that what you are saying, that you saw his ghost?"

"Oh, I don't know – I thought about that on the bus on the way back. Why would I go my whole life without seeing any ghosts to suddenly seeing a ghost? It doesn't make any sense. All I know is that Garfield just flipped into this other guy and then flipped back again, and it can't be a problem with the TV signal 'cos you and Mal never saw anything."

Xiu pauses for a second, and redeems her hand from Catherine. She takes a deep breath.

"Honey, I don't know what to say. But I do believe you, don't worry about that. It's just that I can't imagine what you saw or what it means. No-one else we spoke to this afternoon has mentioned anything like that, and there is nothing on the TV or radio about Garfield flipping out, so I guess it's maybe just a few sharp-eyed crew members like you that noticed anything."

"I guess," Catherine replies, now beginning to feel some relief that she has confided in her friend.

Wendy continues, "Now look, I'll give Mal a call just to check with him. He can ask around and we can get a handle on whether anyone else on campus is talking about this."

"OK, but don't mention me, Wendy. I don't want anyone coming on to me 'cos they think I've weirded out."

"Relax, honey. I'll be discreet. Me and Mal will shake some tails and get back to you with whatever we find out."

After tea and further mutual reassurances that the country will right itself again like it always does, Jumeau retreats to her room, opens the window and draws the curtains. At first she sprawls out on her bed, but after a short while she begins to curl up and wraps the duvet around her so that she is cocooned from the outside world. As her eyes grow accustomed to the dark under the covers, the image of Garfield's twisted features comes rushing back and she feels claustrophobic. Her head pops out of the covers and she gasps for air. There is no escape from this reality. She looks at the clock. It's only 6pm. The day isn't even over. She desperately wants the clock to go back, for this whole thing not to have happened, for her anxiety to subside, for her President to be in his office as usual.

It dawns on her that this day has changed her forever, but in what way she cannot fathom. Eventually she drifts into the comfort of her sleep, where she can dream about the way things used to be the last time she went to bed just a few hours earlier.

Around 9.30pm a noise outside wakes her – it's the sound of two young men, most likely students, arguing down below as they emerge from a nearby bar.

"Of course it was an inside job!" says one.

"Bullshit," says the other, "it's always the same with you types, always looking for a conspiracy. Well I bet you there isn't, and it turns out to be some crazy. You'll see."

"Fuck that. This whole thing smells worse than the end of a fish market. *No-one* believes the lone gunman story any more, not since Kennedy. And those security threads said that so far they can find no prints, no evidence, no CCTV, no nothing. I mean, come on!"

"How do you *know* that? You think you're in some sort of CSI replay here? I'm tellin' ya…"

The two men continue to remonstrate as they walk away, but not before Jumeau hears one of the men mention that Montgomery will be sorely missed.

This rang true with Catherine Jumeau. When Montgomery won the Presidential nomination for the Democrats a few years earlier, she had listened to his acceptance speech from start to finish without batting an eye lid. Oozing charm and obvious integrity, Montgomery was easy with every type he met, from press and rival politicians through to military servicemen and tough guys from rough neighborhoods. He commanded a respect rarely seen in the modern world of politics. As the second black President with parents of mixed faiths, Montgomery knew what it meant to be on the receiving end of stereotyping. Sidelined twice in his younger days when trying to run for Congress due to press 'leaks' of his affiliation to radical religious groups and dalliance with prostitutes and drugs, he had to battle hard to clear his name and prove his innocence. He had conducted his own defense in a case brought against him for illegal drug use and trafficking, having taught himself law as a younger man, and famously admitting to the judge that he had smoked marijuana when he was at college, not only inhaling the smoke but getting "as high as a kite" before feeling faint and spending an hour in the john with the door open as his college friends took photos of him with his trousers at his ankles. The judge, sensing Montgomery's humiliation and personal vow never to get involved in drugs and public life simultaneously, was convinced that the man could no more be a trafficker than himself, and so ruled in his favor.

To say that Montgomery was a breath of fresh air in American political life would be an understatement. Having campaigned against the folly of unsound investment of the nation's wealth in risky get-rich-quick schemes in burgeoning new markets in the far east, where economic competitors were being paid to create better businesses than at home, he championed investment in the US' own infrastructure. That meant that incentives to manufacturing and technology companies, and to scientific research were priority. His ruthless approach to health reform and improving welfare for the nation's underclasses had rung a clear and precise note across the land – that America is going to look after Americans first and foremost. In effect, he had pulled off a renaissance in core economic activity at home: oilfield production in Alaska and the midwest were being cut back; the nation's approach to transport was transforming to a much greener focus with smaller cars becoming a statement of allegiance to the flag; healthcare at the point of need was made a legal obligation on providers, with the cost of new drugs on the marketplace capped to avoid further imbalances in life chances for those unlucky enough to need costly medicines; and 'green research' was made a priority so that clean energy sources, new types of materials and a deeper understanding of the world around us emerged much more quickly than would otherwise be possible.

Of course, this approach didn't suit some. In particular, the military and financial sector elite struggled with the limitations brought to bear on investment and intervention in other countries' economic and political infrastructures. As wealth-generating strategies, these were tried and tested and many vested interests were hurt in the process of change to a new way of thinking about the future. Many saw the pre-occupation with internal infrastructure and Montgomery's 'Heart of America' initiative as denigrating value in overseas investments and necessary military interventions. Montgomery had effectively said to the world that America was not interested in being the arbiter of stability in world order, but rather that America would always be strong and capable of protecting itself and its way of life. One result of this was that some investment banks refused to offer terms for potential investors in major internal projects like the wind-farms along the Eastern seaboard and Gulf of Mexico.

Against this background, Montgomery had struck the young Jumeau as the kind of beacon of hope that North America needed at a time of global uncertainty. Coming from Montreal, she had experienced what it was like to travel across the border and into a different culture, albeit similar to her own. She always felt an outsider, never making the transition to living in the U.S. as fully as others. She would put this down to an engrained sense of being more of a European. Jumeau's father, Christophe, was an academic of French extraction and her mother, Mary, emigrated from Scotland immediately after qualifying as a nurse. Both parents now taught at the Université de Montréal, in Physics and Healthcare respectively.

In reality though, she knew it had been a permanent feature of her life; a sense of being somehow separated from the world around her. Friends knew how odd she could be, at times seeming to be somewhere else when in company; but they would put it down to the 'brilliant mind' syndrome where unbounded intelligence issues you a passport to the wispy, ethereal surroundings of Cookieville.

But her eccentricities were tempered by a gritty determination to make her own way in life and embrace Boston as her new home, at least for the duration of her PhD. Catherine, or sometimes 'Reen' after she babysat for a friend whose kid couldn't say her name properly, had her mind set on following in her father's footsteps as an eminent physicist. Christophe Jumeau originally studied the science behind black holes with some notable contemporaries, subsequently progressing to conduct research into the nature of reality, and modelling ways in which humans perceive physical dimensions.

Catherine Jumeau had passed all her High School exams with flying colors and, by the time she finished, various assessments around IQ and intelligence put her at genius level at the age of eighteen. Given the importance of her abilities to people around her, and in particular her father, who had encouraged her to get onto the academic ladder as early as she could, it all became too much. After all, she was a girl growing up like any other, or at least that's how she wanted it to be so desperately. Being bright came at a price; the cost was some of the simple and visceral pleasures in life, most of which had eluded her while studying in her bedroom or cramming for exams. So it was much against the advice of her father that she decided to take some time out to stay with relatives in France who ran a modest vineyard, working during the day and going with cousins into the local town of an evening.

She had really wanted to go around the world, without any constraints, but Mary Jumeau had convinced her that France was far enough from home and that there would be plenty to distract her there. So Catherine consented just so that she could get away. Her mother, relieved that her daughter wasn't going to a big city or some far-away remote island, knew that Catherine would be safer in a rustic setting with familiar people.

Mother and Father didn't know exactly what she got up to there during that time, but guessed that she would probably enjoy the local distractions and return within a few months. They were right on the first count at least. Catherine Jumeau not only added a few boy-notches to her belt but also spent weekends in various European cities, marvelling at the culture and architecture around her. Mary and Christophe Jumeau visited during two consecutive summers, managing on the second visit to persuade their beloved daughter that she owed it to herself to at least see how University life might suit her. And as it happened, a month before the Jumeaus arrived in Paris, Catherine had split from Marcel, a young student she had been seeing in Le Mans. Unbeknown to her parents, she had been staying with him at weekends and enjoying the nightlife there. But the couple had lasted only three months before he had become besotted with Catherine, making her feel claustrophobic and anxious. Things had become awkward, and it seemed the right thing to do to leave. By the time she returned to Canada, her father had already sorted a place for her on the Physics degree in Montreal. All she needed to do was turn up in October for classes, by which time she was aching to get out of her parents' house.

In many ways, Catherine's journey on the degree course was unremarkable. She coasted for most of the time, preferring to make friends and enjoy the social aspects of University life than to spend her time in the library, which came naturally after her time of discovery and independence in France. But she did like tutorials and workshop sessions, taking great pleasure in demonstrating her deep understanding of all aspects of the Universe and the way it is believed to work. It was in those tutorial sessions that she met Wendy Xiu. Wendy was feisty and knew her stuff. She had first got interested in astronomy as a little girl growing up in Saint-Simon, further toward the sea on the St. Lawrence river. The sky was amazing there, so clear and vast. As she shared a room with her brother, Lei, who had been given a good-quality telescope as a birthday present one year, it was only a matter of time before her fascination with the stars drew her to the lens. Lei was a couple of years older than Wendy and more interested in playing basketball or table-tennis than watching stars, so it became very easy for her to stare out into the night sky for hours on end once it got dark. For a while her schoolwork suffered as she became more and more tired in the mornings after stealing away from her bed night after night to look through the telescope. Eventually her father took it out of her room, and told Wendy that she could only have it back if she passed her major exams before the summer that year. Being determined, yet respectful of her father, she calculated that it was a fair trade if she could spend the summer researching her universe without constraints. She achieved distinctions in every exam that year except History. And that single exception was annoying to her. But there was no doubt that she was an incredibly bright student, and it was just a matter of course for her to go to university and find out more about space and the stars.

At first Jumeau and Xiu were very wary of each other, both being exceptionally gifted students and yet often at odds over some of the less understood and speculative aspects of the nature of black holes, reality and quantum mechanics. They loved it really – amidst most of the Physics students who were struggling with what it was all about, both young women saw the other as a route to gaining excellent passes in their exams and assessed work, and often deliberately started arguments and debates just for the sake of it in order to stimulate their minds and push some boundaries. They knew that it was intellectual jostling, and that they probably came across as a right pair of geek-divas to others around them, but to a large extent they didn't care as the alternative was to sit in lectures and tutorials being bored witless.

At home, Catherine would seek understanding from her dad. Christophe Jumeau loved these moments, and was very good with his daughter, letting her explore in her own way whatever topic was on her mind. Multi-dimensional space, the nature of essential elements in physics like quarks, event horizons, time-travel, super-positioning; whatever it was, Jumeau senior would patiently offer knowledge and opinion while beaming inside at his daughter's progress in learning and understanding. They became closer as a result of this, and the rebel energy in Catherine seemed to have found an outlet in a fascination with unanswered questions about the Universe we inhabit. It was like looking in the mirror and seeing himself as a younger person.

When it came down to it, choosing Harvard wasn't really that difficult a choice after she passed her degree with first class honors. For that was where Professor Walter Melrose headed up the Physics department and would become her PhD supervisor. He led the world in research into quantum mechanics and what is known as 'super-positioning' of the smallest known units of the Universe – essential particles. Jumeau used to tell her non-physicist friends that this was like when you play 'Deal or No Deal' and there are just two boxes left with cards inside them that say '$1' or '$250,000'. Each box could have either value until we actually open one of the boxes. So, when we don't look at the contents, and don't interfere with either box, either box can be $1 or $250,000. Until we look inside it. It's only when we look in one of the boxes that the value is revealed. At parties, this story would usually only get to the second sentence before someone forgot what the game was, or objected on the grounds that the monetary value is absolute for each box, but nevertheless Jumeau liked it, as it made a funny kind of sense to her.

Melrose was important to both the Jumeaus. To Catherine he represented the pinnacle of understanding in Physics and a centre of knowledge and insight that she just had to tap into. Although he was sometimes a difficult person, she put this down to his genius and frustration with anything bureaucratic or mundane. In fact, her place on the PhD programme only came about after several reminders to the professor that he had unopened mails from prospective students to which he hadn't responded. Many budding graduates wishing to conduct research would write to the professor with amazing personal statements and PhD proposals, but the programme allowed only three in any one year, as that is all that Melrose would commit to, such was his attention to his own research and elevated position within the University. Catherine was one of those, and Melrose knew she had talent. He had made efforts to steer Catherine's research in a direction that would feed into his own, although sometimes this led to disharmony and fallout. Despite this, and the history with her father Christophe, Melrose gave Catherine the impression that he cared about her, and she often felt his avuncular charm to be similar to her dad's, so in his absence Melrose probably took on a bit of a father figure role for her.

To Catherine's father, Melrose was the reason he despised Academia. Melrose and Jumeau had worked together as younger men on military research programmes centering around quantum physics. In particular both men shared a fascination for the nature of reality and how we perceive time and space within what is commonly known as 'space-time'. Some twenty-five years ago,

Jumeau had been working on the 'SPEC' project (Super-Positioning and Enhanced Communication), and deduced from experimentation that the instances of a particle that is simultaneously in two different states or positions (super-positioned), do not actually communicate between themselves *per se*, but rather receive and react to the same external information, as if from a third, originating and universally present information source. His findings suggested that it was as if all information was encoded into the very fabric of the Universe around us, and not dependent on the speed of light in order to travel from one part of spacetime to another.

Although Jumeau made this discovery as part of government-funded research, Melrose had been networking particularly well with the hierarchy of managers within the programme, and was given the job of the write up of the findings that Jumeau had brought to the team's attention. As with several other important published reports from SPEC, the subsequent paper listed Melrose as the chief researcher. Further downstream, Melrose's academic career blossomed on the back of this, and more than one eminent present-day physicist would be entitled to hold a grudge against him. Jumeau was, in the main, a sanguine and mature professional of undoubted integrity. Getting involved in public spats was not his style, and close colleagues knew that he had little respect for Melrose.

So it was unfortunate that the best place in the world to study Physics and all matters to do with the Universe and the nature of reality, was at Harvard under Melrose. He had never disclosed to his daughter the full nature of Melrose's treachery, nor did he feel it would be helpful to her. Christophe Jumeau lived with an ambivalent tension between, on the one hand his daughter conducting research at the most reputable and well-funded of all establishments, and on the other the possibility of her research being stolen or usurped by Melrose for his own greedy ambition. It was a terrible compromise for him. All he could do was drum it into Catherine that her intellectual prowess - her thinking and her insight and her conclusions - should be kept private at all times and only shared with Melrose when she had already registered with someone else any new revelations that might bring her success which is hers and hers alone. Relatively inexperienced in the business end of academia, Catherine paid little attention to this at first, putting it down to 'Dad's thing about intellectual property'. But as her knowledge and understanding in the field grew, deep down she understood the principle.

Besides her father, Professor Melrose and Olly, her ex-boyfriend, there aren't many significant men in Catherine's life. Yet at this time, on this day, in this year, she feels that she has lost someone special in Montgomery. Suddenly things come into focus, and she realises she hasn't yet spoken to anyone outside her two fellow PhD students. So Catherine reaches for her phone. There are five missed calls; one from her mother, two from her father, one from Olly her ex-boyfriend and one call that is from a withheld number. Bleary-eyed, she tells it to read her voicemail…

"Hey, it's me. Terrible news, huh? Can't really take it in. Anyway, just wondered if you were around, so call me when you get this." It is the voice of Olly Reikjard, her ex-boyfriend. She resents his over-familiarity at times, as his tone gives the impression to others that they are still together. Still a pair. But they have been apart for some months and Catherine has moved on, the distance giving her clarity of thinking and feeling about what they were like as a couple.

Olly was quite a domineering sort with old-school attitudes about men and women, and, when they were together, someone who always seemed to overshadow Catherine at social gatherings with his magnanimity and covetous displays. Initially she had felt flattered that this academic 'jock' had chosen her to pour his attentions on, and thought he was a genuine type of guy. But as time went on she began to realise that Olly Reikjard, wealthy young intellectual as he was, lacked any kind of emotional intelligence. Collecting trophies seemed to be his raison d'etre. Girls were good for display and organising things. His approach seemed to be entirely functional, and unbeknown to her at the time, the charming young man she met at the sorority bash drew on a very limited set of well-worked moves to attract the opposite gender. She had fallen for it, and taken the best part of a year to realise that he was a bit of an idiot. Worse, he had cheated on her without even worrying about her finding out.

After a heavy exhalation, she hits '3' – delete.

Next message is from her Mum, but rather than listen to any of that, she stops voicemail and calls home.

"Hi, sweetie, we've been so worried about you," Mary Jumeau blurts out before Catherine could even say Hello.

"Hi Mom - sorry, I meant to phone you earlier but I fell asleep and..."

"Your father is on his way down to see you, you know," she continues.

"Huh?" Catherine quizzes.

"Yes, we got a call from Wendy earlier to say that she was worried about you."

"Well, that's good of Wendy but I am fine, Mom, really....listen, I'll call him. He doesn't need to come all that way."

"You're too late, honey, he left a good while ago.

"OK, but it's really late and I don't have anywhere for him to sleep or..."

"It's OK, he said he'd stay at the Plaza. He'll probably just pop by and say Hello, then maybe you two could spend a bit of time together tomorrow. You know what he's like."

"Yeh, I do," Catherine reflects.

Mary Jumeau changes tack. "What a horrible mess with Montgomery. He was a good man. What are they saying down there?"

"Uh, to be honest I haven't heard much except what Garfield said earlier. Did you see that?" her daughter replies.

"Yes. I thought he was a bit like a rabbit in the headlights. He looked awful – God knows what he has gone through."

"I guess."

There is a pause for both women to think again about Montgomery.

"He'll be missed," Mary says softly.

"Yeh, I know – I really thought he was a decent man with some great qualities. I feel so sad that good people always seem to get hurt."

"Now, now. That isn't true. Bad people get hurt too. But I liked the man, in as much as I could tell what he was like. At least he didn't seem to be two-faced like some of the others."

Catherine Jumeau's face goes pale. "What?" she asks.

"I said Montgomery just seemed to be just a straightforward person."

"Yeh, he wasn't two-faced, was he?"

"Exactly," Mary Jumeau replies.

"Mom, did you notice anything funny this afternoon during the Vice President's address?"

"What do you mean, honey?"

Catherine pauses slightly. She wants to test the water. "Well, I mean, what do you make of Garfield? Do you think he's two-faced?"

"Uh, well, I don't know. I don't really know much about him," her mother replies.

"Mom, did Garfield appear normal to you. Em, not 'normal' I mean, but did you notice anything about the way he looked or..." Catherine trails off to see if her mother has seen anything strange.

"Not really – like I said, he looked terrible. Really ashen and obviously stressed, but then I should imagine that's what happens when you get shoved into the spotlight like that and have to talk to millions of people live on air. Why are you asking, dear?"

"Oh, nothing. I thought he was acting a bit strange is all...it's probably just me."

"Catherine, listen, that man is probably some jumped-up administrator who doesn't know what's hit him. I wouldn't be at all surprised if he is acting strangely. I think anyone would in his position."

"Hhmm. Well, we'll see, I guess."

"Look, sweetie, your father will be there in a couple of hours. Just grab a warm drink and wait until he gets there. You can talk to him. Now, I must go, the dogs are barking again. That cat next door drives them mad! Take care, and I'll phone you tomorrow."

"OK, Mom, thanks." Catherine puts the phone down and walks over to the window, pulls the curtains back, and looks up at the sky. It's a clear night and the stars are resplendent. They mean more to her than most, and she starts to think of the way we are all made from the same stuff that stars are made of. One of them suddenly races across the sky.

——-

"Mommy?" a small voice asks. It's Lauren Garfield, the Garfield's seven year-old daughter. Her mother is concentrating on applying makeup and doesn't respond.

"Mommy, where did the President go?" Lauren and Julie Garfield are in one of the upstairs guest rooms at the White House getting ready for dinner. Lauren looks intently at her mother as she applies mascara carefully to her eyes.

"Did what, sweetie?" eventually her mother responds.

"Um, well, did President John have an accident today Mommy?"

Julie Garfield looks at her daughter's face in the mirror, noticing how wonderfully symmetrical it is, unchanged through the looking-glass. And then she looks at her own, very different, face; one that has seen enough of life to be somewhat off-centre and almost a different person in reflection. For a fleeting moment her heart sinks at her daughter's realisation, and the gravity of the situation comes flooding in.

"Why yes, sweetie, he did. And it's very sad, but Daddy is President now..."

"I saw the President inside Daddy on TV, Mommy," Lauren whispers.

There is a chill in the air as Julie Garfield's expression freezes in a confused frown. "Uh, you did?" she asks, nodding her head slightly as she reasons that her daughter is going through a difficult moment too; that young children are not immune to a desire to rationalize very traumatic events in their own ways. "Well, as far as I know, honey, it was just Daddy on the TV today," she offers by way of both an explanation and attempt to get off the subject. "Now, how does Mommy look? Are we ready to go down to dinner now?"

"I guess, Mommy..." Lauren trails off, sounding deflated.

Reacting to her daughter's obvious disappointment, Julie Garfield reaches out and exclaims "Oh, my baby, come here..." as she grabs her daughter and hugs her tightly. "Things will be OK, don't worry. President Montgomery was a great man, and I'm so sad he has gone too, but Daddy has a very important job to do now, and we must be strong for him. You know?"

Lauren Garfield turns and looks at her mother. She is open and vulnerable and unable to lie. "I think the President is still here, Mommy. I saw him with Daddy today."

Julie Garfield stares at her daughter, trying to reason what could be going on in her mind. Suddenly there is a knock on the door. It breaks the silence between mother and daughter, and together they move silently towards it.

—-

After what seems like an eternity, Catherine hears a familiar tapping. Two taps, then two more taps. She recognizes the pattern; it's her dad.

"Hi, Dad!" she sounds relieved.
"Catherine…"

They hug each other tightly. Christophe Jumeau is a large man; six foot two and around two hundred pounds. Despite his size he's a gentle sort; apart from an early outing on the ice as part of the hockey team at college, and a couple of scrapes at school even further back, Jumeau has never used his physical presence to his advantage. Now in his mid-fifties, he looks distinguished and youthful at the same time; something not many men achieve at that point in life. His genes transferred particularly well to his daughter, as she stands five foot ten inches in flat shoes and has a robust healthy aspect that seems to be a constant, even if tired or hungover.

He adores Catherine. Like most other dads, he sees her as the little girl he would strap in to the kids' car-seat, cuddle when she fell over and hurt herself, and watch with pride and joy as she would open presents at birthdays. But Catherine is very special to him in one other important respect. She does what he does. As a professor of Physics at the Université de Montreal, Christophe Jumeau has, among other things, pioneered advances in understanding how humans perceive dimensions of space and time. Famously, and independently of Walter Melrose and previous research programmes he had worked on, he showed how principles of stereo 3D vision in mammalian species such as humans can be applied to telescopes in order to build multi-dimensional images of space incorporating aspects of time. This is important because, although images received by telescopes are essentially 2D at the point of hitting the flat lens, science needs to interpret these into further dimensions in order to model the space-time around us. The outcome of the research has allowed physicists and mathematicians to suggest potential shapes of the universe – from something that might resemble a horse's saddle to a series of intertwined tubes which could form a continuous circle.

The tubes model has been the subject of much further work, particularly in relation to what are known as worm-holes, as it is here that the prospect of time travel becomes theoretically possible.

Now that Catherine is doing her PhD in an area of quantum physics that's very close to his heart, he feels exceptionally proud of her and what she is doing. As an accomplished academic, the tendency would be to jump in and coach his daughter, guiding and holding her hand. But the relationship is built around Catherine's strength of character as much as anything. And this is growing all the time. Although she came a little late to her vocation, Jumeau senior is delighted to see her standing on her own two feet as an independent, and critical, thinker.

"Come in, you must be tired." She moves to take his coat, but he takes her arm instead, giving her a look of intense concern.

"Listen, I just came straight here because I was worried about you. This country...." he trails off for a second before recovering his train of thought. "I've booked in at the Plaza and wouldn't mind getting settled over there really. How about you grab your coat – we can chat in the car and relax at the hotel."

"Yeh, good idea, I can always get a cab later on," she agrees.

They leave the apartment and head over to the Plaza, about thirty minutes away across town. They repeat how awful the news of the President's death is, and perhaps in an attempt to lighten the journey, catch up on bits and pieces of news from back home. It's mainly insignificant in comparison to the events of the day, now coming to a close.

After dumping things in his room, they enter the bar at the Plaza. It's late and the place is quiet, with the odd businessman and smooching couple dotted about. The mood is predictably sombre, and this is reflected in the music. In the background David Gray's 'Other Side' is playing.

'Meet me on the other side...' comes through the speakers dotted around the bar.

"Large cognac and a glass of that Rosé, please," he orders, pointing to a fine French wine he knows his daughter likes.

As they sit down in a dimly lit corner, Catherine's father takes a good swig from his glass. "Well, I guess like me you are wondering what the hell is going on in this country."

"You know, I feel so weird right now, Dad. Sort of numb to the fact that he's not with us any more. Can't believe it."

"Yeh, this country always seems to choose the self-destruct option. He was a good man in my judgement, someone with a real agenda. I think it will only come out in time how much he'll be missed."

"So," she fishes, "what do you reckon is going on? Who do you think would do this?"

"Well, there are plenty of suspects to choose from. I mean, if you track what he has done since being in office, it's spectacular and downright dangerous in equal measure. The guy was a railroader with balls – to do what he has done in such a short space of time took a lot of guts and he *has* to have made a few enemies along the way. Some of those guys would be really powerful too."

"Like who?" she asks.

"Well, I mean you're talking about half the military and air force being on his case. He got rid of half the Defense budget and took thousands of military personnel out of action, so those military chiefs aren't exactly going to have him at the top of their Christmas lists. Then there's the overseas developers who lost contracts, staff - sometimes their entire businesses - as he re-grouped and focused inwards with the economy. They have got to be hurting hugely. Of course, that's not to leave out the Republicans, the Intelligence agencies and right-wing extremists who think he's further to the left than Marx. I mean, there are possibilities wherever you look, I guess..."

"It's sad for his family. He had three kids," she reflects.

"Look, I have seen American presidents come and go, and he was by far one of the best in my opinion. But that probably means he was bound to be ruffling too many feathers and going to prompt some form of retribution. I just didn't think it would be this harsh. It reminds me of Kennedy but it's a bit different – these days we have digital technologies, CCTV, sophisticated surveillance and security. Someone knows what has happened, and there are two ways it can go. It's just a case of whether the powers that be deem that the public get to find out the truth. Personally, I doubt it."

Catherine and her father stare into their glasses for a second. Her dad is just about the closest person to her, and she seizes the moment to tell him about her experience while watching Garfield's address.

"Dad, I need to tell you something but it's a bit difficult to put into words," she is looking expectantly into his eyes and desperately needs him to be receptive.

Sensing her vulnerability and fear, he takes her hands in his. "Catherine, it's OK, I know you must feel like the world has gone crazy. You can say anything to me. I'm your dad."

Letting out a long sigh, she is reassured. Her dad always says the right thing. Always. She smiles hesitantly before continuing.

"Well, it's just that I had a really strange experience today when I was watching Garfield's address to the nation. I'm really afraid." She suddenly realises through saying the words that it is very real. Despite being with her dad, usually the safest place on the planet, she is acutely aware of the adrenalin rush in her stomach which is both stimulating and unpleasant.

"Afraid?" her father quizzes.

"Uh, yeh. I am not sure why. I saw something when I was watching Garfield. His face seemed to change while he was talking, like Montgomery was there too. Like both of them were in the same person. And I noticed that the clock on the screen stopped when that happened. What do you think that means?"

Christophe Jumeau is showing concern. "Honey, are you saying that you think Montgomery is alive? Is that what you mean?"

"Oh, I don't know what I mean, Dad. That's the problem. I don't think I'm the sort of person to see ghosts or anything like that, but I wasn't hallucinating or anything, I know that. Garfield just changed into this very dark creature very suddenly and he frightened me....I can't explain it." For the first time, Catherine Jumeau begins to cry, and her father comes round to her side of the table to sit with her and give her a cuddle.

"OK. OK. It's alright now," he offers soothingly. She feels safe and reassured in that moment. Her dad is there.

As she wipes away the tears, she is filled with the need to understand more. Regaining composure, she carries on.

"Dad, I know this sounds stupid, but I am beginning to think that I am the only one who witnessed what happened with Garfield today, and that just makes me feel even more strange. Am I losing my mind?"

"Of course not, honey. If there's one thing that you cannot do, it's that." he insists. "Listen, just take your time and let's break this thing down like we know we would if we were in the lab. If I can get a handle on the sequence of events then that gives us the maximum probability of coming to some sort of opinion about what is going on."

Catherine perks up. Somehow the idea of conducting an experiment seems to make the best sense and ignites a child-like enthusiasm for a split second that catalyses a change in mood. The young scientist goes through the events in precise detail, including the fact that no-one else seems to have seen what she saw.

"Yes, I have to admit I saw the TV address and did not share your experience," he acknowledges. "So not only have we got some strange phenomenon here, but it seems to be quite specific to you. It's a puzzle, but listening to you now I am confident that you are thinking in a measured way and as a true scientist, so I have no worries that you have perceived an event which is real."

Catherine smiles in relief.

"But you have to be careful, honey," he adds. "If I were you I might not share this with too many people until we know if in fact any one else did see what happened. If you are alone in seeing this, and something is going on with Montgomery and Garfield then it's probably better that you don't advertise it. At best, folks might isolate you as a flaker and at worst there may be danger in some people finding out what you saw."

"Danger?" she exclaims.

"Ssshhhh," he interjects and in softer tones says, "I just mean that it might be best for us to think through what this might mean for you. Who else knows about your experience today?"

"Oh, right. Well, I mean I have only, like, told Wendy. She knows. She said that she and Mal could check around campus just to see if anyone else saw what was going on."

"Hhhmmm. OK. Well, let's see what they say. Has she been in touch about that?"

"Actually no. I'll give her a call."

"Not now though, it's really late and we need to get some sleep," instructs her father. "Listen, stay with me tonight. Here. There are two beds in the room and we can chat some more over breakfast. I don't want you getting cabs at this time and I don't snore quite as much now that your mother got me those tablets." He smiles warmly and they laugh together.

"Aw, Dad. I guess that makes sense. I'm really tired and you must be too. They'll have some posh shampoo I can grab too!"

The pair finish their drinks and retreat to the hotel room for the night. It's past one o'clock in the morning, but earlier elsewhere across America, and the news broadcasts relentlessly repeat the news. Ticker tape scrolls across every screen, at every event, at regular intervals.

......President Montgomery pronounced dead at 1:17 p.m. ET...Body taken to Washington Memorial Hospital...Vice President Garfield orders full investigation...No suspects confirmed...Washington police and Intelligence agencies at scene...

These messages run across Catherine's mind as she falls asleep, this time the anxiety mitigated by the knowledge that Dad is there with her.

Next morning, the Jumeaus breakfast at the hotel, but neither eats much. It's around 8 a.m. Over coffee, Christophe wants to explore possibilities with his daughter. He grabs some sugar and begins putting one, two, three sugars into his coffee.

"Dad! Mom would kill you if she saw how much you're putting in there!" Catherine exclaims.

He smiles broadly, lets out a chuckle and says "Honey, thanks, but your mother isn't here and you didn't see that," and ends with a fatherly pseudo-frown which makes Catherine smile. Christophe Jumeau leans over towards his daughter. "Listen, I've been thinking. It's best you come back with me to Montreal for a couple of days. Your mom was so worried and I know, given what happened, she'd be desperately anxious about you being here on your own. Come home and spend some time with us, just until things calm down a bit. That make sense?"

"Uh, well, I don't know, Dad. I mean, I have lots to do here and Professor Melrose was going to see me later today and all my stuff is at home and..."

"OK, what's the meeting with Melrose about?"

"Oh, he had asked for a catch-up to find out how the experiment went yesterday."

"Well, he can wait," her father says firmly, "and we can drop by the house to get your things. Come on, it will be good to get a break and right now no-one is going to be worried about work when the President has just been assassinated."

The mood suddenly chills again on the mention of killing. It makes Catherine feel uneasy.

"Yeh, OK, that sounds like a plan. You'll see Wendy when we get back to the apartment too - she hasn't seen you for a while."

"Great, let me get packed up and load the car, and I'll meet you in the lobby in 20 minutes."

Catherine and her father walk into the lobby, and while he goes back to the room to pack she picks up the Boston Globe.

'MONTGOMERY 5th U.S. PRESIDENT SLAIN BY ASSASSIN,' reads the headline.

So it was definitely murder, she thinks. No chance of an accident or natural causes. He was killed, and probably in cold blood.

Sitting down in a comfy chair, she scans the first ten pages for any reports relating to Garfield's TV address, but there is nothing other than a brief mention of the intention to conduct a full criminal investigation into the murder. She's on page twenty of the special supplement when suddenly she is startled by a strange voice.

"Excuse me, madam," someone says from behind the paper. It's a deep male voice, and it sounds, incredibly, like Garfield's. She is almost too afraid to look over the top to see who it is.

"Madam?" It comes again. She gingerly pulls one corner of the paper back to see who is talking. A porter is standing in front of her, smiling. "Good morning Madam, can I get you anything?"

She lets out a huge sigh of relief.

"Would you like to take coffee or a light beverage here in the lobby, Madam?" the porter asks.

"Uh, no, no thank you. Thanks. No," she stutters to get the words out, feeling somewhat confused. The porter's voice sounded just like Garfield's. What the hell is going on? Before she can analyze anything, another voice comes at her from the side.

"All set?" Christophe Jumeau says, as fathers do, even although she has been ready to go for the last half hour.

"Yep, let's get out of here," she sighs in a relieved tone, looking back to see where the porter has gone but he's nowhere to be seen.

Thirty minutes later, around 9.30am, they are back at the girls' apartment in Allston.

"Hi!" Catherine shouts as she opens the door. No response. "Hey, Wendy!" she tries again.

"She must have gone in today," she says.

"OK, well, call her and just let her know you'll be away for a few days," Christophe says.

"Yeh, I will," she responds.

"Hey, this is Wendy. I can't take your call right now, but leave me your name and any message and I'll get right back to you!" It was Wendy's chirpy voicemail. But Catherine doesn't leave a message, instead choosing to text her and Mal both to ask them to get in touch immediately.

"Hhhmm," She says.

"No joy?" asks her Dad

"No. It's strange, she always has her bio-cell on unless she is in the lab where there is no signal."

"Well, I guess that's where they must be, honey. Now, have you got stuff you need to get together before we leave?"

"What? Oh, yeh, give me five minutes, Dad."

In ten minutes the pair are about to leave.

"I'll just leave Wendy a note for when she gets back, just in case she is in the lab and doesn't check her cell," Catherine says. She goes into the kitchen and grabs a sticky note and pen.

As she turns to put the note on the little kitchen table, out the corner of her eye she notices something red. It's the fridge magnet shaped like a fat red bunny, and it's on the fridge door. She slowly moves towards it and stops. It's supposed to be a thing of humor, but she stiffens and turns cold very quickly. From their days in halls at university, Wendy had developed a secret alert system for her and Catherine involving badges and fridge magnets. If she stuck the big 'I love NY' badge on the front door of their shared room, it meant that she had a boy back and Catherine needed to knock and give them a bit of time to dress. The big yellow pineapple magnet was used by each to signal to the other that they were up early the next day and not to make too much noise if they came back late. And the red bunny rabbit was the one used in emergencies; when one would leave a sign for the other that something was very wrong and to get in touch immediately. And this was it. There had only been one occasion that it was used before, when Mal's mother had been involved in a terrible car accident, and she and Mal had to rush off in an emergency.

Catherine doesn't know what to think, but is scared. She runs into Wendy's room and stops in her tracks. Wendy's normally immaculately tidy bedroom is a mess; both the work-desk and table lamp have been knocked over and the bedclothes are strewn across the floor. It's enough to scare Catherine.

"Dad!" she cries.

"Catherine?" her father responds. "What is it?"

"Oh Dad, I don't know, it's Wendy, I think she might be in trouble or something. It's the magnet, on the fridge...and her room is all messed up. Something's wrong!" She stares at her dad, not knowing what to say next.

Her dad looks confused. "What's going on? What's this about Wendy?"

She explains what she has found in the kitchen, and in Wendy's room, and what it means.

"Listen, we should report this to the police, but we can do that from the car. Come on, honey, just get your stuff and let's get going."

There is now a tension and anxiety in Christophe Jumeau's voice, and it unsettles his daughter, who quickly grabs her backpack and small shoulder bag as they both move towards the front door.

As she looks back toward the kitchen, she hesitates. "But what about Wendy? Oh God, what's happened to her? Where..."

Jumeau senior takes hold of Catherine's upper arm, and squeezes. He's a strong man, so a little effort on his part jolts his daughter out of her panic. "Catherine", he says in a quiet tone, "the *first thing* we need to do is get out of here. Do you understand?" He looks at her piercingly, a look that she knows from her past, when Dad isn't messing about.

She nods silently. He cradles her head for a second, before taking the key, locking the door, and leading her down the stairs. By nightfall they would be back in Montreal.

* * * *

CHAPTER 2: MISSING

Jagger's voice is bouncing round the room.

'Start Me Up' by The Rolling Stones is coming through the speakers and getting steadily louder. Keith Richards' guitar punches like a heavyweight left-right combination, and Jagger's vocal chords sound like they've been spring-cleaned with a bottle of moonshine. The crack of Charlie Watt's snare drum resonates and echoes around the large loft space above the disused DiCesare Art Gallery in downtown Boston which is, among other things, bedroom to the slumbering figure sprawled diagonally across a large double bed, head down and making noises that only remotely resemble breathing.

The alarm is going off. It's 8 a.m. and Denton Gill is slow to respond, even with the advanced sound dynamics that reverberate around the room.

"Beth?" he mutters, as the noise envelopes him and makes the hairs on the back of his neck stand on end.

Finally he tries to grab the nasty little piece of work that's just brought him back to the real world. After another couple of attempts, he manages to silence it.

He looks at the time in big bold numbers on the screen, and promptly slips back into his recurring dream. He's in a field of tall corn - so tall it's at least a foot above his head and he is lost below in a sea of golden waves, undulating in the wind. A cacophony of rustling reeds fills his ears and he can feel the air pressure intensifying. Directly above the sky is a mix of deep purple hues. There is a storm coming. The nerve ends in his nose detect musky perfume in the air the like of which he has never smelled before, and he can hear a distant cry across the field. It is a girl's voice, at once sensuous and vulnerable. The words are unclear, only the tone and timbre seem to be present but they swirl around his body in a wash of energy and seem to light up his entire being, the frequencies pitched so that every atom, every particle in his body is subject to some external pull that begs him to move through the corn towards the source. It is empowering and yet he feels weak. He can barely resist, struggling to control his movement as the corn stalks begin to gently sweep by him. At first he digs his heels into the earth to fight the intense and invisible force reining him in as if he were an unwilling water-skier, but as the movement quickens and the corn starts to rush by at ever-increasing speeds, the golden yellow of the cornstalks becomes a bright blur above him and he cedes control to the voice.

"Gill." The charming lilt is calling him, and his heart feels like it is answering 'I'm coming.' He feels warm. The panic he felt just a second ago has subsided, giving way to a euphoria as he is catapulted across the field and the voice becomes louder. Somewhere up above there is a bright light breaking through the darkness of the oppressive sky. It is a star unlike any other, the luminosity overwhelming as it reveals itself and descends towards him. He is engulfed by blinding white light. As it falls to Earth, he comes to a halt where the corn has given way to a clearing and he can feel nothing else around him.

All is quiet. The sound of the wind, the rustling, the girl's voice and his racing heart; all gone. He is perfectly still, perfectly exposed. The air around him is thick with expectancy. It's tangible. Something is going to happen. And it does. The air around his right hand is disturbed by another. A smaller, smoother, gentler hand fits neatly into his and Gill trembles as it grasps. His soul is lifted, and he knows. This is the hand that is attached to his other half, his soulmate. This is what he has been waiting for. This is where paths cross, and time and distance don't seem to matter. This is where anything can happen.

Gill wants to see. His need to discover is so great; at his core he is a scientist, exploring the universe. Who is this that is holding his hand and what happens next? His eyelids feel like they are welded shut, but he focuses all his willpower on lifting them. 'Come on. Come on.' An impossibly small slit opens up and white light begins to give way to a rich blue, as if he is suspended high above the earth looking down on an azure ocean. He moves his head to the right and can detect the form of another person, but she loosens her grasp and is beginning to move away. His heart starts to race again, and he begins to hear the beat in his ear. 'Come on,' he says to himself. And as his eyes open and adjust to the light, he can see the outline of the girl's face. He can't make out her features, knowing only that she is an angel, and she has come to hold his hand. He is desperate not to lose her, but she is moving further away and beginning to fade into the blue as darkness begins to surround them.

"No," says Gill out loud, with an anxiety and sadness in his voice as he reaches out to grab the figure moving away. "No!" he is shouting. He is shouting but she can't hear. He can't move to go after her. He is rooted to the spot. And she has gone.
"No! No!" Gill is still shouting.

It is 8.55 a.m. and the opening distorted lead guitar and detuned piano chords of 'In The Mirror' by Field Music have been hammering out at full volume. It's Gill's old favorite and his ringtone for calls from work. He doesn't have a ringtone for anything else; it's the only change he has made to the default settings on his bio-cell device so that, at the very least, the calls from the Precinct sound good.
'Think about me, that's all I'm asking for...' It's nearly a minute into the song and the words coming from his phone seem to connect Detective Gill back to today's reality. Reaching for the cell, he sees it is the main department number down at District. It's likely to be a 'where the heck are you?' call, which happens at least twice a week on average. In a good week he can sleep in until nine most days unless there is a major development which necessitates his presence at a crime scene. He's never been a morning person.
The room is dark; the thick, velvety curtains block every ray of light if they are closed properly, and Gill often feels that these are one of the best investments he has ever made. The bio-cell would let him do many things, like taking high-quality pictures at crime scenes, identifying unknown tunes when he was out and about, navigating him to any location, monitor his health, and, of course, watch the NBA. It let him down, however, with pesky calls from work. Unlike the bio-cell, the curtains never let him down. Once those were closed they performed their function perfectly without

any downside. If he had to get rid of one of them, it would be the cell - no contest.

'I wish I could change and make new rules....conduct myself better,' continues the song before the sound is cut off suddenly on the press of the call button. Gill doesn't speak, preferring to reach for a half-empty glass of water on his bedside table that has been there for a couple of days.

"Wait, please..." comes the woman's command on the other end of the phone. It's Amy Ashbrooke from the Downtown office, and there is a series of rustling and grating sounds before a gruff voice announces itself.

"Gill? Where the hell you been? How come you don't answer your phone?" comes the voice of Lieutenant Lester Young, the ranking officer at Downtown and Charlestown. He's narked, and for him to call it's got to be something important. The rangy, disheveled detective Denton Gill covers the phone and clears his throat before trying to sound as if he has been awake for some time by inflecting at a higher pitch.

"Lieutenant, good to hear from you," he says, in a strangely chirpy tone.

"What?" Young replies, but doesn't wait for an explanation. "Listen, Gill, get your lame, lazy ass down here, now. I have something for you."

"Yes sir, no problem. I just need to…"

But Young has hung up. Gill looks at the bio-cell as if it's at fault for Young's brusque tone, then chucks it on the bed as he musters enough vertical momentum to get up. He is in his boxers, which is good as that means he actually managed to take the rest of his clothes off before hitting the sack last night. Yesterday there was only one crime worth concentrating on, so instead of getting on with filing and routine work at the station, he followed events surrounding the President's assassination on the big screen TV in his local bar from about lunchtime onwards. By the time he got home it was well after 11 p.m. and this meant he had had a skinful. But either the gravity of the country's situation or the arguments going on in the bar as to who was most likely to have commissioned the assassination, or both, must have stimulated his brain too much, as he even remembers the pizza delivery guy coming to the Gallery door downstairs.

His hair looks like a party has been going on in there during the night; tufts of thick, dirty blonde mane form into a mix of wavering shards pointing outwards and skywards in equal measure, making him look quite comical. Catching himself in the mirror, he runs his fingers through to calm it all down and in one stroke does a pretty good job of taming it into something half-presentable, if not exactly trendy.

He shuffles over to the kitchen area which is a good twenty-five feet away, and switches on the light. Wincing from the harsh florescent smack that lands on his face, he stumbles over to the sink, turns the tap on to fill the kettle and flicks the switch once it's back in its cradle. He is on automatic. Next, it's over to the crockery cupboard where the electric shaver lives, and the daily attempt at mowing his face hair commences in a somewhat random pattern which may or may not trim his stubble evenly. He coughs. Despite giving up cigarettes some years back, there is still the lingering memory of that first nicotine hit of the morning that really sets you up for the day; even makes the coffee taste nicer. But those days are gone, and instead the routine is much cleaner; stepping out of the shower marks the official start to the day.

Denton Gill used to be a good athlete, playing basketball in college and swimming competitively as a younger man. Now forty-two, his body remembers its former glory. He looks good, despite doing very little these days to keep it that way. Being in decent shape, and in possession of chiseled looks that seem to suit him better as he gets older, work in different ways; women like him in a sort of 'he needs a woman' kind of way, but some are wary of him too, thinking he's a player. Apart from one or two male colleagues and family who know him well, men either tend to admire him or compete with him. In the former category are that group of men who tend to be comfortable with the fact that Denton Gill is just a different breed of male, independent but lonely, cold-hearted yet kind, strong and weak, all at the same time. These guys don't feel competitive with Gill - they like him exactly because he embodies the essence of an independent American male. Maybe a Jesse James or Jack Kerouac; iconic figures who liked to flout rules and live for themselves and not others. The latter category is that group of men who don't like someone else being in the limelight, or at least getting the attention of people around them without seeming to try very hard. They misconstrue Gill's rather effortless confidence and rugged charm for arrogance, and for the more testosterone-led and alcohol-fueled, this is galling enough to make them push for a confrontation. On several occasions in the last few years Gill has had to extricate himself from potential fights in bars, after having a few too many or hustling at the pool table with the wrong types. Alcohol has become a steady addition to his life since the break up of his marriage some years back, and is a key reason he stays up late at night and sleeps in most mornings.

Gill's dress sense is casual by anyone's standards, only succumbing to pressure to wear a suit when someone higher up the department notices that he looks even more out of place among his peers and insists on something a bit more formal. He usually conforms for a couple of days, then reverts back to what he actually likes to wear. The exception of course is when in court or at a formal event. Because he has just the one suit, it doesn't make sense to wear it too often. The Department doesn't have a 'policy' on this to speak of, but Lieutenant Young and his superior, Captain Todd Sanderson, are old-school guys who still believe that non-uniform cops need to look like they mean business. Today it's an old black leather box jacket, olive wide-collar shirt and low-slung grey jeans. And to complete things, odd socks and a pair of Converse trainers. He is good-to-go, some forty minutes after receiving the call from the lieutenant.

A little while later he is pulling up in his reconditioned Oldsmobile Delta '66 coupé outside the police department in one of the free bays there. There is barely a mile between the gallery where he lives and the Department, but Gill isn't much into public transport or walking, and he may need his own car today. He ascends the stairs to the building and walks through the front door. It's 9.55 a.m.

"Well, well. Good *Morning*, Gill!" says Officer Sandra Chandry, who is on the front desk. She is always on the front desk. In her mid-thirties, of African and Indian heritage and a very proud mother of three gorgeous children. And tough like leather. She won't put up with fools or people who don't pull their weight. Although she is Officer grade and, apart from the admin staff, on the lowest rung of the ladder Downtown, you wouldn't know it. She is very smart and takes pride in her clean-pressed uniform. She's also ambitious and exudes a practised air of authority and scrutiny more akin to a Supreme Court judge than your local policewoman. Like everyone else, she is coming to terms with the President's death, but unlike some, her way of dealing with that is to make everything as normal as possible at her workplace. "My, my, Detective..." she looks him up and down, "...you *do* look smart today, sir."

Gill gets what she is doing. Her sarcasm hits him every day, and every day he smiles at her and asks her for a cup of coffee, black, no sugar. So he does that today too, just like they always do. And like every other day, she ignores this request as it's just his comeback line. The two get on, but Sandra has worked hard over a number of years to get to where she is, and she loves her job. Why anyone who is doing his job - a *fascinating* and *exciting* job - isn't eager enough to come in to work early and dress for the part escapes her, and in many ways she resents his unkempt looks and slovenly habits. She imagines him to be a slob, but she doesn't need to imagine how good Denton Gill - or just 'Gill' as he is known – is at his job. Over the past few years Gill has proven to be uncannily good at solving complex crimes. While no-one has an insight into how he achieves this, it's a fact that when a difficult or high-profile case such as homicide, kidnapping or arson is reported, Downtown and Charlestown's best is often required across the city to advise or assist in investigations.

With so many public servants taking time off to be with their families in the wake of the tragic events of the previous day, the Department is poorly staffed with only five of the eighteen detective-grade staff reporting for duty. Progressing through to the main open office space of the building which is usually a hub of activity and cacophonous at times, Gill is struck by the relative quiet.

"Harry," he nods over to Harry Chambers, the longest serving detective in the Department and the only other detective like Gill who hasn't been promoted since taking up the post.

"Gill, what you doing in this early?" Harry jokes. He is reading the local newspaper and continues, "Things don't change much, huh," pointing to the headline 'SHOCK AROUND THE GLOBE AT MONTGOMERY'S ASSASSINATION.' They are both quite cynical in their own way, without lending any professional time to the emotional.

Gill nods. "...even though they do," he finishes.

"Let's grab a beer later, man. We can cook up some conspiracies together. You know the Lieutenant has a little present for you? He's been pacing around cussing at you up there. Hilarious."

"Yeh, I know," Gill comes back. "Any ideas what we have here?"

"Oh Lord, we thank you this day that I have so much paperwork to do. There is no 'we' in 'Johnson' Gill, and you are just about to have yours pulled. Good luck." Harry's tone is somewhat sarcastic and, as usual, he doesn't want to get involved.

Gill shrugs and offers him the kind of half-smile intended to convey the thought 'Well, there ain't much I can do about it now, can I?'

"Hope you get to see some nice pictures in among all that paperwork there, Detective," he says as he heads towards the stairs.

Lieutenant Young's office is on the first floor, and any time you get called up there, it's usually to get a dressing down or because he's got an assignment. On this occasion, Gill knows from his earlier phone call that it would be a new case. Although he is beyond getting excited about new cases, intellectually it's a lot more stimulating than most police activity. The only thing better than a new case was a solved case, and with one or two exceptions, he usually managed to solve the cases he was assigned. Detectives usually work in pairs, and up until three months ago Gill's partner, Dee Szymanski was his fourth and only pregnant partner to date. But with the baby now nine weeks old and the Department low on staff, Gill has been operating alone of late. This suits him, though; the only partner he really had any form of rapport with was Grady Jones, and he had been transferred a while back. Since then Gill seems naturally just to do his own thing, making practically all breakthroughs in investigations without help from others. Colleagues would say that the way he thinks and works is quite unique, often demanding time alone to really get into the psychology and motivational factors behind a crime or going off to visit people that appear to be completely unrelated to the case. In fact, it has become a feature of Gill's success that he is most likely to break a case precisely when he is somewhere else other than at the Department or with his partner.

"Godammit, what time do you call this? When I say get over here now, I mean *now,*" blares the lieutenant. It's gone ten already.

"Calm down, Lester. What's the beef?" Gill and Lester Young have a volatile relationship, and like most in the Department, Young doesn't have much time for Gill at a social level. But, Gill is good. The Downtown and Charlestown District has proved to be a top performer state-wide and much of that comes down to the wayward, yet brilliant, detective. His insights have been sought throughout the city on different cases, and on balance Young is happy that his home base is right here, Downtown, not least because it puts himself and his boss, Captain Sanderson, in the good books with Boston's Police Chief.

"Missing persons. Two students over at Harvard. I've had the Pro-Vice Chancellor and some professor on the phone all morning asking what we are doing, and you decide to have another lie-in. It's not on, Gill."

"OK, OK. I'm sorry Lester, it's just that with all that went on yesterday I guess it was pretty late by the time all of us got to bed. Wasn't it the same for you?"

The Lieutenant doesn't respond.

"Besides, why have we got this when it's over in Cambridge?" asks Gill.

"It was called in here – don't know why - but it's our baby. Besides, there's no-one over there who can deal with this. They struggle with bike theft, you know…"

Gill grins, and goes to the lieutenant's ever-present coffee jug to pour himself a black coffee. There isn't any sugar to go with it, and Gill hates sugar-substitutes. He winces for the second time this morning, the bitterness of the Department's somewhat suspect bulk-buy filter coffee washing around his mouth leaving no area untouched.

"Mmm, nice…" he asides, before getting to the point. "So, what do you have so far?"

The Lieutenant is calmer now, seated in his pseudo-leather recliner. "About half-nine this morning a research student at the

Physics department over there calls in to report her flatmate missing. Evidence of a struggle apparently. Turns out the missing girl's boyfriend can't be traced either. Neither are returning calls and it looks like they've gone AWOL..."

"OK. Who reported this and how long have these two been missing?" Gill interrupts.

"Uh, Amy has the details on names etc, ask her for those before you get back to your desk, and the timings, let me see..." He looks in the thin folder, which contains one piece of paper so far – the Missing Persons report completed by Sandra Chandry earlier that morning. "Yeh, here it is, the girl said her flatmate left her a message to tell her that she was in trouble and found her room turned over. They are all PhD students apparently, under Professor Melrose, and according to him the two should have been there for a meeting at 9 a.m. this morning. It sounds pretty routine. The pair probably had a fight and will turn up later, but we need to go through the motions in the meantime...keep everybody happy."

"Can I see that?" Gill asks Young. The Lieutenant hands him the report and Gill reads through the four paragraphs quickly, before looking down at his cheap coffee and then over to Young again.

"This doesn't feel right," he says.

"Uh?" the Lieutenant retorts.

"Lester, most of the country has been in shock for the last twenty-four hours. It's really fresh in everyone's mind. Who would want to kidnap a pair of students just after the President was assassinated?"

"Yeh, exactly. But it's high profile stuff so I want you to at least get over there and check it out," the Lieutenant says.

Gill frowns. "Hhhmmm. Sounds weird. I'll get over there as soon as I can."

"OK, and remember you're representing the Police Department across there. Act like a policeman, not a hippie. And keep away from the girls." Young winks at Gill, and the two take a sip of their respective coffees, both barely able to suppress their disgust at the acrid burn of roasted chicory.

After checking on Professor Melrose's availability and collecting some basics back at his desk – a couple of pens, some paper, and his forensics kit – Gill approaches Sandra Chandry at the front desk.

"Hey, Sandra," he says.

"Hey Gill. Quiet, huh? Terrible business..." she offers.

"Listen Sandra, the call this morning from, uh..." He looks down at her report, "...Catherine Jumeau. How did that conversation go?"

"You mean like did she sound funny or anything?"

"Yeh, anything that you might think I should pick up on?" Gill was complimenting his junior officer here to get some reward.

Chandry perks up. Gill is a good detective and he's asking her for an opinion. She likes that, and thinks hard for a second.

"Well, she sounded concerned alright, that bit seemed genuine. When I asked her why she was so sure her friends were in trouble, she ranted on about finding a fridge magnet that was a secret warning sign – between her and the other girl who she shares the flat with – if there was an emergency. That, and her friend's room being turned over – evidence of a fight of some kind."

"So she had tried to contact both of the others then?"

"That's right, but she said that her friends must be in trouble because the only place where they wouldn't or couldn't take a call is in the Physics labs, and that she had made sure that they were not there before calling in here to the Department." There is a slight pause while Gill looks again at the report.

"OK...did she offer any suggestions as to why they might have disappeared?"

Chandry shakes her head and slowly drops her eyes. Gill bends down to try and catch her eye.

"Sandra?" he prompts.

Chandry feels like it would be good to report something concrete here, but errs on the side of caution. "Well, not really. I did ask of course, but she kind of broke down at that point, and what turned out to be her dad spoke to me just to say that his daughter was exhausted and that we really ought to get onto this straight away. They wanted to get away from the place, so I took the cell number in case we needed to contact them." She points to the little box where she has scribbled the number.

"That's very helpful Sandra – thanks," he says, and gives her a big smile.

"No problem, Gill. You headed over to the University?"

"Yeh, think I'll check out the labs and speak to the honcho dude over there, see what I can find out. You wanna come with me?" he adds in jest.

"I wish, Mister. Make sure you take good notes in class now," she smiles again as he disappears into the bright sunlight streaming through the front doors.

Before setting off in the car, Gill punches the number on the report into his bio-cell and saves the contact as 'C Jumeau'. As he does so, it asks him if he wants to assign a particular ringtone. Without hesitation and just on instinct, he selects 'Help Me', by K.D. Lang, in a sort of twisted attempt at phone humor. At least he'd know if he got any calls from her.

He calls Catherine's number. It rings out, until there is a standard automated voicemail.

"You have reached the voicemail for oh-four-seven-one-nine-two-two-four-one-two-one. Please leave a message after the tone, or hang up if you wish to try again later." Gill hangs up. Then rings again. "Uh, this is Detective Gill from Boston Police. I am trying to contact a student at Harvard named 'Catherine Jumeau' regarding a missing person report received earlier today, April eleventh. If this is you and you pick up this message, please call me back on the number showing on your cell. Thanks." Gill hates voicemail.

Heading over to the University he chooses not to have the radio on. The only sounds come from the engine, air rushing by, and other cars. It's such a clear day that it makes Gill think how one could revel in the beautiful enormity of a big city. As the buildings come and go, he recaps on what he knows about Professor Walter Melrose, who heads up the Physics department at Harvard. Often in the public eye, he won some award – was it a Nobel prize? – and has appeared on local TV at various fund-raising events for the University and various charities. And of course he remembers President Montgomery's visit to the University a little while back, as he was part of the local security operation. He is sure Melrose was part of the welcoming party that day too.

Although never struck by celebrity, Gill has time for scientists. They explore the world, look at the detail of what's actually going on as opposed to what we think is going on, and understand the depth of knowledge required to make any form of conclusion with authority. Gill had a love for experimentation as a kid, and was himself a gifted student as a younger man, studying forensics and latterly forensic psychology. But despite the popularity of forensics as a career, and its somewhat glamorous place in the public eye, he never really felt at home in the lab or the mortuary, preferring instead to use the scientific and psychological training as tools in more direct and varied detective work. There were fewer post-mortems to attend that way.

Gill's parents, Joe and Shirley, had to come to terms with Denton's tendency to experiment and wander from the straight and narrow, coping with a few scares when he was a young child. In fact, they got a bit of a bad reputation in Gill's hometown of Newport in Oregon. During the food and wine festival one year, their little Denton, then aged eight, separated from the rest of the family and was reported missing to the organisers of the event and the police. Out of their minds with worry, the Gills were at the police station some hours later when their son walked through the door.

"Denton!" his mother cried as she ran toward him, "where have you been?"

"Hi Mum. I don't know. It was a nice place though," Denton replied, somewhat serenely. "And I knew to come here to find you."

It turned out that he had been reported to the police after being found under a table in one of the wine-tasting tents, just sitting upright and motionless. Of course, the assumption was that the young Denton had managed to pilfer a glass of wine or two and crawled under the table feeling a bit worse for wear. But he had no recollection of drinking, and after double-checking and a cursory examination by the police doctor, the young Gill was found to be absolutely fine with no signs of having drunk any alcohol at all. Despite various attempts over subsequent weeks to find out what happened during those missing hours, the boy couldn't remember anything apart from being in a yellow field of corn. Even though corn is grown in the state, this didn't make sense as there wasn't any ripe corn in the fields at that time of year. In the end his parents put it down to a dream he had while asleep. But the lack of clarity on what happened disturbed them, and unbeknown to them this was not the first, or last, time that Denton's whereabouts were uncertain.

As he became a teenager, Gill outgrew his peers pretty quickly, standing over six feet by the time he went to junior high and already shaving by that time, unlike some smoother-skinned peers. A superbly gifted basketball player and the youngest player in the school's premier squad, he never seemed out of place, looking somewhat older than his years. But there were some lessons he had to learn. In particular, some of the more 'alpha-jock' types were always looking for opportunities to rib and tease younger students. And Gill kind of stood out as an easy target.

One time during a league basketball match, Gill was on the bench and just seemed to be glued motionless watching the hoop and not following play. The coach called to the young Gill and asked him to get his tracksuit off and prepare to go on. Gill stayed motionless and didn't respond. It was only when he was nudged sharply by a fellow player that he came to and proceeded to the court. This was taken as day-dreaming and absent-mindedness, and although it didn't happen every time, it happened often enough for the word 'Denton' to become infused with new meaning for some in the school. To get a 'Denton' came to mean 'to become transfixed in a day-dream during class'. And of course, pronouncing 'Dent-on' like 'hard-on' didn't help his cause very much. For a time it was a bit of a joke around the school, but like most things it didn't last – just long enough for Denton to really dislike hearing his name spoken out loud. So, as a coping strategy he decided not to be known as Denton, and quickly started to persuade friends to call him just by his surname, and introducing himself as 'Gill' with new friends or on social networking sites; in fact in any social setting.

For a couple of years he also found himself retreating to his room on a frequent basis, preferring to be alone. This was to be his laboratory. From a young age he and his twin sister, Beth, had talked about traveling in their minds to other places, often not knowing if it was a real place or a dream-world. The experiences *seemed* very real, and it also seemed that being in two places at the same time wasn't so far-fetched an idea for them. He had made a pledge to his sister that he would find out more about their strange ability to 'dual' as he named it, taking the lead in order to shield her from any risk that may accrue from experimentation.

At first, his research led him down the road of Astral Projection. He read about all the independent instances where people in certain meditative states could 'project' themselves across the world and 'see' things as they happen there. This is what he convinced himself that he and his sister could do, and somehow that was almost reassuring because it meant that they were not unique in this respect. Less freaky. In fact, early in his voyage of discovery, he let his sister in on this and she seemed to welcome the news with great relief.

So, in the spirit of scientific endeavor, Gill set up a series of experiments to test his Astral abilities. First, he started to focus on going to a particular place. One evening around eight he began the process he would usually go through. He'd close his eyes and picture the field of corn from his early dreams, and start to move through the cornfield until the overpowering light would stop everything around him and he would come to the clearing. This would be the space where he had to control what was happening. He felt that intuitively. Once there, he would need to navigate to where he wanted to go. So he waited. And waited. And finally decided to force himself to open his eyes. He could only force them open a tiny fraction. But there, in blurred and indeterminate form, he could see what looked like several pathways leading out of the clearing and into more corn reeds. The overwhelming sense at work was touch. He couldn't explain why, but he sensed that time seemed to have stopped, and gravity was rooting things to the earth beneath him. He had barely enough strength to move his limbs. But he knew that was what he had to do. Making a gargantuan effort, he used his right arm to claw forward like a sprinter coming out of the blocks and taking the first step in a one hundred meter dash, only in super-slow motion. It was like being stuck in a pool of the thickest, heaviest syrup, and desperately trying to escape. But eventually, the slightest momentum led to further movement and Gill's steely determination to gain ground paid off. There was a pathway straight ahead and it was getting closer.

Momentum gained, Gill disappeared into the reeds and followed the path. But rather than a sea of corn around him, suddenly he found himself back in his room. As if nothing had happened. At first he checked himself to make sure he was OK, nothing missing. All good. He looked around his room. It all seemed the same. Desperately disappointed, he wondered what it had all been about. What was the point of the pathway out of the clearing if it just led back to where he started? This was very frustrating. So much so for the sixteen year-old that he decided to go grab one of his Dad's beers and talk to his sister.

Going downstairs, Gill called out to Beth. No response. He noticed that no-one was in the house. This was strange. He was talking to his Dad a little while ago and there was no mention of folks going out anywhere. He checked the kitchen, living room, the garage, and then up to his sister's room before descending again. No-one. Flicking on the TV, he got a shock. Live news coming from CBS was from the night before. He flicked over to ABC, then to his local channel. All reporting that it was Tuesday, not Wednesday. Could he be wrong about the day and the date? The previous night he had watched the Bulls take on the Celtics in the NBA Eastern conference. He even knew the score. Flicking to ESPN, sure enough, Chicago at Boston, first quarter. If it really were Tuesday then no-one *would be* there because his parents had gone with Beth the night before to see her perform with the school orchestra.

Suddenly it hit. He had travelled back in time. He started to sweat, went very pale, and felt sick before heading to the bathroom to throw up. It was all too much to take in. After a little while recovering, Gill splashed some cold water on his face and looked at himself in the mirror. He looked the same, he thought, though he was a day younger. Was this travel permanent or...'

There was a knock on the door.

"Bro?" It was Beth's voice.

Beth was a cheery type, and to Gill she was his little twin sister, even though she was only two minutes his junior. Despite being twins, the gender differences, and elements of nurture mean that the two don't look identical. Facially the two are very similar, but Beth is like a smaller version and very obviously female; a good-looking young woman, and fairly typical as teenage girls go.

"What you up to?" she said chirpily, but immediately stepped back when she saw his gaunt and haunted face.
"Oh, eh, nothing, do you want into the bathroom?"
"What?"
"Oh, sorry, I have been a little bit sick there."
"Are you OK?" His sister looked bemused.

Sensing something odd, Gill looked around. He was in his *bedroom*. Now it was his turn to look puzzled. There was a pregnant pause before he started to realise what was going on.

"Beth, have you been out at all tonight?"

She looked at him with a sisterly smile, like he was having a laugh at her expense. "No, you know I haven't. What's going on, what have you been up to, bro'?" she asked.

"I don't know, really."

That night Gill told Beth about what had happened, checking that she and Mom and Dad had been in all night. Beth was scared and fascinated in equal measure, telling him that she had been asleep and dreamt that Gill was in trouble, so came to check on him. They discussed what it might mean to have the ability to travel through time or space or whatever Gill had just done. One thing was for sure. This was not to get out. Mom and Dad were not to know. No-one was to know. And although they agreed that he wouldn't be trying this again, ultimately his thirst for experimentation and knowledge was too strong for this event to be unique.

Over coming months, Gill would spend many evenings with his door locked, on his travels. And Beth would get updates on what they both came to name as 'dualling'. On one occasion, Gill travelled in both space *and* time, and ended up in a nearby fishing trawler that was moored in the harbor at Newport earlier that day. This was particularly frightening, as he had no control over exactly where he located to. The shock of the shift spooked him and he promptly fell overboard into the sea. His shouts alerted a family on a nearby boat, who, after spotting him, called the coastguard. Coming back with a start in his room, he spent the next day checking the newspapers and local radio and TV for stories of someone falling overboard at the local harbor, but there was nothing reported.

The Gill children also used some careful questioning to see whether or not their parents had passed on the special ability via their respective families, but it became apparent that this was something that appeared only to occur in the brother and sister. They became convinced that, although some people might have some innate ability to be in two places at once, it was probably the case that, like Beth, many wouldn't know it without someone else making them aware of the fact.

It was also the case that Gill felt another presence when he got to the clearing in the field. He assumed this would be, in some way, Beth because she was his twin, but somehow instinct told him otherwise. He had taken the next step in thinking. Where Beth had accepted that space and time travel was an anomaly akin to Astral Projection, and that this wasn't anything supernatural or overly profound, Gill knew that the ability was the *result* of something else. He couldn't pin this down; it always eluded him. At one point he thought that it could be something extremely spiritual, then at some other point found it extremely frightening if it could be related to dark powers or the forces of good and evil. Going down this alley wasn't a good move. In fact, it freaked him out for a while, and it was only once he rationalized that it was more about the nature of reality and perhaps some quirks in our understanding of the physical laws of the Universe that he calmed down. That version gave him confidence and appealed to him as a would-be scientist. The Universe is real; we are made up of matter and have the ability to think. Maybe he was the next stage in evolution? This is when he would put the brakes on, squint his eyes like Clint Eastwood, and whistle the melody from the classic western 'The Good, The Bad and The Ugly'.

After a year of experimentation and some frightening near-misses – including a random jaunt to the smelting plant in the next town – Gill was getting the hang of co-existing in different realities. For that is what he believed he was doing – exploiting some anomaly in his make-up that allowed him to exist in more than one position in the Universe of space-time at once. And it transpired that there were several limitations to this, at least up to that point. First, in terms of actual distance and time, he couldn't yet travel far; everything seemed to be local and within a short period of time either side of now. Then there was the problem of control; actually getting to a particular junction in space-time was the holy grail for a reason - it was extremely difficult to achieve. It would be easy to get it wrong and end up in some weird situation. Side-effects were difficult to avoid – perturbing energy fields and physical reality would show up in different tell-tale signs such as local space-time warps where people or objects may exhibit strange characteristics as they are impacted by nearby dualling activity. Maybe most importantly, Gill intuited that an absolute constraint was set by others; if, in either location in which you are dualling, you are observed – as in that very first experience where it seemed that opening the door to Beth brought him back to her reality - the whole dual-existence deal collapses. However, his lack of clarity on that made him nervous; by extension, there may be circumstances in which he might not be able to return to his original reality.

Although the more flippant and overwhelming temptation would have been to try and locate to some event in the past like a boxing match, football game or horse race where you already knew the outcome and so could make vast fortunes on betting, the problem was that of multiple universes or realities. Gill realised that winning a fortune in one reality didn't mean that it would be so in his original reality. So unless you could actually take a decision to stay in an alternative reality for the rest of whatever time you have, or more dangerously were trapped in that reality, it seemed to him that you'd always come back to this world. That was the one he knew and, despite the usual trials and tribulations that everyone faces, loved.

Of course there were endless questions about dualling, and he'd share some of his musings with Beth. If you were to travel further in spacetime, would things change in the original world, like when astronauts go into space and travel far into our solar system, they age less than we do here. Would Mom, Dad, Beth get older, more quickly the more Gill did this kind of stuff? Could you go very far forward in time and see what things might be like in our world in ten, twenty, or a hundred years? And so on. Gill's mind sometimes felt it was going to explode with questions.

One thing he couldn't know, or try to find out, was if something happens to you and you die in an alternative universe, would you die in this one. Would there be no *you* anymore. And then there was Beth. He knew that even though she hadn't tried anything so far, she had the potential to dual too; and despite his experience, and relative good fortune, to date, he knew that there are real dangers in attempting dualling. In the end, so strong were his love and protectiveness towards Beth that he kept such insights from her, and insisted that she never try anything like this unless and until he knew more about how it all worked and fitted together. It was hard for Beth though. They were alike enough as twins that she shared his taste for adventure and new experiences. But for now, she saw in his eyes that there were still so many uncertainties, and she always remembered the haunted look on her brother's face that first time he dualled.

By the time Gill was in the twelfth grade, he had begun to put dualling to some use. Having finally gotten some level of control over where and when he was locating to, and also now able, to some extent, to handle the two existences side by side by splitting his behavior and attentions to those around him as situations demanded, he managed to get a sneak of the science papers for his final high school exams. This was important because he had made his mind up at that point that if he didn't make the NBA draft then he was going to try and put his skills and knowledge to use in solving crime. In many respects, Gill was a good kid, having inherited core values centering around fairness and equality from family and friends. So the time that he cheated by gaining advance knowledge of exam questions, he really did have a bad time with his conscience afterwards, and vowed never to misuse dualling again. Of course, there were times when things still went wrong though. If he were ever in two places and both demanded lots of his care and attention at the same time, he found it impossible, and would sometimes have to find an isolated spot to re-locate back. This was the final skill he needed to manage a lot better – getting back. For so long he had been unable to dictate when he would revert to single existence, but now he was beginning to realise that this seemed to be easier if others were not present, and if he managed the mental process of fighting his way back through the heavy, gravity-laden slow-motion journey across the clearing in the field. By using this vision and determination, and sheer strength of will, he found that he could manage the process better.

Accepting a place at Portland State University in Forensic Pathology, to all intents and purposes Gill pegged back on dualling for a while, instead giving his undivided attention to three other things; study, music and girls. Such pleasures were uneasy bedfellows, but whether he was cutting up a corpse, blowing notes out of his beloved saxophone, or having a romp with one of a string of girlfriends, he took full advantage of the system. Rid of any lingering labels or nicknames, in many ways university suited Gill to a T. Where some failed to balance things out, he knew that his career choice depended on his total understanding of forensics, and the mindset of the criminal.

Completing his degree with first class honors, he crossed over to the University of Portland to do a Masters in Forensic Psychology. This would complete his training before setting foot into the world of crime and the U.S. legal system.

It was during his second year in the Crime Scene Investigation lab in Seattle that he learnt of his sister's disappearance and assumed death. Gill's parents were distraught; there was no note left, no evidence of Beth being kidnapped or hurt, and most importantly of all, no body found. After years of deference to him, he knew that Beth had tried and succeeded in dualling, but something went wrong so that she was trapped in a different reality. But this didn't help him, and it wouldn't solve anything for his parents. They all knew that Beth had been unhappy, having problems with her long-term boyfriend who had persuaded her to go to Boston with him instead of completing her studies in Phoenix. On hearing that news, Gill decided to go to Boston for himself to talk to the boyfriend and get a sense of where she might have gone. He took a job teaching Chemistry for a while, which allowed him time in the evenings to try and find his sister somehow. But after a year of trying he became tired and his teaching became so poor in class that he was given notice that he needed to find somewhere else to work.

After some months out of work and hitting the bottle, Gill applied to join the police force, thinking that he might have access to criminal investigation files, local criminals, lawyers...anyone that might have a clue as to his sister's whereabouts if the worst-case scenario were to be true. Officer Denton Gill took up his post and began to employ his ability to dual again. Slowly at first, careful not to arouse any suspicions or doubts about his performance as a cop. It was largely a thankless and fruitless task, the only outcome of which was that his knowledge of the city's underworld, patterns of crime and the legal system really became encyclopaedic. This helped him to gain a reputation as a solid performer to whom others would turn for information and insight. It saved time, and meant they didn't need to use computers.

After three years, and still without any trace of his beloved sister, Gill's father was diagnosed with Alzheimer's, aged just fifty-eight. Although there were new drugs available, the inevitable onslaught of symptoms took its toll on Shirley Gill, and he reluctantly took a prolonged leave of absence to go back and help out and spend time with his dad. Joe Gill had become a broken man;

the sense of loss at the disappearance of his cherished daughter Beth left him sad, vulnerable and lonely. Gill tried hard not to relate Beth's disappearance to his dad's condition, but it was hard to avoid. The Gills eventually got a home help in the form of Consuela, a lovely Mexican woman with expertise in looking after those with mental health problems. Her arrival perked Joe up, and Shirley managed to get out to work, and also to play golf like she used to, so the whole situation became more manageable in many ways. It didn't stop Gill from wondering whether Joe would ever recognize Beth if she eventually returned some day, and this made him re-double his determination to find Beth as quickly as he could.

On Gill's return to Boston some months later, he managed to get a placement at the Downtown District, this time manning the front desk at the station. It was mainly form-filling but he could never dual from there as he was almost always dealing with people and difficult interactions, so he put in for patrol duty again, and got back on the trail for Beth. It was only once Lester Young was appointed Lieutenant for the District that Gill got on the radar of management again. After some time, Young decided to put Gill up for some aptitude testing and trials as part of a partnership with Grady Jones. Gill passed with flying colors and soon the Jones-Gill pairing was by far the best at Downtown and Charlestown, and probably across the city too. These guys cracked a number of high-level and public cases over several years, and this was mainly without Gill seeking recourse to dualling. The only thing Gill did do was cover his ass good and proper by locating to the Mayor's office every so often to catch up on what the Mayor and senior cops were up to. He had enough ammunition to protect himself, if he ever needed to, and so he felt particularly secure in his role as detective, avoiding anything more public-facing further up the ladder. Besides, his spare time was spent playing sax with his chums in the jazz quartet The Horizon, and the odd night chasing women with Grady, even after Jones had been reassigned to the Allston District.

——-

Gill's ageing Oldsmobile bumps clumsily over the speed humps. The chassis scrapes the concrete and the sound is like screeching chalk for a second.

"Shit."

As he drives over to the car park, he sees a bunch of students laughing as they walk between classes. It takes him back, and he smiles. He parks up and heads over to the 'Heisenberg' building, slightly ahead of schedule. The building is very grand, with super-massive digital welcoming screens offset against a mix of impressionist and cubist hangings. A strange combination, he considers, yet somehow quite effective in this environment.

The main reception isn't busy, so he makes some small talk with the receptionist before taking a seat and waiting to see Professor Melrose.

"You can go up now, Mister Gill – room two-two-one on the fourth floor," the receptionist smiles broadly at Gill.

As he waits for the lift, he notices that the numbers go in the sequence 4, 2, 3, 1, before reaching the ground. Odd, he muses to himself, not thinking any more of it at the time. Two men in security uniforms and caps are in the lift as the doors open. Both men step out of the lift while Gill stands to one side. He doesn't notice their faces, but they both have beards and the taller of the two men gives Gill a half smile before they walk off towards the main door. He presses '4', and the lift doors close.

Professor Melrose has his own secretary, and after she puts a call through, he finds himself in Melrose's spacious office with great views across the campus.

"Now, you are..?" Melrose enquires in his indiscernibly middle-English accent. He is a smallish man, slightly rotund - most likely as the result of too many occasion lunches and dinners – and wearing a rather bright cerise waistcoat which seems at odds with his rather more demure beige chinos. The look seems studied though, and Gill guesses that the professor likes to be known as somewhat eccentric and flamboyant, with a taste for the finer things in life.

"Gill, Sir. Detective Gill from Downtown District. I called earlier to get some time regarding the two students reported missing this morning."

"Ah yes, of course, take a seat would you, Detective. Can I get you anything to drink?" The Professor moves over to a large globe in the corner of his office and opens the top to reveal his collection of spirits, wines and sherries.

Gill raises his hand to signal his abstinence, adding "I'm good, thanks."

Melrose shrugs, and pours a glass of his favorite Port.

"So I assume you haven't found them yet, or I would have been informed. I called in earlier today as they missed a very important meeting. That's unlike them, but then I thought Malcolm and Wendy may just have bunked off for a few days...you know, taken some time to get away in light of all the bad news floating around. I wouldn't blame them – quite fancy getting away myself."

The Professor sounds remarkably upbeat, taking everything into consideration.

"You think so, sir? I mean, according to the report Mister Baines and Miss Xiu have not been contactable all day, and there are no signs that they packed any clothes or toiletries before leaving. If they did plan a break." Gill wonders how much information the professor has been given.

"Oh, I...I didn't realise that," he reflects, sounding a bit more anxious now. "A policeman called earlier on the phone; he said that Catherine had notified you that something was wrong, but beyond that I didn't think it would be anything sinister," the Professor trails off, inviting Gill to update him.

"Well now, Professor, we may not have to label it as that just yet. But is it your experience of Mister Baines and Miss Xiu that they take unannounced leave from classes and their work here?"

"Absolutely not, Detective, but I think we may be dealing with extenuating circumstances here. Look, I know both these people fairly well, and I know they are impressionable and idealistic young students who must have looked up to Montgomery as an icon of radical progressive politics. In their minds he could have been an idol, who knows? I mean, if the President gets assassinated then maybe some younger people might think that the world was coming to an end, or simply that America isn't for them. It's a possibility."

"That's a good thought, sir. It might just be like that." Gill pauses, and looks around. Melrose's book collection is extensive, and ordered precisely. A larger volume entitled 'The Twins of Space and Time' catches his eye, and he moves to the large display cabinet to view the author. It's by Christophe Jumeau. "But," he continues, "I think it unlikely that they wouldn't leave a message or take some provisions with them, most especially if it were a longer journey."

"Well then, I defer to your judgement, Detective Gill," Melrose responds in a rather sagely manner, bordering on the patronizing.

Gill is sensitive to senior academics and the need to avoid ambiguities in questions, meaning and answers. It's not easy terrain normally, but it somehow feels a little too difficult here.

"Now, if there is anything else..?" the Professor adds by way of inviting Gill to leave.

"Just one thing, Professor, if you would. You were here yesterday when the news broke about the President?"

"Yes."

"And you are not aware of any threats to either Baines or Xiu that came about yesterday or beforehand?"

"What do you mean, 'threats'?"

"Perhaps a grudge from someone in the past, or an incident that you might have witnessed which could mean that the two had enemies on campus?"

"Afraid not, Detective, I think they would have let me know if anything like that had taken place. We were quite a close knit little group, you know."

"Were?" Gill prods.

Melrose straightens up, and gives Gill a cold stare. "I very much hope that the group gets back together as soon as possible. Now if you don't mind, I have another appointment..."

"I understand, Professor," Gill says, deciding not to go in for the rebound, instead opting for a throwaway to close out the conversation. "Oh, that's what I should have asked right at the start. What is it that Baines and Xiu are researching?"

"They are both looking into black holes, gravity…that sort of thing." The Professor pauses slightly, before adding "Are you interested in physics, Detective?"

"Oh, just in passing, Professor; I am afraid my knowledge of such things is confined to how gravity affects me when I get home after a shift on duty." Gill smiles broadly, and Melrose reciprocates.

"Good luck with the investigation, Detective – do let me know when you find them. I have kept this quiet so far, as I think everyone here would be terribly distressed if they thought that anything was remotely wrong."

"Of course, I'll do just that, sir. Good..." Gill is interrupted by what sounds like an afterthought by the Professor.

"And I meant to ask you, Detective, where is Catherine at the moment? Is she OK?"

" I believe Miss Jumeau is safe and well at the moment, Professor. I am due to speak with her this afternoon," Gill responds.

"Oh, I see, well, if you see her will you please ask her to get in touch with me as soon as possible? She isn't answering her bio-cell either."

Gill hesitates a moment, not knowing exactly how to respond. "I'll do that, sir," he says, and tries to sound convincing.

Gill exits, reflecting on how his chat with Melrose seemed to resemble some sort of medieval jousting match. Maybe it was just him, but he definitely got the feeling that the Professor seemed distracted and eager to keep the discussion as brief and information-free as possible.

He asks the receptionist if he can get access to information on Baines and Xiu, and a few minutes later, the student records office manager brings him copies of their student registration forms, along with ID photos. During the wait he takes the opportunity to ask the receptionist if she might like to grab a coffee or something stronger some time at the weekend, and arranges to meet up downtown.

Leaving the Physics building he decides to go to the student refectory and have a coffee. It's coming up to lunchtime but the place is very quiet. There are one or two groups of students sitting quietly. After a quick call back to the department to find out if there is any further news, he strolls up to one of the tables where a mixed group are chatting quietly.

"Guys," he greets them. They nod back, checking him out.

"Sorry to interrupt – I guess like me you are all coming to terms with what happened yesterday, huh?"

"Yeah," says one of guys in the group.

"Listen, do any of you guys know Wendy Xiu or Malcolm Baines over at the Physics building?"

"Doesn't ring any bells, dude," another answers.

"OK, well, thanks anyway," he offers as he leaves.

He tries the same routine on the other tables, but no-one knows the PhD students. On the last table he uses the ID photos to help, which kind of gives away that he is a cop but by this time he can't be bothered to hide it, and doesn't really care if students get spooked by the fear of a kidnapper on the loose, considering that it might make them more vigilant.

Drawing a blank, he wanders over to his car, and sparks up the 4.2 litre engine. Not exactly eco-friendly, and guaranteed to have no renewable sources of energy associated with it whatsoever. He loads his favorite mix on the new sound system he's had installed. 'Livin' in the U.S.A.' by Steve Miller starts to blare out, and makes him nod in appreciation. Gill's love of a 'tune' started very early, and has been a constant source of pleasure in his life.

As he begins to draw out of the parking lot, a young student waves him down, clutching what looks like a rolled-up newspaper.

"Hi," says Gill out the window as he comes to a stop.

"Hi!" the young man is dressed in smart chinos and a pink shirt, more reminiscent of a businessman than a student. He leans in toward Gill. "I heard you asking about Malcolm earlier?"

"Yeh, I was. And you are?"

"Oh, sorry, I'm Lamar. Lamar Merriweather."

"OK Lamar, have you seen him then?"

"I saw him last night, yes. He's in our quiz team; we are going to a quiz tonight but I can't get hold of him either. It's not like him really to miss one of those – he's pretty well organized, and good at keeping in touch usually. I just thought you might want to know."

"Right...so, I guess you have left messages for him and he hasn't got back to you, huh? Did he mention anything last night or give you any indication that he might be planning on taking off with his girlfriend?"

"No, not at all."

"So, where did you see him last night – here, on campus?"

"Yes, just back at the refectory there. We were supposed to be meeting to discuss quiz stuff but we were all just talking about the assassination."

"That figures. Does it seem odd that anyone would just suddenly up and off without letting people know? I mean, did Malcolm seem particularly affected by events yesterday?"

The young student thinks for a moment, then looks at Gill hesitantly. "Well, he seemed to be more interested in Garfield really. He kept asking if we had noticed anything strange about him during the time he was on the big screen there."

"And..?" Gill prompts.

"And, well, none of us had, so I think he just dropped it in the end and said he was heading off to see his girlfriend."

"So he was trying to find out if you had seen *what* exactly?" Gill can't really get a handle on what Lamar Merriweather is telling him here.

"I don't know, Sir," Lamar goes on. "He mentioned something to do with Garfield's face appearing to change or something like that. And something about the clock on the TV stopping, but like I said we all watched the Garfield address and none of us saw anything like that."

Gill shifts in his seat as he hears that the clock had stopped. Suddenly things get more interesting. He had experienced time grinding to a halt before. He leans out of the car window to Lamar.

"Lamar, that's very helpful. Will you be around campus over the next few days? I might just need to make contact again if that's OK."

"Sure thing, uh, is it Detective?"

"Gill. Detective Gill. How can I contact you, Lamar?"

"I'm over at the Structural Engineering Lab most of the time now. And my team are at the Star and Shadow quiz on Wilshire tonight too, if....?"

"Great. Might see you there, Lamar. Here's my card in any case. If anything else comes to mind, get in touch." The two smile at each other and, shifting into Drive, the Delta '66 rumbles down the slip road and disappears round the corner.

K.D. Lang's velvet tones fill the car. 'Help Me' is coming through on his cell.

He delays answering the call for a second as he realises that it is Catherine Jumeau on the other end of the line, and partly too because he needs to pull over, having forgotten to twin his bio-cell with the car. Parking up, he silences the stereo.

"Gill speaking..."
"Detective Gill, it's Catherine Jumeau."

Gill is silent, and the silence prompts Jumeau to check whether he is still there.

"Detective Gill?" her voice comes through again.

The tonal qualities seems strangely familiar to him, but he can't process the sound quickly enough to understand any more.

"Catherine," he says in a soft, aerated tone, neither asking if it is her nor following up with smalltalk.
"Yes, it's Catherine Jumeau, Detective Gill. I got your voicemail. I'm sorry for the delay in getting back to you."

Things seem odd enough right now, but the sound of Catherine Jumeau's voice is confusing him even more.

"Are you there?" it comes again.

He clears his throat, and tries to picture Catherine Jumeau, but can't. He didn't think to get an ID for her at the student record office. The voice is all he has.

"Uh, yes. Yes, this is Gill. Uh, thanks for getting back to me, Miss Jumeau, I was worried about you," he blurts out.
"Well, that's good of you, Detective, but I am fine, really. It's Malcolm and Wendy that I am worried about. I just know something is wrong. Do you have any news?"
Gill is hesitant. "There have been no developments so far, I'm sorry," he says, as he begins to think about how he can meet her in person. This seems important.
"Oh," comes Catherine's stifled response.

"A bulletin has gone out to all police patrols, transport operators and hotels across New England, so if they have decided to take off somewhere then we stand a good chance of tracking them down. And of course there are no reports of anything more sinister, so we have to stay positive at this stage. Right now we do not have any evidence of a crime having taken place, so we need to take things one step at a time. I'm sure you understand."

"Yes, but her room...I mean..." Jumeau says.

"Yes, well I certainly need to have a look at that. May I ask whereabouts you are at the moment, Miss Jumeau? I understand that you are not at the apartment?"

"That's right Mister...uh, *Detective* Gill. My father drove me home this morning, so I am back in Montreal now. He thought it would be safer that way."

"Listen, you guys did the right thing – until we clear up what is going on it's probably best to play it safe for now. However, I would like to get access to the flat to check for fingerprints, any traces of DNA...things like that. Anything that may help us figure out what might have happened if there was a break-in. And I need to talk to you too. Do you know when you will be back?"

"I can come back first thing tomorrow, Detective; I don't feel right being all the way up here when Wendy and Malcolm are in trouble, and I understand that you need to take statements and so on. I only came back here because I got frightened and felt really strange. I guess things should be safer now, do you think?" Her voice trembled slightly as she seeks comfort from Gill's response.

He doesn't hesitate. "I would hope so, but in any case you'll get full police protection over the coming days, Miss Jumeau, just as a precaution. If for any reason you still feel uncomfortable at the apartment, we can find you a safe house. We have several of those which are very discreet and extremely secure."

"That makes me feel better, thanks. You have a very reassuring voice, Detective - I suppose lots of people tell you that."

Gill half-smiles in embarrassment. He wrestles with the need to ask more about Catherine, but pins down the urge, realising that it might make him sound like a flake. "Actually no, but thanks. You have my number now, so you can call me any time. But text me when you are close to the city tomorrow, and I'll meet you at the apartment."

"Sure. See you tomorrow then," Catherine says before ending the call.

Gill turns the stereo back on, shuddering involuntarily as he hears Catherine's voice in his head. He stares out the window at the traffic whizzing by, and at the crossroads ahead. The lights seem to be at red for an eternity, before eventually turning to green, at which he shifts into Drive, and rejoins the traffic heading downtown.

That night Gill spends a little time down at the Star and Shadow, partly because he wants a drink and partly just to check that Malcolm Baines hasn't shown up to play the quiz with Lamar Merriweather. The last thing the University needed was any further disappearances. No sign of Baines, so after a couple of drinks and a stint at the pool table, he heads back downtown to his open-plan apartment. It feels very empty. It always does. Like something is missing. Pouring himself a nightcap, he slumps down on the sofa and flicks on the news. No further developments in the investigation into Montgomery's assassination, and a couple of interviews with Garfield aired that afternoon. Most news focuses on Montgomery's life, his background, his family, his achievements, testimonials from home and abroad, and arrangements for his funeral. He switches the TV off, and grabs a notepad and pen from the large old desk in the corner of the main living area.

He makes a note of things he needs to do tomorrow:
1. Check Downtown – leads/reports
2. Student Records – ID (Catherine)
3. CJ apartment PM
4. Request police presence/guard for CJ
5. Check Melrose – background check/follow-up mtg

He's just about to put the note down and head to the bedroom area, when he realises he has forgotten one important task.
6. Review Garfield TV address/get video

And with that, he heads off to bed, his head swimming in a lake of emotions and information that threatens to drown him. As his head hits the pillow, and his eyes begin to close, he heads back out to the cornfield.

* * * *

CHAPTER 3: ENCOUNTERS

Mitch Nicolescu is chatting to the on-duty surveillance officer in the main CCTV control room in the White House. The badge on George Beston's uniform reads 'SS' from a distance, which is an unfortunate oversight by the Security and Surveillance team in the design of their uniforms. Screens one through six show key locations along the perimeter fence surrounding the nation's Presidential seat. On screens seven, eight and nine are the three main entrances to the building, and ten through twenty cover all major internal connecting doors and all main service centers – catering, mailroom, cleaning, clerking, reception and, of course, security itself. On screen twenty-one, Ellis Garfield is sat at his desk in the Green Room. He looks to be studying papers, the ends of his fingers resting on his forehead, and so covering his face. On screens twenty-two through thirty, all adjacent annexes to the Green Room are covered. There are another thirty CCTV positions, and the Security and Surveillance team number some sixty personnel, all of whom are rigorously checked for background, political activity, mental stability, aptitude, fitness, weapons handling and something called 'Security IQ'. Ironically, the elite nature of these sixty men and women means that they are probably at once the greatest protection and greatest threat to a President, should there be an attempt on his or her life.

The entire staff complement throughout the White House has undergone special examination in the last thirty-six hours following the assassination of Montgomery and you can cut the atmosphere with a knife. Everyone is on edge due to apparent failures in the field which resulted in Montgomery taking two shots to chest and head in quick succession two days ago.

"Anything to report?" he asks Beston.

"No, sir. We may have a little problem with screen twenty-one but I've asked Schwartz to look into it," Beston replies.

"Uh-huh. You know what it is? Did you have signal loss?"

"No, it's fine sir, I just had a bit of static and jitter on screen a couple of times, but it seemed to right itself. It's most likely a connection that needs fixing."

"OK George, keep me posted on that one. Well, it's getting late and Phil is already here, so I'm just going to inform the Vice President of security arrangements."

"You mean 'President', Sir," Beston says with a friendly smile. Nicolescu nods. "Of course."

Everyone at the White House, while still in shock over Montgomery's death, knows that Ellis Garfield is no match for the electric and powerful presence of his predecessor, but they have to work with what they've got. Most think that Garfield will only be there for a short while before there is either a forced contest for the Democratic leadership or an election called early next year. Whatever the case, Garfield is, most presume, going to have a horrid time getting the confidence of the public while dealing with the many outstanding national and international issues.

As Nicolescu takes a last look at Garfield's lonely figure on screen before departing, he mutters "poor bastard" to himself, and heads off towards the Green Room.

Walking down the main corridor to the central atrium, the place is teeming with staff darting in and out of offices, and shouting over each other to be heard. It sounds like a madhouse and Nicolescu has always wondered what the hell all those people actually do, apart from run around like headless chickens all day. He sees Phil Kirkland with two of the senior clerical staff at reception, and they greet each other affably. Mitch and Phil have worked together for years and run a tight operation at the White House, along with colleagues Dave Brewis and Al Mason. These four are the most senior security personnel that have direct and daily access to the President, Vice President, all members of the cabinet, Chief of Staff and senior advisors. The four permute in-house and in-field co-ordination so that each is always up to date with procedures and developments across all areas.

It was Kirkland and Mason who were in-field on Tuesday when the President was killed at the Senate, but all four security chiefs know that something extraordinary happened that day. It is unthinkable that an outsider could have got in to the restroom where the President was found shot dead. So it seems kind of obvious to everyone that it was an inside job. This is intensely worrying, as it most likely means that one of their own was involved in some form of pre-planned plot. This is a hair's width away from conspiracy, and it makes them extremely nervous, arousing suspicions about everyone they have hand-picked, and in whom they have placed their trust.

Right now though, they have to come together as a team while an external investigation is carried out by the special agents, mainly brought in from the secret services and Homeland Security. Everyone is mindful of those guys, because their whole existence revolves around a ruthless stealth in rooting out any individuals or groups involved in action against the United States. If you slip up just once with them, they are all over you and you can kiss your career goodbye at best, and at worst end up being permanently detained if they suspect any part of your story may not add up.

"Shall we report?" says Mitch Nicolescu.

"Let's do it," replies Kirkland, and both men walk purposefully over to to the Green Wing, before arriving at Garfield's office.

Kirkland knocks on the door. It's the security knock – a sequence of one, then five, knocks with the emphasis on the fifth of the five latter knocks. It's done that way so as it's quite counter-intuitive to other common forms of knock. There is no response. Both men wait for a few seconds before Kirkland knocks again. Still no response. Instinctively they both reach underarm for their pistols and rush in, fearing something may be wrong. Garfield is at his desk, staring blankly out the window.

"Are you OK, *Sir*?" Nicolescu raises his voice on the 'Sir', much like he would do in his Army days. His voice retains that strong and attention-grabbing authority that demands a response. Kirkland has already darted to the windows and is checking for any sign of illicit entry, but comes up with nothing.

Garfield looks up, his pupils so dilated that his eyes appear black. It's an unsettling look, distant and cold. For a second, the two security officers are mesmerized Then Garfield, eyes slowly returning to blue again, seems to come to his senses, bewildered by the fuss that's being created.

"Is there a problem, Sir?" Nicolescu is shouting this time.

A second later, Garfield responds. "Uh? No, no....I am fine, Mitch. Sorry about that, I think I must have dozed off for a second there. Were you knocking at the door for long?"

Kirkland gives Nicolescu a glance which says 'what the f...?'. Nicolescu raises his eyebrow and turns back to the now-President. "Sir, my apologies. When we didn't get a reply we just thought there may be a problem, Sir."

Garfield seems to be back in the land of the living. "Understood. Better safe than sorry...but I suppose I should get some rest."

"Sir, as you wish. If you need anything else, the security handover has taken place and I'll be on personal alert through till eight tomorrow morning. Just dial two, here..." Phil Kirkland informs the new President.

"Thanks Phil..." Garfield trails off before adding, "and I appreciate your vigilance guys. Keep up the good work."

Both men nod purposefully, signalling the end of the exchange. Once outside, Kirkland turns to Nicolescu. "What the hell was that?" he says.

"Search me, Phil. I guess the guy is just zoned out. You'd be too if you've been thrown a curveball like he has." Nicolescu makes it sound like it was nothing.

But Kirkland, having been on duty when the President was assassinated, is keen to avoid any slips or errors in security. "Maybe, Mitch, but all staff are briefed on these things. It should be second-nature to respond to a security knock, and he must have known we'd be reporting. Do you think it worth talking to Hart about this?"

Abe Hart is the Secretary of State for Defense, and the guy the security men look up to as the most senior military in the government. If they had a beef, Hart was usually willing to listen, and gives much more respect to the security forces than the rest of the Cabinet.

"Come on Phil, the guy is just exhausted, that's all. What's he gonna be doing in there for pity's sake?" Nicolescu's palm-off comes back, and Kirkland seems assuaged, at least for the time being.

The two get back out into the atrium and go their separate ways, while George Beston is calling his colleague Hank Schwartz to get an update on the technical situation with the main CCTV camera in the Green Room.

——

"You look just awful, honey," Julie Garfield tells her husband as he walks through the living quarters with some papers. For the former Vice President, now President after being sworn in, this is home right now. Cleaning and Service staff were very efficient the day before in moving the former President's personal belongings, along with those of his wife and children, into storage in another part of the building. Garfield and his wife, Julie, will eventually move in, something that she finds particularly distasteful, but for now they are temporarily using the Presidential living quarters to freshen up and prepare for meeting the press. In many ways it feels very strange for Julie Garfield; she never imagined she would be anything other than the Vice President's consort and public-facing advocate for good causes she and others were involved in. Her husband is clearly finding it difficult to come to terms with what has happened, and she knows he isn't sleeping, often elsewhere during the night. This is far from how she imagined life might be, but as is her duty she has determined to support her husband through such difficult times, despite their problems and his demeanor, which sometimes veers toward malevolence.

Ellis Garfield says nothing, instead reaching for the coffee pot which he has ordered catering staff to refill every hour, on the hour, until he tells them not to. Here is someone who had been pushed into the role as leading man when his entire career to date has been as a member of the supporting cast. Someone who has spent the last three years in the shadow of a great man, arguably the boldest national leader the U.S. has ever had the fortune to have in office. Someone who, until the President's demise, has been barely recognized in the street and was, in many ways, the new kid on the block and an unknown quantity to the general public, carrying out lower-priority duties alongside the President.

Garfield knows all this, and he also knows that the reason he was picked as Vice President was as much to keep the centre-right factions of the party happy as anything else. Coming out of Florida, with its natural resources, tourism, wealth, and not an insignificant traffic of drugs and 'laundry', Garfield, a time-served soldier with several tours of duty in the Middle-East, had cut his teeth first as an aide to the mayor in Naples, and started out as a Republican. But the staid and somewhat tired state of the party back then, having suffered at the hands of some excellent Democratic candidates, made him disillusioned, and after taking a short sabbatical, he returned with an insatiable appetite for political life. So much so that he made a life-changing decision to re-locate to Wisconsin, as far from the lush everglades as he could get, where he was encouraged to seek nomination to run as a Democrat for a seat in the House of Representatives.

A slightly odd mix of sharp, rugged features and clean-cut appearance, Ellis Garfield looked the part for the predominantly hard-working people of Wisconsin back then. Somehow, by dressing in ill-fitting suits his tall and lean frame would disappear within, giving him the look of someone who only wore a suit because he had to, and was actually more used to dressing down than dressing up. This was an endearing feature for most. It certainly won him lots of sympathy votes which were directed against the forthright, tailored bunch from the Republican party, as did the development of a harder Northern lilt which helpfully replaced his otherwise indecipherably middle-American tones. All in all, Garfield seemed to be a bit chameleon-like, adapting himself and his public persona to ensure his continued rise in the world of politics. But it worked.

Julie Garfield, née Westbrook, completed the picture of the all-American family. Marrying Ellis while he was in the army, she had brought their two children into the world. And now in the limelight, at Julie's insistence, they are kept away from public events as much as possible; her thinking being that they should remain free from outside intrusions and scrutiny for as long as possible. She clashes with Ellis all the time on this; politicians' children are, in his mind, part of the deal. They should be seen in public to show how politicians are fathers and family men as well as cold and calculating decision-makers. Ingratiating himself with the hierarchy in the Democratic party in Wisconsin, he played things diplomatically and always made sure he garnered support from the more right-wing factions on issues like immigration, foreign policy and defense. As long as nothing went wrong, it was only a matter of time before he would run for Senate, that being more related to experience and age. At forty seven, Garfield was one of the younger Senators, and now, some three years on, the spritely and lean fifty year-old had achieved what very few dreamed of, the highest office in the land. When he was sworn in yesterday, and heard the words 'President Ellis Garfield," a satisfied grin surfaced on his face despite the circumstances in which the pronouncement was made. It didn't matter what other people thought; he had made it. He is number one.

A little while before Nicolescu and Kirkland barged in, Garfield had been in a meeting with Maria Ortega, chief of Homeland Security. He had called her in to discuss her interim report on investigations into the assassination. Ortega, a strong and shrewd lawyer for a long time before running for office, is not only one of the best cabinet members for years, but also, to the surprise of many - including herself – a powerful icon for many women, dressing in bold and sometimes provocative outfits as a statement of both her femininity and authority. She is also someone for whom Garfield has much respect, for she is fiercely loyal to Montgomery and the party. They have battled many times in Cabinet, and her scant disregard for his authority perturbs him. In Garfield's mind this is surely about to change, given the circumstances, and he wanted to use the earlier meeting as much to lay down the 'new rules' as to receive the report. But today's encounter didn't go according to plan.

In fact it ended up making Garfield very uncomfortable. Ortega's report highlighted two main things. First, the conclusion was that there was no-one capable of getting into the men's room at the Senate building with the President, firing two shots with such precision, and then escaping without the security services knowing. Each one of the serving officers that day had been interrogated in depth. In fact, their families and friends were too. And they were searched thoroughly. All the available CCTV footage showed absolutely no sign of unusual activity. There were no tunnels into, or out of, the building, let alone the men's room. Secondly, there was no indication that there had been a plot to kill the President that had been carried out with the knowledge and backing of the security services. There was simply a lack of substance to the whole thing. This effectively meant that the investigation would have to explore other avenues, involve the FBI further, and therefore also remain open and inconclusive.

Together, these conclusions effectively mean that there isn't going to be any rapid closure on the investigation. Moreover, Ortega has got her teeth into this; she stated that the loyalty she feels towards Montgomery will drive her unwaveringly to find the truth behind the assassination. Admirable as this is, it means that he, as President, will have nothing immediately to report to the public, and will have this hanging over him and his cabinet for a while. Worse, not only will it make him look ineffective if the case can't be closed off, but he may also then face challenges to his Presidency. Earlier, as Ortega left the Green Room, she told Garfield that Montgomery would not rest in peace until his killers were found. And now, as the new, and prematurely beleaguered, President re-reads the report, he realises that he will need to get involved in the investigation personally.

—-

Back in Boston, Sandra Chandry is at the desk next day when Gill arrives around 10 a.m.

"My, my. Now what *have* we got here, I wonder?"

"Morning Sandra, make mine black, no sugar and very strong."

"Comin' right up, *Sugar.*"

They both smile before Sandra brings out some papers and slaps them down on her desk.

"I got the background check on Melrose you asked for, and a couple of reports of sightings of young folks that match the Baines and Xiu descriptions, but if you ask me they ain't too reliable."

"Uh-huh – can I see?"

"Here you go, Detective. Knock yourself out..."

"Thanks."

"Oh, and the Lieutenant says there isn't any capacity among the officers for one-to-one protection, so you're going to have to sort that one out yourself."

"Great. First he drags me out of bed because the case is priority then he ducks any additional resource..."

"Well, I guess that's why he's the loo-ten-ant," she quips, stressing the 'loo' part of that phrase.

"Is he in?" asks Gill.

"Yeh, he's with the Captain though."

"OK, Officer Chandry, that'll be all," he says with a sly grin on his face as he makes his way inside.

Chandry smiles to herself.

Gill is approaching his desk. "Harry," Gill nods at Harry Chambers, who is at his desk, as usual.

"Hey Gill, how's it hangin'?" Chambers' line in chat was fairly rudimentary, and although Gill liked Harry, the guy represented everything that was wrong with policing these days. As part of a squad of detectives with a fair trade in homicides and serious crime, Chambers is lazy. Physically and mentally. It annoys Gill because he imagines that at one time Chambers was keen and had a good nose for hunting down some criminal elements. But these days Harry brown-noses with the Captain and gets to cherry-pick which cases he takes before they are handed out to the others. That way, he gets to sit at his desk more and avoid any physical activity. Half the time his partner, Bob Heskey, is out on patrol on his own, which strictly speaking shouldn't happen. And Heskey, Gill thought, is more than likely on the take from the local mob. It all boiled down to values. And in Gill's mind, neither Heskey nor Chambers have many good ones left.

"Proud, my friend. Proud." It was Gill's little put down for Harry.

Gill goes over and pours himself a coffee and then sits back down at his desk. His face creases up the way it would on smelling a rancid corpse. He has taken his first sip of the day. "That'll come in handy for unblocking the drain," he tells Chambers, as he places the cup down on the table.

There are two folders in front of him; one is marked 'FIELD', which he assumes is the sightings of Baines and Xiu, and one is marked 'MELROSE'. He's requested both in paper format as he finds it a struggle with screen and projection-reading. His gut tells him that the sightings will probably come to nothing, but he takes a quick peek inside. There are two reports of a young couple that fit the all-points bulletin distributed the day before. The first is from Reginald Johnson, a ticket salesman at Braintree station who claims that a young Chinese woman and her boyfriend got off at the station and asked how to get to Providence. The report, however, states that they were wearing heavy back-packs, like they were travellers. So, at least on the face of it, this doesn't sound too promising. The report finishes by saying that the local department over in Providence has been put on alert and are 'actively pursuing'. 'Bullshit,' he says to himself. 'Actively pursuing' rarely means that in his experience, but at least something is happening over there. The second report is from Bridget Reisenberger, the head librarian at the Peabody Institute library, who says that they have a member named Wen Xiu who took a book out the previous day called 'Calligraphy and You'.

Given the fact that he can't really do much about those right now, he closes the folder and picks up the weightier of the two, marked 'MELROSE'. Inside is a collection of documents grabbed off the Internet. There's a printout from Wikipedia, which isn't particularly helpful as half of the interesting stuff is only accessible via linked web pages, a couple of Newspaper articles on Melrose's Nobel Prize nomination and a fund-raising event for the Harvard Department of Physics, and a Departmental Request for the Presidential visit back in January. A Departmental Request – D.R. - is a record of a request for police action or involvement in matters of dignitary or public safety, and this one was sent directly from the Professor to the Mayor, which was then forwarded to Captain Sanderson. The request was for a local security presence on the 20th January, when the President visited. As Gill reads the request, he notices what looks like Sanderson's hand-written scrawl across the bottom. He can't read it very well as the captain's writing looks pretty much as if it's from a pre-school infant. He turns the bit of paper at an angle and reads the words to himself. "Mel host VP prior. Sec – no req dept."

He re-reads the note. It seems to say that Vice President Garfield stayed with Melrose before the President's visit and that security was waived for the VP's stay there. Could this be right? Maybe Melrose and Garfield know each other from somewhere in the past – well enough for the Professor to host the Vice President at his house with minimal security? He decides to test the water on the lieutenant, running upstairs and tapping on Young's door. He and the Captain are just finishing a discussion and both greet Gill with nods.

"Lieutenant. Captain." Gill nods to both. "Do you have a minute?"

"You want me here, Gill?" says the Captain. Gill pauses before confirming with a nod.

"You know I am looking into the disappearances at the University? Well, I met with Professor Melrose yesterday. Do either of you know him?"

The Lieutenant nods slightly before the Captain responds."I see him at some events, and I know he raises a bucket load of cash for his research," the Captain says. "Why, what's on your mind, Gill?"

Gill decides to wade right in. "Captain, I noticed that Vice President Garfield came to Boston on a pre-visit before the Presidential visit. Do you know what that was about? It seemed to be very low profile...under the radar, so to speak."

Sanderson looks at Young and then back at Gill. "That's right, Gill, as I understand it Garfield and Melrose go back a way, and so we are sometimes briefed as to private visits, just so that when the VP's security guys are in town, we don't mistake them for the mob."

Lieutenant Young lets out a stifled chuckle and moves over to Gill. "This may not surprise you, Gill, but we don't advertise when the Vice President of the United States is in town if we don't have to..."

"Sure, I get that, sir. What's the history there, do you know?"

"Think it's something to do with Melrose's days in the military. I know Garfield served in the Middle East and had some role in Intelligence before running for Office. What's the angle, Gill?"

The Captain presumes Gill has a theory – he usually does – but on this occasion Gill doesn't have much in the barrel.

"It's not an angle, sir, I just read that Melrose had hosted the Vice President and wondered if it had been in an official capacity, that's all."

"OK, well, let us know when you've got something to report, Detective," the Lieutenant wraps up the conversation before turning to Sanderson. "Thanks, Captain," he says to signal it's time to break the little gathering up.

The Captain and Gill leave the Lieutenant's office and go their separate ways, but once Gill sees that the Captain has gone he returns and knocks again on the Lieutenant's door.

"What now?" Young asks Gill.

"Uh, I understand that you denied my request for a patrol presence for Miss Jumeau, is that right?"

"Who?"

"Miss Jumeau, the student who filed the missing persons on the two over at the University."

"Oh, uh, yes, sorry Gill, no can do. There's no-one around."

"Can't you draft in a couple of officers from Allston or Cambridge? I mean, it's more their patch than ours and my feel on this is that she may need some protection in the short term."

"Look, the priority tag on this is so you get it sorted out in double-quick time, but look around you – we have hardly any staff to cover even the basic functions, so you are 'it', Gill, unless you have something more concrete to go on here?"

"Uh, no, not really sir, not as such. But listen, I'm going over to the apartment this afternoon, and I'll be doing a forensic examination. She's convinced that her flatmate is in trouble, and she is definitely spooked. Can we agree that if I confirm evidence of a struggle, or anything else suspicious, we escalate and put a couple of guys on her – what do you say? I mean, we wouldn't want anything nasty on our hands here sir, if you get my drift."

Young thinks about what Gill has just implied. "Hhmmm. OK, Detective, but I'll need something to go on. So far we have a couple of youngsters that have split up after a fight, and their friend who thinks this means that it's a doomsday scenario. It happens all the time, and it don't mean a thing, until it means a thing. You know that."

Gill lets out a heavy sigh. "Yes, sir," he says. Like Chandry said, that's why the Lieutenant is the loo-tenant.

When Gill gets back to his desk, he notices a missed call from 'C Jumeau'. "Shit," he mumbles. He presses the call button to ring her back. The opening chords to 'If I Needed Someone' by the Beatles ring out on Catherine's bio-cell. She is a huge Beatles fan, like her dad. She takes the call while Christophe Jumeau points to the sign for Prospect Hill to let her know where they are.

"Hi. It's Catherine here," she declares. There is a bit of background noise and the signal isn't great, but even so it's unmistakably her. The greatest struggle right now is to try and stop himself from getting distracted by the soft Northern lilt in tone and intonation when she speaks.

"Miss Jumeau, Hi, it's Detective Gill, I'm sorry I missed your call earlier. Where are you at the moment?" Gill is worried that she might be at the apartment on her own.

"Oh, that's OK, Detective, I just rang to let you know that we'll be hitting Boston in about twenty minutes. Do you want us to come straight to the apartment?"

"Uh, yes, I can make it over there in twenty, but please wait outside in the car. I will need to carry out some tests and so we should be careful not to disturb too much. Who else is with you, by the way?"

"My Dad's here – my parents are worried about me so he wanted to drive me down."

Gill nods his head. "That makes sense. Listen, I better get moving if I am going to reach you in time. I will call you when I arrive."

"OK, well, um, see you soon!" Her intonation rises at the end to convey a sense of optimism, and she is genuinely pleased that the Detective is taking things so seriously. Last night she tried to think back to whether or not she might have met a Detective Gill, maybe when all those policeman were at the University for the President's visit. But she couldn't picture him.

Catherine's dad pulls in and parks the car in the nearest open space about fifty yards down the street. "Honey, I'm just going to go over to check if it's clear," Christophe Jumeau informs his daughter.

"Oh, Dad, you don't need to, really. I mean, Detective Gill is going to be here any minute and it's better if we just wait for him, don't you think?"

Before he can reply, Catherine's cell rings, and Gill says he is at the entrance to the building. They look over and up the street they can make out a tall figure, carrying what looks like a small leather briefcase, standing in front of number forty-eight, Nile Street. As they get out the car, Christophe's cell goes off. It's Mary Jumeau.

"You go on, Catherine, I'll be across in a second," he tells his daughter, "But wait there for me. I want to check this guy out before we go back into the apartment."

Catherine hasn't the inclination to argue. She knows her dad is just being protective, but at the same time she is intrigued by the figure in the doorway, and leaves Christophe to take the call, checking for traffic before skipping across to the other side of the road.

Gill is kicking himself because he didn't get the student ID for Catherine, so he doesn't know what she looks like. As he turns around and looks back down the street, he sees a figure skipping onto the pavement. It's a normal enough scene to anyone else, but it's Catherine he is looking at, and the shock hits him instantly. As he looks at her form coming towards him, she is engulfed in a ball of bright light. A bustling street full of movement is transforming; all the figures in the frame are beginning to slow down. Catherine must be no more than twenty feet away, moving towards him. And he is transfixed by her. She is glowing, a spectacular aura embracing her, and for a moment he wonders if he is in a dream. The world around them is grinding to a halt. Even the wind that rustles the awnings of the shops up and down the street stops blowing. But Catherine and Gill are the moving dimensions that stand at an angle to everything else. And with every step Catherine takes towards him, the slower the motion gets.

The intense white light surrounding her broadens out and diffuses, creating an interior from which gracefully emerges the most exquisite and stunning vision that Gill has ever witnessed. Somehow she seems so familiar, as if it were a reunion rather than an introduction. Time has slowed to allow him to understand this, to take it in. To embrace what is in front of him. Confined to his dreams, she has been, until now, a figment of another world, another universe, another reality. But here, now, in the real world, he is frozen to the spot as everything seems to have come to a stop.

As Catherine skips onto the pavement, she sees Detective Gill's hair being blown by the wind that is funnelling down the street, then his hand reach up to pat it back down before noticing his purposeful scan up and down the street. Coming closer she can only just make out his face from the side, but the outline is classic and she senses a strong presence. As she gets within a few yards of Gill, he turns to face her and she is caught in the headlights of his piercing blue eyes. Her walking pace slows as she is hit by the realisation that this man is very important. She doesn't know why. A physical sensation of being very slow and heavy washes over her, and she begins to think she might be hallucinating as she sees the detective in a soft haze of light as if he is some sort of savior. She should be upset and worried by this series of events, but instead is calm and receptive. Her nerve-ends are tingling; her fingertips sense the change in air pressure, the atmosphere itself thick with anticipation. She has become super-sensitive to that which is around her.

As she gradually gets closer to Gill, a wonderfully open and optimistic smile spreads across her face. He *knows* something. About *her*. No, he *knows her*. They are intimately connected but they have never met, but this is where her knowledge ends. Regardless, she doesn't want the sensations to stop; nothing else seems to matter right now except the man in front of her. Catherine comes to a halt opposite Detective Denton Gill.

To passers by, it would look odd perhaps. Gill and Catherine are stood outside number forty-eight, Nile Street, absolutely still. They are looking into each other's eyes, smiling at each other, in silence. Some time passes; perhaps a second, or possibly a minute.

"Detective Gill!" comes a distant voice that reverberates around them. It is the catalyst for a break in the atmosphere and both slowly snap out of their apparent catatonia. The static picture is reignited into motion, and the street picks up life, the hustle and bustle beginning to reach full pace. It is Christophe Jumeau, scurrying up the street to catch the two before they go to the apartment. For a moment the two can't break the stare. "Detective Gill! Catherine!" he calls again, this time raising his voice.

"Is everything OK? Have you guys introduced yourselves? Are we ready to go up?" Christophe Jumeau enquires.

It is Gill who comes round first. As he adjusts, he moves his head toward Catherine's father, but his eyes won't move away from Catherine's. It is veering towards an awkward situation. Christophe begins to look concerned about Catherine and quite firmly says "Catherine," as if she were being reprimanded as a child. She too snaps out, and turns to her dad.

"You must be Professor Jumeau," Gill directs his assertion confidently at the older man, and salvages his initial command of the situation.

Professor Jumeau seems distracted by Catherine's well-being for a moment, but Catherine's smile lets him know that she is fine, and he turns to Gill. Being a bit more formal than either of the other two, he is more bound by social etiquette and only if pushed would create a scene.

"Detective Gill. My pleasure," he says and extends his hand to Gill. "I see you've already met my daughter?"

Gill shakes the professor's hand. "Uh..." he doesn't know how to answer that, as actually he and Catherine have not done anything as mundane as say 'Hello' yet. Gill and Catherine give each other a look, and smile. There is a tacit agreement to play out the real-world scene before them and to quell the urge to embrace and figure out what the hell just happened. Nevertheless, the pair are on a heightened plane and and it takes all their determination and presence of mind to refrain from grabbing hold of the other's hand. The hesitation in doing so only strengthens the anticipation of what may come.

It's Catherine's turn to salvage something, her filial duty of care and respect for her father coming to the fore. "Yes, Dad, we were just wondering if we might already have met each other." Her inflexion seems so child-like and innocent that her father senses how positive she is, and immediately relaxes.

"Oh really?" he smiles.

"Uh-huh, it might have been during the Presidential visit," his daughter muses.

Gill, detecting that this conversational thread can serve no immediate purpose, switches into detective mode. "Anyway, I guess you guys are pretty tired after a long trip, so what do you say we head upstairs?" at which the other two nod and the trio go inside, led by Gill.

Outside Catherine's apartment Gill carries out a couple of quick checks on the two different locks, dusting for fingerprints and using an ultraviolet light to check for any signs of blood. Then he asks Catherine to unlock the door, which she does and Gill moves inside. It takes a little while for Gill to thoroughly check the entire apartment for prints, blood stains and any damage.

Catherine and her father wait patiently in the living room while this is going on, discussing plans for the coming days.

"Was Miss Xiu here when you left for the Plaza hotel with your dad the other night?" Gill asks Catherine as he emerges from the kitchen.

"I don't know, but probably not is my guess. She went to meet Mal, I know. We left for the hotel pretty late. So she must have come back very late indeed."

"And you didn't notice the fridge magnet and the state of her room that evening, only the next day?"

"I don't think I was in the kitchen after we both came back from the University, and I only checked the bedroom the next day before I left with my dad, so no, I wouldn't have noticed anything at that point," she responds.

On the face of it, there are no obvious signs of break-in. So what happened after Catherine went over to the Plaza to meet her dad seems a mystery. And why Wendy sent a coded message to her flatmate rather than call the police or Catherine is still unclear. Gill becomes convinced that, at the very least, Xiu - either alone or with Malcolm - felt threatened and was very possibly forced out of the flat.

Gill looks at Catherine and smiles at her, thinking how beautifully vulnerable she is right now. It's hard for him to remain detached and think straight, but he knows he has to if he is to help her.

"Catherine, how long had Wendy and Malcolm been dating?"

"Oh, since our days in Montreal, why?"

"And they were, as far as you know, happy and content?"

"Yes, very. I mean, they have their little spats every so often like most, but they are very strong together."

"Uh-huh, so no big fights or anything..." states Gill rhetorically, giving enough time for a comeback, but Catherine just shakes her head.

"And when you called Wendy and Mal, did it ring out, or did it go straight to voicemail?"

"Uh, it rang out on Wendy's I think, but not on Mal's."

Gill is thinking that if Wendy's cell had run out of battery or was broken, any calls would go straight to voicemail, so it was likely that Xiu either wouldn't or *couldn't* take a call. And it does seem strange that Wendy hasn't called.

"Just one more thing – if it is very late at night, who else would Wendy let in here apart from you or Malcolm?"

Catherine thinks for a second. "I can't think of anyone, apart from Wendy's parents or at a stretch Mal's dad, but they don't live here, so no-one really."

"OK. So I guess the only other person with keys to this place is the landlord or his building supervisor, is that right?"

"Mm-hmm. That's Vinnie though - he looks after most of these right down to the corner of Nile and Stretton. He's really friendly. He's getting on now, and complains about his arthritis and how difficult it is to get up and down the stairs."

"What about neighbors – you know any of them well enough to come round for drinks or a chat at that time of night?"

"Not really. I mean, we get on OK with the neighbors, but we don't socialize with them. Do you think Vinnie or the neighbors have something to do with this?" she asks.

Possibilities were running out, and Gill decides to get the Jumeaus in on his thinking so far.

"On balance, no. I'll need to check the results of prints and bloods when they come back from the lab, but my guess is that whoever was here was not known to your friends."

Christophe Jumeau shifts in his seat, and an increasing sense of unease pervades the room.

In his mind, Gill came back to the point he put to Lieutenant Young the day before. Why, on the day the President was assassinated, would anyone kidnap two PhD students form Harvard? Unless this was already carefully planned and was for some sort of ransom or revenge motive, it stood to reason that something must have happened that day to initiate the action to kidnap the two. But what?

"Catherine, I'll need the bio-cell numbers for Wendy and Mal from you. We'll get the cell company to check activity over the last forty-eight hours," Gill states, and Catherine indicates her agreement.

Gill now turns to Christophe Jumeau, who has been listening intently to the questioning. "Professor, could I trouble you to help out for a second?"

The Professor perks up and nods at Gill eagerly. "Yes, of course."

"Well, I think it's probably better if Catherine is based somewhere else for a few days - just until we have a better idea what happened to Catherine's friends. My suggestion is that you book a room at a hotel somewhere for a few days under a different name – locally though, so we can ensure you are safe. Do you think you can sort something out?"

The Professor lifts his head and looks piercingly at Gill. "Of course, Detective, I'll book a suite at the Plaza."

"No," instructs Gill. "It will be safer to base yourselves at one of the lesser known hotels, and you need to book in under different names. Try somewhere like the Roquefort or Burlington – you'll be less conspicuous."

"I see. So you *are* convinced something sinister is going on?" the Professor quizzes Gill.

"I am just covering the bases at this stage, Sir. Until I have a better idea of what is going on, I have to assume the worst-case scenario and act accordingly." Gill sounds textbook, but his professionalism is dwarfed by the absolute commitment to ensure Catherine is safe from harm. "So, if you can make a start on organising that, I have a few more questions I'd like to ask Catherine?"

"No problem, Detective, I'll get on to it straight away," the Professor assures him, and begins to forage in his coat pocket for his cell.

"Catherine?" Gill ushers Catherine towards the large French windows that dominate the room and lowers his tone to a whisper as the two are silhouetted against a view of Boston high-rises. "Did you feel what happened there?"

"Yes," she replies, but she cannot offer anything more. Her sparkling turquoise eyes are searching his.

He wants more from her, but right now he figures they just need to have some time together away from her father, which won't be easy as Christophe Jumeau is rightly worried about his daughter and won't want to leave her for a second. He will have to be patient, not a known quality of his.

"I can't explain what just happened, but I know it happened, and I know that you are very special to me for some reason. If you feel the same way, just let me know."

She holds his gaze the entire time, locked into his presence. It could be an affirmation from Catherine, but suddenly she becomes self-conscious, fighting to understand what is happening. She looks away, and then back at Gill.

"Who *are* you?" she says, not knowing what to expect as an answer.

Gill opens the windows and signals to Catherine to follow him out onto the balcony. His voice is soft and low, merging with the drone of the traffic from outside. "We must be connected in some way, that's all I know," he explains, and lets out a heavy sigh. "When I heard your voice on the cell, I couldn't figure it out at first, but it's the same voice that I have heard for years in my dreams, and when I saw you walking up the street just then, I recognized every particle in your body even though I've never met you in person before."

Gill pauses. Catherine can't take it in, and he realises that this is scary stuff.

He continues, "Listen, I know I shouldn't say any of this. I just figured you'd understand if you felt what I felt..."

"I don't think I understand anything right now, Detective. I really don't know what happened there, it's so strange - like I am in some weird dream. And I am terrified for my friends..." Catherine declares.

It makes Gill feel strange too, as he wants her to open up more. But he gets it. She is overloaded, and her mind is protecting her. She has very real concerns in this world, this reality. And she doesn't even know anything about him. He decides to peg things back a bit.

"Yeh, look, let's focus on finding Wendy and Malcolm first, but promise me one thing," he says, making sure Catherine looks at him square on.

"Yes?" she replies, still faltering.

Gill hesitates. He wants to say 'promise me that we will spend the rest of our lives together' or 'promise me that we will explore the universe together' or, at the very least, 'promise me we can spend some time together this evening'. But something prevents him, probably thinking that it might pressure her.

"Promise me you'll call me Gill from now on?"

There is an imperceptible pause before Catherine chuckles as Gill's quip relieves the tension, and she offers him a welcome relaxed smile. "OK, *Gill.*"

Professor Jumeau's voice becomes more prominent in the room as he confirms with the hotel. "Right, thanks. We'll be arriving around seven."

Gill and Catherine move back into the main room, before Gill asks them to sit down. "OK, so I apologize in advance about this, but I need to understand more about events as they happened on Tuesday. I understand that you were all together last during Garfield's TV address, and that Wendy and Malcolm had thought something had happened to Garfield?"

Catherine looks at her dad, and the Professor in turn addresses Gill. "How did you hear about that, Detective?"

"Well, it wasn't too difficult – some students in the refectory told me that Malcolm had been asking them if they thought there was anything strange about Garfield on the TV, but it sounded like no-one knew what he was talking about." Instinctively he turns to Catherine. "Did you know about this?"

Christophe makes a face to suggest to Catherine that she shouldn't say anything. She knows why. If she says it is *her* that witnessed the event then she will be drawn in and could be at further risk. But the reverse is also true. Wendy and Malcolm didn't see anything that day; it was her, and her sense of honesty and fair play takes over. Another factor comes into play too. After meeting Gill, all those minutes ago, for some reason she doesn't want to hide anything from him.

"Look, Detective. *Gill*. It was *me* who freaked out at Garfield's appearance on TV. Wendy and Mal were just asking around if anyone else saw what I saw. They were doing that for me." Her voice falters a little. "All because I didn't want to sound flakey and look like an idiot."

"OK, Catherine. It's fine - those guys were just being friends, that's all. Don't beat yourself up." He inclines his head to catch her eye, and she puts on a smile for him, but he knows she's upset at the thought that if her friends are in trouble then it might be her fault. "If you can, just give me the order of events, as they happened. That way I can gauge what we are dealing with here."

Catherine relays in detail what happened, as she had done with her father. But this time she paints a graphic picture of how Garfield changed.

"I really need to watch that again - it was like Garfield just wasn't *there* at that point," she concludes.

Gill stiffens and straightens his back. Catherine's account has chilled him and he is struggling to remain collected. It's difficult to know how to respond.

"Well, that sure sounds strange. And you're right – we need to track down the video of the TV address. I would have been freaked out too, so I understand your anxiety." He pauses. "Look, I don't know about you two, but I could do with a coffee or something stronger."

Christophe Jumeau takes the opportunity of a break in the conversation to suggest that they make their way over to the Burlington and grab a drink somewhere over there. Catherine appears exhausted just by recounting everything again. And Gill is wading deep in confusion; in the space of a few hours he has been through the gamut of emotions, taking on what should be a trivial case which has turned out to be life-changing. Most of all, he is desperately trying to make sense of two things; on the one hand finding Catherine, and on the other the significance of Garfield, who now seems to hold some sort of clue as to why two young people have gone missing.

As Catherine packs some things for a short stay and her father visits the bathroom, Gill looks around the main living room. It's modern, yet homely. Bright, yet subtle. There's a good quality copy of The Glass by Picasso on the wall. He loves Picasso, especially his Cubist pieces. He moves closer to see the quality of the canvas used. As he does so, he notices a very slight angle on the vertical of the canvas, pushing it out from the wall. Squinting to see in the slit between the wall and the painting, he sees a black wire. Gently, he grips the lower corner of the canvas and uses his index finger to nudge it away from the wall further. It's a bug. Plain as day. He hesitates. 'What the...?' he thinks, steeling himself not to say anything out loud. Their entire conversation has just been recorded. Whoever was at the flat planted a bug. Or had it been there for a while? 'Shit'. Gill's internal dialogue can't get any more eloquent on this occasion.

This is nasty. Game-changing. No, the game has already changed. But this means organized surveillance, and danger. If Catherine was only a bit-player before, she is centre-stage now. Deciding not to interfere with the bug, Gill awaits Catherine and her Dad, and, once he has checked they are ready to go, ushers them out of the apartment. As they walk downstairs, he wonders if he needs to report this to Lieutenant Young downtown. For now, he decides against. Instead he focuses on the immediate need to get the Jumeau's safe. There was nothing for it, but to get them somewhere hidden. If whoever was listening thought they were going to the Burlington, it wouldn't be long before they'd come looking.

Obviously Catherine would be some sort of target, and he guessed that if Xiu and Baines were being held somewhere, they would have told their captors that it was Catherine who was witness to Garfield's performance on screen. What was the connection? Paranoia is creeping in and as they leave the building, the bright light outside brings Gill round to thinking about going into hiding.

The detective scans the street for any obvious tails. He can't see anything. "Where are you parked?" he asks Christophe.

"Just down there."

"The blue Fusion over there?"

"That's it, yes."

Gill lowers his voice and gets closer to the Professor's ear. "OK, don't ask me any questions but I am going to lead in my Oldsmobile, just there. We are going south, not north. I'm going to take us to a place that will be safer than the Burlington."

"But I've booked us in there..." Jumeau comes back.

"I know, it's just safer this way. Please trust me on this one."

The Professor looks surprised, but doesn't argue.

Gill accompanies the Jumeaus over to their car and checks underneath and inside the car for bugs. He tells them it's just routine and not to worry. He then goes back down the street and draws away in the Oldsmobile. The Jumeaus follow him. After Gill has taken a couple of odd turns and is happy there is no tail, both cars head south out of the city.

—-

Gill's bio-cell is showing a picture of Grady Jones. "Grady?" he says, as the connection kicks in.

"Gill? Hell, good to hear from you, man. What's happening with you, brother? Bizarre times, huh?"

"Bizarre. Listen, I'm not far from your house, man, and I need a favor..."

"Uh, sure. What's the score?"

"Got a couple of good people who I need to hide for a couple of days. They are straight, nothing heavy. Can you give them the spare room?"

"Uh, yeh, I guess."

Grady Jones' wife left him about a year ago and Grady has a three-bed over in Dorchester.

"I got Monique here, but we got space. You going to be around too?"

"Yeh, I'll update you when I get there, man. And thanks – I wouldn't do this, you know..."

"Yeh, Yeh, Gill. Tell me about it. Glad to help, you know that."

—-

"Dad, where are we *going*?" Catherine asks.

"Not sure, but Gill insisted we go south and not to the Burlington," her dad responds.

"Dad, I'm scared. This is all making me feel..."

"I know, I know, honey. Look, do you trust this guy?"

"Gill? Yes I do. I..."

"Well, I do too. Don't ask me why, but my gut tells me he is a good guy and he's genuinely worried about you. I'm inclined to go along with his plans until Wendy and Malcolm show up and things get back to normal. He doesn't strike me as the kind of man who would do things like this unless it was necessary."

Half an hour later Gill and the Jumeaus are at Grady Jones' house. After introductions, Grady and his girlfriend Monique pass round some Schlitz beers, and they order in some pizza. Catherine's anxieties subside for a while as she begins to warm to their friendly hosts.

"So, you and your dad are kinda mad scientists, right?" Grady asks cheekily. They are in his home, he doesn't know what's happening. He has the right to ask whatever he likes until he's told to shut up.

Catherine takes a slug of beer, and gets to it. "Yeh, we are. We just developed a time machine," she says, jokingly.

Christophe Jumeau hasn't been in this kind of environment since he was a student and, relaxing into the discussion, offers Grady an explanation of what they do.

"We basically do tests on tiny particles like electrons and photons to see how the world really works, in minute detail. The funny thing is, this also explains how the Universe works too."

"You mean like stars and shit?" Monique comes in.

"Exactly," the Professor answers.

"Wow, I love all that stuff, man. I don't get it, but I love it!" Grady adds.

After a while, Monique shows the Jumeaus where they'll be sleeping, and she and Grady get off to bed. Soon after, Christophe and his daughter go to the larger of the two spare bedrooms. As she enters the room Catherine looks back towards Gill, and raises her arm in a hesitant attempt at a wave. Gill opens his mouth as if about to say 'goodnight' or some such thing, but nothing comes out, and instead he smiles at her, wishing that she would just come over and hug him. But her father calls her and she disappears into the room.

Checking in with District, there is nothing new on Baines and Xiu, and the cell records won't be checked until at least noon next day. Gill lets them know he and the Jumeaus are out of town, without specifying where. Right now, he isn't ruling anyone out of his suspicions, including the likes of Captain Sanderson. As he considers the Captain and Lieutenant at the precinct Downtown, he resists the temptation to go down the conspiracy route. But he does remember that Sanderson said that Garfield was a friend of Walter Melrose. So Garfield has a history with Melrose. And Melrose is the mentor for the PhD students at the Heisenberg building. Here is a direct link between Catherine and Garfield. As he ponders this, Christophe Jumeau comes back into the large kitchen area.

"Just getting some water for us," he says, as he looks for glasses.

"Professor, what's Walter Melrose like? Do you know him?" Gill asks.

"Detective, I am not the right person to answer that question," comes the response.

"Oh yes? Why is that?"

"Well, I have to admit to a great bias, which will probably color your impression too much."

"Hhhmm. Well, why not let me be the judge of that. Do I detect that the bias is negative?" Gill already knows that Christophe Jumeau is indicating his dislike of the man.

"It's like this. Walter Melrose and I go back some way. When I completed my postgraduate work I was approached by the Defense Department to carry out some work into new military technologies. It was a real opportunity for me at the time, so I enlisted in the military, got plenty of funding to do what I was researching, and was able to get my teeth into some real gnarly problems."

"So where did Melrose fit into all this then?"

"He was one of the overseas research physicists brought in. Bit like me. But he started brown-nosing and soon became Head of the team. He was a real jerk. I mean, he'd make bad decisions and sometimes stop projects that were absolutely ground-breaking. All the things that people who don't know how to manage think they should do, he did, and most of his decisions turned out to be flawed."

"What about Garfield, was he about then?" asks Gill

"No, I don't know where he fits in with Melrose, except that it's common knowledge among some of the old crew that Walter is getting huge amounts of funding for some projects that he is working on, and most of it is approved indirectly through Garfield. I know Garfield spent some time in military intelligence. I heard that somewhere, maybe at an old reunion or something."

"OK, so help me out here. You can't stand Melrose, but he's supervising your daughter's PhD. That's got to be bad, right?"

"Not really. Look, I don't like the man. He took the credit for some real breakthroughs we made back then, and then he piggy-backed that credit onto funding applications so that he could afford to conduct leading-edge research programmes, and get the best brains to work for him. *But*, Catherine is a genius. She deserves the very best facilities and sponsorship she can get, because I believe one day she will head up one of the major research organizations in North America."

"So you supported Catherine's application to Harvard." Gill pauses a second before adding, "And she doesn't know about Melrose's thievery and greed?"

"No. Well, she might, but it won't have come from me."

"OK, Professor. I get it. But what about the actual research? I mean, what is it that you and Melrose discovered back then? Can you tell me?"

"I'm not supposed to mention anything about that research, Gill. It's just an oath we take, and we are sworn to secrecy as it may affect the defense of the country itself."

"Hhhmm," sighs Gill, "that makes it difficult for me. I need some sort of starting point to understand what Catherine witnessed when Garfield was on TV. Do you have any notion of what that might have been – you've heard her account twice now, right?"

Jumeau ponders for a second, looking down at his feet. "You know, I don't....I have never heard of anything like that before, so it's a difficult one to analyze. It looks like no-one else saw what Catherine saw, so from a scientific point of view, the probability would be that it is nothing. But I believe my daughter. It might be that she has some sort of heightened sensitivity to certain forms of light, or waves, or more generally, broadcasts. But if that were the case then she'd have seen other things, not just this. If I were looking at this logically I'd say that whatever she saw was caused by two reagents – Garfield on the one hand and Catherine on the other. My worry is that it is *only* Catherine that has witnessed Garfield's behavior. If that is the case, then you must be thinking, as I'm thinking, that she is in some sort of danger if Garfield was up to no good. That is why you have brought us here."

Gill gets up from the kitchen table and moves closer to Christophe Jumeau.

"I am beginning to think that Catherine has witnessed something that is..." he hesitates, trying to find adequate wording, "...incriminating. My conclusion so far is that this can only be on the part of Garfield. That unbeknown to an entire TV audience, except Catherine, something happened to Garfield during his address that made his face appear to change and take on the appearance of John Montgomery. But if Montgomery is dead, then I don't know how to characterize this. I can't quite believe she saw the ghost of Montgomery. But if that really was Montgomery, then is he still alive?"

"Detective, you don't strike me as the sort of person that believes in ghosts, and I doubt very much if John Montgomery is alive. Why would they say the President has been killed if he is still alive? That makes less sense than seeing ghosts."

"I know. You're right. There has to be something else." Gill is fighting his own mind now. He knows the professor is correct, but doesn't want to jump to conclusions about Garfield. One thing that is bugging him - the apparent time-out Catherine reported during the address. Maybe it was a malfunction, but if that were the case then other people would have noticed that, and it would appear in the video. He begins to create, and then discard, hypothesis after hypothesis, thinking each one so bizarre that there needs to be a simpler explanation. As a true scientist should.

"What is it that Melrose got his Nobel prize nomination for?" he asks the Professor.

"Oh, he and a colleague at Cambridge – the one in England - got that for showing how large objects can theoretically move through time.'

"What, you mean like time travel?"

"Yes, only in theory though. I did a lot of work on this before Melrose knew what he was talking about. All he did was come up with the summary of what several people had already proven."

"OK, so in practice it wasn't possible?"

"Well, that's the question. Mainly because the only way in which dense objects with significant mass could travel in time - including us humans if that is what you are thinking - require that circumstances mimic the event horizon at a black hole, where normal physical laws of the universe are subjugated to quantum mechanics." The Professor notices that Gill hasn't been thrown by some of the parlance, so after a brief pause, carries on with the explanation. "Black holes hold a lot of promise for us as scientists because they exhibit some of the most extreme conditions found in the Universe. The interactions between gravity, mass and light are not particularly well understood. If we can understand what happens in such places, we might be able to understand our physical world better, and some of the anomalies that apparently exist within it."

Gill considers the Professor's somewhat measured response, his eagerness for explanation getting the better of him.

"OK, suppose those conditions could be created artificially, here on earth. Could someone or something travel through time that way?"

"Well, that's what many of the colliders around today try to do. They simulate the conditions of, for example, certain aspects of black holes. But of course they operate using tiny particles rather than large collections of billions of particles like us."

Jumeau pauses a second, much as he might do in a lecture in response to a two-part question. "But I think you, and many others, are asking the wrong question, Gill. For me, a more attractive hypothesis is that time travel can actually be independent of local constraints."

"How's that?" Gill squints at the Professor.

Christophe Jumeau looks at his watch. It's gone 11 p.m.

"Forgive me, Detective, but I'm afraid I've become rather tired. Can we pick this up again tomorrow? I'm very happy to discuss these things; it's just that I suspect Catherine would like her water and I have driven a long way today."

Gill is embarrassed. He has kept the Professor from his daughter and was following a selfish line of thought at the expense of a worried father. "My apologies, Professor. I get carried away by my fascination for such things sometimes. Don't let me keep you any longer."

"Very well. Good night to you then," and with that the Professor ambles off to his temporary bedroom at the other side of the house.

It's been a long day for everyone. As Gill dumps down on the camp-bed Grady has put out in the box room by the garage, he begins to reflect on all the different strands of his exploration so far. Right now it seems like he's in the middle of a fog of possibilities. And not being able to be with Catherine is killing him. Actually being with her, instead of having to grab little fleeting moments between running away from...well, who? Who the hell is bugging Catherine's place, and what do they want? Are Baines and Xiu just bait for him and Catherine? Why Catherine?

As his head hits the pillow, he wonders if he might meet Catherine in his dreams...

* * * *

CHAPTER 4: SPECULATIONS

'MONTGOMERY AUTOPSY: CLINICAL SHOOTING HALLMARK OF HITMAN', reads the front page of the Boston Globe.

CNN is on the TV and anchorman Bill Sherman is on air.

"As the investigation continues into the untimely death of President John Montgomery, government officials revealed late last night that an autopsy carried out by the Chief Medical Officer for the District of Columbia reported the cause of death to be two gunshot wounds, one to the chest and one to the head. John Hooper, leading the State's efforts to find the killer, or killers, had this to say:"

The screen switches to an outside broadcast unit where Hooper, a pallid, slightly-built uniformed gentleman approaching middle-age, reads out a prepared statement to reporters in a distinctive southern drawl.

"I can confirm that the President was killed with a .22 calibre pistol, most likely a standard issue weapon widely available commercially, and found in most military and law enforcement agencies across the country. The nature of the injuries inflicted suggests a clinical hit-and-run, most likely carried out by someone experienced in handling firearms. So far, forensics have not shown up significant clues as to the identity of the attacker, or attackers. I will be releasing further statements as the investigation continues…"

"Mr Hooper, sir!"

A cacophony of shouts from the assembled press follows, before the news channel cuts back to the studio.

"Well, as we heard there, investigations still obviously underway and, as yet, inconclusive as to the exact nature of the attack on the late President. We will bring you more throughout the day as we hear it. Meg Donnelly has more over at the White House. Meg, what's happening there?"

"Well Bill, so far there has been no further public announcement from the White House Press Secretary and Chief Spokesperson for the government, Shammi Sarin, on developments here, but I understand that a full internal investigation is underway within the White House itself and that this is being carried out by a combined FBI and Secret Service unit specially selected for this task. Out here, the Capitol building is still under heavy security and a slow and thorough sweep of the entire area is being carried out both within and outside up to and including the security perimeter. As you can see behind me, the place is still inundated with security men and army personnel, aided by local police. It looks a little chaotic, Bill, but we are assured that everything is under control. Despite that, I doubt very much we'll have any answers for people at home by the end of today, but obviously we'll report back as soon as we get any breaking news. Back to you in the studio, Bill..."

"Thank you very much, Meg, for that update, I'm sure we'll be back with you before long. Now, in other news today..."

Grady Jones flicks off the TV with the remote.

"Sounds like they got themselves a whole lotta nothin' goin' on down there, huh?"

"Did she just say that her sorry ass ain't got a clue as to what the hell is happening? I think *sooooo...*" adds Monique as she trails off in a sarcastic drool. "Looks like it's gotta be an inside job. What a surprise."

"Shit, man, how difficult can it be? The man went to the John, and got pumped by some CIA Secret Service Navy Seal who got paid by the Republicans to get rid of Montgomery's ass and make sure we go back to the dark ages," Grady offers.

"What makes you so sure it's the Republicans?" Catherine asks Grady.

"It's *obvious,* preppie, I mean who else has the motive and the method to be able to get around the guy's entire security team? I mean they got past the starting line-up *and* the bench and still dunked on his ass. You don't get to the paint like that unless someone fucks up big time or they on the take to throw the game. And I'm tellin' you there is a whole science behind throwin' games..."

Catherine doesn't really follow what Grady is saying, but gets the gist.

Gill is just finishing some juice before coming into the conversation. "What is obvious is that Montgomery didn't stand a chance," he says.

Grady has the bit between his teeth."Either there was a conspiracy or there was one guy who nailed him. And my bet isn't on the 'lone gunman', no sir." Grady is half-kidding and Monique chuckles sardonically at his reference to Lee Harvey Oswald.

Gill shakes his head. "I'm not so sure. It's just...well, we just don't know what the hell happened in there. My guess is that there could *only be* one or two people tops who could have been present, and there's a whole bunch of people who had a beef with Montgomery, so 'The Right' won't cut it with me until we know a bit more." He gets up and goes over to the coffee pot and fills his cup. As he takes a sip he looks surprised. "So this is what coffee is supposed to taste like..." he reflects, and then gives a little satisfied look to himself.

Christophe Jumeau comes over to the table and addresses Grady and Monique. "I just wanted to say thanks for putting us up here – we were very comfortable last night." He nods.

"No problem, man," Grady replies.

"So, Detective, what are our plans for today?" the Professor asks Gill.

"Well, I have a few calls to make, and then I think I need to get into the city to check out some leads. I'd be grateful if you could stay here and be vigilant. I think we should put a call in on the hour every hour until I get back. That sound OK?"

"Yes, of course, if that's what you think is best. We'll do whatever is necessary."

Gill has thought through an itinerary of activity for the day. "Grady, can you see if you can access as much inside information on the assassination itself? I need to get a handle on the exact sequence of events at the Senate. You have your contact in the service, don't you?"

"Yeh, she's still there. I may have to go through the family though, rather than direct. What sort of things do you need to know?"

"I need to know exactly where the cabinet was at the time of the murder. Who was actually at the Capitol building, what was going on, and why security failed at the exit of the chamber and entrance to the washroom. That's critical - if you can get me some intelligence on that I'll get us tickets for the play-offs."

"Sure thing, partner."

"Monique, I need you guys to be especially vigilant. The Jumeau's will need to stay here most of today, so if you go out for any reason, use the security knock. One-two-One, you know the drill Grady. Catherine, Christophe, you get that?" Everyone nods. It's fairly simple.

"How long will you be?" asks Catherine, clearly displaying a sense of anxiety.

"Not long," he says and gives her a big smile. "I'm just going to pick up any messages from work, get the forensics reports, and some clothes from my apartment. I should be back in a few hours," he assures her.

Grady turns to Monique. "Sugar, you know where everything is, right?"

She nods. It's obvious to everyone what he means, but nothing further is said. He grabs his jacket and heads outside to the car. Within a few seconds, the car rumbles into action and takes off toward the city.

—-

Gill has a dilemma. He doesn't want to leave Catherine but he really needs to get things done, not least of which is his intention to dual to Melrose's offices to see if he can find out more about the projects he is running. But first he needs to talk to Catherine. While her dad is being polite and helping Monique in the kitchen, he asks Catherine to step outside into the back yard. It's quite large, with most of this week's washing on the clothes lines and Grady's motorbike chained up over in the corner. There's a worn basketball hoop and backboard before a narrow back alleyway between the houses. He checks up and down just to be on the safe side, and approaches Catherine. He resists the urge to touch her, instead smiling uncertainly as he struggles with his emotions. She can see that he is uncomfortable, and immediately wants to help him.

"Listen, about yesterday and what you...what is going on with us. I know that we can't go there right now. I understand that," she tells him.

Gill musters strength to control both his emotions and the physical environment around them as he moves to stroke her cheek. But as he does so, things inevitably begin to slow down, as they did yesterday, and seeing that this is beginning to happen, Gill retracts his arm and turns away.

"Gill." Her voice is like velvet, and he is drawn back. There are things he must know, and if he is to make progress, Catherine holds one of the keys.

"Your Dad is very protective," he says.

"He's always been like that; he cares about me so much," she replies.

"You're very lucky. He's shrewd, and obviously a very loving father. We talked briefly last night. I didn't realise he knew Melrose?"

"Yes, they were colleagues once, I think. Dad doesn't talk too much about him, but I know they worked on various projects together. Professor Melrose says he is one of his greatest influences."

"I'm sure that's true." Gill pauses, stumbling awkwardly into asking Catherine more about Melrose. "I guess what might help me is to understand what sort of things you are all researching across there with Professor Melrose. Can you give me some sort of idea?"

Catherine is far less circumspect with her research than her father, mainly because she hasn't reached that stage in academic life yet where she has published major papers or had negative experiences of confidentiality agreements. "Well, I can sketch things out for you – do you know much about any of this stuff?"

"Not really. I'm not totally ignorant though. I did forensic science at university so I know a little bit of all the sciences, and am a master of none," he smiles.

"Yes, of course. Forensics. I always thought that would be an exciting thing to do," she says, and continues on before Gill has time to raise any objections to her mis-placed assumption. "Well, it's all very boring really. I mean, when you get to the point where you are researching very small niche areas in physics, very few people understand exactly what it is you are doing."

"Try me. I'm a glutton for this kind of stuff, and if I fall asleep on you I promise I'll never ask again."

Catherine gives him a candid and knowing smile, clearly drawn by Gill and his somewhat earthy humor. "OK, well my dad and Walter did lots of research into what's known as particle super-positioning. That's where a single particle – say a photon of light – can actually exist in more than one state at a time until some measurement or observation of that particle causes its super-position state to collapse. It's a quantum mechanics thing really – for very small particles and small localized environments it has been proven that we don't really know enough about the state of anything until we observe it. Even then, it's a compromise. Have you heard of Heisenberg's Uncertainty Principle?"

"That's where if you aren't certain of something, you still bullshit in any case?" Gill quips.

"Yeh, OK, well the bullshit function in the equation relates to the fact that, for a photon or an electron, if we try and measure its speed, the more accurate we get with that, the less accurate we are likely to be about knowing its location, and vice versa. Come on, you know that part don't you..?" She looks at Gill with a frown of suspicion. Gill nods in conformity, as if she's his teacher in science class.

"Yes, Miss."

"Right, well pay attention to the next bit, 'cos this is where it gets more interesting. We also know that if you take a proton source, and use a light splitter so that a stream of photons is split and kept apart – in other words that there are photons from a single source which end up totally separated and unconnected to each other – you can see that a change in the behavior or status of one of the photons immediately affects the behavior or status of its equivalent, even although they have no way of being in contact with each other."

"So they are like twins in effect. From a single mother, and later in life if one does something the other also does the same thing?"

"Sort of. It's even weirder than that though. My Dad in particular has worked on the nature of the apparent, or virtual, connection between the two. It's the 'how' part that interests him. *How* does one know what the other is doing if it's billions of light years away on the other side of the Universe? The answer seems to be encoded at source rather than dependent on any physical laws we know of at the moment. Even Einstein, who was a classical physicist and strangely down to earth despite what people said of him, could only explain such a phenomenon by calling it 'spooky'. Not exactly the most scientific term, huh?"

"OK, so what can you do with all this knowledge then? What are you and Walter Melrose cooking up over there at the labs?" Gill prods.

"Well, where my Dad is interested in the *entanglement* between two twinned particles, Walter is more interested in the practicalities of super-positioning of one particle. I don't know all the details but they disagree on some fundamentals around how super-positioning is possible in the first place. In any case, I'm investigating how super-positioning might apply to different *groups* of particles, as opposed to individual photons. So, taking an arbitrary classification of small particle groups, we could see how big a collection of particles we can have before super-positioning becomes impossible."

"Sounds fascinating. And are Wendy and Malcolm doing this stuff too?"

"Yes, they are going down a slightly different route though, trying to look at the minimum conditions necessary for super-positioning in terms of external factors, rather than the internal mass and type of particles involved."

"So, how far have you got with this?"

"Well now, *Detective*, I'd need to kill you if I told you that," Catherine jokes.

Gill offers her a laugh and a smile. She could make any joke and he'd laugh really, but actually she is quite cute on the humor front, as it turns out.

"Aw, come on. I don't know enough at the detailed level to be any risk to you or Professor Melrose. All I'm trying to understand is how important this stuff is, and whether or not there may be others who are interested enough to try and grab hold of the intelligence behind it."

This statement makes Catherine pause for thought, and she recognizes instantly that of course Gill is trying to help her and her friends. She doesn't hesitate.

"Well, the way it works is that our PhD projects will combine with the Professor's own work to form the most advanced profile of super-positioning and long-range communication and control ever known. He's incredibly proud of what we are achieving."

Gill detects a real sense of admiration in Catherine for Professor Melrose, which takes him a little by surprise. According to her dad, the guy is a weasel and rubs his nose where the sun doesn't shine in order to maintain a standard of living most bank bosses would find it tough to payroll.

"Yeh, but I mean, what is that going to be used for? What's the American public paying for here?' Gill asks, feeling like a little pushing might tease out any issues for Catherine in the process.

"Uh, well, I don't get too involved in that side, but let me give you an example. If we could get a small surveillance device – and I mean something nano-technology size here – to super-position, then we could theoretically gain access to any location around the globe and listen or watch anything that was happening there. That's just a security thing, but it's only the start of what might be possible with this. Imagine one day being able to see what it is like at the other side of the Universe, or at the beginning of the Universe, without having to move from your seat!"

"Now you really have got me," he admits, not fully getting her last point. "But I've got to admit, this is pretty powerful stuff, huh?"

"Yes, you could say that. That's why my Dad and Walter do what they do I guess, and why I'm still a struggling student who is nearly thirty and can't afford holidays." She smiles and looks at Gill intently. "It's really about unravelling phenomena which we know exist but can't be explained by classical physics or what we might think is 'common sense'. Like, before Einstein came up with the fact that a tiny bunch of atoms can have a huge amount of energy, we couldn't conceive of the nuclear bomb or nuclear power. Well, right now, it seems like super-positioning is something that might not only be very important, but something that we can use to good effect in the future."

"So, no nuclear bombs with this stuff then?" Gill probes Catherine's assertion carefully.

"Not if we are careful and the scientific community controls development," comes the retort, but it reveals Catherine's lack of political awareness, which worries Gill.

Gill senses it's time to move on.

"So what is Melrose investigating then. What's *his* bag?"

"Well, none of us knows exactly what he is researching, but I know it must be important. My guess is that it's around detecting when particles are super-positioned – you know, like, how you would actually *know* if something was actually in two places at once. Usually, if eminent scientists keep things close to their chest it's because they are about to announce some breakthrough or revelation to the scientific community in an 'of-the-time' paper; a 'hitter' as they say. Either that, or they can't tell you because it is to do with intelligence, like the stuff my Dad and Walter were involved with back when..."

Gill takes a deep breath. 'How you can tell if something is in two places at once' he says to himself. The ironies are ripe for the picking, but he stores the information for now. "OK. Last question, then I'll shut up. How close are you to getting small objects to super-position at your command, and how long will it be until large objects follow suit?"

"That's two questions, Detective Gill.....We are there with smaller objects - but you didn't hear that from me - and, well, I don't know about large, large objects. I take it you mean us, bodies, people? I really don't know about that. I mean, it seems such a leap for such a large collection to have come from a single source. There are two problems. We can *manufacture* an inanimate object of certain size and properties which we can super-position because we could originate material from a single source in the lab, but obviously that won't be the case for humans. We can't create them in the lab and split them in two with a photon splitter! And the probability that we could find two large-mass objects that were entirely made up of particle equivalents from a single cosmic event or source in the Universe is, well, practically nil."

"Well, Miss Jumeau, I could talk to you all day about this and other matters of the Universe, but I guess that'll have to wait a while," Gill says as he becomes aware of the need to get over to the precinct downtown.

"I'll look forward to that," Catherine says, adding "Oh, and will you promise me one thing?"

"Sure..." says Gill.

"Promise me you'll call me Catherine from now on?"

They both laugh as they move back toward the house.

—-

Over at the Downtown and Charlestown precinct, Captain Sanderson is on the phone.

"Professor Melrose, good to speak to you again. What can I do for you?"

"Captain, I am calling with regard to the missing students in my department. I really need to know what is going on and I didn't get much from your colleagues, so I decided to talk to you in person about this. Do you realise that, as of today, I have no PhD students here at the University? I really would like to understand what has happened to Miss Xiu and Mr Baines; they are, after all, the subject of an ongoing investigation, I believe?"

"Of course, Professor, I completely understand your concern. Although we are under some significant pressures with regard to resources, I want to assure you that we have prioritized this here Downtown. I currently have three full-time officers and detectives on the case, and we are following up all leads."

"Yes, yes, Captain, I am sure that you are. It's just that it's been two days now, and we don't seem to be any further forward. And now, this morning, I have not seen my other student, Catherine Jumeau, who was due in for a meeting. That means that all of my students are now missing. I have to say that this is not only worrying but really I need to have a more detailed picture of how your investigation is moving."

The Captain is left floundering. He has not been made aware of the detail of the case and cannot give any firm answers or reassurances. "I can assure you, Professor, that I share your concerns, and that we are doing everything we can. I was not aware that Miss Jumeau has been reported missing. Have you filed a missing persons report on that?"

"Of course not, Captain, I am reporting that to you now!" the Professor snaps, sounding both irritable and anxious.

Sanderson chooses to assuage as best he can. "Ah, well I will, in that case, make sure that we have that recorded, and someone gets over to you to take the relevant details. As it happens, I am due to meet with the relevant officers here within the next hour regarding developments and we will update you immediately on progress. Will you be around for the next couple of hours?"

"Yes, I will be contactable all day. I would expect to be updated by yourself or someone senior there, Captain, given the seriousness of the situation," Melrose insists.

"Very well, Sir, I will try and make sure that happens, but I'm sure you also understand the current pressures within the system which prevent us from being able to make promises we may not be able to keep. My duty here is to provide the best service I can under the circumstances."

"If you would just contact me, Captain, as soon as possible, I'd be very grateful," the Professor retorts, unwilling to mitigate his request on the back of the Captain's reasoning.

"I'll be in touch," says the Captain, and puts down the phone.

"Lieutenant!" Sanderson screeches at full volume. The piercing vibrations reverberate around the precinct, shattering the relative peace and quiet of the morning shift. Lieutenant Lester Young scurries out of his office and along the corridor to Sanderson's office.

"Captain?"

"Lester, I know we are at full capacity here, but if I have to take one more call from Professor Walter Melrose I'm not sure I will be responsible for my actions.... Now what the *hell* are you doing about finding his goddam students, huh?"

"We are flat out on it, Sir. Uh, and we have a bit of a breakthrough too. Phone company records show that the girl...uh, a Wendy *Xiu*...has made several calls from her cell since she was last seen, so it is likely that they are OK. We also have reports that Miss Xiu's parents have received a text from her, so we are hopeful that we can track them down at some point today. We just need time with this, Sir, that's all." The Lieutenant sounds chipper and upbeat, as he always does when he's getting heat from superiors. It's a sort of blanket 'what could possibly be wrong when we are doing everything we are doing' argument. Quantity over quality. We are working hard, so you can't criticize us, whereas the actual argument is not about working hard, but about being clever.

"And Miss Jumeau, you realise that she is now being reported as missing too?"

"Ah, now that's not a missing persons, Captain. We decided to make her safe yesterday, just in case. She is fine, just laying low as we didn't know if there was anything sinister going on. Sounds like things should return to normal pretty soon," he concludes.

The Captain likes Young. He always provides answers and tries hard to keep the ship steady. He knows running a high-profile department like Downtown is a bit of a game, but he couldn't do without Lester Young. "In that case, Lieutenant, could you make a point of calling Melrose and updating him with the latest information? May be best to send one of your guys over there too, if they are in the area. That would complete things nicely."

"Sure thing, Captain, I'm on it."

The two nod to each other and Young retreats back to his office. "Goddam students..." he says out loud to himself, and takes a glug of his cool, acrid coffee. "Goddam," he repeats.

Downstairs Gill is just walking into the precinct forecourt. Sandra is there. She's always there. At least she was always there when he was there. He couldn't remember having seen Sandra Chandry anywhere else apart from there, on the desk, and has a fleeting thought that she might not even exist other than when he comes in and out of the building.

"Officer Chandry," he states.

"Detective Gill, how *marvellous* to see you," Sandra says in a mock Marilyn Monroe accent.

'Damn, she is good at that,' he says to himself. "Sugar?" he enquires.

"Coming *right* up." She reaches under the desk, as if she has magicked up a coffee for him, and for a moment he thinks she might *actually* have the most foul-tasting coffee of all time waiting for him under her desk. But instead she pulls out a file with the words 'XIU' written on it. "Looks like you might have to stand down on this one, Gill," she says as she passes him the folder.

"Gee. Thanks," Gill says as he troops off towards his desk.

Harry Chambers is at the desk opposite Gill's, like he always is. Is Harry just a figment of his imagination too? He's never anywhere else it seems. Gill is kidding with himself, but there is a semi-serious side to all of this. Actually, how *would* you know if the person you see in front of you wasn't also somewhere else? How could you tell?

"Gill, you in a party mood today?" Harry asks.
"Wha?" Gill doesn't have time for Harry right now.
"Because the Lieutenant sure is going to have some fun with you, my friend," he adds.

These superficial 'quipicisms' really grate on Gill. If you asked Harry what he meant, he probably wouldn't be able to reveal any detail. Because he doesn't know anything. He'd just give another form of the same quip, like 'You feeling itchy today, Gill? Cos you sure going to get scratched by the Lieutenant, yes Sir', or some such thing. It's meaningless dribble, and Chambers seems to have plenty of it.

Gill flops the file down on his desk, and goes over to grab a coffee. He smells it, scrunches his face up, takes a sip, shivers involuntarily, and sits down. Inside the folder his attention is immediately drawn to a couple of lines in the first of two briefings, each less than two paragraphs long. 'Phone company records show Miss W. Xiu has received and made two calls during last 48 hours, latest reported at 19.57 on 14th April.' That was last night. This is heartening. The next report is even more so. That reads 'Report from Mrs Maya Xiu @ 21.18 on 14th April, mother of Wendy Xiu, to say daughter texted - she and boyfriend visiting relatives in Atlanta, GA.'

Gill looks at this again. Odd, he thinks, that Xiu and Baines would wait several days before thinking to call anyone, and not inform the Professor about their decision to travel south. On the face of it, though, this is good news, and a relief. His plans for today are that he and Catherine watch Garfield's TV address, that he goes to the University to see if he could see Professor Melrose again, and then gets to his flat for a shower and a change of clothes before heading back to Dorchester. He'd now be able to give the Professor the news in person – it would be his excuse to get into a conversation about the work going on there, and any links between Melrose and Garfield. This still intrigues him – what exactly is the nature of their dealings?

After calling Catherine to make sure she is alright and let her know that Wendy has been in touch with her mother, Gill is checking his e-mails. He eyes one from Shirelle Stevens, another officer at the precinct. The message subject reads 'Garfield video'. Gill doesn't like the fact that she has done this. He specifically asked her not to mention the nature of the request in any communications, but instead she's made the subject header a giveaway. There it is, boldly obvious in case anyone cares to look at it. His curiosity gets the better of him and, rather than waiting for Catherine, he clicks on the message and in it there is a link to the CNN footage of the TV address. Rather than doing any background checks and online research about Garfield, he decides just to see what this man is like. How he comes across on screen. As he watches the footage, he makes a few notes.

Garfield's sharp features make him appear naturally quite serious; his voice has no distinguishing features save a very slight tremor; his face is pretty expressionless, even with the gravity of the situation; the backdrop of a mesmeric rolling U.S. flag and mildly-textured studio board is most likely designed to offset the traumatic nature of the address. Put together, the whole thing induces a sense of torpor, that's for sure; there is nothing spectacular here. He re-runs the footage. A couple of purses of the lips, yes. No clock stops. No mad moments. And no sign of John Montgomery. So Gill can't detect anything that Garfield was up to via the video. Now, does that mean there wasn't anything to detect, or just that *he*, like millions of others, can't detect it? He is rather disappointed. Somehow he thought that if anyone could detect something that Garfield demonstrated during that address, then it would be him. After all, he and Catherine were closely connected, like they were two forms of the same entity. Why couldn't he see what she saw?

He sits back in his chair. Then he sits up. This can't be. He re-runs the footage again. There's nothing. "Shit," he says out loud, determining that he needs to get Catherine to watch the video again as a check. He sits back in the chair once again, and takes a few moments to think things through.

Why would Catherine see something and he wouldn't? The only difference is that she witnessed the event live. If you could only see Garfield change form in real-time, or in other words, a direct point in spacetime, then a video of a past event isn't going to show anything. And funnily enough, that would also likely hold true if Catherine watched the re-run. What would happen if he could travel back to the point of the address? The more that Gill thinks about the entirety of the situation the more he determines that he will have to dual to find out what is going on. It's been a while since he has felt the absolute need to do this, but it is becoming increasingly obvious that nothing is particularly obvious about this case. Or cases. It seems that the Baines/Xiu missing persons is just the tip of an iceberg, and that the timing around the assassination of the President of the United States is most likely turning out to be causal rather than co-incidental. There are two immediate tasks left for today. Get to his apartment to freshen up and grab a change of clothing in case he needs to stay at Grady's house another night, and see if Walter Melrose will agree to an impromptu meeting at the University.

"Gill!"

It's the Lieutenant. Gill heads in the direction of the stairs, but stops at the bottom when Lester Young appears at the top, looking down on Gill. "I want you to get over to the University right away."

"Oh yes?"

"Yeh, uh, the Captain got a call from Professor Melrose this morning. He reported Catherine Jumeau as missing. You think you can sort that one out?" The Lieutenant was referring to Gill's preoccupation with protecting Catherine Jumeau and the fact that the Captain has been embarrassed by not knowing about this. The onward suggestion is that it was over-the-top, and now that Baines and Xiu are reported to be OK and just visiting relatives, the Lieutenant is delegating the awkward task of telling the Professor that Catherine is not missing, to Gill.

"Sure, I was planning on heading there anyway," Gill comes back.

"Good. You can update him on the sighting of Baines and Xiu as well then."

"Lieutenant, they haven't been sighted. A text is all we have so far."

"Whatever, Gill. You know what you have to do."

"Sir." Gill realises the Lieutenant has de-prioritized the whole thing and just wants Gill to wipe up the mess. And that Captain Sanderson doesn't get caught short on any more calls from Walter Melrose.

—-

At the loft apartment Gill makes a call to Catherine and, knowing that she is safe and well with Christophe and Monique, puts on his favorite playlist, pointing his bio-cell at the stereo. 'Waiting For My Real Life to Begin' by Colin Hay, comes on.

He gets into the shower and breathes a deep sigh of satisfaction as the water hits him hard and begins to revive him. There's a line in the song about a mask wearing thin. "Mask" he says out loud. He looks up at the wide shower nozzle and the individual channels of water powering relentlessly down on him. He can't feel any particular stream hit him, but the overall effect is to coat him with a membrane of insulation against the outside air. This is why showers are so good. He thinks about the clearing, and whether he'd ever be able to touch Catherine like a lover would. He ached for her, and yet they seemed to be as separated as they were before they met, prevented from being normal by their connectedness. How insane. Physical connection preventing physical connection. How could they surmount the obstacles between them? Maybe it wasn't about that. Maybe they both had to just let go and make their way to the clearing. From there they might be able to go off to some other place where they could be together like normal folks.

It strikes him that Catherine was doing all this research into dualling – super-positioning as she would call it – and yet didn't think that this might be something to do with him, and therefore her, and the reunion that he felt happened when they met. Catherine could dual, right? Well, if he was right then she must be able to, but yet there was no outward sign that this is something she had ever considered. Maybe, like Beth, she had some strange dreams where she dualled, but got freaked out or instinctively knew that it was dangerous. Because it *is* dangerous, that much is true. Has she unmasked something? What does she feel? He has to find out...

Gill's internal dialogue seems incessant, and only the slight downward shift in water temperature brings him round, as the shower turns lukewarm. He steps out and begins to get ready. Grabbing a small overnight bag, some clothes and toiletries, he switches the stereo off and puts on his bio-cell. He thinks about calling Catherine again, but decides against. He doesn't want to suffocate her. He thinks about Beth, and where she might be. There are two women in his life that need his help. One he can see, one he can't. He has perhaps been waiting for this opportunity his whole life. Maybe that's what his *purpose* is. Maybe that's why he is here.

In the car on the way over to the University, Gill winds down the window and listens to the roar of the passing traffic, the hum of the engine and every bump of the chassis as it goes over humps and potholes in the road. He is traveling through spacetime. In an Oldsmobile. It's an interesting thought. By the time he gets to the University, Gill's hair is stood on end like he has just touched a Van de Graaff generator. He uses his right hand to sweep it down and in one motion makes a pretty good attempt at getting the whole thing under control.

He's parked in the same spot as he was last time he was there and Lamar Merriweather told him about Malcolm. He half-expects Lamar to come kicking up this time too, but there is no sign. In fact, there's no sign of anyone. The campus looks dead. He gets out, and walks through the neatly designed concrete path to the Physics building. It says 'Heisenberg' on the outside. 'Mmmm', he says to himself, as he gets the reference now.

Inside, he is dealing with Laura again, the receptionist at the main desk. He has a sort-of-date with her at the weekend, which is awkward given that Catherine is obviously the only woman in his life now. However, their arrangements seem so trivial compared with recent events that he decides against any conversation about canceling. Like a true detective, he never knows when it might be useful to have a warm contact.

"You're in luck, Detective, the Professor is free and will see you now," says Laura, with a flirtatious smile.

"Thanks, Laura," he says and returns the smile.

On the way up, Gill prepares for what will be potentially a difficult conversation. He needs to understand more about Garfield, via Melrose. This is tricky, as he has no idea of the kind of link between the two men. If he had had more time, he would have researched this thoroughly, but he hasn't, so he's going to have to be light on his feet.

At Melrose's office, he hesitates slightly before knocking.

"Come in," comes the stifled shout from behind the door. The dulcet English tones seem so benign, yet Gill is swayed by Catherine's father's account of this man.

Gill enters but sees that Melrose is on a call. The Professor puts up two fingers to signal that he'll be two seconds. Or minutes. Gill isn't quite sure.

"Very well, 5 o'clock then. See you later," the Professor finishes the conversation. "Detective Gill! Do come in. Take a seat."

Gill walks over and takes a seat. "Professor, I'm sorry to intrude like this but I have some information and thought it best to update you in person," he says.

"Oh yes?"

"Yes, it looks like Wendy has contacted her mother and apparently the message is that she and Malcolm are visiting relatives in Atlanta."

"Well, now, there you go. I knew that they had maybe just decided to get out of the city for a while given all the furore around recent events. I am *so* pleased to hear that, it's such a relief, Detective."

"We cannot confirm as yet that this is one hundred percent verified, and I would caution that we still haven't had direct contact with the two, but it could be good news, Sir."

"So, any idea when they are coming back? We have work to do here, you know."

"Well, actually I would have thought that one of them would be in contact with you regarding their return. You haven't heard from them I take it?"

"Not as yet, Detective. Now, as I told your Captain earlier, I have another problem which I hope will resolve the same way. Catherine Jumeau, my other PhD student, has not reported in today, and that isn't like *her*. First Wendy and Malcolm, and now Catherine. It's *most* unusual..."

Gill clears his throat. The fact that direct contact has not yet been made with Baines and Xiu is lingering on his mind. "Yes it is. Have you had any contact with Catherine over the last couple of days, sir?"

The Professor looks at Gill in a somewhat sneering peer over his half-rimmed spectacles. "Detective, I have just told you that my student has disappeared. I wouldn't have reported that if I had seen or heard from her in the last couple of days, now would I?"

"I understand, Sir. When was the last time you talked with Miss Jumeau?"

"Well now, let me see, it would have been the day of the assassination, just before she went to the lab with the other two. So, yes, the same time as I last heard from Wendy and Malcolm. Is this significant? Do you think Catherine is visiting her parents too?" the Professor asks. The irony is apparent to Gill.

"I have no idea, Sir. If I can be specific about Miss Jumeau's disappearance then I can file the missing persons report and we can go from there."

"Very well. That would have been around 10 a.m. on Tuesday morning. As far as I know she was around that day as some other people here reported seeing her, but beyond that, I can't offer anything else."

Gill needs to turn this conversation towards Melrose's relationship with Catherine and the work they are carrying out. It seems to him it's the only way to understand its potential significance to someone like Garfield.

"Yes, the assassination seems to have taken everyone by surprise. We are extremely under-staffed down at precinct as a result. As a matter of interest, Sir, did you see the Vice President's address that day?"

"I beg your pardon?"

"I was just asking, Sir, if you saw Vice President Garfield's address to the nation that day. It seems like that's the last time your PhD students were seen together."

"Oh, yes, as a matter of fact I did see that, Detective. Very moving, I thought, and a good tribute to Montgomery. He will be missed, that is certain."

Gill is wondering if this guy has been a Shakespearian actor in some previous existence, because if he's lying and knows what has happened to Catherine, and the other two, he sure is hiding it well.

"Indeed he will, Sir." Gill decides to go straight for the throat. "In fact someone at Downtown mentioned that Garfield himself is a frequent visitor here." He leaves the hook floating pregnantly for a second, saying nothing by way of follow-up.

"Well, I wouldn't go as far as that, Detective. Ellis Garfield happens to be a major supporter of our work here. He has visited the University several times, and in fact persuaded the President himself to grace us with his presence, as I'm sure you will be aware."

Melrose is trying to switch focus of the conversation, and Gill has spotted it. There is more to explore here.

"Yes, I remember it well. A very successful visit - I was part of the security operation that day. And by all accounts your department was being heralded as a key contributor to thinking on things like super-positioning, is that right?"

The rising tension is palpable, as Melrose shifts slightly in his seat. The man has played politics his entire life, and is not about to let a minor league policeman bowl him out, no matter how big he is or how well he can throw a ball. "You have done your homework, Detective Gill, but who would have told you about our work here?"

'Fuck' Gill says to himself. By attempting to force the Professor's hand on the link to Garfield, he has had to reveal that he knows about the type of work going on here. Only Xiu, Baines or Jumeau could have done that, unless it was publicly available. Gill will have to bluff. "Well, after our last chat, Sir, I decided to do a bit of my own background research so that I wouldn't look like such an idiot in such matters," he smiles at Melrose, who gives him a very unconvincing smile back, like that of a laughing hyena about to tear the ribcage out of a wildebeest.

"Oh yes?"

"Yes, well I spent a little time asking around about what Miss Xiu and Mister Baines were studying, just to see if that might be significant," he says, drawing attention away from Catherine and towards Xiu and Baines. "You guys seem to be at the forefront of research in this area." This time he is not asking for information, but stating fact. And he knows it. Melrose has to come back on this, or sound like he is evading questions. It's like a game of chess, and Gill has the upper hand right now over the older, and one would assume wiser, of the two men.

"Yes, we have a number of ongoing projects here, all of which utilize innovative research to solve unresolved issues in physics. We are proud of that fact, and my PhD students are conducting research which we feel is both important and timely. Now how does that help with Miss Jumeau, Detective?" Melrose's irritation is obvious. Clearly he finds Gill's stubborn and somewhat indisciplined line of questioning irksome at best.

"Well sir, to be blunt, we are concerned that two missing persons reports in as many days might be related to the type of work that is carried out here rather than being attributed to random events. And by that I mean that we already know that you are carrying out classified research that is not for public consumption, and that this research could potentially be of use in counter-intelligence and covert surveillance operations." Gill leaves this hanging in the air, just as time used to slow down when you watched Dwayne Wade hang in the air on a pull-up shot before releasing the basketball. There is a second of complete silence as Melrose absorbs what Gill has just said.

"Well. You *have* done your homework, Detective. I can see that." All of a sudden the benign figure of this ageing academic takes on a more menacing demeanor. "But let me understand what you are saying here. You think that my students are disappearing because they are involved in sensitive research? If that is the case, then I think we need to reconsider the way this conversation is going."

Gill goes in for the slam. "What I am saying, Professor, is that it's rather hard to believe it's co-incidence that *all* your students would be reported missing when you are on the verge of a major breakthrough in the development of technologies that may be of a game-changing nature in the global theatre of war." Gill's heart is beating fast, and he can sense beads of sweat beginning to seep out of his forehead as he lets his words settle. He has just bullshitted the Professor into thinking that he knows that there is a major new technology about to be reported to the U.S. military, but which could be of extremely high value in the hands of any enemy of the State. It is a proposition of the highest order in terms of national security. And that's why Gill is struggling to keep his nerve.

The Professor throws Gill first one intense stare, then another. Then he walks over to this large window looking across the Boston cityscape and down to the river. He is thinking, trying to work out what is going on. You can *feel* it.

"Look, Detective, mmm, *Gill*. Let's get something straight here. I don't know how you have accessed this information, but you are overstating the case by a long way. What we do here is academic work. We don't make any military weapons here. Do you understand that?"

"Yes Sir, I do. But I also understand that Robert Oppenheimer was carrying out very important academic work."

The significance is not lost on the Professor. This is turning out to be a difficult encounter, and so far the Detective has wiped the floor with him. He decides to call the Detective's bluff in a last resort to salvage the situation and not be forced to give away any additional information that might draw outside attention to the sensitive nature of the work going under his tutelage.

"I can assure you that the projects we have going on here are all vetted carefully by the government and anything that requires security clearance is given the necessary approval by the relevant authorities. If you are trying to suggest that some sort of covert or subversive research is going on then I'd be very careful if I were you, as you could land in very hot water!" Melrose's fuming retort is edging Gill towards calling off any further exploration of Melrose's activities. The professor's outburst seems genuine to him, but he still doesn't really know what the connection is between Melrose and Garfield, and that's what he needs to get to.

"Oh, I am certainly not suggesting anything like that. But since you clearly do require security clearance for some aspects of your work, then it's not a stretch of the imagination to consider your PhD students potentially valuable to those who might wish to exploit the knowledge base that exists here. Wouldn't you agree that your students know an awful lot about your work and the experimentation which is sponsored directly by the White House?"

"What do you mean 'directly by the White House', what are you talking about?"

"Well sir, it is common knowledge that the current President, President *Garfield*, has visited your establishment and is well known to you. The assumption is clear – that Garfield has a special interest in the work that you carry out, and has sponsored you to undertake sensitive and important work that could be of importance to our National Security. To have PhD students privy to that knowledge is dangerous, do you not think?"

Melrose is incandescent with rage. And then it comes. He points his finger at Gill and moves towards him. He is as much as a foot shorter than Gill and would never be any physical match, but he is older and wants to stamp his authority on the conversation. It is where Gill has led him. "Now listen here, I don't know who you think you are or where you get off pushing people around like this, but let me make it clear to you, Mister, you are playing with fire here. If you are implying that I have endangered my own researchers through the type of work we carry out here, then I consider that to be worth you and your Captain being put in a sling and catapulted straight to the unemployment queue at best, and at worst a prison cell so that you can consider the grave mistake you have made here. Do you understand me *now*, Detective?"

Melrose's rant is designed to shake him up, but Gill has been around the block one too many times, and, while the Professor can no doubt pull some strings with the White House and maybe the local Mayor in order to make his life a misery, there is no doubt in Gill's mind that the Professor is hiding something about what is going on with Garfield. It was time for one last shot.

"OK, Professor, so are you saying that your PhD students don't know about your secret work for President Garfield? Is that what you mean?"

The Professor knows this is a trap; that he's one move away from checkmate and needs to come up with some move that allows him a way out. But he is panicked, and even his quick and erudite mind can't refuse the question, which is the culmination of a master strategy, designed as a one-way ticket, and due to its validity requires an answer.

"That's right."
"I beg your pardon, sir?" Gill didn't expect that.
"You heard me, Detective, I said that's right."
Gill can hardly keep his composure, but he has to nail it. "I see. And you are not prepared to talk to me about the nature of that work, Sir, is that right?"

The Professor is silent. He goes and sits at his desk, obviously shaken. Still no reply. Gill has to do something. He hasn't got what he wants. He thinks of Catherine and pictures Catherine's innocent face as she explained what they do at Melrose's place.

"I mean, I obviously understand, Sir, if there are national security reasons why you cannot discuss the details of your work. I am just trying to clarify that Wendy Xiu, Malcolm Baines and Catherine Jumeau are unaware of the specific nature of that element of your research. Can you at least confirm that with me? It could be important to my investigation."

He waits. The professor takes a moment, and then raises his head up to look at Gill straight in the eye.

"That's right, Detective. My students are unaware of any such activities," he whispers though gritted teeth, like it is a struggle even to get the words out.

The storm is over. The clouds break and the sun comes back out again. Gill has got what he came for. He nods at the Professor, turns and goes towards the door. He grabs the handle, turns back to Melrose and quietly utters the words "Thank You," and leaves.

As he goes down to the ground floor in the lift, he notices the floor order goes 4, 2, 3, 1 before hitting the ground floor. As he comes out of the lift, there are a couple of tallish security men, about to get in. They look at him, much like security guys do when they are on duty and checking everyone out as they go about their duties. Gill nods at them, and says "Fellas," before walking over to see Laura at the front desk. She's on the phone, but smiles at him as he mouths the word 'thanks,' smiles, and then departs.

As he walks across the open space towards the car park, he thinks about Catherine. Then Melrose. He was beginning to realise that, if Melrose was using Catherine to further aspects of his privately-funded research, Catherine really could be at great risk. For that would be valuable to other groups, and not just the U.S. government. Things were pretty complicated, that he could tell. But right now, Catherine's safety was dependent on her *not* knowing as much as some might think she does. Gill pauses for thought as he gets in his Delta '66 coupé. There are two main problems.

The first is the protection of Catherine. She is at real risk if someone found out about her admission that she is the one who witnessed something strange about Garfield. And he had found the bug in her apartment, which means somebody out there would most likely know about Catherine's experience and Wendy and Malcolm's intention to question fellow students around campus. He makes a mental note to follow up on Baines and Xiu – finding those two now becomes critical to gauging the threat to Catherine. He also makes a mental note that it could be that one or more students at the University are there on surveillance for either Melrose or possibly even Garfield. That would make some sort of sense if Garfield's vested interest in the research being carried out required him to place his people on campus.

The other problem is that he is getting drawn into the business of national security. Clearly Melrose is involved with Garfield, and in some way that is, at the very least, worthy of investigation. But if whatever is going on goes right to the top, then Gill is beginning to think that he is out of his depth. Although Melrose caved and told him that he was involved in state-sponsored secret research, he would doubtless waste no time in relaying this to Garfield's people, so that Gill and Catherine would become a renewed focus for them. This wasn't good.

Gill decides that the most important thing in the short term is to keep Catherine safe. There's no point in taking her back to the city yet. She mustn't talk to anyone about Garfield. He is going to have to find out who took Baines and Xiu, and he has to get the information from Grady on the assassination. Finally, he decides that he is going to have to go to Washington. If he can get inside the White House, then he might be able to witness for himself what is going on with Garfield.

'Heavy...' he says to himself, and sparks up the Oldsmobile.

––-

Catherine is checking her bio-cell back at Grady's house in Dorchester. Missed calls from Mary Jumeau, an unknown number and 'Prof M'. One voicemail message.

"Dad!" she shouts into the bedroom where Christophe Jumeau is reading. He asks her what she wants. "Did Mom call you earlier?"

Her father comes into the living area. "Yeh, it's fine, honey, she wants us back home but I said that we are good here for a couple of days. I mean, 'here' as in the city. I didn't mention actually being here."

"OK, that's cool. I'll just text her for the moment."

She says "voicemail - 1", and listens to her message.

"Oh, hello, Catherine! It's just Walter here. I hope everything is OK with you – a bit worried as you missed our meeting and now I can't seem to find you anywhere on campus either. Can you just give me a quick call when you get this, just to let me know you are OK. You know how I worry! Anyway, bye bye for now."

Walter Melrose sounds like a protective uncle phoning his favorite niece. He is neither an uncle nor kindly according to her father. Yet she doesn't know much detail behind the seeming dislike her father has for Walter; something that reflects his pragmatic concern for her working relationship with the man, and future career. In other respects, Melrose is keen on keeping his little team of postgraduate doctoral students – his real *talent* – close to him. It makes sense. They are valuable to him, and he is valuable to them. The deal is that they play ball and share their thinking and findings in return for kudos, guidance and the best facilities in the entire country.

So far, Walter has tended to be a little controlling, but Catherine reads that as his eagerness to help steer her towards a better overall product at the end of her write-up. Melrose is a little older than her dad, but of that generation and of that extraction; rather suave and deliberate men, confident in their own thinking and exuding an air of mature authority in their day-to-day dealings with people around them. Catherine imagined Walter as a bit of a catch back in his day at university in England. He had apparently excelled as a young graduate and was in a group of around twenty academics from around the globe who took part in multi-national workshops aimed at bringing the best in the world together to solve seemingly intractable problems in physics and mathematics, such as the Higgs-Boson project or anomalies such as dual forms. This would have been a hey-day in some respects. The U.S. government in the last twenty-odd years has focused on many other priorities and it is only recently under Montgomery that engineering and physics research has started to get serious backing from the state and some public-private initiatives. By galvanizing efforts in multiple fields of enquiry, Montgomery's vision is to create a whole that is greater than the sum of the parts. It is a grand vision, but so far the jury is out on the outcomes of this new injection of energy.

Melrose is also a very social beast. A consummate and witty after-dinner speaker, and a very media -friendly 'front-end' for Harvard, he commands much respect and has endeared himself to many public figures including actors, sports people and politicians. The man knows how to network and win friends in high places. While Catherine knows that her dad isn't too enamored with that kind of character, her take on things is different. She figures that if Melrose is doing all that public-facing stuff, then she wouldn't have to, and could just get on with her research. Maybe it would come to her one day to do all that, but she doesn't need to worry about that now. And when there had been a do at the Heisenberg, she and Wendy would have a laugh and a joke with the Professor, sometimes edging into flirtation but in a very innocent kind of way. All in all, she considers Walter a nice man who had toughened up over the years and was fronting some of the most advanced research in the world. And she, for one, is really happy to be part of that setup.

She decides to call him.

"Hi Professor, it's Catherine!" she gushes, being deliberately upbeat.

"My goodness – Catherine! Are you OK? I've been asking around all over for you – I...I even called the police to report you missing after what happened to Wendy and Malcolm. Are you OK?" The professor sounds very relieved to hear from Catherine.

"Yes, yes, I'm fine. I'm fine....it's so nice to speak to you. I was really worried about Wendy and Malcolm but I heard that they are OK."

"You did? Well, that's interesting because I've just had a policeman round to here to let me know that too. Did they get in touch with you then? And where the devil are you?"

Gill hasn't raised any potential suspicion of Melrose in Catherine's mind up till now, so she is not thinking that Melrose could be involved in some shady scheme directly sponsored through Washington. He's still just her PhD supervisor, mentor and occasional father surrogate.

"I'm just in town – I spent a bit of time at home after what happened on Tuesday; guess I just felt a bit low. I did mean to call you..."

'Oh now that's OK, my dear. I understand – it was all a fantastic shock to everybody. I am just glad to hear from you; your voice never sounded so lovely! Now, what are you up to and when am I going to see you, then?"

Catherine thought about Gill's phone call earlier telling her that it looked like Wendy and Malcolm were safe and well. She wanted to believe that the situation had probably settled down now, and that perhaps things had been blown out of proportion over the last couple of days. That what she saw in Garfield might have been her imagination running wild after all. Most of all she wanted things to get back to the way they were before the horrible news of the President's assassination. Being cooped up in Grady's house wasn't much fun, and although it was good to be with her father, there was no way that she could take much more of sharing a room with him, or his snoring.

"Well, Professor, I think I might be in town tomorrow."

"Great, let's meet – how about Black's on Devonshire around noon then?" the Professor replies quickly, without checking his diary.

"OK, that sounds good – look forward to seeing you, Professor."

"And you. Oh, and Catherine!" he adds

"Yes?"

"Keep your chin up – the show must go on!"

Catherine smiles to herself; this was the sort of chipper person she remembers first meeting at the University's open day the year before, and she really does have a soft spot for him.

——-

'If I Needed Someone'. It's Gill.

"Hi, it's me. Glad I caught you this time."

"Um, Hi. I am too. Are you coming back soon?" she asks him.

"Yeh, I am on my way over now. Should be with you soon. Everything OK?"

"Yes, everything is fine. I'm playing my fifth game of Scrabble with my dad, and Monique made some fantastic soup for us at lunchtime. It's very exciting."

"Ha ha. Believe me, you don't want it to be any more exciting than that. And I've had Monique's soup before, so I'm surprised you can still talk."

"Ha ha, I know, I think she misread the recipe..."

"...and put four times the amount of pepper in, yeh?" he finishes her sentence.

Catherine chuckles, "Think it was at least five."

She can hear a faint bleep in the background on the call.

"I'll bring some ice back. See you soon," he signs off.

Gill has another call coming in, from the crime lab.

"Gill."

"Detective Gill?"

"Yes."

"Oh, hello, Detective. It's Angela Giordana down at the crime lab. I have the results of the tests you asked for on samples from the Jumeau apartment?"

"Great. What you got?"

"Well, not much really. From what you gave me I can identify four sets of fingerprints and there don't appear to be any signs of blood from the swabs or IR shots. I'd really need to get a team over there and do further testing if you want some more detailed collection and analysis done."

"And there are no matches on the fingerprints?"

"Not to anyone on our database."

"OK, thanks Angela. I'll let you know if I need a team down there," he says.

Gill thinks about Catherine's place. It's bugged, so putting a forensics team in there will be very obvious and ensure that whoever placed the surveillance device in there will know what is going on. The four fingerprints are most likely to be Catherine, Wendy,

Malcolm and Catherine's father, and Gill will need to get fingerprints from each of them to verify this. That sounds less than feasible right now, and on balance it doesn't look like he's going to get anywhere down that route. This is frustrating, but perhaps not surprising. Whoever broke in and bugged the apartment was experienced enough not to leave any trails.

Thinking this through makes Gill realise that the break-in and the bugging were most likely part of the same act. But of course, that's still supposition only. What if the bug had been put in the apartment some time ago? Before he gets any further with this train of thought, the phone goes yet again.

"Gill!" It's the Lieutenant, and he's shouting. Gill isn't in the mood.

"Lieutenant. It's good to hear from you."

"Gill, I just had a complaint from Professor Melrose."

Gill interrupts before Young can get any further. "Lester, the Professor needs to understand that when people are reported missing, then we expect the people we interview to tell us the truth. The guy was trying to hide the fact that Baines and Xiu are involved in some sensitive research that could be related to national security. Something like that is pertinent to the case, don't you think?"

"Now listen to me, Gill. The Professor is a very well-respected figure not only here but across the world. Of course some of his research is sensitive – his unit is highly regarded for its work in advanced engineering and physics, that's why they get funded and that's why they are envied so much. And that's why you storming in and using bully-boy tactics is not the right thing to do. You realise that the mayor called Captain Sanderson about this? Shit, Gill, you got to watch what you are doing, or you are going on disciplinary. This is a verbal warning; I don't want you near the Professor again in this investigation. If you need anything from him, let me know in person, and I'll deal with it."

'Jeez...what an asshole,' Gill thinks to himself. It applies to both Young and Melrose at this point. He lets out a weighty sigh. "Will there by anything else, Sir?" he asks.

"What you up to anyway? Sandra says Xiu has been found, and nothing came through from the forensics at her apartment. You ready to put this Jumeau thing to bed now?"

Gill didn't like the inference the Lieutenant was making to his intentions with Catherine, although that's undoubtedly what it was. Ever since Gill had a short-lived fling with a victim of robbery a few years back, he had been labelled as a bit of an opportunist. It was unfair, but that does't matter in the police force. You get labelled. Full stop. You can only hope it isn't malicious or debilitating, and his was neither. He lived with it. Some thought he was cool as a result, some thought it hindered his ability as a detective, but the majority didn't care or had forgotten. Some, like the Lieutenant, didn't care but used it situationally; for when he felt the need to patronize Gill or remind him of who had the power in their relationship.

'What an asshole,' the thought comes again, before he continues with the Lieutenant.

"Well, I wouldn't put it like that, Sir – we still don't know what happened to Xiu that night. I'll be happy to conclude things once I can confirm that Baines and Xiu are not only OK, but that nothing happened to force them to leave. We still haven't heard from them directly. In fact, I was going to go down to Atlanta to check things out for myself."

"Nonsense Gill, get them on the phone, or liaise with the guys in Atlanta, but you don't need to *go* there, for Christ's sake. The mother says they are fine – what more do you need? Besides, we are still short-staffed and we got other cases lined up, so you get yourself back here and we can close things down on this one."

"Lieutenant, I just need a couple more days on this and I'm sure things will be wrapped up by then, OK?"

"I'll give you the weekend, Gill. I want to see you in my office Monday morning - nine a.m. - for a briefing. You got that?"

"Yes, Sir, understood," says Gill, playing the game. In the end he managed to get some breathing space from Young, despite the Lieutenant's obvious irritation at Gill's performance with Melrose.

Gill pulls over at a drug store to get some ice-cream for Catherine. As he gets to the counter to pay, he notices that the Washington Post is on sale. A sub-heading reads 'GARFIELD DOUBLES AS VICE PRESIDENT.' He picks it up and reads the fine print.

'President Ellis Garfield is doubling as the Vice President, the post he held before the death of John Montgomery, as the Democratic party and the Cabinet consider candidates for the role.'

He really has to get to Washington. He shifts into Drive, and heads onto the Southeast Expressway out of Boston.

Back at Grady's house, things are quiet. As he pulls into the drive, Gill is excited about seeing Catherine. Literally, the particles of which he consists are excited, responding to her proximity. He is slowly coming to terms with the control of this. It is the sweetest frustration that he has not yet been able to touch Catherine without them creating some form of vortex in which everything slows to a stop around them. He understands why this is. Time effectively comes to a halt at the clearing; it has zero value. That means that the clearing acts as a wormhole. Or rather it does if you can get out of the sticky mess, the pool of thick molasses syrup that weighs you down and all but prevents you from moving in that space. As long as he remains out of direct contact with Catherine, they can both remain in the real world - this world. No-one around them will be aware of any changes even if they did, because for others time slowing down to zero for Catherine and Gill will be a relative function and imperceptible. To all intents and purposes, as long as he and Catherine can manage their time without touching, for now, then they can be together in the same location with only mild side-effects. One of those is the tingling sensation and craving to touch. It is temptation personified, and the sense of anticipation and longing in their interactions must be noticeable by now, although no-one has commented as yet.

Grady is still at work, and it's been an uneventful day by all accounts. Catherine is happy to see him and they share a little joke about playing things cool with each other, really just a throwback to Monique's soup, without offending Monique. It turns out that Christophe Jumeau has taken to Monique, and that they share several interests, including cooking, so they have been enjoying their time together.

Gill is keen to pick Christophe's brains about Melrose, but this time he wants Catherine's input too. Monique is enthusiastically preparing some Jerk pork for dinner, in her own little world singing along to 'Chase the Devil' by Max Romeo and moving rhythmically around. Christophe is enjoying watching the scene.

"Professor?" Gill has interrupted his enjoyment rather forcibly, and the Professor's expression quickly changes to slight annoyance as he straightens up in his chair. He clears his throat. "Yes?"

"I'm sorry to butt in, but could I borrow you for a second?" Gill asks.

"Uh, yes, sure. Monique, just let me know if you want any help, will you?" he offers.

Monique gives the Professor a warm smile and raises her hands, currently full of spring onions and garlic cloves. She nods and sings about going to outer space. Jumeau laughs and nods back.

The two men head over towards the Professor's temporary bedroom, where Catherine is sat on one of the beds having some ice-cream.

"Guys, I need to pick your brains a bit here. It's about the kind of research that is going on at the University, or maybe more accurately what Professor Melrose might be developing. Can you lay that out for me? I think it would be useful for me to get a handle on this stuff."

The Jumeau's look at each other. Christophe turns to Gill.

"Well, I can only guess on that one, Gill. Catherine is closer to that side of things these days, aren't you?" he asks as he looks back at Catherine.

Catherine throws her dad a glance designed to rebuke. "Like I said yesterday none of us knows exactly what he is doing. His own research is done in another lab, usually Lab One or Lab Three. He's the only one with keys to those, and, well, we've never been in them."

"You mean that Melrose has never even given you a clue as to what he is actually doing? I can't believe that someone as eminent as the Professor would be able to keep research concealed like that. Surely you know the nature of some of it, don't you?" Gill is keeping his own understanding to himself right now. He wants to hear directly from the two experts in front of him what they think Melrose's research is actually producing.

"Well, some of it, I suppose. I mean, I know that he is looking at the way in which super-positioning actually happens. Like, how it *actually* takes place and why an observation in one body automatically affects the other. Is that what you are getting at?" Catherine helps out.

"Kind of. Look, I know that this is the most advanced research of its kind, and it sounds to me that if you can have one object in front of you, appearing to be here, when in fact it's someplace else, that could be used for many different purposes. But one of those purposes could be military, dangerous and potentially game-changing for a country in terms of its security and defense programmes, not to mention how useful it would be for criminals if they needed an alibi when they were actually off robbing banks."

Catherine smiles. She loves the fact that Gill is interested, and she is becoming aware that he knows more about physics than he first made out. But it is Jumeau senior who picks up on Gill's implications.

"You're right at one level of course, but let's just deal with science *fact*. Yes, it is possible to super-position objects in spacetime. I have been involved in that side of things too. But what you are getting at is what a lot of people like to imagine; that somehow we can make people be in two places at once, and jump to different parts of the universe, or back in time, and so on. Now I know it's not what you and others might want to hear, but there are very real problems with these kind of leaps in imagination. First, we are dealing with quantum mechanics here, and this is very much of the microscopic rather than the macroscopic. So, as scientists we can't pinpoint where an electron is if you ask us, because it's uncertain where it is at any point in time. But we can say where *you* are in terms of location and time to some degree of precision, because large objects like you usually act in very predictable ways. When we looked at super-positioning back when, we were able to get very small objects to appear to be in two locations, but as soon as you measure the location of one, the whole thing collapses and the dual-state phenomenon disappears."

"So if no-one is *looking* for a dual-state object, it can be in both places, right?" Gill comes in.

Catherine sits up on the bed, and her movement causes a break in the conversation. Both men look at her.

"Yes, but if you think about it differently, it might help. There is only one object here, remember. It's just that with super-positioning, a version of that object is in a different spacetime location, which is like a different reality. As soon as you look for it in one or other of those places, the super-positioning collapses."

"So, it's more about the fact that there are multiple realities out there than the fact that we can split into two?" asks Gill.

"Yeh, it's like paths in the forest. At any point in spacetime a new reality can emerge based on a decision to go down one path or another. Super-positioning is a bit like running down one path, finding out what that reality is like, coming back, and then running down the other path to see what that reality is like. And if anyone spots you on the way down one or other of the paths, then you are stuck taking that particular path." Catherine's explanation is a bit clumsy and not entirely accurate, but it works for Gill right now.

"OK, OK. So what about where this could all go in terms of research? Is it impossible that a person could super-position? I mean, with respect, Professor, I thought that Wendy and Catherine were looking into precisely how groups of particles that may form larger objects can do this and what conditions might be necessary for it to take place."

Gill's questioning is forcing Christophe to come off his perch. As the senior guy at Montreal he has to be pretty circumspect in what he says to colleagues, managers, externals and the press alike. It's engrained in him now. But here it feels different, and he is with his daughter who he knows may be privy to knowledge that could be dangerous. This is what has struck him of late, and what makes him anxious for her. Now might be the time to open up a bit, if he can get past his oath of security.

"Gill, let me help. I know you are trying to understand this so that you can gauge the level of threat in the current situation. I really appreciate that. So, what I am about to tell you will go no further than this room. Do I make myself clear?"

Gill nods. "I need all the help I can get, Professor."

Catherine looks at him. Despite his size and obvious competence as a policeman, Gill seems strangely vulnerable in his need for knowledge, and as she watches him look expectantly at her father, she realises that she is beguiled by his truthfulness.

"OK, so you pass the test for stubbornness and stealth in your questioning, Gill. I like that." The Professor smiles, then continues. "The situation is that Walter Melrose has managed to get most of the entire military research budget for advanced physics research, and that, although some of that does go towards a rather lavish lifestyle, he is nevertheless in the privileged position of being able to devise and conduct some of the most leading-edge experiments of our time in this field. I happen to know that he has already documented an experiment in which he has successfully super-positioned both inanimate objects, such as nano-tech bugs and cameras, and has made a first attempt with microscopic animate objects. The latter is I think based around low cell-number and static life forms. I can also tell you that, as I understand it, the animated tests have been entirely problematic, mainly because with living organisms, the entirety of particles will be changing much more rapidly in terms of movement, cell division, reaction to external conditions, even basics like the need to photosynthesize, and so on. So, in short, while your investigative intuition is correct in that Melrose is probably conducting sensitive research, don't be fooled into thinking that he has been able to crack human time travel or anything like that. The route he has gone down will not lead to that outcome."

Gill looks at Catherine for her take on this, After all, she is looking at just what exactly *is* able to super-position. She takes his cue.

"Well, I don't really know about that. The only thing I can add is that there is some preliminary evidence to suggest that some collections of particles – some objects – are more likely to super-position than others. That's what I am looking into, and that's what Walter is really pushing me to report on."
"What makes you so sure that Melrose won't be able to develop something much more sophisticated like instant travel around the world, or even a time machine. What is it about his research that makes you so sure?" Gill asks Christophe.

Catherine looks at her dad. She has had this discussion before.

The Professor pauses for a second, probably wondering about the best way to come at this. "Well, my daughter knows my thoughts on this, maybe she should tell you," he says.

"Dad, come on..." Catherine says in a daughterly reprimand, before her dad continues.

"Well, here's the thing. A long time ago I realised that Walter was hell-bent on pursuing super-positioning as an end in itself. I know this because we were quite close colleagues at one point and I remember his absolute joy at the first successful experiments we carried out to prove that super-positioning of microscopic objects was not only possible, but that we could have some degree of control over the location of the take-up position."

"Take-up position?"

"Yes, the target location where we wanted the version of the object to locate to," the Professor clarifies.

Gill is very excited by what he is hearing but doesn't want to show it. Did Melrose and Jumeau discover dualling? Are there others...many other people who can do this? It's all rushing through his mind but he can't get ahead of himself on this one. "I see," he mutters.

"But in his frenzied pursuit of this I began to see that he was missing something."

"And what was that?"

"The *why*," Christophe states.

"The *why*? I don't understand," Gill replies.

"What I mean is that Walter Melrose doesn't really want to ask why things super-position. At microscopic level, in the quantum world, particles behave somewhat randomly and cheat us. They can be in more than one state at a time, in any number of positions in spacetime, heavy or light depending on context, and so on. In other words, just looking at super-positioning in itself doesn't really get us anywhere apart from being able to deal with small things. The fact that he has spent twenty years and millions of dollars in research to get to the point where he can super-position a tiny nano-tech device is probably good for national security and the criminal fraternity if they got hold of the capability, but not a major breakthrough in terms of our understanding. At least not in my opinion."

Catherine interjects "Oh for goodness sake! You make him sound like some sort of street magician. Everyone knows that this stuff is difficult and complex. It takes time to devise the right experiments, learn from some things that didn't go quite right and then get to the next stage. But I guess you've forgotten what it is like, Dad," she trails off. It is a bit of a rant, Gill concludes, which reveals quite a difference in approaches and opinions between father and daughter.

Catherine puffs hard and seems to be leaning towards a huff. "Listen, I've heard this before, so please excuse me...I think I'll go and keep Monique company for a while," she says and gets up off the bed. As she starts towards the door, Christophe Jumeau is looking down at the floor, silent.

Gill guesses this is a reaction he has had before. "Catherine," he says, but she shakes her head at him as she leaves. Gill really wants to go after her. Her frustration seems to have rubbed off on him. He is tense, but he needs to hear what Christophe has to say.

"Professor, I've come to realise that some aspects of 'hard science' can actually be a matter of opinion and relative truths. I would like to hear your take on these things. In fact, I'd go so far as to say I have a personal interest in making sure I understand better. I think it might be related to the case."

The Professor looks at him intently. "Yes, I am beginning to think so too. How much do you know about Melrose, really?" he quizzes Gill.

"Enough to know I think he is hiding a lot, and that he is intimately connected to the current government and possibly the security services in some way."

"Yes, I thought you might say that. It is no surprise to me that he has continued to milk that particular cow, or that he is potentially up to no good. I think he lost whatever moral backbone he had some time ago."

The two men begin to relax a little more, helped by the fact that Gill is bright enough to pick up on things quickly, and a gentleman. Instinctively, Jumeau likes Gill. He knows that, as a man approaching middle-age, Gill will probably have some things in common with himself. Yet, Catherine is his daughter, and it is obvious that she is attracted to Gill. There is a natural tension, at least to Christophe, whose concern for his daughter's well-being has never been as acute. So Gill has to tread carefully, and not assume anything.

"So, where do you and Melrose clash then, as physicists?" asks Gill.

"Good question. I have a fundamental problem with Melrose's starting point really. He sees the world, the Universe, reality, whatever we want to call it, as a bunch of discrete elements that we can investigate in their own right. So, for example, he will focus on super-positioning as we test and measure it – so we can witness reality, in effect, by looking at one part of it. I happen to believe that reality is much more profound than that; that, for example, super-positioning happens as a result of other phenomena, which we can't perceive."

"OK, now you've got me. Can you unravel that?"

"Sure. It's a bit of a brain fart, I know..." he smiles at Gill, relishing the challenge of putting into a simple and concise statement what the hell he is talking about. "Listen, I'm not saying that Melrose is wrong, per se, let's get that straight from the start. But he is investigating the symptoms of a universal phenomenon, rather than the cause. That's why I think he isn't a true scientist. He just wants to use a small kernel of understanding that we hit on many years ago, to create practical applications which he can sell to people that don't understand enough to know the value of what they are buying. They just think it 'kicks ass' because it is the most sophisticated of what is on the market. But the truth is that the market is not sophisticated at all, and seems to be about quantity rather than quality. Let's make something bigger and better, and more powerful...and so on."

"Yeh, that's believable alright. You are talking about what he is developing for the government, right?"

"Yes. He is building bigger and better technology so that he can put surveillance devices at any location on the globe without anyone having to place them there physically. He entertains the notion that one day he'll build a machine that will transport people to another location instantly using this methodology. The thinking behind this is the same as the basic quantum physics experiments that showed us that particles can be in more than one state at a time. This is decades ago. Splitting a single particle like a photon of light so that it appears to be in two positions at once, that sort of thing. You have heard of super-positioning, obviously..."

"Yes, I have, and in fact it was a pet interest of mine at one point. Carry on..." Gill encourages Christophe.

"Well, in my research, I looked in some detail at what's known as *entanglement*. In the Universe – let's take the one we are in now – particles can be entangled with other particles. Perhaps those particles are in some other place in the Universe, some other 'bit' of reality. That means that when they were created they shared some source information - or are part of a more holistic entity that exists somewhere - that gives them 'sense'. I use that word advisedly. What I mean by 'sense' is that the state of each of a pair of entangled particles is dependent on the other. We have proven this – that if you change the condition of one of them, the other reacts as if it has been sent a message telling it about the other's change of state. Am I losing you here?"

"No. It's fine. So what's the issue then? If the message is sent then the other one changes. I'm not sure what that in itself means," Gill replies.

"Ah, that's just it. I said 'as if' there were a message sent. But there isn't any such thing. We know this because any real message would be limited by a constant called the speed of light. Now even though that is incredibly fast, it's not fast enough to allow a message to pass *instantaneously* between two entangled particles that are millions of light years apart. And that's the weird thing. We know that the communication between particles is not limited by the speed of light, and this breaks classical physical laws."

Gill is beginning to sense in himself a realisation. He has done his homework on this stuff, and knows the basics of quantum weirdness, but the idea of entanglement has only just begun to centre in him since discovering Catherine. He feels in his bones that he and Catherine are from the same source, the same material. Are they a sort of human equivalent of an entangled pair? The parallels need to be explored.

"Fascinating, Professor. I talked to Catherine about super-positioning yesterday and I likened the splitting of one into two to that of identical twins being born and sensing exactly what the other one feels and does throughout their lives. Is that what this is too?"

"Not quite. Rather than splitting something into two respective independent parts, I think super-positioning is actually a feature of just one thing. So the problem he has is that as soon as someone looking for a bug finds that bug, then the connection and information is lost, the original bug disappears, and the remaining bug is trapped in the place that it was observed. So what he needs to come up with is not only a super-positioning machine, but also a way to avoid detection. Others will find ways of detecting a super-positioned surveillance device, just as they will detect ordinary surveillance devices. He can't really get beyond this at the moment."

"Hhhmm. Think I get that. So what's your take on the whole travel thing? How do you overcome those limitations, if that's where you are going with this?"

"Yes, that's the question. But I am not trying to build a space or time machine, Gill. What I can bring to this is some less commercial sense, if I can put it like that. I am not driven by building things, so my mind tells me that there are certain phenomena in quantum physics that are simultaneously higher level and more profound. Entanglement seems to be more than just two *instances* of one thing; it's about the link between those instances too. The information and communication between them is not dependent on any known restriction that we are aware of. So, being in two places at once is possible without any machinery if there is no space between you and where you want to be. There is an opportunity for unrestricted travel through spacetime via the opening of a channel between the pair, but either or both of the pair may be able to exploit the limitless possibilities that arise from that."

"Sorry?" says Gill, struggling now.

The professor pauses, sensing he has gone too far too quickly. "I don't think about super-positioning in the way Melrose does. I think that if a particle or object is entangled, then it has an equivalent somewhere else in the universe, and if the channel between those two objects is open, then it's like there is no space between them. They may as well be in the *same* space. The distance is immaterial," he says, pausing before adding in a somewhat hushed tone, "Have you heard of wormholes?"

"Yes, like little holes in the Universe where you slip through and come out somewhere else in an instant? Yes, I mean I've watched a whole lot of science fiction on TV..."

"Well, in a way, a wormhole can also be looked at as the communication channel between two entangled objects. That's what I have been working on, and that's what I think is far more interesting."

"But you haven't shown that large objects can be entangled, have you?"

Jumeau pauses for a second. He is thinking about his response, and Gill detects a hesitation. "It's not a case of experimenting with this stuff, Gill. Things are entangled if they are entangled, so my research is more about how to tell if an object is entangled with another object even if you haven't deliberately created a pair of entangled objects in the lab."

Gill is silent. He is thinking of himself and Catherine, and not about what Melrose might be up to. What does all this mean?

"One way to think about things is to imagine what it might be like to be an entangled object. You might act unpredictably at times, or suddenly find yourself in a new situation that seems to have arisen spontaneously," the Professor continues.

"You mean like if I were an atom or something bigger than that even?"

"Well, the combined set of particles that make that object would need to have a great enough level of entanglement with another object. Moreover the entanglement would have to be *specific* to those two large objects. But I see where you are going. You are asking yourself if two people could be entangled at a sufficient enough level to allow them to demonstrate quantum-like behavior Well, funnily enough, I have pondered this on many an occasion. The odds should be astronomical – sorry for that – but think about it. Realistically we are talking about particles that came from an event or source that happened back in time that have somehow re-grouped in some way within a terrestrial object with very specific spacetime co-ordinates. It's not an impossibility, but I imagine it would be rare. However, it could be that something we don't know about could bring those particles together in some way. Maybe a meteor or asteroid that contained very specific particles from a supernova, or even the Big Bang. Or it could be that those particles were never that far apart. Given that the distance and time elements of entanglement are basically unrelated to the behavior that either of the pair exhibits, my feeling is that it is the entanglement alone that allows the channel to be created to spacetime. It's like a door through which you can get to anywhere; like a wormhole, as I said."

"Jeez. That's some serious juice right there. So, just say for a minute that two people could be entangled. What would it be like for them?" asks Gill.

Jumeau pauses for a second, looking over and out the window. "I don't know. I can guess though. You might not be able to explain some actions you have taken or thoughts that you have, or think that you don't necessarily have control over your destiny – that other parts of you sometimes dictate what you do and how you feel about things. Sometimes it might be that you get what we know as déjà vu, or feel the presence of someone else beside you sometimes, or perhaps feel that you have a guardian angel, or maybe are connected to other people in a sensual way. You may feel that you are missing something in your life – that there is someone out there who will really know you and understand you, because they are your true partner in the Universe. I could go on..." the Professor leaves his thoughts hanging.

"Yeh, maybe look like someone else?" Gill asks.

"Yes indeed. That feeling that when you see a face it's actually someone you know. I hadn't thought of that one. That's good!"

"Jeez." Gill is speechless. This is what he should have studied. This is what he is. Entangled. It makes perfect sense. "Could it also mean that you could super-position?"

"Of course. That would be fairly low-level stuff if you were entangled, I would think. Mainly because entanglement for me is only a manifestation of something even more profound."

"I don't know I can go any deeper, Professor," Gill protests in jest.

"Ha ha. Come now, I know you want to go down the rabbit-hole, Gill. We have come this far – let's see what's beyond the blinding light, shall we?"

Gill's expression slowly changes from a frown to a wry smile. "Take me there, Prof," he says, delighted by the invite.

"OK, well, so far I have kept things nice and simple." He smiles at Gill, like he is about to really devour him in some predatory intelli-frenzy. "I have studied quantum weirdness all my life. From a boy I was fascinated by the greats like Bohr and Einstein, then Hawking and others - many others. Those insights into black holes, Big Bang, string theory, branes, dimensional overlap and so on, they all got me charged up. I realised back in the day when I was getting funded to research practical applications of quantum weirdness that looking at these things from a classic scientific paradigm wasn't going to work. We are taught to break things down, to look at the respective parts of things, the components; to understand what they do, how they work. In our mechanical and technological world, that makes a lot of sense, and science has helped engineers to build...stuff. Cars, buildings, planes, washing machines. Great. All very useful. But in terms of opening up the potential of our Universe, progress has actually been really slow in relative terms. We still rely on the same machines as we did one hundred years ago. So all this nonsense about the rate of development speeding up, we have to take with a pinch of salt. There are many reasons why development doesn't happen quickly enough, but one of them is demonstrated well by the likes of Walter Melrose. The way to get your head around this stuff is to think big, and think *connected*. I happen to believe that one of the reasons we witness super-positioning is that each instance of an entangled object is a projection. So, having a surveillance device in a lab in Boston *and* in the Kremlin, or wherever, is about the same object having a projected instance of itself beamed into another place. The source remains the same. But the reason one object might react to what is happening with its entangled partner in some far-flung corner of the Universe, or even just down the road, is because they relate back to a unifying information source, or what you might call *base reality*."

"This is getting a bit trippy," says Gill, sensing that the Professor might just have gone off on one.

"Yes, I know, but hang in there," the Professor urges Gill. "In a way it is a big trip, this. There is quite a lot of evidence now to show that the Universe, or reality as we know it, as we experience it, could be more like a hologram, or projection, of something that happens at the very edges of our Universe, and that there may be many possible variations of that *base reality*. It's not so much science fiction as mathematical probability. It is likely that we are living in a 3D projection, or simulation, of a reality that is being played out in two dimensions, but with features of a hologram. You might not know this, but if you create a hologram of yourself, then the image of you remains whole even if you divide the hologram in two, or as many pieces as you like. Each little bit of that hologram will contain an entire you. So if you were to break up that hologram and chuck the different bits all over the place, then there would be as many instances of you as there are pieces of the hologram. Where it gets really interesting is if you think of what the *source* is. Where you *originate*. Is this source just a *single object*? What if the source is *entangled*? We know that entanglement is more likely the closer things are to one another, in terms of vector space. Entangled objects may therefore easily display variances in the holographic projection of themselves."

At this point, Christophe pauses. The silence is calming.

"Whatever the nature of the projection, I believe that entanglement could be, in fact, quite common. That's why entanglement and super-positioning are not 'weird' any more for me. In fact, the weirdest thing about reality is that it isn't any weirder. But here's the thing. It's when entangled objects reunite that we face a new unknown," the Professor concludes.

There is a long pause in which Gill is staring at Professor Jumeau. Gill is thinking 'if that is real, it's weird enough for me.'

"OK," Gill says. "OK, I need some time with that, Professor. That's a bit of a head-mash." He slouches back in his chair and looks up at the ceiling. Christophe Jumeau, older, wiser, gets up and heads towards the door, before turning towards Gill.
"You want a beer?" he asks.
Gill nods his head, unable to do much more.

That evening, with Grady back, everyone sits down to Monique's jerk pork. Catherine and Gill immediately reach for their beers as soon as they take their first mouthful. Christophe is trying to get some cool air into his mouth while reaching for the jug of water.

"Yikes," Gill says. Catherine can't get any words out, but makes a stifled 'hoh' noise several times.
Grady laughs. "Monique sure likes her Scotch Bonnet," he announces. The unlikely bunch start to laugh uncontrollably around the table.

* * * *

CHAPTER 5: NO SECRETS

'Start Me Up' at full blast.

"Jesus, dude, you got to get a better tune than that to wake up to!"

It's Grady's voice, struggling to be heard over Mick Jagger. Gill reaches over to his jacket which is hanging on the back of a chair next to his makeshift bed. He manages to silence The Stones mid-flow.

"Coffee is on, man," Grady says. "You want some?"

"Hhhmm," Gill exhales, enough to be a 'yes' for Grady.

Catherine and her father are in the kitchen with Monique having some breakfast. As Gill arrives Grady pours him a coffee. Gill is still a bit drowsy but his first sip of decent coffee brings a change of expression to his face, and he nods to folks around the table, as much to say 'I'm now officially awake.'

"How are you this morning?" Catherine asks.

Gill smiles at her and replies in a husky tone "Fresh as a field of corn." The connection between them is tangible in the room, and Catherine's father turns to look at Catherine who has a broad smile on her face as she holds Gill's attention for long enough to make it awkward for others in the room.

"So, what are you guys' plans for today?" Monique interrupts. Everyone looks to Gill.

"Uh, well," Gill stumbles, trying to get his mind in gear, "first off, I need to know what you got on the assassination, Grady – you said you had some stuff for me to look at last night, right?"

"That's right, man, anytime you are ready," Grady confirms.

Gill nods and turns to the Jumeaus. "Catherine, Professor, I'll be checking in at the precinct today. You going to be OK here?"

"Well, I got a call from Mary, my wife, this morning. I ought to get back home really, and I'd like Catherine to come with me if that's OK," Christophe Jumeau states.

"Well, I figure it's best to keep Catherine here for now, Professor, but I understand if you need to return to Montreal." Gill gives the Professor a look which indicates that he knows what he is doing is best. Jumeau senior looks disappointed. He is torn between getting back to his wife and staying with Catherine. His daughter senses this, and takes his hand.

"It's OK, Dad. I'll be fine – I'm not in danger here and everything seems to be working out OK. I need to get back to my apartment and get my stuff and then I'll come and see you and Mom in a few days." Catherine manages a broad smile for her Dad. "Besides, me and Monique still have our game of Scrabble to finish." She smiles over at Monique.

Monique smiles broadly. "That's right, honey, but you know, I'll miss all those fancy words that the Professor here knows. Damn." She chuckles to herself. She and Christophe have been on the same team and having the best time together.

The Professor laughs heartily with Monique. "OK, well I guess I should get back. I'll call you regularly Catherine – if I get just one that you don't answer I'll be back here before you know it." He turns to Gill. "And if I can be of any further help, Detective, please do call me?" his intonation rising at the end to ensure Gill nods in agreement. With that, Christophe decides to get off early so he can get back to his better half for dinner.

—-

A little while after breakfast, Grady is updating Gill on what has come out of the investigation into the President's death so far, mainly gleaned from one of Grady's friends who is fairly senior in the Washington police.

"Damn G's man, gotta be an inside job. No doubt," Grady spits out with some venom. He has previous history with government agents following an alleged leak of security information when he was with Special Forces. Nothing was proven, but it was enough to get Grady a commendable discharge and emerge embittered and deeply cynical about his own government. These days, since leaving

Downtown district, he is pulling his weight over in C-6, otherwise known as South Boston.

"Evidence?" Gill prompts.

"Some real giveaways. We got a big morning session at the Senate, so it's packed. Lots of security. In fact, security at every turn, even at the washrooms. Watertight." Grady smiles a wry smile. "No-one could have got in, not even to the john, without being seen. So it has to be from within."

"What about motive, weapon, forensics...there have to be clues there, huh?" Gill asks hopefully.

"You kiddin' me? Motive – about half the Senate have motive, as well as most of Wall Street and most of the military. Weapon – none found. Nada. Forensics – traces of shrapnel discharge in the immediate area around the body and splatter tests show he was shot at point blank range. One stopped his heart, the other right between the eyes. He didn't stand a chance."

"And bloods?"

"Only one, Montgomery's."

"Anything before or after that might raise suspicion?"

"Not really. Before going to the washroom, Montgomery was reported listening to Senator Willis' speech on Terrorism before going to the ante-room to the main chamber with Senator Nash and Vice President Garfield. From there he proceeded directly to the john where security reported that he seemed fine as he approached them and went in. He was the only person reported in there at the time, and security did not encounter anyone else after they went in to check what was happening – apparently there was a good four minutes between Montgomery entering and security realising that he'd been in for too long."

"Could it have been those security guys?" asks Gill.

"Well, they were the prime suspects of course, but from what I hear, they just ain't connected anywhere and certainly didn't hatch no master plan, if you get my drift..." Grady says as he points to his temple.

"What about the last person to go the washroom before the President? Who was that?" Gill continues.

"Well, now, that would be Senator Shawn Maybury from Louisiana. He's been questioned three times now by police and special investigators, and that guy checks out on all levels. Even conducted forensics on him to see if there was any evidence of gun-handling that day. Nothing." Grady pauses in reflection. "You know, the security guys are the chief suspects, and two of those guys are still being questioned by special agents. But there's nothing - they totally check out from what I understand. So it looks like we are either dealing with a massive cover up, with multiple groups co-ordinating a coup d'etat in the john of the Capitol Building, or somehow someone fooled security to get in there, took out the President, and had a planned exit route which wasn't out the front door."

"And what about that then – any signs of another exit?" questions Gill.

"No. The only thing that was reported was a slight smell of cologne in the room, which one of the guys said didn't seem the same as what the president had been wearing when he went in. Nothing else."

"OK, so the hit-man smells nice. That's good to know," muses Gill. "Man, this is weird, huh?"

"I don't like it, Gill. If the security guys are for real, then you got a major problem 'cos you got an ice-cold hit-man who vanished into thin air."

——-

"We're ready!" Catherine shouts from the other room. Gill and Grady join the others and, after farewells and thanks, Gill and Catherine are in the Oldsmobile heading back into the city. Gill seems pre-occupied, and he is. Information overload, again. Decision time, again.

"So, the idea is that I stay at the apartment with a police guard, while you go to Atlanta to track down Wendy and Mal, right?" says Catherine after a couple of minutes.

"Kind of. I need you to stay at the precinct for a short time while I go over and just make sure the apartment is safe. I'll be able to brief the other officers on security issues that way, so you are totally safe."

"OK, if thats what you think is best. I need to get a couple of things from the shops so you need to relax your regime for about an hour. I'll be fine and will stay in contact though."

"What do you mean 'things from the shops'?" Gill asks.

"Detective, just stuff. Stuff that girls need. Stuff I can't do without. Understand?" Catherine delivers a little rebuke to Gill and you can hear the determination in her voice.

"Oh, right," he says, a little embarrassed. "Well I guess if it's just for a short while, but I need you to be contactable at all times. Check your bio-cell for signal regularly – you should be fine in the city though. I'll call you to make sure you are OK."

"My God, you sound like my dad now," she says, a little wry smile on her face.

Gill raises his eyebrows involuntarily. "I just have your best interests at heart, dear," he says sarcastically. They both smile, and sit back in the all-in-one front seat. Gill likes those – you can get four people on there if you want, or have your girlfriend snuggle into you while you are driving. Old school thinking, but then that was Gill.

At the precinct, Lieutenant Young is in his room as Gill and Catherine approach.

"Ah, Gill, now who do we have here?" asks the Lieutenant.

"Lieutenant Young, Catherine Jumeau," Gill introduces the pair.

"My pleasure, Miss Jumeau, glad to see you are safe and sound like your fellow students. Now Gill, what can I do for you?" the Lieutenant asks, being very business-like in his delivery.

Gill turns to Catherine, smiles at her and says softly, "Catherine, would you give the Lieutenant and myself a couple of minutes?"

Catherine flushes slightly before replying, "Oh, sure, I'll grab a coffee downstairs."

"Feel free to use my desk," Gill adds.

When Catherine is out of sight, Gill ushers the Lieutenant into his own office and shuts the door.

"Here's the thing, sir. I think Catherine is at risk here. I'd like to put a detail on her for a couple of days while I try and get hold of Xiu and Baines in Georgia. I understand that they still have not been confirmed as found?"

"Jesus, Gill, what exactly is the risk? I mean, Xiu and Baines have called in, Miss Jumeau is not missing after all, and nothing's been taken from her apartment. Just who do you think is after these students?" The Lieutenant is calm, but irritated.

"I don't know, but there's a bunch of things that don't add up on this one. First, I have a pretty strong feeling that Baines and Xiu are not OK, even though they are supposed to have texted the mother. Why would anyone travel long distance to where their relatives live, then spend several days without letting their work know? Second, there's now no doubt in my mind that at least some of Melrose's research - and those PhD students' research - is maximum security stuff, and potentially valuable in any currency. And last but not least, I found a bug in Catherine's apartment the other day." Gill leaves the best to last.

"What?" Young exclaims, now unsettled.

"That's right. I haven't touched it, but thought you ought to know. My guess is that it's either someone snooping for any conversations Xiu and Catherine might have had about their work, or that it was planted when Xiu and Baines were taken the other night so that they could find out where Catherine is."

"If you are sure about this, then how come you can't tell me who 'they' are? What's going on here, Gill?"

"Listen, Lester," Gill makes his approach to Young more determined, "Fuck knows what is going on here, but it's not good in my book and I don't want us to be sorry for not doing the right thing. I need to find Xiu and Baines, and we need to protect Catherine until we know more. It's our duty, and now that you know the detail, you have to give me some resource to work with." Gill trails off and leaves the Lieutenant pondering the situation. He gets them both a cup of fresh coffee from the Lieutenant's pot in the corner.

The Lieutenant is a little lost. He's not used to cases with so many unknowns, maybes, unquantifiable risks. He's uncomfortable enough with things that he decides the best way is to defer to Gill, who at least has the energy and personal interest to run around finding out what might be happening.

"Look, I'll give you a two-man detail but that's it. Get your ass down to Atlanta and find those kids – I don't want any mess here. I've had Melrose in my ear way too much, and the Mayor might just pin my dick to the desk if we don't calm the Professor down. Two days though – that's it."

"Done. But I get to pick the guys on the detail. I'm not having any rookies on this one," Gill asserts, and the Lieutenant nods in agreement.

"What about that bug though? You gonna leave that be?"

"Yeh, I guess, for now anyway – I'll sort that when I get back," Gill confirms.

The two men are frowning and staring at the floor. They take a sip of the worst coffee money can buy and immediately contort their faces before managing a nod to each other as Gill departs. Gill is pretty pleased. He's got what he wanted from the Lieutenant, and makes his way back down to his desk where Catherine is reading The Globe.

"Hi," she greets his return with a certain amount of uncertainty in her voice. "Is everything OK?"

"Hi. Yes, fine. I just need to get over to your apartment, like I said. We can make everything secure by mid-afternoon once I have sorted out the officers who will be guarding the place. Will you be OK for an hour or so?" he asks, and adds before she can reply, "I'd feel better if someone else could do that shopping for you." Gill knows he's got no chance of getting anybody from the precinct to go shopping for Catherine, and he's regretting not bringing Monique into the city so they could keep each other company. Too late for that.

"Look, I'll be fine. I'll be in that shop across there, and I'll grab a coffee just down there. I'll have my cell on the whole time, and I'll wear my dark glasses. I'l even buy a headscarf and wear that if that makes you feel better. No-one will even notice me."

Gill doesn't pick up on her perfunctory attempt at humor straight away. "OK, OK. You win. But call me or text if *anything* – and I mean *anything* – is wrong. Promise?"

"Promise," Catherine responds.

Gill is too caught up in his own thinking to realise the impact his concern is having; she feels uneasy at the urgency of his manner but reassured that his attention is on her safety. On balance, Catherine thinks that being over-protective is Gill's way of showing her how much he cares, and she likes this. So much so that she is part-blinded to the danger she is in. And it's for this reason that Gill has chosen a different path for them to go down. But first he has to get across to her apartment.

———

On the main road, Gill looks in the window of the second-hand music store beside the entrance to the small block of apartments where Catherine lives. 'Cover Me', by Merz, is filtering out into the street, its progression from floaty aesthetic to gritty electric coda catching Gill's attention. He imagines what he could play on top of that on the sax. He imagines playing. It's been too long since he has heard from fellow band members, and he makes a mental note to get back into the swing as soon as this case is over.

He enters and nods over at the young owner behind the counter, who looks unfeasibly cool.

"Alright?" he says.

"Alright," Gill repeats. "I was just wondering if you could help me. Do you know the girls that live upstairs?"

"Uh, you mean the college students?"

"That's right, you know them?"

"Not really, but they've been in a couple of times and bought some vinyl. They seem really nice."

"Yeh, they're sweet, man. You know most of the guys in the block here?" Gill pursues his thread a little while longer.

"Well, yeh, I guess I probably do. I mean, there's only a few anyway. I know Marty best, he's the little fella on the top floor. Mad on jazz he is. And then there's the old couple. I don't know them but I see them come in and out. A couple of other guys, tech geeks maybe. How come you are so interested, man?"

"Well, it's just that I am a close friend of Catherine's – she's the tall one – and we think that someone tried to break into the apartment a little while back. You didn't see anyone a bit odd – you know, like they are really not from around here - looking around outside or going in and out recently, did you?"

"Can't say as I did. I mean, lots of people come in here, man."

"Sure, I get that. But you're observant, yeh. I mean I noticed you checking me out the other day when I was outside, right?"

The young guy smiles, then breaks into a laugh. "Ha ha. Hey, *you're* the observant one. But yeh, I checked you out. You guys looked like you are into each other, yeh?"

It's Gill's turn to smile. "Yeh, you could say that."

"Look man, apart from you, the only unusual thing I remember is seeing a couple of beefy-looking dudes in surf gear the day after they announced the President had been killed. I remember because hardly anyone was around that day and I was sat outside. I just remember thinking that they didn't look right. I mean, bad hair, pale, shocking taste in clothes. More like dodgy golfers than surf majors."

"So, did they enter the building then?"

"Yeh, they just went in and came back out really quickly. Just a few minutes I would say, so they must have been looking for someone and when they weren't in, they came back out again. I didn't really think anything of it. You a cop then?"

"Yeh, like I said my girlfriend's place got broken into, and I'm trying to figure out who would do that kind of thing. Here..." Gill says, handing over a standard issue business card from Boston Police.

"Man, I wouldn't have guessed just from looking at you. Hope you get to the bottom of it, dude."

"Me too. Listen, thanks. Appreciate you taking the time. I'll take a proper look at your stuff the next time – I'm Gill, by the way," Gill says pointing to the business card.

"Josh. Take it easy, man."

Gill goes upstairs to the apartment, and uses Catherine's key to get in, taking care not to make any sound. Going straight to the living area and to the Picasso on the wall, he disarms the sensor. It will be only a matter of time before whoever is monitoring the apartment realises that the bug is incapacitated and they send someone over to check. If this happens within half an hour he'll check out who comes, and if not, he'll ask Josh to give him a call if he sees anything odd again. He balances a bottle on the front door handle so that it will smash if the door is opened, sits down on the sofa and takes in the painting, which is captivating. Then he calls Catherine to make sure she is OK. She tells him she is in the department store and all is good.

But she's not. Actually she is on her way to meet Professor Melrose on Devonshire. Catherine figures that Gill wouldn't approve of her meeting Melrose, but she is fond of her boss and her professional responsibility has kicked in. At Black's coffee shop she spots the professor over in the corner. Unusually for him, he has dressed down to what might be deemed normal clothing for a middle-aged man. Much more downbeat than his usual flamboyant waistcoats and his penchant for brightly colored clothes.

"Catherine! My dear!" he exclaims. He is obviously pleased to see her, and she reciprocates by giving him a hug before she sits down. After ordering a black coffee and settling in, the Professor enquires about her whereabouts. "I've been worried sick about you, my dear. After Wendy and Malcolm disappeared I didn't know what to think. Obviously the President's assassination has affected everyone really badly, yes?" The Professor is angling to understand more about why all of his PhD students went missing, post-assassination.

"Oh, Professor, I am so sorry for not being in contact. That day the three of us were in the lab until the afternoon and I guess no-one thought to tell us what had happened. So we just caught the whole thing on the news. It was really shocking."

"So what happened to you then – did you all go off somewhere to take stock? Where did you all go? I heard through the police that Wendy and Malcolm are now in Atlanta, for God's sake. Why on earth would they go there? Have you heard from them?" There is concern on his face.

"No, I don't know. It's..." Catherine pauses. She is trying to answer several questions and is caught between keeping her story to herself or sharing it with the man who has been mentoring her and with whom she has shared her research. The man who is the key to her future, and someone who she *has* to trust.

"What is it my dear? Are you OK?" the Professor prompts.

"Yes. Yes, I'm fine. I haven't heard from Wendy so I still don't know if she is OK. It's just that I had a very strange experience that day. Wendy took me home as I wasn't feeling well."

"Oh yes? What sort of 'experience' my dear? Sounds like it shook you up..." he trails off.

"Yes. It did. It really did. Look, Professor, I feel pretty silly about the whole thing, and I need to know that you won't think me an idiot if I tell you. Can you understand that?"

"My dear girl, I have seen many strange things in my life! I am not going to be shocked by anything, let alone think any less of you for telling me. Besides, I am so intrigued now that you can't possibly keep me hanging on a thread like this!" His jest breaks the tension and Catherine lets out a nervous laugh before continuing to recount her experience.

"Professor, you know Ellis Garfield, don't you?" she asks.

This isn't what the Professor was expecting. He looks bemused, and can't find any words.

"Professor?"

"Uh, yes, yes I do. He is a supporter of our work, you know that. I'm sorry, what is this got to do with your bad experience the other day, my dear?" He looks puzzled and is clearly struggling with the tangential thinking required.

"It's to do with his address to the nation. Did you see that?"

"Yes, I did," the Professor answers.

"Well," Catherine starts, looking around her and quietening her voice, "I saw something very strange when he was speaking. It was as if Garfield and President Montgomery were the same person. Like Montgomery was there, shouting at me. But I couldn't hear anything. It was so odd. I was very sad afterwards."

"You mean you saw the ghost of Montgomery during Garfield's speech? Well, I think a few could lay claim to such a thing, my dear. I mean, many people were mourning his death and it is often the way that people see what they want to see after being traumatized like that. I remember once…"

But Catherine is tired of people telling her what something is, or what it isn't.

"No!" she blurts out, loud enough that people nearby look around. There is an awkward pause in the corner of the coffee house. Returning to a less dramatic tone, Catherine explains. "No, it's not that. That's what everybody says to me, but it's not. This was real. I felt it in my bones. I even saw the clock on the screen stop while this was happening. That made me think about time stopping and the implications from a scientific point of view. Please don't tell me I was seeing things, Professor – of all people you should know that I am level-headed and wouldn't tell you something if it weren't true."

She is almost pleading, trying to get her boss to understand that this isn't some enchanted wishful-thinking ouija board session, but that she, as a scientist, observed something that was *real*.

"You say the clock stopped?" Melrose asks.

"Yes. It just stopped while this metamorphosis happened. Why would that happen?"

"Hhmmm. I don't know. But it's odd alright."

The Professor distracts from the conversation by calling the waitress over. Catherine takes *this* as odd. He orders two more coffees even though Catherine has almost a full cup in front of her.

"Professor?" she raises her eyebrows and looks straight at Melrose.

"Uh? Oh, yes. You said 'metamorphosis', Catherine. Why did you use that word?" comes the question.

"Well, because that's what it was like. As if Garfield turned into Montgomery for a minute, or at least that something of Montgomery was inside Garfield. I completely freaked out. Did you see it too?"

"Oh, no. No. No, I didn't see anything like that," the Professor now sounds a bit distant and troubled.

"Professor, what is it?" Catherine asks with some trepidation.

"Eh? Oh, nothing my dear. I am just thinking. Listen, did Wendy and Mal see this too?'

"No. That's the point. It only seemed to be me that actually saw it happen. At first I thought that I had just been so tired and emotional – you know, like what you said earlier – but I know it wasn't that. I know myself well enough to know that it wasn't a hallucination."

The Professor reaches across to Catherine and takes her hand. "My dear, don't worry. You are an extremely talented student and I am certain you wouldn't make anything like this up, so *don't worry!*" The ageing academic has regained his composure quickly and sounds very reassuring. But he isn't finished yet. "Have you told anyone else about this, my dear?" he asks.

Catherine hesitates for a moment. The Professor's reaction has given her pause for thought. She reflects on the conversation for a second, and judges that, on balance, it wasn't a good idea to tell him after all. Like a child who can't keep a secret and wants an adult to make everything better in an instant, she is disappointed that he is taking so much time to reflect and is obviously working out the implications without telling her what he is thinking. When someone asks you 'who else have you told about this?', it is always an uncomfortable question because it can only come from a pattern of thought which is concerned about the risk involved in other people knowing. It is always loaded. And Catherine is shrewd enough to know this. Either the Professor is worried for her safety, or worried for others. And either way, it just serves to make her more nervous. So she backs off.

"Just Wendy, really. I thought it was so silly that I didn't want anyone to think I was an idiot," she answers, convincingly.

"Well, maybe that's just as well, my dear. Obviously when it comes down to the Vice President – I mean, the President of course as he now is – he would be concerned if people thought that he were somehow psychologically or physically damaged and could not do his job properly."

"Excuse me?" Catherine exclaims. She has no idea what he is talking about.

"I mean, it's obviously a strange time in any case, given that Montgomery is no longer with us. We don't want to be spreading any rumors about the new President as being somehow two-faced or debilitated in any way. He will most likely need all the support he can get."

Catherine is looking at the Professor very intently. She can't figure out how the conversation has turned to the new President's well-being and public profile rather than the science behind what she saw. It is unlike the Professor to be unconcerned with the scientific aspects of anything that looks strange. She and Melrose have had several spontaneous conversations on quantum weirdness in the past, and these have been very enlightening.

"Well, I guess," she says, "but how would you explain something like that, from a scientific point of view, Professor?" she enquires.

"Oh, you know, I wouldn't know where to start, my dear. I am not so sure there would be any science behind seeing the ghost of

Montgomery in someone. My best guess is that it is nothing other than something very non-scientific – emotion. I think you don't know it but you were probably grieving in that moment, and your mind gave you something to hang on to which makes you think Montgomery might still be alive. I mean, that's where this is going, right? That you believe he is still with us?"

Catherine shivers. She is turning cold and is now very uncomfortable. The Professor is refusing to entertain the prospect of any scientific viability about what she has seen. This disturbs her so much that she is beginning to realise what a mistake she has made coming here. She thinks about Gill, and how much safer she feels with him. She would like to be with him right now. Sensing that she has revealed too much, she decides to get back to the police station as soon as she can.

"So, my dear. Please, just relax. This must have been very traumatic, I am sure. But honestly, think about it. Your mind is such a strong instrument. It can give you results that you want, rather than what is real. My guess is that on this occasion it has got the better of you. And I *understand* that. It's perfectly natural, so don't be too upset at yourself. Now, the most important thing for you is to get right back into the swing of the research, and to join Wendy and Malcolm in the lab again. Let's all get back to some sense of routine at least. Come in tomorrow at around ten and we can review where we are with everything, and make a fresh start on some of the work. How about that?" Melrose says.

Catherine gets herself together enough to play the game. "Yes. Yes, that's probably best, Professor. I'll do that. And if you hear from Wendy or Malcolm will you let me know?" she asks, deliberately making her voice sound feeble and searching for a positive response.

"Why, yes of course. Of course I will. Now, what are you up to this afternoon. Can I offer you a lift anywhere?" Melrose asks.

"Oh, that's very kind, but I have some shopping to do. Girl's stuff," she says, hoping that the 'stuff for girls' tag is enough to dissuade Melrose from pursuing the line.

"Ah, I see," he says as he signals to the waitress to get the bill, "well, I shall run along then. That should take care of the coffees. And don't forget," he says as he takes Catherine's hand again, "we all see things differently, my dear. It's best to work through it rather than dwell on it. Take it from me." He smiles as he feels satisfied he has managed a reassuring ending to the conversation, oblivious to Catherine's newly-laid suspicions.

If nothing else, Catherine could stay cool when she needed to. But as soon as the Professor leaves, she phones Gill.

"Catherine? What's going on?" Gill asks.

"Uh, when are you getting back. It's just that I am finished in town now and wondered if you can come back."

The tone in her voice is different, and Gill responds with calm. "I can come now if you like. I'm finished here."

"Yes, I...that would be good," she says. It's enough for now. They both know that he needs to get Downtown.

Gill has been at the apartment for long enough to know that de-activating the bug has not caused anyone to come rushing over. The surveillance on the apartment is most likely secondary, or at least organized and operated from a more distant location higher up the food chain.

He pops back into the record store downstairs and asks Josh to give him a call if he sees anybody lurking around outside or going up to the the girls' apartment. Driving back in to the city, Gill hears the rush of the traffic past his window. He is thinking about Catherine, and who would bug her flat. He calls Grady to ask him to check the bug he has taken from Catherine's place, to find out how this kind of device might be used, and by whom. Grady says it will take a few days but that he'll drop by the precinct later to pick it up.

Back Downtown, Gill parks at a bad angle right outside the front entrance and runs up the stairs to find Catherine. Sandra Chandry is on duty, but this time she just nods to Gill, seeing that he is in a rush.

"Officer Chandry." Gill still takes the time to acknowledge her.

"Detective," comes the reply over his shoulder as he whizzes by and into the main open office. Catherine is at his desk, looking somewhat anxious but otherwise fine. Unusually, Harry Chambers isn't around. It's a bit of a first, but just as well, as he wants to have some time with Catherine alone.

"Hey, you OK?" he asks her.

"Hey, yeh I'm fine – just needed to see you, that's all."

Gill feels a sense of wonder. He immediately moves towards her to hug her but he is forgetting himself. As he does so the weirdness of time and movement begins to take hold and he has to resist. For now. She feels it too, and they look at each other for a moment as things return to normal.

"What *is* that?" she asks him.

"Us," he says, and smiles at her. She reciprocates, before he gets to the point. "So what's up then – why the call? You sounded...well, worried."

"Yeh, well, you're not going to like this..." she throws him an awkward glance, at which he does nothing other than raise his eyebrows in a motion that says 'carry on...'

"I met Professor Melrose briefly when I was out in town. I just bumped into him and he invited me to have coffee with him. I hope that was OK?" she says, with a big rise in intonation at the end of her sentence which suggests she really needs him to say that it *is* OK. But it doesn't come.

"Nice. So what's the problem?" Gill says. Catherine seems to be both reassured and confused by Gill's reaction.

"Well, it wasn't a good meeting, let's put it that way. He seemed to be in a weird mood and I ended up feeling quite strange by the time I left." She hesitates while she looks at Gill, wide-eyed and vulnerable. "In fact, I...I felt..." she breaks off, unable to finish her sentence.

Gill senses that she is fighting something. "Listen, this is *me* here. I don't know if you realise it yet, but you and I aren't going to be able to keep away from each other for any length of time, so you'd better get used to trusting me. You got that?" he raises a half-smile and a nod from Catherine.

"Yep, I've got that, Detective," she says. "So here's the thing. I think I made a mistake with the Professor. I told him about what I saw with Garfield and he got all defensive on me, and sort of ignored what I was saying. The strange thing was that he got very emotional, and it's just not like him to react like that. Think I hit a nerve. Ended up just needing to get away from him."

"I see," says Gill, "so what part of your story seemed to cause him the biggest problem – the fact that you saw something weird or the fact that it was Garfield that you saw?"

Catherine gives this a little thought, before answering.

"Hhmm, actually it was as soon as I asked him about Garfield being his friend. That was when he first started to get edgy. He just tried to trash the fact that I had seen anything, saying that I was probably stressed out and overly-emotional. But he knows me better than that, so it kind of spooked me that he reacted that way. I didn't know what to think except maybe that I ought to get away as quickly as I could."

"Ok, from now on, I need you not to do stuff like that. You probably already guessed that your Professor gets ten out of ten for bullshit quality in my book, and possibly more for deviance. He is closer to Garfield than anyone cares to admit, and I know that Garfield has visited him on several occasions. It's all related to his secretive research, and it's why I think you and your friends are in very real danger. I'm not messing with you; in my professional judgement you guys need to be protected until we can get to the bottom of what you witnessed, do you get that?"

Catherine looks at him intently, into his piercingly honest blue eyes. "Yeh, I get it," she says, "but why do *you* believe so strongly in what I saw? No-one else does. I mean I'm glad you do, but I don't understand why you buy into it so strongly."

Of course, this is it. This is what she needs to know from Gill. He has followed up on her story almost unquestioningly when only her father dared to believe that she actually witnessed something that could be important beyond just the immediate weirdness of a TV address. So what is it that Gill knows that led him to this? Or is it just that Gill is head-over-heels with Catherine and so besotted that he can't reason properly?

Gill takes a second to frame his response, anxious to be clear and dispassionate in his delivery. "OK, good point. And perhaps it's about time I made myself as clear as I can with you. First off, I'm sorry if I have been overly protective. It must sometimes seem like heavy-going for you, and I guess that's down to me. But the reason I am convinced about your story is that I think I may have an explanation, even though I might not be able to frame it in the kind of hard scientific language that you need. I mean, I do actually think that something happened during that TV address and that you witnessed Garfield doing something that I think might be, well, criminal at best, and possibly conspiratorial at worst. And because I believe in justice, I know that it is somehow down to me to find out if Montgomery was the victim of some form of coup, most probably led by Garfield." He pauses. Catherine is looking at him, silent and without breaking her stare. He decides to carry on. "So, although I feel there is something incredible between us, I'm not being blinded by that. In many ways, I wish I hadn't met you under such circumstances. That things might have been very different in another reality where we just met. I mean, just *met*, normally. At a party, or in a bar, or at the library. It might have been very different. But we are here, now. And I'm the only person that can really do anything to understand what is going on with Melrose, Garfield and you. I don't want that to scare you either – I know you are going to be OK as long as I am around."

Catherine begins to cry, and Gill reaches for her. Everything slows, as it does. But he doesn't care, he wants things to slow down for them right now. All he wants is for them to be alone for a second and for her to know that he is the person who will protect her. He feels himself being drawn into the field and he can hear her voice calling his name even though her lips are not moving. He is losing sight of the current situation at his desk in the precinct and gaining the vision at the clearing in the cornfield. They are there together, and have the chance to travel to wherever they want. It's only his utter conviction and loyalty to the current reality, and people's lives there, that makes him stop and decide to go back. Catherine is used to the cornfield in her dreams but she's never really understood what it means. She has to be guided, but knows that they are there together. He can see her face for the first time in the dream state when he starts to dual. He knows that she has the ability too, but just hasn't learnt how to do it yet.

He leads her away from the clearing, and they return together to now. Things start to speed up, and all around them becomes clear. They are back in the main office, at his desk. The tears have disappeared, and Catherine is smiling.

She leans across the desk so that they are close, but not touching, and says, "You know, we really must stop doing that in public." It breaks the tension, and they both have a chuckle. After a few minutes, Gill announces that he is going to talk to the two officers who will be patrolling outside Catherine's apartment, and that they'll leave when he gets back. On his return, the pair leave the building and drive off in Gill's car.

"What did you mean when you said you have an explanation for what I saw?" Catherine asks Gill in the car as they are stopped at traffic lights for what seems like an eternity.

"Mmm, well, of course I'd need to kill you if I told you," he says, jokingly. But this time Catherine isn't laughing, and he realises. "Sorry, "he says, "it's just that it's going to sound ridiculous to you. Do you still want me to try?"

"Yes, Detective Gill, I do," she comes back with a hint of irritation in her voice. "Otherwise I'll come across there and hug you so hard we'll never get away from these lights."

"Woah, OK, OK," he chortles, the chemistry between them adding to the physical attraction. There is a long pause before Gill gathers himself. "Right, so what if I said that the reason that Garfield appeared the way he did to you was related to the fact that you and I slow time down and have some kind of physical – I mean, literally physics-related - connection?"

Catherine can't take her eyes of him, even though he is looking forward waiting for the lights to change. They are still at red. "Carry on," she instructs.

"Well, basically I think Garfield was dualling when you saw him on TV."

"Dualling?" she sounds puzzled.

"Uh, super-positioning," he says, leaving a second or two for this to sink in. Catherine's face is a picture of concentration as she begins to take in what Gill is saying. Gill carries on. "I think Garfield used his ability to go back to the scene of the crime at the Capitol building while he was on air. My guess is that he had left some evidence there, and used the exact moment when everyone - even security - would be away from the scene watching the TV address to take a chance and go back to clear up."

"Haha. You're joking right? I mean, that's just ridiculous. No-one can do that kind of stuff – I know, I am looking at this and I can tell you..."

"Stop. For a second," Gill interrupts sharply, which has the strange effect of calming Catherine down before she gets too uptight. "Listen, I know this sounds mad to you, but the reason I'm guessing this is because I know that super-positioning of a large object is possible. I've seen it."

"What? Are you serious?" Catherine sounds skeptical and more than a little undermined. After all, she is the expert, not Gill.

"Just go with me for a second. Please. Here's the thing..." Gill looks across at Catherine, deep into her eyes. "I know, because I can do this."

There is silence. Catherine can't speak. All she can do is look at Gill, and wonder. More silence. Gill is comfortable with it, but it is the only way to move forward. Eventually, he decides to pursue his thinking out loud. He has let the cat out of the bag, there is no turning back, and he needs her to know what he is thinking.

"I started when I was young. I didn't know what was going on at first, but I took a chance and practised lots. I nearly came unstuck on more than one occasion and I guess was lucky too. But I got to the stage where I would go into a dream-like state and find myself in a different reality. Sometimes it would be the same place, where things are familiar, sometimes it would be back or forward in time, sometimes it would be a weird place, but that felt more like an actual dream. I've been doing it – I call it '*dualling*' - for years, but only for work really. My sister is the only person apart from you that knows."

"Your sister? You...I...Gill, what the hell are you talking about? I mean, it's just not possible. You, Garfield, super-positioning? I can't believe that you...I mean, if you could do that, you could change history. My God! Is that what you are saying – that Garfield was in front of the camera, in front of millions of people, *and* at the scene of the crime where you say he murdered the President? Have you any idea how fantastic that sounds?"

Catherine is imploding, and Gill fully expected it. It's just too much to take in at once, for anyone. She needs his help and support, otherwise she will just go into denial and reject both him and his hypothesis.

"Yep. It's ridiculous, right? But remember what your dad says about this kind of stuff. That it's not a matter of thinking about the physical limitations in the laboratory. He knows that if matter – us – comes from the same place and is entangled, then all sorts of possibilities open up. Why is it so fantastic to think that larger objects could be entangled at a significant enough level for a channel to open up between them which may allow for journeying in space-time? That's what I think is going on here. In fact, until I heard your dad talk about his own research and ideas, I didn't know what all this was about, but I think I'm beginning to piece things together. Don't you see? Me, you, Garfield, the assassination. It might be coincidence, but if it is, it's got to be the weirdest coincidence that has ever occurred."

Catherine slumps back into the padded front seat in the Oldsmobile. Her mind is processing the information furiously. She has only barely heard the last part of Gill's synopsis about entanglement, but she already knows at one level she is entangled with Gill. She is yet to fully understand what this means. Right now, she's more engaged in her own experiences and how they might be related to her research, and herself. Her brain is coming up with challenges.

"OK, Mister, so just hang on there. Let's just say that people – big people like you – can super-position and be in two places at once. Surely this will only be possible if you are not observed, and there were millions of people observing Garfield when he was on TV, so there's no way that your theory holds up there."

"That's just it though," Says Gill, "Garfield wasn't observed. He couldn't have been, because there was no-one with him who was measuring his activity in real spacetime when he was addressing the nation. Even if there was a cameraman on him, they'd only have seen him through the lens of the camera. At least for the split second that he brought time to zero and was off doing other things. I reckon the entire audience were precisely *not* at the same location in spacetime when he was super-positioning."

Catherine ponders this. It makes some degree of sense, with one important omission. "Well, you can't explain why *I* observed him then, can you?" she argues. Her logical side of the brain has kicked in.

"Well, you know, I think I can," he asserts, before adding, "and this is what might be difficult for you. Are you sure you want to hear this?" he begs the question but knows that she has to comprehend her own unique place in this unravelling story.

"You're going to tell me that I am super-positioning right now?" It's almost a joke, but she knows that it isn't, and that the silence that follows from Gill leaves a void which is filled with her own realisation that the fact that things become so strange when she touches Gill might be because they are actually very similar. Or the same. There may be trouble ahead. "You're saying that I was the only person to witness Garfield super-positioning because...?" she adds. She can't fill in the gaps. Gill will have to propose the solution.

"Because you can see things others can't, Catherine. Not only do I think you can dual, but I think you can see in different dimensions," Gill explains.

Catherine is silent for a moment, then lets out a chuckle.

"Oh, come *on*! Now you are just being silly. So I was the only one who saw John Montgomery because I can see *souls?* Very scientific, Detective."

It's Gill's turn to be silent. He realises this is pretty leftfied, and the words 'soul' and 'science' are uneasy bedfellows. Catherine breaks the air.

"So I'm special and you're not? If we are so connected, why didn't *you* see anything?" she questions.

"Well, I'm pretty sure that I didn't witness it because I didn't see it in real time. Maybe you saw it because, even though you were not in the same location, you were sensitive enough to witness the time dilation; maybe that was enough for you to see into a higher dimension of activity that others couldn't. Maybe I could have seen the same thing if I was there with you. I don't know; this is where my understanding breaks down. But I think the reason that thousands of people have not come forward to say that they witnessed some weird shit when Garfield was on TV, is that very few – maybe no-one – can see what you see. There might be some sort of connection between you and Garfield. Or even Montgomery if you saw him as you seem to have..." Gill trails off, his thinking turning to that question. The *why*? Like Catherine's father had said, sometimes it is important to ask that, but right now he doesn't have more to offer.

The lights change to green at last, and after a blast of a horn from the car behind, Gill is startled into action, and pulls away. The pair are silent as both reflect on what has been discussed. It's not exactly easy terrain, and Catherine is taking it quite badly. If Gill is right, this is life-changing for her, and so laden with potential risks and exposure to danger that she can't quite bring herself to go down that route in full. She decides to think things through, and look into how she can prove or disprove any of the possibilities that he has raised. One good thing has come out of this though. It now seems even clearer to her that she was not mistaken in her assertions about what happened that day at the University. She feels vindicated, albeit with enough accompanying baggage to fill the hold of a large jet.

As Gill pulls onto the freeway, Catherine looks around at the road signs. "Hey! Where are we going?"
"Washington," he replies.
"What? I thought we were going back to my apartment. I have my stuff there. What's going on?"
"It's just better that you stick with me right now. You're one of the few people that can help me solve this thing," he says, before adding "and I couldn't stand the thought of leaving you there."

The whole situation seems to be taking such a frenzied series of turns that Catherine is beginning to lose the ability to analyze and prioritize the facts and opinion before her, and also the will to stay awake for much longer, so tired has she become with all that has gone on.

"So why Washington? You'll be telling me that you're going to talk to the President now, right?"

"Not exactly, but you're pretty close. Once we're through there I want to head to Atlanta so we can track down Wendy and Malcolm since you're still not getting through by cell. Sound good?"

"Uh? Nothing sounds good right now. I'd like to have a bath in my own bath, and go to bed in my own bed. And my father is going to go berserk when he finds out that we're so far away." Catherine is stressed, tired and now moody. Gill decides not to respond, and instead puts on one of his mixes on the stereo. As 'Back to Life' by Soul II Soul drifts out of the speakers, Gill puts his foot on the gas and the car speeds down the freeway, south towards New York.

—-

"Steve? Is that you?"
"Yes."
"Where are you?"
"Location six."
"OK, wait there."

Walter Melrose leaves the Heisenberg Building, gets into his Jaguar XJ12, and pulls out of the car park. Forty minutes later he is at Belle's Diner just outside Mansfield on highway ninety-five south of Boston. Inside, the man at table fourteen has his head in a newspaper. He looks like a trucker, with a Red Sox cap, ill-fitting leather hooded jacket, baggy jeans and boots. His beard is heavy and you can't see his eyes behind the thick-rimmed tinted spectacles high up on his nose.

"Howdy," the man says.
"Hello," Melrose replies, as he takes a seat opposite. The waitress, 'Mandy' according to her name badge, looks too young to be working, never mind in a trucker's diner. "Black coffee, please," he orders.
"So, what have you got for me?" the man asks.
Melrose leans over and whispers, "I don't like what is going on."
"OK, what is the concern?"
"Where do you want me to start? I mean, first of all of my PhD students disappear, then I get a particularly aggressive policeman threatening me in my own office, and then when my best student

finally shows her face, she says that she witnessed you change into John Montgomery while delivering your address." Melrose's voice is becoming animated and breaking out into a canter.

"Keep your voice *down!*" orders 'Steve', pseudo-trucker and President of the United States, heavily disguised and trying to keep his own voice in check.

"Sorry," says Melrose, "It's just...I don't know what's going on and I have never felt so out of control, what with Montgomery's assassination, and now all this. I needed to let you know that people are asking certain questions. About you. You have come up several times in conversations that should be about my missing PhD students, but all end up leading to your name. Now why is that Ell... Steve?"

The tension is palpable. 'Steve' looks around. The diner is so low-key that any little disturbance would cause the whole operation to come to a sudden halt.

In a hushed and composed tone, Ellis Garfield addresses Melrose "Stay calm, Walter. We need to be focused, and I need you to give me what detail you have on this. There is nothing to worry about; it will all blow over but right now I need you to give me detail. Exactly who are you talking about? Are you talking about the young Jumeau girl and the Detective...uh, Detective Gill?"

Melrose looks surprised. "You know Catherine and Detective Gill?" he asks in a hesitant tone.

"Why yes, of course, they are both familiar to me. I guess through my visits to your place and the University."

Melrose does not recollect ever talking to the Vice President about either of the two, but isn't certain. Besides, he is reluctant to argue or resist anything from Garfield right now, so he defers. "Oh, OK, well yes, that's right. First of all this Gill fellow, a most dislikable chap – very, how-do-you-say, 'in your face' – has found out about the maximum security research that we have been doing."

"Hey, back up there Walter. What do you mean 'has found out'? Just exactly how has he found out about any of that. And what exactly has he found out? Does he know about Unitron?"

"I don't know. But he knew about military super-positioning and my funding. I suppose he could have been bluffing but it didn't sound like it to me. He knew that you were involved, for example."

"What?" Garfield exclaims and this time it's his own voice that carries over to other tables. He angles his head down into his coffee cup for a few seconds, just long enough for anyone turning around to have a glance, and look away again without incident. "Have you told him that I am involved in your research? What do you mean?"

"No. No. I mean, I haven't told anyone anything I can promise you. No, he must have got hold of documents or something. He just seemed to *know*, that's all." The Professor can't be any more specific right now.

Garfield lets out a sigh. It's the first sign that he is struggling. "Right, well, for now we can't do anything except keep an ear to the ground. He could be bluffing you. You aren't a good card player, Walter, and if he has bluffed you, then we may need to bluff back. Can you use your influence with the local police to get him taken off the case?"

"I'll see what I can do. But if I were you, I'd be more worried about what happened during your TV address. Surely you weren't 'in transit' at the time, were you?" Melrose quizzes his long-standing test subject and funder.

"Of course not. What have you been told?" Garfield asks.

"Well, I met with Catherine Jumeau today – she turned up after going missing for a couple of days. She is a very bright student, you know, one of the best. Her research is into..."

Garfield interrupts sharply "Walter."

"Oh, yes, right. Well, anyway, she reported seeing you, or rather your face, doing very strange things during the TV address last Tuesday. Do you know anything about that?"

"Well of course I don't. What the hell is this about, Walter? Are you saying that some girl saw my face move on the TV screen and that this is a major issue for national security?"

Garfield is testing Melrose, and Melrose is beginning to realise that Garfield is playing a game here. He has known Ellis Garfield for a number of years, including when he was much younger and just out of special forces abroad. He has a sense of the man, and intuitively knows that Garfield is hiding behind his words as well as the heavy disguise.

"*I'm* not saying anything, Ellis. It's what she is saying that is important here. She says she saw Montgomery's face in you that day, and that it shook her to her bones. Now, I know Catherine pretty well, and she is just not the sort to make this stuff up. If she says she saw something, then I think she saw something. The interesting thing is that no-one else did. Just her. Do you think she saw a ghost?"

"Probably. Young girls liked John – he was like a big brother type. That's all. She obviously saw what she wanted to see. Why are you so bothered by this?"

"Because not only did the people she told about what she saw go missing, but she has obviously informed the police and now they are going to start an investigation into Unitron and what that may mean. We stand to lose a lot if this were ever to be made public. We both know that."

Garfield shifts in his seat, uncomfortable with the truth that Melrose is offering. He grabs the salt jar and plays with it in the cup of his hand as an imitation stress-relief ball. "OK, leave this to me and the project team. We'll take things from here. I don't want you to mention the name of the project again. Any documentation you have must be bagged; my guys will call in for that. We close things down for the short term. There will be nothing to find. *Nothing*. Do I make myself clear?" The voice is hushed and now very menacing.

"OK, if that's what you want. Listen, Ellis, are you involved in something here? You can talk to me. We've been friends a long time. Are you mixed up in some sort of plot or are you in trouble of some kind?" Melrose asks, naively thinking that Garfield might confide in him.

Things have moved on significantly in recent days and Melrose is rapidly becoming surplus to requirements. What he doesn't realise is that Garfield's goons are active on campus, and picked up on Xiu's questions to fellow students on the *same* day they were asked.

"Thanks Walter, I appreciate your concern, I really do. But let me reassure you that nothing is going on that can't be handled internally in Washington. What I need you to do is ensure that local police don't get the chance to go off the deep end. It'll be bad for them, for you, and for the good work you and your students do at the University. You don't want anything to jeopardize what you have there, do you?"

"Well, no, of course not. I mean, I've worked hard to build that up, and you and I have..."

"Exactly, Walter, you have built up a marvellous department there. So don't spoil the future – get your people under control and stop all this needless meddling on the back of some flimsy hallucination and gossip about TV programmes. There is important work to do, and we're not getting any of it done by worrying about all this, are we?" Garfield sounds like he is on the TV, or at least addressing someone other than the Professor. It makes Walter Melrose exceedingly uncomfortable.

As the new President gets to his feet, he throws down a ten-dollar bill and leans down to whisper into Melrose's ear. "There. Now, take care of things in your backyard, Walter. It needs a good clean. Don't contact me again until you've tidied up, OK?"

Melrose nods his head and turns to the window as the hooded figure of Ellis Garfield shuffles across to a black pickup parked on the far side of the car park.

* * * *

CHAPTER 6: COME TOGETHER

Heading south on highway ninety-five, Catherine is slumped against the passenger door in the front of Gill's trusty Oldsmobile, grabbing some sleep. As they are passing a diner, Gill has to swerve violently to avoid a pickup exiting from the slip road at high speed. Catherine wakes up with a start.

"Jeeezuz!" Gill exclaims, "What a dick!" No sooner has he managed to right the car to avoid hitting the median strip when the pickup growls as it accelerates to speed past. As it draws parallel, Gill senses something very wrong. The vehicle is quite close. He looks across and sees an enormous burly type in a dark suit and sunglasses. It's getting toward dusk, and the sunglasses are definitely not required. Then, suddenly, Gill's whole body begins to become so heavy that it feels like he is slowing his own car down just by virtue of a rapid increase in gravity acting upon him. It's crushing his chest, and it is almost impossible to take a breath. At first he thinks that Catherine must be touching him, but moving his eyes to his right he can see that she is still three or four feet away. Both vehicles slow to a snail's pace but perversely Gill feels like a test pilot experiencing some ridiculous level of G-force. As things become ponderously slow, he manages to look again into the cabin of the pickup and sees another figure, hooded and hunched up. The figure looks like it is struggling to raise a hand. For a fleeting moment through the darkness inside the hood, Gill sees the glaring white and red of what looks like an oversized eye. The picture is framed by the side window of the pickup and the figure looks straight at him. Gill can't look away. He is transfixed by the charged undercurrent of menace behind the stare. For the first time in many years, he feels fear in every nerve-ending. For a chilling few seconds the two stare at each other, motionless. But then that eye shifts forward. To rest on Catherine.

Breaking Gill's stare interrupts the sequence, and the hooded figure slowly moves further forward to focus on Catherine, and she is caught like a rabbit in headlights. Never having looked more vulnerable and in danger, she is clearly petrified. For a fleeting moment, she locks stare with the hooded figure. And momentarily, to her utter astonishment, a glow of light radiates within the darkness of the hood, exposing the earnest face of John Montgomery. Her fear is suppressed in that instant, but before she can assimilate the vision in full, the eye suddenly changes to red, and throw a defiant dagger back to Gill before turning to the road, where the pickup edges forward so the vehicles are no longer parallel. The vehicle is moving ahead much faster now, and it is only by jolting himself physically that Gill manages to get his faculties together and press the accelerator pedal.

"Catherine!" he shouts.

"Gill..." she slowly responds, still shaken.

"Get...get the number!" Gill blurts out but barely manages it, his mouth still trying to regain normal function.

But it's too late. The pickup is now speeding off into the distance at a rate of acceleration that resembles that of a dragster. Catherine vaguely remembers a D.C. plate, but couldn't be sure - it was so much of a haze.

Gill decides that they both need a moment to recuperate, so he pulls in to the hard shoulder to speak to Catherine.

"What the hell was that?" he asks her.

"I don't know. That man, the way his eye..."

"Yeh, OK. I got that too. Listen, just let's take a breath here. That was so weird, I think it must have been something to do with another force, trying to communicate with us, or maybe warning us."

"No," says Catherine, "No, he wasn't doing that," she states.

"How do you know?" Gill comes back at her.

"I just do. That was Garfield in that car. I just know."

"Garfield? That can't be. I mean why..." Gill trails off, realising that of course if Garfield *is* a duallist like them, there is nothing to *stop* it being him. "You're sure?" he asks Catherine to confirm.

"There is no doubt in my mind."

"Shit," Gill says. Things are turning very strange indeed, but right now he needs to focus on his plan. "OK, listen, we're still going to Washington. We'll stop when we get outside New York and by late tomorrow we'll be there. The way the pickup sped off makes me think that whoever was there didn't want to hang around, so I doubt if we'll see them again. You going to be OK?"

"I wonder if we are ever going to be OK at this rate, but I know what I'm witnessing and I am beginning to think that you and I are somehow destined to be involved in this. There's just too much coincidence," Catherine replies, before adding hesitantly, "Wendy and Malcolm – they really are in trouble, aren't they?"

Gill looks away. "We're going to find them, Catherine," he reassures; it's all he can do right now.

A few hours later Gill sees the sign for Elizabeth on the New Jersey turnpike. It brings back a picture of his sister Beth in his head, and for a moment he sees her sweet face and hears her voice the last time he saw her. He feels a shudder in his body, and pulls into the local motel-diner. 'The Woodbridge' suggests a somewhat more upmarket version of a motel than it actually is. But Gill in particular needs some rest. He has used the journey to try and clarify in his mind where things stand but that has taken quite a bit of effort, and more than one wrong turning, so now is the time to eat, and sleep. He books two single rooms, but since they have very little luggage with them they don't even bother to look at what the rooms are like, instead just heading to the diner to eat.

As they enter, Field Music's gritty guitar fills the entrance area and people turn to look at the couple. They look good together, probably too good for the diner. The noise is causing some degree of perplexity, as if Gill deliberately wanted to announce their arrival. Nothing could be farther from the truth, and he hurriedly retrieves the phone from his pocket and presses the answer button. Catherine is left at the entrance, somewhat perplexed herself and trying hard not to flush as people stare at her.

"Gill."

"It's Grady. Got the report on that bug, man."

"What you got?"

"Well, you might not be surprised to know that it's plain old agency issue. I traced the ID on the chip back to Fairfax, so it's standard specification. Looks like the Feds have been tracking her for about nine months – more or less when she and her friend moved in."

"That's if it *is* the Feds. Anything on signal feed? You know, like where the sound was being sent?" Gill asks.

"Mmm...hmm. No. Only thing is that they might have installed a repeater locally too, which means the signal would have been boosted possibly. My best guess is that this was surveillance at a distance – just eavesdropping."

"Right. That's helpful, thanks. What about the apartment – you been keeping watch?"

"Listen, man, I been in a couple of times just to turn the lights on and make it look like folks are there, and I ain't seen or heard zip. Nothin' on the answer machine either, or from the trace on Xiu's cell phone," Grady trails off and pauses before adding, "Uh, just one other thing partner - my old lady, she's givin' me stress on this, so I figure on getting' back home soon unless staying here is priority. You got the patrol there anyways, right?"

"Yeh. No problem. You go home. It sounds like our federal friends are a bit slow off the mark on this one, or know that there's not much to see there. One of the two."

"Man, I ain't let on to no-one. No-body."

"That's cool. I'll take the hit from Monique for keepin' you out late. Speak to you later."

Gill gets back to Catherine in the diner and slips into the seat opposite her. "Still nothing from Wendy or Mal?" he asks her.

"Nothing. Still straight through to answer machine. I've left a dozen messages by now," she replies.

"OK, I've got a trace on her phone, so as soon as it is turned on, we'll know where the signal is coming from. Once we're through in Washington, we'll head down to Atlanta like we planned."

Catherine is anxious for Wendy and Mal, but recognizes that there is absolutely nothing they can do right now. They break off to order beer and tacos from the waitress. As Gill munches his way through a taco, Catherine thinks back to Gill's revelation and ideas about Garfield.

"How do you know if you are, you know, 'dualling'? Do you experience both worlds at the same time? How do you concentrate on doing two things at once?" she enquires of Gill, who has inadvertently spilt some ground beef down his chin. She instinctively wants to take a napkin and wipe it off, but resists and merely points instead.

After wiping, Gill replies, "Well, it doesn't just happen. I mean, you have to want to do it, and it's normally better to be alone when you do try it. I used to think I was dreaming, but realised that it was probably more like meditating. I can get into a meditative state relatively quickly now, and with me I always end up at the clearing in the cornfield. Probably some personal metaphor that I like. The clearing, I think, is where time stops, and I get the chance to choose where to go in spacetime. I hear you calling to me when I am there, you know."

Catherine looks at Gill a little sheepishly, mainly because she has had the same dream for many years where she is in that field and can feel a presence there. Even though she cannot remember ever calling Gill's name, the connection between them through recent events has convinced her that it could have been him in her dreams. It's very strange. This man is right in front of her, has just spilled chilli beef down his chin, and seems really down-to-earth. But he says he can travel through space and time, and in the car he said 'it takes one to know one' when talking of Garfield dualling during his TV address. This is what has caused her most worry; that somehow she might be some sort of duallist like Gill. Or Garfield for that matter.

"So you can travel back and forward in time doing this?" she asks.

"In theory yes, but my experience is that the further into the future or the past that you try to travel the harder it is to get back. I don't know why that should be – it can't be to do with anything physical. My guess is that your mind realises how far away you are from 'home' and makes it more difficult to find your way back."

She presses on. "But what about other worlds? I mean, where time stops there is the potential for a worm-hole to open. To anywhere in the Universe. Why don't you just get lost when you super-position? I mean *dual*?"

"You mean I might end up randomly on Zorg Nine in some different galaxy? I thought about that lots of times too. For some reason the time dimension seems to be easier to control than space. And even that is difficult in itself. I have often thought that I'm just too scared to try it; that I'd probably die. I mean, if I consciously tried to locate to the other side of the Universe, I would have absolutely no control over where I landed. I'd have to have some sort of knowledge of another planet or location which supported life like ours in order to even try that. Well, until the day comes that we know where there is another planet with an atmosphere like ours - with air and water - I tend to focus on local spacetime." Gill pauses, and Catherine can tell in his eyes that something has just made him incredibly sad.

"What is it, Gill? What are you thinking?" she urges him.

"Uh, it's...it's just that I know that it can be really unsafe to travel too far," he replies.

"You lost someone, didn't you? Who was it?"

There is a long pause, and Gill's emotions come to the fore. There is a hint of a tear in his eye. "Beth," he says.

Catherine understands that this is his sister. She gives him a moment, desperately wanting to hug this big bear of a man but unable to follow her heart and do so. The waitress arrives to clear the table and she orders two more beers.

Gill opens up. "It's been so long, and I've looked for her so many times. I don't even know where to start. My parents' lives have been destroyed by her disappearance and, well, the easiest way for them to understand it is to believe that she is dead. Any other way is torture. But I know differently. I know she is out there somewhere, in a different reality, living her life but unable to return. That's what's scary about all of this."

"It must be hard. I don't have any brothers or sisters but if my parents thought they had lost me, it would devastate them utterly," Catherine says, as she thinks about Gill, Beth, and her own mother and father.

"Yeh. It seems that I always put the people I care about in trouble..." He looks at Catherine with a resigned apology written on his face. It is unsettling, but makes Catherine carry on. She wants to get to the bottom of her involvement, however scary that might be for her.

"OK, so there are a few people in this world – our world, here and now – that can super-position, or dual. And you and Garfield are two of them. But you said that 'it takes one to know one' when you explained why I could see Garfield's face contorting on the TV. What did you mean by that? Do you really think I am like you and Garfield? I mean, I can't do what you can do. The farthest I've travelled is in my dreams and even then it is only to that damn cornfield. I've never super-positioned in my life and don't intend to start now." She hasn't realised it, but as she has been talking she has sat up and clenched her fists again, classic signs of a 'Catherine moment'. She is worked up and fighting a truth that she knows is coming.

The waitress comes across with the beers. "There we are, you two. Two beers for the two travellers," she says in an ingratiating and friendly tone. Catherine looks at her for a second, speechless. Unwittingly the waitress is underlining what is coming from Gill. There is no escape. The waitress gives a little shrug after not getting any reply to her friendly comments and goes back behind the bar.

"You know what I am going to say, don't you?" says Gill.

"No," Catherine lies.

"I'm about to tell you that you and I are both able to do these things. You must be capable of dualling because we are virtually the same matter, the same stuff. We have met before. I know it. It's just that we hadn't ever recognised each other until I heard your voice on the phone the other day."

"Stop saying that!" she raises her voice loud enough to get the waitress's attention again. She smiles nervously at the waitress who signals to ask if Catherine wants her to come back across. Catherine shakes her head and tries to broaden her smile, without success.

"Look, whether you like it or not, you and I meet in that field because we open up a worm-hole between us. Ask your father. Heck, ask your Professor. It's what happens when two objects are entangled and communicate. Their states reflect one another, and the channel of communication that opens up allows information to pass between them wherever they may be in the Universe," Gill states.

"So you think, Gill. But we are two feet apart at this table. We are in the same spacetime, so your theory goes out the window. You can't prove anything."

"But that's why we are experiencing all this, Catherine. Don't you see? It must be very rare to have an entangled pair in the *same* spacetime location. This is why I think weird stuff happens when we actually touch. In my head all I can figure out is that this is the reunion – I mean, the actual, physical reunion – of particles or matter that might have been created at the beginning of time or from some black hole. So bringing those back together could be incredibly powerful. The way I see it is that both of the pair can use the channel that opens up at the clearing in the cornfield to decide where they want to go. So even though you haven't tried, my guess is that you could probably dual if you wanted to." He smiles at her.

He is one confident man, she thinks. For an instant she acknowledges to herself that it is perhaps true. "So, what's to stop me from trying to do this and ending up dead?" she asks, but already knows what the answer is. Gill just looks at her, allowing her to work it out for herself. She tries to answer her own question. "I mean, so I would go to the clearing with you, and then you would let me go and I'd have to try out a move, say, to a specific place or time?" she asks.

"Or both. Yeh. But there are risks, and unless you have to, I wouldn't try it. You might be better off leaving that to me for now."

Catherine takes a slug of her beer. She is naturally rebelling against the idea that only Gill can and should use his ability to dual. Why should he be able to do that and she shouldn't? But when it dawns on her that she is actually contemplating trying this, she shivers and looks over at Gill. No. No, she'll leave all that to him. It's *his* thing.

"You want any more beer?" Gill asks her.
"No, I'm beat. Think I'll turn in," she replies.

The pair get back to reception and walk round the enclosure of motel rooms until they get to rooms thirteen and fourteen, adjacent to each other.

"Well, goodnight then..." Catherine announces after a short pause.
"Listen, Catherine," he says, realising that she has never looked more in need of company than right at this moment. "If you need

anything, I'm right here. Lock your door and keep your phone on, but don't answer it unless it's me. Understood?"

Catherine nods silently, lowers her eyes from his, and opens her door before turning and looking back at him one more time. Palpable tension is streaming through the air between them. They are both desperate not to do things this way, yet resigned to the fact that it is the only way. Gill smiles, and opens the door to number fourteen.

—-

"Walter, Steve here."
"Oh, Steve. Hello there. How are you?"
"Good, thanks. Listen, I can't talk for long but I just wanted to check whether or not you found the papers you were looking for?"
"Pardon?"
"The papers – you know, the ones that went missing. Were you able to track them down?"
"The papers? Ah yes, no, I haven't been able to locate them as yet."
"OK, well you know how important they are obviously."
"Yes, of course. I'm sure they'll turn up."
"They have to, Walter. My life's work depends on it – you do understand that, don't you?"
"Um, yes. Sure, I understand."
"It's important to have everything tidy, Walter, that way you don't run the risk of losing things. I'm sure you appreciate that. I remember one time someone got the police involved as some of my papers went missing. It was a terrible affair – the police really didn't understand what we were doing and they were very unhelpful. In the end, the person responsible was sacked, then just plain disappeared. No-one knows to this day what happened to him. It was most unfortunate."
"I...I...yes, that sounds awful. Well, I will have everything in order very soon, I can assure you."
"Well, I do hope so, Walter. It's been good talking to you, and thanks for all your hard work. Cheerie-bye."

The voice on the other end of the phone is menacing and mocking at the same time. Walter Melrose is still transfixed as the caller hangs up the phone. After a second or two, he puts down the phone. Then immediately picks it up again, and gets his secretary to place a call through to Lester Young at the Downtown precinct.

"Downtown." It's Sandra Chandry's voice.
"Is that Lieutenant Young's office?" Melrose asks.
"No, Sir, this is the front desk. Who's calling please?"
"This is Professor Melrose calling from Harvard University. I need to speak to Lieutenant Young straight away please."
"Just one moment please. I'll try and connect you."

There is a muffled sound, and some distant shouting, before the sound turns to 'Hanging on the Telephone' by Blondie. It has been chosen as a joke by one of the more technical guys and has gone un-noticed for weeks as nobody from the Precinct actually *calls* the precinct switchboard itself. Walter Melrose catches his rotund frame in the reflection of an abstract picture hanging on this wall. Realising his thinning, sandy hair is tussled and unusually messy for him, he tries to pat it down as he waits. He is not amused. After a few seconds, there is a sudden boost in volume as a man's voice shouts 'Jesus!" at top volume, then further rustling, and eventually the same voice, in a much more hushed tone, comes on.

"Lieutenant Young."
"Ah, Lieutenant. It's Walter Melrose. At the University."
"Ah yes, Professor, how nice to hear from you. What can I do for you?"
"Lieutenant, I need to speak to you about my students and your man there...Gill. Detective Gill."
"Oh yes?"
"Yes, I know that my students are OK now, so there is no need for the department to put any more effort into this one. So you can tell Detective Gill to stand down. I'm sure you'll appreciate freeing up the resource, yes?"

The Lieutenant is a bit slow to comprehend. The Professor sounds so personable, with his polite English accent, that he is nodding his head in agreement about freeing up staff before he realises that it's actually his decision as to how things go. But on balance, this is perhaps a bit of good news.

"Well, that's very good to know, Professor. So you have spoken to Miss Xiu and Catherine then, and all is OK?" he asks the Professor.

There is a slight pause on the phone. "Oh, yes, indeed. Indeed. All is well, Lieutenant."

The Lieutenant responds, "Ah, well that is good news, Professor. I'm especially glad that your students are back at the University. I'll have someone call around tomorrow just to make sure I can close the reports with statements."

The Professor doesn't know what that means, but nods and says, "Surely. Thank you for all your good work, Lieutenant. Young." To all intents and purposes he has got the police department off his, and most importantly Garfield's, back.

—-

"Gill?" asks Reynish Eckhart.

"Yeh, who's that?"

"It's Reynish."

"Hey, Rey. What's up?"

"Just wanted to let you know we been called off the job," Eckhart informs Gill.

"Oh yeh? Why's that?"

"Don't know. Lieutenant wouldn't say. Got the order to stand down and go home about ten minutes ago. You OK if we do that?"

Gill thinks about the patrol officers. Gill knows both of them well, from days gone by, and knows also that they have families. This was a bit of a cushy number for them, but nevertheless he doesn't have a need for them right now.

"So, you didn't see anything at all?" Gill quizzes Rey.

"Nothing. If there were spooks about, they were so good we didn't see them. But hey, we got our own bug in there too, so we'd have known if there was anyone in."

"Right. So you will take that out of there before you leave, right?"

"Sure thing. So you OK if we scoot?"

"Yeh, man. It's fine. But if anyone asks, the apartment was occupied and people were in there, right?" Gill asks.

"Of course, man. As per."

"Thanks, Rey. Appreciate it. See you soon, man. We gotta play soon or I'll forget the set," Gill says with a smile. Rey is the bass player in his band, The Horizon.

"Haha. You got it, man – stay sharp."

—-

Ellis Garfield is in the Green Wing, talking to Phil Kirkland.

"How's things going with the investigation, Phil?" he asks the security chief.

"Slow, Sir. We haven't got very much to go on at all. Feds say there is an unusual mark on the mirror in the washroom, but no prints anywhere, no weapon. The post-mortem on President Montgomery showed an unusual problem with the eyes. At first it looked like the gunshot to the head caused the eyes to cloud and go white, but the pathologist has ruled this out."

"What do you mean when you say the eyes were white?"

"Well, the initial report shows that the President seems to have been blinded by something. When exactly that happened we don't know. But it's not a direct consequence of being shot," Kirkland explains.

"OK. Well, you'll let me know of any developments immediately they happen, right?"

"Sure thing, Mr. President."

Garfield liked being called 'Mr. President.' It has a fantastic ring to it. He has called Kirkland in for another reason though. The new President is extremely anxious about Walter Melrose. He is a weak link and of great potential danger to Garfield's mission.

"One more thing, Phil. Have you received any reports – from anywhere – regarding sightings of Montgomery post-assassination?"

Kirkland gives Garfield a quizzical look.

"Beg pardon, Sir?"

"I know it sounds strange but my wife mentioned to me the other day something about people seeing John's face on the TV and such things. Do you know anything about that?" Ellis Garfield is taking a risk by enquiring of Kirkland if anyone other than Catherine Jumeau has seen him super-position live on TV. For that is what he is effectively asking.

"You mean, 'are there any reports of people seeing President Montgomery's face on TV after he was dead?'"

"Yes, I guess that's what she was talking about," Garfield responds.

"Well, no, Sir. At least, not that I know of. That's like people seeing the ghost of Montgomery? Well, I wonder if a few people might have had that vision, Sir, it being an emotional time an' all." Kirkland is finding it difficult – he deals in facts, not speculation.

"I understand, Phil. It's a stressful time for everyone, so I guess that was just the emotion coming through like you say. So, nothing officially reported about sightings of Montgomery on the TV or during any news programmes, that sort of thing?"

Kirkland is really struggling with this line of questioning, but tries to remain as professional as possible. "No, Sir, nothing reported like that."

"Ho Hum. OK Phil, that will be all. Keep me closely informed at all times," Garfield instructs the smartly-dressed Kirkland, who turns and is just about to leave the room when he seems to remember something, stops and turns back to face Garfield.

"Yes, Phil?" Garfield asks.

Phil Kirkland smiles at Garfield. "Oh, nothing Sir. It's just that President Montgomery used to say that a lot – 'Ho Hum.' Funny, huh?"

Garfield flushes, something he doesn't do often. "OK, well, thanks for letting me know," he says, smiling awkwardly at Kirkland as he turns and leaves the room.

Garfield makes a note to himself to look in the mirror, and to ensure that Walter Melrose and his other student are taken out of circulation.

—-

Walter Melrose, meantime, is panicking. It is beginning to dawn on him that amidst the confusion and disappearances, something is linking everything. His logical brain tells him that there could be many coincidences of course, and not to jump to conclusions. Yet he has adrenalin surging into his stomach, and his heart is pounding too hard. The flow of oxygen to the brain sparks some connections.

The Professor has worked with Garfield on his abilities over many years - ever since Garfield got out of the military - so he knows only too well that Garfield is exceptional, if not unique. The deal has always been that Garfield funds multiple areas of research while Melrose helps Garfield develop his super-positioning capacity in secret. For the latter, Melrose uses a series of anonymous test subjects, all of whom are Garfield with different pseudonyms. Melrose's locked lab is used to determine environmental and physiological changes happening when Garfield duals. To date, this has been relatively fruitless in terms of practical development of the power. By its very nature, trying to measure anything around super-positioning will paradoxically negate any effect. So Melrose has developed a series of surrogate sensors and recording devices that do not seem to interfere with the process of super-positioning. Neither man has ever referred to the process as 'dualling', that being something unbeknown to them.

That Garfield may wish to develop his capacity to super-position for criminal purposes is something that Walter Melrose would never have imagined. Until now. What *is* clear to the Professor is that Garfield will go to whatever lengths necessary to prevent any knowledge of his abilities being leaked to anyone else. In fact, Walter Melrose realises that he is the only person with that knowledge. Except possibly for one other. Catherine's story about Garfield, and his subsequent reaction, has made Melrose exceptionally nervous. For if Catherine has detected something in Garfield which may be related to his abilities, then that would mean that either lots of people like her could have witnessed the same thing. Or, more worryingly, that if she is the only person that has witnessed this, then she presents a risk to Garfield's secret. Right now all the connections are coming together for the Professor and he is beginning to realise the danger that he, and his PhD students, are in. This of course presupposes Garfield's intent is malicious, but the Professor's recent encounters with his long-time test subject certainly lead to that conclusion. The man has changed; as if suddenly time is of the essence.

In his study, he paces up and down nervously, desperately trying to figure out what to do. As long as Garfield believes that Wendy, Malcolm and Catherine are no direct threat to him, then they should be alright. And he should be alright. Wendy and Malcolm are safe, according to the police, and hopefully Catherine didn't think anything of his rather flippant dismissal of her story about Garfield. That only leaves the arrogant detective Gill – he was fishing deep when he came to the University, and it is really his involvement that is potentially going to ruin everything. He is the key, Melrose decides. If the Mayor will take him off this case then that could get him out of the way. He must be taken care of.

—-

In the White House, Ellis Garfield is back from his little trip north. The CCTV cameras record a slender, still figure staring out at the White House lawn. They record him there, unmoving, for twenty minutes. The new President is reflecting on Melrose and the reported vision of his student, Catherine Jumeau.

So far, Garfield has been unable to see what happens to himself when he super-positions, because any footage of him is then viewed, not in real-time, but post-event. So just as anyone watching the video of his TV address to the nation last Tuesday would not have seen anything noticeable in the man, so too no scientist can witness first-hand a person dualling. For that would, of course, trap them in just one reality. This conundrum has been at the heart of Melrose's thinking for some time. But what he has lacked in observational proof for super-positioning, Melrose makes up for in looking at secondary effects that can happen around Garfield. For example, he has begun to understand the physiological changes best, and has recently been looking at Garfield's bio-measurements, cells and DNA. This is why he put his best student, Catherine, onto a project to look at larger groups of cells and how they can super-position at large object level. A big discovery was the ability of Garfield to slow time when he super-positions, allowing him to operate in an alternate point in spacetime while appearing to be functioning normally. But it isn't all plain-sailing. Both men also know that, due to the recorded loss of mass experienced by Garfield when super-positioning, there is energy drain involved which means that he has to limit the frequency of his activity.

Of course, Garfield feels that Melrose now suspects him of some involvement in Montgomery's assassination. That is unfortunate. Melrose is Garfield's passport to finding out enough about his ability to use it to travel further in spacetime. Right now he is confined to relatively small jumps back and forth. Enough to go back to the scene of the assassination and attempt a clean up while everyone was watching him on the TV. If Melrose or any of his bunch suspected that he was super-positioning during that TV address, he is in big trouble. His own secret service team, fiercely loyal to Garfield and known to him from his days in Antarctica some years ago, have successfully secured and held Xiu and Baines, who are now locked in a basement of the safe house just outside Washington. They are currently looking for Catherine Jumeau, who is now known to be out of the city. Garfield thinks back to the incident on the highway on the way to Mansfield airport last night. 'That *must* have been Catherine Jumeau' he thinks.

"Damn," he exclaims. It is picked up on the CCTV and George Beston looks up at the monitor. He has the sound up on camera twenty-one. Ellis Garfield has just realised that he has missed the opportunity to silence Catherine Jumeau and her detective friend. And then comes the follow-on. He is so far down the rabbit hole now that it is inevitable that others will have to be sacrificed if he is to avoid being caught and unable to carry on with the research needed to save him. But he can't lose Melrose, for he is the savior. Who else knows so much about super-positioning? It seems very clear what needs to happen now. He is going to have to take Melrose and his students out of circulation and make them work for him directly and in secret. Combining all efforts is the way forward, he thinks, even if it means holding all of them against their will until such times as they figure out how he can master his powers to escape.

So, he is staring out the window at the White House lawn, and after twenty minutes has come to the conclusion that the first priority is to hunt down Miss Jumeau and the detective before they get up to anything troublesome. It's late, so tomorrow he'll also invite Walter to dinner in Washington, as a gesture of his appreciation for all he has done for him, so far.

At the Woodbridge Motel, Catherine is lying in bed, thinking of the boy next door. And Gill is lying in bed, worrying. It would be safer if they were together, but he is afraid of confusing everything further. And there's always the danger that they might actually touch, and things get out of hand. 'Now we wouldn't want that, would we?' he thinks to himself. Then he thinks again. What exactly would be the worst thing that could happen if they kept touching? They would dual, and as long as she was with him, they could travel together? No, that wouldn't work because they might observe each other dualling in the world they traveled to together. Hhmm. So they meet at the clearing in the cornfield, like he has always dreamed of. Then they would have to go their separate ways. Catherine, being totally inexperienced at dualling would almost surely never return without his help. So the worst that could happen is that they lose each other forever. That's serious enough for Gill to turn onto his side and resign himself to a restless night.

Catherine's world has turned upside down in the space of a week. Lying in a motel room isn't her idea of fun. If it weren't for Gill she wouldn't be here, but on balance she knows that, ironically, this is probably a good thing. So many strange things have happened that she finds it difficult to separate out the pieces of the puzzle, never mind attempt to put it together. So far she has witnessed the most important man in the United States morph into his dead predecessor live on TV, had her two closest colleagues and good friends disappear, been taken under police protection, seen her boss turn on her, and then watch in shock as what looked like the bogey man drove past them on the highway. And she has fallen in love. A busy week by anyone's standards. But what of Gill? He believes Garfield can super-position, and that she saw Garfield change in front of her because she has some special vision related to dualling. This seems so incredible that she somehow needs to say it out loud, and mutters "incredible" to herself. But could this be true?

She closes her eyes and starts to think about what happened when she touched Gill. The electricity, the force, the dream-like quality of what happened. It was unbelievable. Like what girls believe love is about when they are still young enough to be driven everywhere by their parents. She begins to drift off, the vision of Gill in her mind, and as she does so she begins to feel the light touch of air on her face. Gently at first, then more of that warm breeze flows over her as she looks up to the cornflower blue of the sky above. The sounds of the reeds of corn flowing in the wind rush toward her and suddenly she is moving. Slowly at first and then picking up speed and unable to prevent herself from being pulled along through the corn. Her heart is beating maniacally; she is out of control and beginning to get dizzy. She thinks she is going to be sick. Just then, everything comes to a stop. Her eyes have been forced shut by the speed of movement and the need to stop things rushing past so quickly. Now she can open them. As she does so, she is in a marvellously peaceful place. It is the clearing. She is so heavy that she cannot move. It is almost as if she is drugged, on some form of opiate, she imagines. Is this what a trip is like? Is that what's happening? She becomes aware of a presence beside her. She can't turn her head to see who it is. She is desperate to know who it is. She senses it is a man. Gill? She tries to move her eyes and does so by a mere fraction. It is a man, a dark figure beside her. Why is he moving? She struggles against the listlessness of her own being. She must weigh a ton at least and the slightest millimetre movement is taking an almighty, gargantuan effort. After what seems like hours she has begun to move a little more easily, but it's torture. She has no idea of time right now – it seems like she is in a completely different world. But, the need to move is strong because she senses that not to move would be to become trapped in the clearing because of the sheer weight bearing down on her. Pushing forward seems to make her lighter and lighter as eventually she can see that she is getting to the far side of the clearing where there are a number of pathways visible. For some reason she seems to know which one to choose. Is this her decision or is it already chosen for her? She can't decide. She takes the path.

—-

'It Takes Two', by Marvin Gaye and Kim Westonn, is on the radio in Gill's room. He is thinking about Catherine still. But as the song fades out he becomes aware that something is not right. There is no sound from next door. He's keeping vigil. It's just a sense that Catherine isn't *there*. What's going on? He turns and sits up. And in front of him is Catherine. She is fantastically beautiful. A vision in a white nightdress who has come to be with him. She silently moves over to the bed, smiles at him in the way that only Catherine can, and places her hand on his forehead, instantly calming him and sending vibrations of warmth into his mind. This isn't like when they met the other day, this is different. This is surely a dream. He reaches out and takes hold of her, and they embrace. The forces at work are so strong that everything seems to float away, leaving them, and only them, on an island floating in space. Barely aware of the separateness of their bodies, they become overwhelmed with each other. At the height of their senses, an explosion of love sends them into a new world. A world where everyone has the ability to find their universal partner, to find true love and become fulfilled.

It is so overwhelming for Gill and Catherine that they spend the rest of the night clutching each other in silence. Neither needing to speak. Neither needing to worry. Neither needing anyone else.

——

In the morning, the pair are one their way to Washington. They seem to have changed after the consummation of their reunion. Little is said. Instead there is an understanding between them that Gill's proclamation of Catherine's abilities is coming true. She dualled last night, and both of them know it. True, it was a few yards, and with no discernible time shift, but she did. The awakening in her has been catalyzed by Gill. He gives her strength, confidence and fulfilment beyond her wildest dreams. It is her destiny now that chance has brought them together. But so too is Gill's imminent journey back to the scene of the murder of the President of the United States of America. He will have to leave her to do that, because she would observe him if she was to travel with him when dualling. So she will be alone for a time. And neither like this. There is a knowing, deep down, that they are on the run. In fact they are in great danger, and neither know what Garfield or Melrose might be up to in terms of hunting them down. For Catherine, it is almost certain that Wendy and Mal have been taken. That is as far as she can go with that thought. Beyond that is darkness. For Gill, it is almost certain that Catherine is right and it was Garfield in the pickup truck yesterday, and that he is at the heart of the President's assassination. In order to reach the point where he and Catherine might be together on any sort of normal basis, he knows that Garfield will have to be brought to justice. For now, his ambition is to try and go back to the scene of the crime, stop Garfield from murdering the President while simultaneously making sure that others witness the then-Vice President attempting a murder, and trapping Garfield in that reality. Difficult. Of course, if that happens, the reality that he is in now will change because Montgomery would be alive. Speculatively, that could mean that he and Catherine do not meet. Does he really have to choose between saving the President and saving his reunion with Catherine? There has to be another way.

'Soul Boy', by The Blue Nile, is on Gill's mix coming over the car stereo. Paul Buchanan's moody vocal pierces the air in the car. The words settle, and Catherine eventually turns to Gill as the outskirts of Washington D.C. come into view.

"So, how will I know how long to wait for you?" she asks.

It is a good question. Gill doesn't know the answer. "I'd give it twelve hours. If I'm not back by then, don't worry about me – things will just be taking longer than I expect, that's all – but if you can, you should find out if Wendy and Mal are actually in Atlanta."

"You mean, go down there by myself?" she asks.

"Yes. Talk to Wendy's mother and find out what was said and how it was said on that phone call that Wendy made. I need to know that – it could be important," Gill replies, giving an edge of importance to Catherine's task deliberately in order to focus her on something positive and tangible in the short term.

"OK, I guess I can do that. Then what?"

"Well, if you can find Wendy and Mal, the three of you need to go somewhere that no-one would think to look for you, and then wait for me to contact you. If you can't find Wendy and Mal, then...then you still need to do that. Get away and stay away until I find you."

"I'll go to my parents' house," she says.

"No," Gill interrupts, "whatever you do don't do that; you'll put them at risk. You've got to understand that Garfield and his people will not stop until they find you. They will automatically be watching out for you there."

"Gill, I'm really scared. I don't want you to do this. I mean, you don't know what will happen and you might change things for the worse." Catherine's tone conveys her anxiety. She is clearly struggling with the possible outcomes of Gill's intervention.

Gill pulls over onto the hard shoulder and comes to a halt. He takes her hand and they have a moment of absolute peace. He lets go. "We have a duty to do this, Catherine," he says, "because we can." His eyes seem to light up as he stares deep into her. "President Montgomery was a good man who was murdered in cold blood. I wouldn't want to lose what we have for the world, but you know that we have to do this, don't you?" His question resounds around the cabin of the Oldsmobile and hangs in the air like an inescapable spray of scent.

There is a long pause before Catherine responds. She drops her eyes from him slowly and says "Yes," nothing more.

About half an hour later the pair check into the Liaison on New Jersey avenue, about a mile from the Capitol Building. It's early evening and they decide to have dinner together. The mood is sombre but relaxed, neither saying much. They are enjoying being together and there are moments where everything seems just as it should. As they get to the lobby of the hotel, Catherine goes toward the lift, but Gill doesn't follow. She turns around and is about to say something, but realises that he is not beside her, and is saying goodbye in his own way. A few yards apart, they hold each other in a visual embrace for a few seconds as the world speeds by around them, and as Catherine's emotions come to the fore, Gill smiles at her and turns towards the entrance to the hotel. She is transfixed as she watches him leave, seemingly in slow motion with his long stride and easy gait. A tear runs down her cheek and as it reaches her lip, she raises her hand to wipe it away before turning to go upstairs and wait for his return. It is going to be the longest wait she'll ever have to endure.

—-

In the White House, Phil Kirkland has a problem. The CCTV monitors in the Presidential office have been playing up a lot recently and despite several visits from the security company, several hours of footage has been lost due to the faulty equipment. In order to correct things, he and the other heads of security are going to have to choose between a complete replacement or installing backups in order to ensure continuous coverage is restored. It is simply unacceptable to have such outages and their jobs will be on the line if they don't sort it out. It doesn't occur to them at this time that it might not be down to the technology.

Ellis Garfield is in the living quarters with his wife and children in a rare moment together as a family.

"Honey, you sure everything is OK?" says the First Lady.
"Huh? Oh, yeh, sure. It's all OK, don't worry," he replies.
"It's just that you appear to be so distant at the moment, I..."
"I've told you. Things are fine. Listen, why don't you take the kids away for a little while. Just take a break and let me get on with things here. There are some pressing issues that I need to sort out, and it can't be any fun for you or the kids being cooped up here with me like this," he suggests.

Julie Garfield, now First Lady Garfield, is struggling with practically everything. It's an impossible position to be in for the wife of a newly-sworn President. Less than a week in office and already the stresses and turmoil of her husband's work have exacerbated the problems that already exist between them. Things have been going downhill for them for years now, especially after her husband's return from Antarctica. Something happened to him there which changed the course of their lives, but she has never been able to find out what that is. And since the assassination of Montgomery, it has been simply awful. Ellis seems to be in a different world most of the time. Just sitting sometimes for hours in his little ante-room office in their living quarters, hardly sleeping and taking terrible mood swings. She'd become used to them, but not like this. Every single second of the day he seemed to be frowning. Maybe this was him planning or worrying whether or not he was going to be next. She just didn't know, because the man that she married all those years ago was a completely different person these days. Someone she didn't know, and sometimes didn't want to know. She felt like a single mother most of the time, and although her friends and family were very supportive, the father of her children and the most important person in their lives was never there. It had become a living hell. Despite the fact that she mourned the loss of the Ellis she once knew, she still had hope in her heart that that man might return. But it now seemed to be a forlorn hope, cast into the fire along with most of her happiness.

"OK honey," she says, "We'll go up to the Cape for a few days. I can spend some time with my mom and dad. The kids will enjoy the break too. You should come soon." She responds as a good wife to the President should. But her stomach is in a knot, and she knows that something is very, very wrong.

* * * *

CHAPTER 7: GETTING AWAY WITH MURDER

In the Capitol Building, there is a a lot of noise coming from the main chamber. The Senate is packed for a crucial reading of the latest in a line of controversial bills put before the house by John Montgomery. The proceedings are proving to be unruly and the house is buzzing in anticipation of seeing the President deliver what will have to be a bulldozing and charismatic speech on the future of defense spending and positioning of military troops in different hotspots around the world. It is quite possibly the most important speech of his Presidency and could make or break him in terms of his re-election.

Unusually, Montgomery is nervous. He is in the main ante-room to the chamber and can hear the hustle and bustle outside. His main speech-writing aide and political advisor Patrick Nash is with him.

"Hey, come on," says Nash, "You've done most of the hard work on this, you just need to relax and be yourself."

"That's just the point," says Montgomery, "I don't feel myself today. Something doesn't feel right. My gut sense is that McDonough and Kahlool have been rounding up our guys and offering bribes. I got a call from General Paterson last night too – advising me that teams with weak offenses always get beaten. Very helpful."

"Look, John, you were always going to have difficulty with this, but no-one gets anywhere by playing pussy with bullies. That's what they are. You know it, and I know it. You are stronger than they are, and you've proven that many times over. Don't let them get to you."

"Thanks, Pat. Appreciate the sentiment."

At this point Ellis Garfield enters, looking concerned.

"John, are you sure you got this right?" he says. "We got a rabble out there baying for blood!"

Garfield sounds excited and worried. Montgomery doesn't respond, instead giving his Vice President a look conveying his displeasure at his untimely and unhelpful interjection.

"Ellis, listen..." Montgomery begins, but is interrupted.
"John, please don't do this. It's madness, you must realise that. Think of the shitstorm that you are about to create!"

Things with Garfield have been difficult over the last three months. First, he seems to be a fair-weather friend, holding private and unauthorized talks with the Republicans on key issues behind his back. Garfield's political history with the Republicans seems to be a form of currency for both. Secondly, Julie Garfield approached him privately to talk about her husband's somewhat erratic behavior and refusal to see a doctor, complaining that he, Montgomery, must be pushing him too hard. This was of course, unsettling, but what made it unusual for the President was the nature of what Julie reported; that Ellis Garfield seemed to be spending much time in the wee hours sat alone in his study in their living quarters both at work and at the house on the Cape. More than that, she had, on two separate occasions, worried that he had overdosed on drugs as she had found him in some sort of catatonic state, only to be jolted out of it and then turning extremely violent, throwing things around the room and accusing her of spying on him. This was very unsettling for Montgomery, who desperately needed to have stability in the ranks, and could not 'carry' Garfield if he was proving to be a liability. The constant nocturnal activity had become almost an obsession for Garfield, at the expense of his family and his performance in his public role. And finally, John Montgomery's security chief, Maria Ortega, had reported an oddity in Garfield that she thought worthy of report. That Garfield had been spending a significant portion of his time with Professor Walter Melrose at Harvard University. Now this would not have merited much more than a cursory check had it not been for the fact that the labs at Harvard Engineering and Physics had received an inordinate amount of funding on the recommendation of the special Senate Committee for Scientific Research, chaired by Ellis Garfield. A powerful committee known to be a vehicle for the pursuit of advanced military technology. At best, Montgomery could not have a scandal on his hands; it would just give ammunition to his enemies and undermine the credibility of his Presidency. At worst, this was worthy of broader investigation, perhaps at the level of the secret service or FBI. For no-one seemed to really understand what Melrose and his staff were investigating.

Actually, for Montgomery, there was something else. He had an innate distrust of Garfield, and never really had a choice in his appointment as VP, ceding to pressures in his own party that Garfield's appointment would appease many Republicans and make his time in office easier because Garfield was seen as 'Republican friendly'. This came to a head just a week ago, when he asked Ellis outright to declare his interest in the Harvard connection. Garfield responded by saying that he had a particular interest in Melrose's work, and that this could change the way we look at counter-intelligence. When Montgomery pushed to explore what exactly he meant by this, Garfield seemed to retract from this position and declare that his own interest was actually to make sure that the government were getting value for money from the work. It was at that point that Montgomery knew Garfield was lying to him. Getting value from the work that was going on could have, and should have, been a key component of an independent assessment through the Senate Committee. It was obvious from the discussion that Garfield had not implemented any independent assessment, and instead was personally involved with Walter Melrose. What was worse, Montgomery had been duped into visiting Melrose's operation, and by doing so, gave a super-legitimacy to the whole thing. So to start to investigate in any formal manner would be to score an own goal and undermine himself as President. The Melrose connection had now become a major issue for Montgomery, and he had signalled to Garfield that once the main Senate work for the semester was complete, in some six weeks from now, he intended to revisit the issue with vigor. Garfield knew what that meant. Basically there would be a very real possibility that the secret nature of Melrose's research would be uncovered, and so leave Garfield open to public exposure as corrupt and pursuing some form of hidden agenda. Montgomery takes a deep look at Garfield, which disarms the Vice President.

"What are you doing, Ellis? We've discussed this. I'm not about to change my mind, you know."

Garfield finds it difficult to contain himself, lost for words. He approaches Montgomery as if about to say something profound.

"Well, listen, I'd brush up a bit first, John. You look like shit. You've got ten minutes before you're on," Garfield says.

Montgomery smiles, genuinely amused. And for all that he disliked Garfield, he did need to freshen up. But before he can acknowledge the remark, Garfield prompts once more.

"Look, take five to gather yourself at least. Go freshen up in the washroom and come out looking your best, huh?"

Montgomery gives Garfield a hesitant glance, then looks over to Nash who shrugs his shoulders as if to say 'Might be worth doing'.

"OK, gentlemen, that will be all. I'll be in the washroom if anyone needs me urgently."

And with that, the two close aides leave the President.

In the washroom, John Montgomery is looking in the mirror. It strikes him that his face has changed quite a bit over the last year or so. He still looks good for his age, but a few more lines are creeping in, and clearly the pressures of being in office are taking their toll. Ironic, he thinks, how he has never felt more alive.

It certainly irks him that anyone in his inner circle would try and undermine him the way Garfield did. Damn that man. He turns the tap on and splashes water on his face a couple of times, almost to try and wash away the irritation that it has caused him. He definitely needs to get rid of Garfield.

As he raises his head to the level of the mirror, and looks again at his own face, suddenly he sees Garfield's face emerge from behind him. The shock freezes him for a second. How did Garfield get there? He wasn't in the room and security had told him that the washroom was 'all clear'. What was going on? As his vision adjusts to seeing Garfield's face in the mirror, his instinct is that something is wrong.

"Ellis?" he says, and turns round to see Ellis Garfield's tall figure not more than two feet from him. As he looks into Garfield's black and distant eyes, the overwhelming darkness penetrates the space between them and he is blinded, only pitch black remaining. Montgomery is terrified. He moves to protect himself, but it is already too late. As he begins to raise his arm, Garfield points the silencer barrel of a .22 calibre pistol directly over Montgomery's heart facing downward. Montgomery doesn't hear anything, instead feeling only a piercing arrow cut through his heart and inflicting searing pain. As he leans forward toward Garfield, struggling for breath and losing control of his body, he feels the cold metal of the hollow cylindrical silencer just above his eyes. The trigger clicks, and Montgomery drops like a stone.

Garfield stands over Montgomery in triumph. He has succeeded. But before he commences the process of re-locating back, he feels something come over him. It is radiation and it is seeping into him. He cannot escape it because he is attracting it. He is the target. For an instant, he hears John Montgomery in his ear. It is a cacophony of all the things Montgomery has ever said to Garfield, rushing into his ear and getting louder and louder. It becomes deafening, and the vibration shakes the whole room. The sound is so loud that he has to shut his eyes and cover his ears to try and soften the blow, but this has no effect. As he opens his eyes, he too is blind. This time by brilliant white light. His heart is pumping hard and fast. He begins to feel very heavy, as if gravity is rooting him to the spot. He will surely be caught. Security outside must hear all of this and be rushing in, right now. He is doomed. Struggling to move his chest, he fights the invasion into his body with all his might. He tries to move his arms and slowly gains a little control. He closes his eyes and opens them. As he does so, he looks into the mirror. He is looking at John Montgomery. His heart is about to burst. He can't breathe. His face, Montgomery's face, is smiling back at him.

And suddenly the crescendo of noise comes to an end. His face begins to morph from Montgomery's to a translucent formless white mask, which would be paralysing if it wasn't familiar to him. He is caught in a trance, confused and exhausted. The experience the same as in Antarctica. It was life-changing then, and it feels just as real this time.

Suddenly he is forced back to the current reality by a loud knock on the door. "Mr President?" a voice comes from outside.

As he turns to face the door, suddenly he is aware of another presence inside the room. It is faint, but there is a shadow forming out of the corner of his eye. Just as he is looking to see what that is, he can hear the door handle begin to turn, and a voice shouting "Mr President, are you OK?"

He has to know who the emerging shadow might be. It is a tall and ominous figure with a radiating aura of energy. It feels formidable, and unfriendly to Garfield, and is revealing itself before him. 'Damn,' he exclaims to himself, worried that there may be a witness. A face begins to appear; and in it he recognises his enemy. But there is no time to find out more. No option before being caught by security who are just about to enter the room. He must overcome the panic. He closes his eyes and takes a deep breath, and in the process regains enough composure to locate back to his car. He looks in the mirror. It is the face of Ellis Garfield looking back. He checks himself for any signs of blood or injury. All OK. Quickly he hides the pistol in the glove compartment, and forces himself to locate back to the chamber.

—-

"Ellis, wake up buddy, this is gonna be interesting," Walt Reinesberg, Democratic Senator for Michigan, nudges him with a wry smile.

"What? Oh, sorry. Mhmm, should be, yes," he manages to splutter out amidst a pseudo-cough, without appearing too distant and disoriented.

But the President doesn't come to the chamber, and within half an hour the entire Capitol Building is shut off by internal security, secret service and local police.

* * * *

CHAPTER 8: THE FORK IN THE ROAD

"Get on the ground, *now!*" comes a bellowing voice that reverberates around the washroom. "I said *now!*".

Gill is standing a few feet from the President of the United States, who is motionless on the ground, blood seeping out of his skull and forming a pool to the side of his head. Two security guards are pointing their weapons and ordering the tall detective to get on the ground. He is in great danger, and about to be shot if he doesn't do what they say. But he knows the drill. He kneels slowly, then lies face down putting his hands behind his back. He is looking directly into the face of John Montgomery, which has been paralyzed at the moment of death. It is a frightening sight. The President's face is contorted in fear with blank, white eyes seeming to look everywhere and nowhere at the same time. And something else. For an instant, Gill also sees the surprise in Montgomery, as if he couldn't believe what was happening to him in that moment. But before he gets any further with this, he feels a kick to his legs as they are forced apart.

"I am a police officer," he responds, quietly and in a tone designed to allay any fear of resistance to arrest.

"Sure, buddy," says one of the officers as he approaches, all the time pointing his gun at Gill's head. As his partner gets the handcuffs and calls for backup, the officer pushes his gun hard against Gill's temple.

"You are going to burn for this, motherfucker. You are going to wish you had never been born."

Gill is shaking, but says quietly again, "I am a police officer. Please check. Please…"

After more security personnel rush in, Gill is manhandled away from the scene, trapped in a new and frightening reality.

As the chamber awaits Montgomery's entrance, a member of the secret service approaches Patrick Nash, and another approaches Ellis Garfield. Maria Ortega and Abe Hart have already been given notice that there has been an 'event'. Garfield looks up to the plain-clothes agent as he leans over Walt Reinesberg.

"Commander Reed, in charge of Capitol Security today, Sir," the agent identifies himself. He is very intense, and frowning. "Sir, come with me please," the agent says, sharply and with such authority that Garfield doesn't hesitate. As hundreds of eyes focus on Garfield, he stands up and follows the agent out of the side door to the chamber. As they approach the main lobby and what looks like a senior uniformed officer, Garfield notices that the entrances are all closed off and security personnel are lining each corridor, quietly funnelling down each passageway. Garfield guesses the same is happening outside.

"What's going on?" he asks the officer.

"Sir, I am reporting a critical-level incident involving President Montgomery." And in the same moment paramedics come rushing towards them. The officer points down toward the east annex and the washroom that Garfield has just visited. A bead of sweat emerges on Garfield's otherwise stony features. "Remember! Use the special exit if you are taking the President out of the building," the officer calls to the paramedics.

"What is he talking about, Commander?" Garfield asks.

The most senior special agent in the building takes Garfield to one side and quietly whispers in the Vice President's ear, "John Montgomery is leaving here in a body bag, Sir. He has been shot twice and there are no vital signs."

Garfield is struggling with the best way to play the situation, knowing what he knows. He has rehearsed this moment, so he is reasonably assured in his delivery. "My God, what happened? I mean, have you got the culprit? Is anyone else in danger?" All good questions, and from an ex-military person, perhaps not an unexpected response.

"Uh, yes, Sir, we have a suspect in custody right now, and we think this is the work of just one person at this time, but by way of security procedure, we do need to conduct a controlled evacuation of the building and we will need to search each and every one of the people here."

Garfield is aware that this will include him. He nods. But this isn't his concern. Commander Reed has just said that his special agents have detained a suspect. This is not part of the plan, and instantly Garfield is thinking about the shadowy figure that appeared just before he super-positioned back to his car outside the building. Instinctively he knew it was the strange detective protecting Catherine Jumeau.

Garfield shivers for a second. The Commander is looking to him for some form of acknowledgement and authority. After all, Ellis Garfield is, by default, the Supreme Commander-in-Chief now. Suddenly Garfield has to react to all this, in real time.

"Commander Reed, thank you for the information. Please carry out your duties as procedure dictates. The Presidential staff and cabinet will offer you all the support we can," he instructs, in as calm a manner as he can manage given his internal turmoil.

"Very good, Sir," Commander Reed replies, nodding slightly and moving off to oversee the security operation.

—-

"Denton Gill, I am advising you that you are in police custody and under investigation for the murder of John Montgomery, President of the United States of America. Do you have anything to say at this time?" Special agent Lenny Charles addresses Gill in a small, featureless cell over at Washington's high-security detention centre, not far from the Capitol Building. Agent Charles is accompanied by two other plain-clothes officers and Gill's hands are handcuffed behind his back.

"No. Now please allow me my phone call," Gill says.

"You will get that shortly, Mr. Gill. But first we need to ask you a few immediate questions for our records. I am now advising you that whatever you say during this session will be recorded, and I would remind you that you are being observed on CCTV cameras. Do not, I repeat, *do not* attempt any form of sudden movement or any action that may give us cause to suspect that you are attempting an act of aggression, as we will not hesitate to take immediate action to restrain you. Do you understand?" Charles says in a calm but menacing tone.

"Yes. Jesus, guys, I am a cop. I know the score, and I know I am entitled to get in touch with my lawyer at the very least. So please, get me out of these things and let me make that call."

Charles moves around and behind Gill, then leans down so that he is whispering in his ear. "You ain't gettin' no call, *Detective* Gill, until we have a nice little chat about how you ended up next to our dead President. Now, you have a choice. You can be a good boy and talk to us openly, or I can make things really uncomfortable for you. It's up to you..."

And with that, Gill proceeds to answer questions about how he managed to be in the washroom with John Montgomery. All of which are based on the premise 'I don't know.' It is only several hours later, after brutal interrogation and a series of humiliating forensic examinations, that Gill is dumped into a padded cell while FBI, secret service and special investigators begin to collate evidence.

The present reality for Gill is stark. It seems he has been observed by Garfield while dualling, and is therefore trapped in this horrific reality where he has taken the fall for the murder of the President. It's the worst possible outcome of his endeavors. Not only is he trapped, with Garfield presumably revelling in his apparent culpability for the assassination, but Catherine is waiting for him back in their original world and she is in great danger from Garfield and his henchmen in that reality. All of this is not to mention the very real danger Gill is now in from possible avengers; that he could be another Lee Harvey Oswald. Although Gill is as tough as they come, even *he* feels a sense of desperation about the situation. On the upside, he figures that they can't have any forensics on him. He just wasn't there long enough to do anything.

As a prisoner at this time, he gives some thought to his options. There is no telling how long he'll be trapped here before he can dual again. My God, what if he can never dual again? Best not to go down that route just yet. Who could help him? Grady and, at a pinch, Lieutenant Young could help him out, but they are just small-fry and all the way up in Boston. He's not going to have any friends in Washington, at all.

He *must* get back to Catherine. She is the one who he might be able to contact back there. Maybe she could see if Melrose or Christophe Jumeau have anything up their sleeves that might be able to help. Maybe pigs might fly, or someone could be in two places at the same time. It's all speculation and a big dose of hope right now. He tries to focus his mind on getting to the cornfield. To hear the rushes, to feel the wind against his face as he speeds towards the clearing. But there is nothing. Just the dark when he shuts his eyes. Maybe sleep will come and allow him to dream. The pictures of Catherine and Beth begin to form in his mind, and it gives him some comfort, for now.

———

"Incoming, Sir."

Pratin Malic is sitting in a black pickup outside the Woodbridge Motel. He is a big guy, his hulking frame crammed into the front seat of the black Ford Ranchero. Beads of sweat run down his brow as he reports to Steve Nelson.

"OK. Switch please," Nelson replies. The pair simultaneously enter a code into their respective bio-cells and the signal is scrambled to all but the direct line between the two devices.
"What you got?" Nelson asks.
"Well, sir, the pair headed south towards Washington. They might be trying to get close. My advice would be to remain vigilant and put Hector and Daniel on special watch," Malic suggests.
There is a pause. "Are you sure?" Nelson comes back.
"Pretty much, Sir. I mean, I don't know what other destination could be in their minds, given the situation."
"Yes. Find them and take them out," Nelson instructs.
"Affirmative, Sir."

———

Steve Nelson puts the phone down. It rings immediately as he does so. It startles him a little, and he sees it is Walter Melrose.
"What do you want?" Nelson asks in an impatient tone, bordering on anger.
"Ellis, I need to talk to you," Melrose says.

"Goddammit, man! We are on open line! Switch now," Nelson shouts, clearly annoyed by Melrose's security breach. The two men switch to secure mode.

"Ah, oh, I'm so sorry. Steve. Steve, listen...listen, I...I need to talk to you," Melrose blurts out, his speech peppered by stuttering pauses.

There is another pause before Ellis Garfield addresses the Professor. "No Walter, *you* listen. I am very tired of your bleating and inept incompetence. I asked you a very simple favor, and you blew it. Not only have you made things exponentially worse by practically advertising the fact that you have been conducting secret research, but you've done exactly what was *not* required. Instead of allaying any fears and settling things down, you've connected the Jumeau girl and her meddling detective boyfriend to me." Another pause. Melrose is stumped, and cannot muster any words, so Garfield continues, this time in a quieter and altogether more threatening tone. "You obviously realise that this has changed everything," he says as a matter of fact rather than a question, and, without waiting for any response, continues "I will now have to deal with things in a very different way."

"Now, now, Steve. I'm sure everything will be..."

"No, Walter, everything won't be. It's a mess. You will have to accept responsibility for that," Garfield's tone is dark and ominous.

"But Ellis...Steve...I haven't done anything wrong. I am trying to help you. I am your friend. Don't you understand?" Melrose is now pleading with Garfield.

"That will be all, Professor. My people will be in contact soon to arrange a meeting," Garfield states, before hanging up.

As the phone goes dead, Melrose's face turns ashen. Garfield has never talked to him like that. As he paces up and down his office, his primary postgraduate students all absent and his research potentially in ruins, he tries to assess what is going on. He is not a strong man. He has no resources other than the intellectual, and he has very few friends without Garfield and his onward connections. But on top of all the damage ongoing, there is an additional factor. A realisation that Garfield, his greatest supporter and ally, is also his biggest threat. Would Garfield order his kidnapping, or worse? It's a very real possibility. And what about his students? Has Garfield disposed of Wendy and Malcolm? Oh my God, they might be dead!

Catherine. His dear Catherine. Such potential and such a likeable student. She is on the run. From Garfield. Everything is wrong. Melrose paces some more. His stomach is churning. And suddenly the pacing stops. He has to get away. Lay low. Yes. He is probably being watched right now! 'Damn,' he says to himself. 'Damn.' His face has gone from ashen to a red flush in a matter of seconds.

"Yes, Professor?" Melrose's secretary asks.

"I need you to book me on a flight to London immediately, Amy. Sooner the better. It's urgent."

"Of course, Professor. I'll see what is available and get back to you as soon as I can."

"OK, but do hurry, my dear. And please, I don't want anyone to know about this, do you understand?"

"Why, yes, Professor. Is everything OK?" Amy asks.

"Yes, yes, it's fine. I just need you to do this quickly. Please!"

The Professor sounds very edgy, and Amy realises that she should not ask anything else.

—-

Catherine Jumeau is pacing too. In room two-two-one of the Pomada Hotel. Twelve hours have now passed since Gill left her in the lobby. As each hour went by excruciatingly slowly, Catherine mulled over everything that had happened up until then. Unable to make or receive any calls on Gill's command, she felt totally alone. And scared. More scared as each hour passed. She is now beside herself with worry, but has to carry out Gill's commands. He knew what he was doing, and now she has to remain focused on what *she* is doing.

As she checks out, she sees a tall man wearing dark glasses enter through the revolving doors, looking around. It's the shape of the figure that is familiar. She can't quite place it. It's enough to make her hurry things up at the checkout. Nervously she fumbles for the cash to pay the woman at the counter. She leaves without asking for any receipt or change. Hurrying across the lobby, she looks back to see the dark figure being greeted by a porter and shaking his head. Panicking, she avoids the lift and takes the stairs down to the underground car park. Her heart is pounding hard against her chest, and she is struggling to breathe. She is in the middle of a panic attack. Everything around her is going blurred.

Exiting the stairwell into the car park, she desperately tries to find Gill's Oldsmobile, but she can't see anything; blinded by acute anxiety. The Oldsmobile is so distinct she thinks, she must be able to find it. And there, across on the far side, is the elegant and familiar dark coupé shape. Just seeing it brings her back from the abyss, calming her down. And as she runs over to it, she smiles. It's not Gill, but it's Gill's. She grabs the keys from her purse and jumps in. Looking around, the car park looks empty. Relief. She tries to get the keys in the ignition, but it's tricky as the keyring is so full of keys that they fall down on the foot-mat. She leans down, grabs them and sits back up, only to let out an involuntary shriek.

The dark figure upstairs has found her. As she looks across the car park, Hector Caballos, henchman for Ellis Garfield, is standing at the lift exit; staring across at the Oldsmobile. As the classic shape of the Delta coupé helped her find the car, so too it has helped him find *her*. He begins to walk over. Catherine screams in panic. "Stop it!" she shouts to herself. "Shit." "Come on!" she tells herself. She fumbles with the keys again, trying to slot the right one into the ignition. Absolute fear has taken over, and she starts crying, trying to see through the gathering pool of tears. Through that watery distorted vision she also sees Caballos, lurching over toward her, within fifty yards now. "Please. Please!" she is encouraging the keys, and herself. "Please!" one more time.

Caballos, takes out a pistol from under his arm. It has a silencer which reflects the light of the neon that brightens the dark underground car park. It catches Catherine's eye. In a strange turn of events, it catalyses a reaction in her; a determination that she is not going to die this way. Not today. She focuses right in on the ignition key, slots it in and turns. For once, Gill's jalopy starts up first time, and she revs up. This makes Caballos start to run, but his pace is slow. His lumbering frame does not allow for speed, and as she reverses out and backs towards him, for an instant she wonders if she could run him down. But she brakes, shifts the lever into Drive, and starts to move off.

Caballos is just feet away, and pulls the trigger. A point .22 bullet shatters the rear window of the Delta '66 coupé and wavers slightly by the interruption of the glass barrier. Sufficiently so to miss Catherine's head by two centimeters to the left, before exiting diagonally through the open side window. Catherine screams as she puts her foot to the floor and the four-and-a-half litre engine's torque pushes down and forward as space is opened up between her and her assailant. Caballos fires again. This time it's at the petrol tank. The bullet dents the metal without piercing, ricocheting off at an angle, hitting a nearby bumper and ricocheting a second time back towards the Oldsmobile. By the time it hits the side window it has lost enough pace that it rebounds off, but not before making a loud 'clack' which startles Catherine enough that she swerves, hits the back end of a Volkswagen Passat and almost comes to a halt as she brakes. Caballos takes aim from afar, focusing again on the head of Catherine on the left inside the car. He steadies his arm and hand, as he has been trained to do from a young man in the military. In his vision, Catherine looks vulnerable and weak. His finger gently presses against the trigger, and pulls. The bullet goes straight towards Catherine Jumeau's head.

Dennis Trevellion is the owner of the Passat. He is livid. Some crazy bitch just slammed into the back of his new car. A car he had saved up to buy. A car that represents his hard work and endeavor for years. A car that makes his wife proud. A car in which he can take the family out to the country, knowing that it will reliably get them back again. It's German, safe, and economical. It's perfect. And he even waited so that he could get his favorite metallic blue color. And now it's been made ugly by a stupid girl who is driving some old banger that probably isn't even insured. Damn those students. Too many of them and don't know the first thing about work, or what it means to have to graft in order to survive. Don't know what it means to have to go to work every day with a smile on your face while you service people in the plush surroundings of a nice hotel. Don't know what it means to earn shit wages for being nice to people.

As he gets out of the car quickly and strides towards the back of the Oldsmobile to challenge the incomprehensibly stupid driver, Caballos' bullet enters his right temple and kills him outright. Dennis Trevellion drops like a stone, never knowing what hit him, and never able to enjoy his lovely new car again.

As the sounds of bullet hitting flesh, and flesh hitting concrete, reverberate around the enclosed underground space, Catherine quickly turns the steering wheel and takes off at high speed, escaping the bullet marked for her. She turns the corner and gets to the exit barriers. She can hear the steady clump of Caballos' black leather shoes hitting the concrete. It's incessant, and her senses pick up on this sound above anything else. The car park ticket is still in the corner on top of the dashboard. She reaches for it, lowers the window, and attempts to run it through the scanner to allow the barrier to lift and allow the car out. She is too far from the scanner. Her heart begins to pound again, this time harder, seemingly about to break her chest wide open and escape, as if it has had enough of being hunted down, and wants out.

She reaches down to pick the ticket up and another shot hammers into the metal of the side door. In a moment of extreme collectedness that surprises even Catherine, she stays down, grabs the ticket and scurries out the car to scan it directly on the machine. The barrier lifts. 'Come on. Come on.' she says to herself. She creeps back into the car, staying low. Another shot rings out as it hits the machine. There are no screams left in her. This time she has had enough, and abandons all. She presses the accelerator hard, and the car lurches forward as she peers above the line of the steering wheel to see where she is going. The car picks up speed as it rises up and out of the car park. She is free.

—-

As Caballos' message comes through to Pratin Malic, he curses loudly. Garfield is not going to like this. Avoiding direct voice contact, he quickly sends a secure encrypted message to Garfield's private number with the details.

Garfield receives the message while pouring himself a drink in the Green Wing. He winces and can't help letting out "Fuck." It's involuntary, but reflects his current state of tension.

Maria Ortega is with him, discussing homeland security in light of the President's assassination.

"Would you like me to return later, Mr. President?" Ortega asks.

"What? Oh, no, no, it's fine. Where were we?" Garfield responds. But he's struggling. The interfering pair of amateurs is really beginning to grate on Ellis Garfield.

As Maria Ortega looks at her new President, she is aware of a new vulnerability. One that wasn't even predicted by his detractors. In effect, he looks weak. Like someone who is desperately trying to control something out of control. And one other, small thing, she thinks. Since just last week when the President was assassinated, Ellis Garfield's face seems to have changed, from the rather taut and severely angular features, to what appears to be a more rounded and somehow more friendly look. This is in direct contrast with his mood and demeanor, however, and this brooding and frowning side seems to be winning the interaction at this time.

"Shall we?" Garfield asks Ortega by way of getting her out of a stare as she takes in the changing face of Ellis Garfield, President of the United States.

—-

In the alternative reality created by Gill in his attempt to prevent the assassination, he is sitting in his twelve-by-eight padded cell. He has tried two further attempts at dualling to see if he can get back to Catherine, or even just outside the cell in order to escape. There is nothing there, and it is getting to him. A little while ago he felt an uncomfortable rush of adrenalin in his stomach and lower abdomen for no apparent reason. His gut instinct, literally, is that this was related to Catherine's situation. Solace is scarce. But, if he can *feel* what Catherine is feeling, then potentially there is still a communication channel open to them. This may offer hope. But can it be reciprocated? His experience is greater, and his abilities much more practiced, so his conclusion is that she will probably carry on to Atlanta without really understanding what has happened to him. And he doesn't want her to try to dual in order to find him, as she will most likely fail and end up somewhere that he can never find her, or even be killed in the process.

It is worse still. He is the one who found Catherine, and he is the one who has put her in danger. He, and Garfield. And Melrose. Men around her, who affect her, have made her chances of surviving the next few hours practically nil. And if anything happens to Catherine, then surely his life is over. He begins to hope that Beth is out there. That Beth might come to him. That his little sister, lost for so many years, might return and makes things OK. And with this,

Gill realises how desperate he is. And fights to regain control. No time for such emotions.

—-

Catherine Jumeau is speeding towards the fork in the road. Her whole body is operating much faster than usual, her senses heightened and heart beating quickly, way above one hundred BPM. The car she is in is also speeding. As she takes an amber, a pedestrian who had stepped out a little too quickly and had to step back to avoid being hit by the runaway Delta, shouts from the pavement.

"Slow down, *asswipe!*"

The words enter the cabin of the coupé and seem to slow down around her ears. That guy was talking about her. The power-steering is so loose on the Oldsmobile that her hands are jumping around from side to side on the steering wheel, like in the old movies where they shot the movie star in a fake car on set, with a video of the road behind in the background. Maybe she *is* an asswipe. Yes, she sure is. For getting into this mess. And for being out of control in a runaway car with no rear window. She brakes. Gently at first, bringing her speed down substantially. Her heartbeat follows suit. It's a lucky move. A patrol car on the side road she just passed doesn't move, but it surely would have if she hadn't braked a block back. That's two bits of really good fortune that she has had.

Passing Carlito's Hire-Car, she comes to a stop a few hundred yards up the street and gets out. She knows the Oldsmobile is just too obvious. And it's got bullet holes in it. Not exactly a guarantee of anonymity. The hire car place has a little Golf on the forecourt, and after giving her details and paying the deposit, she drives off, with 'Running Away', by Roy Ayers, coming on the radio as she does so. The little Volkswagen is easier for her; smaller, more manoeuvrable. As she drives past Gill's Oldsmobile, her heart skips a beat. Somehow she should feel safer, but doesn't.

She heads over to one of the big parking lots outside JFK, parks up and takes the free bus ride to the airport. Her headscarf and dark glasses are a pretty good disguise. Unless they are looking for Audrey Hepburn, then she should be OK, at least for now. At the main entrance, many buses are pulling up, parked, or moving off. As she alights, she has a strange feeling. She is about to travel to Atlanta to see if she can find Wendy and Mal, but in her heart she knows that they are not there. Gill told her to do this. So it must be right. But something in her tells her that this was just his way of making sure she got away. Out of danger. And she knows Gill is in danger. Everyone she knows is in danger.

At that moment, Catherine Jumeau decides that she needs to take a step back. She is in a very public place, so no-one can shoot at her here. Ironically, she feels safer among all these strangers than anywhere else right now. She takes a seat at one of the cafés in the main concourse and starts to think about what to do. As she takes a sip of her Americano, her eyes catch a glimpse of a brightly-colored waistcoat. She wouldn't have thought anything of it usually, but she had just been thinking about Wendy, Malcolm and the Professor. She looks again, squinting to try and elongate her vision slightly. It is indeed the flamboyant colors of Walter Melrose. If it weren't for his dress-sense, she would never have seen him. 'Walter?' she says to herself. Yes. It *is*. He is only twenty-or-so yards from her, walking very swiftly. She still has coffee in her mouth and in the two seconds that it takes her to swallow that, reform her larynx and move her lips in order to shout to the Professor, two suited men move in and seem to visibly welcome him, clearly saying hello and one grabbing his bag. He looks surprised, and in an instant, his cheeks flush brightly. He is embarrassed? No, he is shocked! The men turn him around and start to laugh and joke. But the Professor isn't laughing. They move back towards the exit. As they do so, Walter Melrose looks around, looking disoriented. And then, for a split second, Catherine's eyes meet her Professor's eyes and there is a moment of recognition. Melrose's panic is obvious. Catherine's panic is obvious. He raises his hand. But before he can shout out to her, his eyes seem to glaze and his head seems to drop slightly. In a morbid twist, his face contorts into a smile, the obvious sign that they have drugged him.

Catherine's third piece of luck today. Melrose's flapping signals to Catherine have gone unnoticed by his captors. She watches as the threesome, acting as one, manage to exit through the throng of the crowds unnoticed, then disappear. An ice-cold chill travels from top to bottom of Catherine's spine. She writhes to avoid its clutches, causing people around her to stare. Trembling slightly, she can't decide whether it is herself or her cell that is vibrating. She looks at the phone, and there is a missed call. It's from Wendy! She is overjoyed, for a second. In normal circumstances she would be delighted by this. But she hesitates. This reflects her new-found resilience and mood more than anything. She is operating at a different level now, and somehow Gill's influence and way of thinking has affected her. She resists the urge to call the number back, believing that it might be a trick. Much as she would love that it were indeed Wendy calling, she suspects that it is just a ruse to get her to reveal where she is or what she is thinking. And so, she leaves it. A moment of calm comes, as if a part of Gill is with her. She decides there and then that she is not going to Atlanta. But first, she buys a ticket to Atlanta with her bank card. That's what Gill would do.

—-

"Lieutenant Young?" It is the voice of Christophe Jumeau.
"Speaking," Young replies.
"Ah, Lieutenant, now. Are you aware of the whereabouts of my daughter and Detective Gill? It's just that my wife and I haven't heard anything for a day or two and we just need to make sure everything is OK. I'm sure you can understand."
"Ah, Professor Jumeau. Yes. Well, actually Professor Melrose has reported that everything is OK now and that things are back to normal, so I have ordered Detective Gill onto another case. Your daughter is presumably back at work, no?"
"Why, no, Lieutenant, not at all. We were under the impression that she was still under police protection. Is that not the case?" Jumeau is sounding a little anxious now, and the Lieutenant senses this.
"Ah, now listen, Professor, please don't worry. This whole thing has taken on mythical proportions and really, it is a storm in a teacup. As I understand it, Professor Melrose reported in a couple of days back to say everything was back to normal, that he had met with Catherine in the city, and that his research operations were back on track. On hearing that, of course I took the decision for my men to stand down. We are very short of resources here, Sir, so..." but before the Lieutenant finishes Christophe Jumeau interrupts.

"But Lieutenant, have you actually checked? Have you seen my daughter? And Detective Gill, is he available, I'd like to talk to him," he says, in a somewhat authoritative tone.

"Sir, please calm down. My detectives often handle several cases and are very busy people. The fact that Gill hasn't been in does not indicate..." and again, another interruption.

"You haven't seen him either? Lieutenant, do you realise that now we have four missing persons? Wendy Xiu, Malcolm Baines, Detective Gill and my daughter. I mean, I can tell you that and I'm hundreds of miles away. What do you actually do down there, Lieutenant? You clearly don't have a handle on any of your operations!" The discussion is being escalated by Jumeau, and Young has to go on the back foot.

"Professor Jumeau, I am perfectly aware of what is going on in my precinct, thank you. I'd appreciate you calming down if we are to proceed any further," Young retorts.

"I'm as calm as a father whose daughter has been given police protection only to then disappear can be! I'm sorry, Lieutenant, but I am going to go above your head on this. I do appreciate that you are badly resourced at present, but I consider your performance on this matter to be sub-standard. I will be talking to the Mayor directly."

This spooks Young, who does not want any escalation to his Captain or the Mayor. His subsequent reaction is probably the catalyst for his own downfall, but he doesn't realise it.

"Well, sir, I don't think that will get you anywhere, as it was the Mayor himself that intervened to close down the case," he informs Jumeau in a curt and rather patronizing tone. There is a pause on the other end of the line. Young decides to capitalize on the silence. "So, if there is nothing else, Sir, I believe..." he gets half way through his sentence before Christophe Jumeau responds, decisively.

"Lieutenant Young, I'm going to cut through you right there. I understand that you have just told me that the Mayor of Boston has personally intervened in what I am led to believe has been deemed a relatively low-priority case in order to ensure that my daughter no longer receives police protection. My daughter, who is a witness to information directly related to the assassination of the President of the United States of America. Do you understand how this looks? I'm afraid to inform *you*, Lieutenant, that your responses in this conversation have given me renewed and grave cause for concern, not only for my daughter's safety but also in terms of the collusion and cover-up on the part of the Boston Police department in a potential national security issue. You understand that this warrants national press attention and national investigation? You and your police department will be consigned to the garbage dump after this!" And with that, Christophe Jumeau does not wait for a response, banging down the phone so hard in its socket that the plastic cracks.

Lieutenant Lester Young is left gaping at the picture of the American flag on his office wall, contemplating what this concerned father, who isn't even American, has suggested.

—-

"Switching," Pratin Malic says.

"OK, speak," says Garfield, who is in the bathroom at his weekend home near Cape Wrath. He has come to avoid being in the limelight, but he can only be here for the shortest time.

"We have the Professor. Do you want him in the same place as the others?" Malic asks.

"Yes, but keep them apart. No contact. What about the girl?"

"She is still loose. Hector got close but she got away," Malic reports.

"Godammit, Pratin! This is what I pay you for!" Garfield shouts. It resounds outside the bathroom, and Julie Garfield overhears.

"Honey? Are you OK in there?" she shouts through the door.

"Yes, yes, I'm fine!" he shouts back, and waits to hear her footsteps moving away.

This time he whispers into the mini-phone he has in his watch. "Now listen, you get hold of that girl whatever it takes - get the cop's location before you silence her. No more fumbles. You got that?"

"Sir. Yes, *Sir*." Malic comes back, stoically sticking to comms procedures and remaining unemotional.

About half an hour later, Malic gets a call from Daniel Faye, part of the small ops team Garfield uses for covert security. Faye tells him that Catherine Jumeau has taken a flight to Atlanta on the back of the tip-off that Xiu and Baines are down there. Malic sends Faye and Caballos to Atlanta with orders to take Jumeau out, and anyone at the relatives' house if need be. If they come back empty-handed, he will send them to Montreal to use Christophe and Mary Jumeau as bait for the daughter to come back home.

Gill's lawyer, Chay O'Driscoll, arrives at Washington's high-security detention centre, and he and Gill are accompanied to a private ante-room by two security guards, one of whom stays in the room with them.

"So, Gill, I bet you never expected that we'd meet quite like this, huh?" O'Driscoll says.

"You got it, Chay. It's fucked up. Fucked up big time. Can you get me out of here?"

"Are you joking? Do you realise what's happening out there? For years America has prided itself on offering advanced and superior security to its Presidents in the wake of Kennedy, Reagan and Obama. That was the last time anything remotely like this happened. The public are baying for blood, and the entire security operation around the White House and the Capitol Building are reeling from what is being thought of as the biggest mystery in security history, which is making them look like a bunch of muppets. And you are at the heart of it. Would you care to explain what you were doing in the same room as the President of the United States of America, at the exact time of his death?"

Gill takes a deep breath. What's going to be his story?

"Look. I can't talk with these goons listening in. Everything in here will be tapped. There's no point in doing this until we are in confidence; they want to believe that I did it and right now there's nothing I can do about it. What I *really* need, are the details about what happened before and after the assassination. I need to piece together the bits." Gill's delivery is calm, assured, and credible.

O'Driscoll looks at Gill for a moment, assessing his mood.

"OK, let me see what I can do. It may take a little time."
"I'm like Louis Armstrong, Chay."
"What's that?" O'Driscoll asks.
"I've got all the time in the world," Gill says, ironically.

O'Driscoll smiles, understanding that he needs to move it along.

"I'll be quick, don't worry," he reassures Gill, and before Gill knows it, he is back in his padded cell. At the very least he has bought a little time to be able to try to dual again.

———-

'Catherine, this is Dad. We are just so worried about you now. I talked to the Boston police today and they told me you are no longer under police protection. If you get this, and you are OK, please, please respond. Even if it's just a text to say that you are OK. Please, honey, your mother and I are worried sick. We just need to hear from you.'

Christophe Jumeau sends a text to Catherine rather than call, instinctively sensing that a phone call might alert her captors to her whereabouts. At least a text might just vibrate or not make any sound at all, is his thinking. Mary Jumeau has had to be put on tranquillizers to keep her from stress attacks. Catherine may as well be five years old – it makes no difference to Mary, whose beautiful daughter has disappeared.

Catherine sees the text. She hates the fact that her mother will become ill the longer she keeps out of contact. Of course she wants to get in touch, but Gill's instructions were that anything coming out of her phone that wasn't from him had to be ignored. But for the second time she is going to ignore Gill's wishes. It's a risk, but she needs to let her parents know she is OK. She books into the Parity Motel on the main highway out of Washington. It's low-key, and she registers under a false name adding that she hasn't any ID on her at this point as she is just waiting to get her car fixed. The cash payment seems to carry the day with the manageress, a large bloated woman who spends sixteen-hour shifts sat behind the reception desk, mainly watching TV soap operas through her computer.

Across the freeway is a large shopping mall. She goes on foot and in one of the department stores buys a greetings card with 'Happy Birthday to our Wonderful Daughter' written in big sparkly letters across the front. She sends that to her parents' house, with nothing written inside. Her way of making sure they know she is OK. And, she thinks, by the time they get it tomorrow, she will be away from the area.

She goes back to the motel, feeling tired and anxious at the same time, determining to take some time to think through what is going on, and what to do.

The heat is becoming unbearable in Gill's cell. He is running a temperature and feels that someone outside has deliberately turned the heating up so that he is uncomfortable. He has no watch to be able to tell the time, but it has been several hours, he thinks, since he met with O'Driscoll and is waiting to hear back from him. Still no word.

He wonders about Catherine, and what she is doing. If she has gone to Atlanta. If she has been able to find anything there. What she will do if he doesn't come back. If only he could contact her. He tries yet again to dual, but it's no use. Desperately alone, and with no sign of any possibility of getting out of this cell, things looks pretty grim.

But grim might just be the beginning. Ellis Garfield is spooked by Gill's arrest and detention. Instead of rejoicing in the fact that a suspect has been found, the plan was that this was the most mysterious of all murders and one which could not be solved. He needs to know why Gill turned up at the scene, and after a couple of conversations, understands that Gill is far too dangerous. He needed to be taken out.

At the White House, Mitch Nicolescu and Phil Kirkland are listening to a grainy and scrambled recording of what sounds like Ellis Garfield's voice.

"Can you make any of this out, Mitch?" asks Kirkland.

"Nothing – we need someone to scrutinize it," Nicolescu comes back.

The recording is taken from the CCTV camera in the main hallway outside Ellis Garfield's temporary living accommodation the night of Montgomery's assassination. It seems as if Garfield is shouting obscenities at someone. But the reason it has been brought to the attention of the two security chiefs is because Garfield was alone that night, his wife and children being away. So who was he shouting at? No outgoing or incoming calls had been registered by security that night, so unless he was talking to himself, either someone else entered the quarters, or Garfield has some sort of unregistered device that he is using for communications that he is hiding from security.

"Mitch, I wonder if we should wire-tap Garfield for a while, just to make sure he is OK. I mean, he might be going crazy or something. If that is the case, then we can't have him in charge. You know what I mean?"

Mitch Nicolescu takes a moment before commenting. "Hhmm, I don't know, Phil, that would require authorization, and it might get back to Garfield. He isn't going to look too kindly on that kind of thing."

"Mitch, this isn't about us. This is about him. My concern is that he may prove to be unfit for the job, or make unsound judgements. We are the closest in right now, and someone has to know," Kirkland insists.

"We could talk to Maria?" Nicolescu suggests.

"Of course, that's it, Mitch. She can decide what to do. It's her bag really. I'll set up a meeting." And with that the two security chiefs go their separate ways.

—-

"Are you sure?" comes the voice on the other end of the phone.

"Yes." Garfield's voice is steady, and cold.

"It may be difficult. There is a lot of security there. We will need to get inside help."

"I will make it worth your while. This is a matter of national security, and you will be doing your country proud. This man is evil, and needs to be taken care of before he gets a trial and ends up with a cushy life in some high security prison reading books and cooking for pleasure. If we don't do this, justice will not be served," Garfield stresses his case.

"Do I have a green light for any means?"

"Yes."

"Forty-eight hours. Keep him there."

"No. I can't guarantee that. This needs to be done now. Twenty-four hours maximum."

There is a pause. "I'll see what I can do." The phone goes dead.

——

Back at the Parity Hotel in the world where Catherine and Gill first met, Catherine is lying awake, concentrating on Gill. She has been so lucky to find him, yet so unlucky to lose him almost straight away. This is hard to take. She is thinking through options. It is only a matter of time before Garfield's henchmen track her down. What if they go to Montreal to her parents' home? Oh God. Not that. 'Come on!' she urges herself to leave the emotions out of things. She thinks back to her conversations with Gill about dualling. He told her she saw Garfield super-positioning because she, like him, and like Gill, is a duallist. Maybe the only way to do anything useful was to explore this ability, and track Gill down. She can't stand running, or sitting on motel beds, any longer, and feels utterly helpless, waiting to die at the hands of some calculating killer under Garfield's private control. No. She wasn't going to be silenced in this way, damn it. 'Damn it,' she says to herself.

A crease forms on her brow. She concentrates hard and tries to imagine the corn field and the sky above. She is concentrating so hard, and is so stressed, that she can't do anything except get annoyed with herself. After a few curses, several thumps on the bed and numerous visits to the window and back, an exhausted Catherine Jumeau has to give in to tiredness. After taking a shower, Catherine dresses, just in case she has to leave quickly. Then lies down on the bed, and falls into a twilight world of happy days back in Montreal.

At some point in that twilight world between what is real and what is dream, Catherine feels a rush of wind against her face. It's very much of *this* world, and brings her for a moment into consciousness. She opens her eyes, not sure where she is. Above her is a blue sky. Cornflower blue, and so deeply colorful that it makes her smile broadly. The wind against her face intensifies and she begins to be pulled along, through the reeds. It's not the same as the first time, and it feels better, more relaxing. This is where she *wants* to go this time, rather than being afraid about the unknown. She lifts her feet up so that she does not cause any drag on her movement, and almost immediately she arrives at the clearing. There is no Gill.

Nothing except the weight of the atmosphere. This is the difficult bit. The incredible mass that is sticking to her is the Universe's response to time dilation. Things have slowed so much at the clearing that anything that enters it acts as a magnet to any passing mass. She's at the edge of a worm-hole, at the intercept between this world - the world she was born into - and many different worlds. Realities which might exist elsewhere. She feels the gravity of the situation, and momentarily panics. She is rooted to the spot. She imagines that many people might get to this point and be rooted forever, trapped in some space-goo that eventually makes you implode under the colossal mass that you attract, literally losing yourself by falling into your own black hole.

Regaining her composure, she realises that if she can gain momentum and reach any of the pathways she can see in front of her, then she has a chance of travelling through spacetime. Her determination and understanding of the situation seems to be to her advantage. It's so difficult to move. Like trying to lift a huge weight at the gym, with one hand. But just like the gym, if you imagine someone is helping you to lift the weight, then suddenly it becomes less daunting, and you see that you can lift it after all. Somehow, Catherine feels that someone is there helping her. It's another woman, and she can smell her. This is unexpected, but it gives her a choice. Hang around here and try and find out who is helping her, or take the freebie and get on with the task in hand. She decides on the latter, and within what seems like a few short movements she is beginning to break free from the gloopy mass of molasses pressing down on her. It feels fantastic – cathartic and energizing.

As she gets through to the other side of the clearing, she is faced with the next challenge. Which path to take. There are so many, opening and closing it seems. In fact, there seem to be more every time she looks. This is really disconcerting. Out of the corner of one eye, she sees something shiny. She naturally goes towards it. As she gets closer, she can feel a push from each of the pathways as she goes past, as if each one is repelling her. But just up ahead and to the left she can see the bright sunlight bouncing off something small, and metallic. As she approaches, she sees it is a watch. It's Gill's watch, but it's broken. And in this instance there is a palpable sense that something is very wrong.

She's firing on instinct right now, and seeing the watch draws her inexorably into the dark entrance to the pathway.

—-

Alfredo Gonzalez is taking a leak. He shouldn't be. He's on duty guarding washroom two in the east wing at the Capitol building. His job is to stand outside and make sure there is no-one going in or out unless they have permission. It's been a while since the assassination and everyone knows that no assassin is ever going to revisit this scene. The forensics guys have been over the place with a fine tooth-comb and have done all they are going to do. The only thing that remains there is the large-lettered 'CRIME SCENE' tape that runs around most of the inside of the washroom. But you can easily duck under it, and Gonzalez has been on duty for hours without taking a break, so he's having a fly leak, hoping that no-one will notice. The relief is gratuitous, and he is making noises to that effect.

Behind him, Catherine Jumeau is trying not to make a sound of her own. If he turns around, she'll be seen and that can't happen. Silently she creeps towards the door, and prays that the big security guard will wash his hands before leaving. The door has a big brass handle and it will surely make a resounding noise if she tries to turn it. Luckily for Catherine, Alfredo's parents were insistent on hygienic behavior in all things toiletry-based. As he starts to run the tap, the sound is loud enough to mask the turn of the door handle, and Catherine leaves. She dodges the first CCTV camera which is facing down the corridor away from her. She decides to get out as quickly as she can. After taking two wrong turns and almost encountering several uniformed security officers, she gets to one of the side entrances. There is a TV van backed up against the exit door, with several people to one side discussing coverage of the building.

"Let's wrap this up for today. OK everybody, we need to get this stuff away now!" shouts the director.

Catherine moves smoothly and quickly to the other side of the van and peers through the two side windows at the rather distorted figures on the other side, beginning to pack away their gear. She backs away from the van, slowly. As she gets some ten yards away, she hits something. It's a security guard.

"Alright, Miss?" he says.

"Oh! Hi there. My, you guys are everywhere!" she exclaims, using the best girly-cheerleader voice she can muster.

The guard laughs. "Well, now, that's our job, young lady. Are you with the crew?" he asks.

"The crew?" she says.

"Yeh, the crew over there," he says, pointing to the TV van.

"Oh, yes, I've just started. They don't need me until tomorrow, so I just thought I'd take off. When are you on duty till?"

The guard blushes slightly. "Oh, me? Ah, I don't get off until 11 p.m. Ma'am," he says, leaving the comment heavy in the air in case the lovely young woman in front of him might just come on some more.

"Oh, too bad. They work you hard, huh? I've got to be up really early tomorrow. OK, well, nice to meet you...?" she looks at the guard with her big eyes and he is completely at her mercy.

"Oh, uh, Anthony. I'm Anthony. Will you be around tomorrow...?" he asks.

"Sarah. I'm Sarah. Yes I will be. Look forward to seeing you then, Anthony," she lies. And with that flirtatious farewell, Catherine turns and walks towards the main exit, exaggerating her hip movements shamelessly as she does so. The guard waves to his colleagues at the main gate to let her through.

Half way down the street, and towards a nearby hotel, she enters and goes straight to the washroom there. She splashes water on her brow and pats it dry, trying to collect herself. If she analyses the situation too much, it will become unmanageable. Deep breathing helps. Until someone else comes in and her attention snaps back to Gill. The first thing she needs to do is get some information on what is going on. It is clear that the assassination has already taken place, so she can't figure out how far back in spacetime she has travelled. Get a newspaper; that's what she needs to do.

Through the lobby of the hotel and into the lounge area, she grabs a Post from one of the vacant tables. She orders a coffee and gets to reading all about recent events. And then it hits.

'BOSTON POLICEMAN PRIME SUSPECT IN MONTGOMERY ASSASINATION...'

A new reality, and one of the worst.

There is so much in-depth reporting that she has every conceivable insight, without being witness to actual events themselves. Very worryingly, she reads that Gill is due to be transferred from the East Street correctional facility to the Leavenworth maximum security detention centre in Kansas within the next few days, and so she immediately decides to get as close as she can to East Street. She asks someone the way, and ends up near Eastern Market metro, deciding to grab a coffee and some privacy anywhere she can. This proves extremely difficult, so she goes to the nearest bar and gets into a cubicle in the ladies' room.

Locking the door behind her, she feels quite unwell. Traveling through spacetime has taken its toll for her as a newbie. Although she felt good a little while back, color and verve have been replaced by grey tones and torpor. Blood has drained from her head and as she sits down she feels feint. She reaches for the bottled water she just bought. As the energizing and life-giving liquid runs down the back of her throat, so her willpower revitalizes to forge ahead and try to reach Gill. He is very close, she can feel that much, and this gives her strength. No amount of flippant flirtation with security guards would get her into Gill's cell, she knew that. So it has to be this; dualling. Again.

As once again she comes to the clearing, this time she hears a voice. It is a girl's voice and it is calling for Gill. She cannot make out any particular figure, just the fact that there is a presence there. It is such a familiar tone to her ears, yet she cannot place the voice. And again, Catherine drags herself through the clearing to get to the pathway's opening on the other side. This time, there is no watch, no clue as to where Gill might be. She is so close to him in spatial terms that it seems so silly to have to do this just to jump to where he is. But of course, this is the way. She closes her eyes for a second and tries to feel the way forward. As she does so, most of the openings in the corn-reeds begin to close, leaving only two paths; left, or right. Instinctively she understands the danger. In a moment she could be dead. In a moment she could be with Gill. Which is it to be?

Gill is being transferred early. The authorities have deemed it necessary to get him to the maximum security centre at Leavenworth, Kansas. He is in the back of an armored van, chained to a bar rail by the hands, and his feet clamped together with shackles. The van is stationary, inside the main gate of the East Street complex. There is another van behind, and an armored car in front. The security guard at the main entrance is on the phone.

"Uh-huh. Uh-huh. OK...Uh-huh. Thank you," he says, looking over to the senior security chief in the front van. He raises his voice slightly, given the distance the van is from his post. "Uh, Sergeant? We are just waiting for the police escort. Should just be a couple of minutes."

"What's that, Officer?" shouts the Sergeant.

The officer raises his voice so that it soars above everything else. "I said it will be *about two minutes until the police escort gets here, sir!*"

The officer's voice resonates around the compound, and out into the street, before bouncing back and onto the van Gill is in. He hears it loud and clear, as if it is coming through an old-fashioned megaphone.

And so too does Catherine. As she hesitates between left and right, the sound of the officer's voice floats across from the right, and she immediately knows that is where she has to go. And so it happens. Catherine materializes in the armored van taking Gill to Andrews Air Force base.

Gill can't believe his eyes. He is about to cry out 'Catherine!' at the top of his voice, but she has the presence of mind to raise her hand to cover his mouth to silence him. As he stares at her wildly, eyes aflame with expectancy and delight, she signals to him to be quiet. And in that moment she realises that they are touching, but without the usual effects. He wants to hug her. She wants to hug him. But neither knows what that might mean. Almost too afraid to find out, she moves her hand away and holds a finger to her mouth signalling to him not to speak. Reluctantly, he nods, his eyes never straying from hers.

They are together again, and for just one second, everything is alright. The two are silent, simply smiling at each other. They are going to have to talk to each other without speaking. At first

Catherine tries to make some signals to Gill, almost like sign language, but without any coherence or structure. As if dictated by the sheer need to say something to each other, Catherine talks to Gill in her mind.

'Gill, if you can hear me, I love you. I don't know how I found you, but I did. I saw your watch at the clearing, it was a miracle really. I just want to be with you, whatever happens'.

Gill looks at her. She doesn't know whether or not he has heard her. He just keeps looking at her. He has those big puppy eyes, and for a moment she sinks into them, giving herself just a second of indulgence in an otherwise oppressive reality. As she does so, she begins to see something in his eyes. Or rather, behind them. As she stares, she is mesmerized as Gill's eyes radiate a light that begins to fill her field of vision. She is calm, and focused, but completely under his spell. And as the light pervades the atmosphere around her, words start to appear in her mind.

'So glad you are here. I knew you could do it. Maybe together we can find a way out.' The words are so clear that Catherine reaches out. She can touch them. She picks the word 'together' and holds it in her hand. And grasps it tightly.
'I love you,' she says.

A moment passes, and he smiles at her.

Gill can't move for the shackles and the handcuffs. And now Catherine is here, they are both captive. Realising all of this, the initial elation of their reunion becomes somewhat dampened by the harsh reality that is in front of them.
Then it dawns on Gill. Catherine; if he has witnessed her in this exact spot in space-time, then she too should now be trapped in this reality. "Fuck," he blurts out. She steps away and looks at him for a second. 'Fuck,' she says silently.
And just twenty yards away, in the van following Gill, and now Catherine, is Tomas Schecter, special services marksman for U.S. Army Intelligence in the Middle East five years ago, and now a hired assassin in the payroll of one Steve Nelson, aka Ellis Garfield.

The secure convoy eventually grinds into motion, out of the gates of East Street correctional facility and onto the freeway, heading down towards Morningside and, beyond that, Andrews Air Force base.

* * *

CHAPTER 9: ANOMALIES

Abe Hart, Secretary of State, and Maria Ortega, Secretary of Homeland Security, order coffee at the Lincoln café over at the Capitol building. They move away into the far corner where there is at least twenty feet between them and anyone else there.

"So?" Hart asks.

"So, FYI I've asked for a report to be compiled of his phone calls and a review of all CCTV footage since last week," Ortega responds.

"And this is because?"

Ortega pauses for a second, just making absolutely sure there is no-one within earshot. "Because I have reason to believe that we have a problem. His absences from office and erratic behavior are unacceptable given the situation. Julie has been pressing him to go to the doctors for days now. She says he isn't sleeping, and just sits in his office for hours not doing anything. We don't know what he is doing in there, but it's not showing up in any leadership or authority. The man is floundering and out of his depth."

"I understand. But why would someone struggling with the pressures of office in extremely difficult circumstances warrant a security investigation. Do you think there is a link to the assassination?" Hart quizzes her.

"I simply don't know at this point. I have people on it. Two things for you to take away: the first is that a private memo, which John started to write regarding the association between Ellis and the eminent professor Walter Melrose at Harvard, surfaced yesterday from the criminal investigation. It was part of a routine examination of all John's belongings. In it, John mentions the possibility of covert research being funded without the knowledge of the Treasury, and his intention to start an investigation into Melrose and his crew up there. Now, at the very least that raises a conflict between Ellis and John," she reports.

Abe Hart sits forward in his chair. "Possible motive. Well, well."

"I know. It gets more intriguing. The details are a bit sketchy, but I have information that some of Melrose's staff have gone missing. I don't know if this is linked, but it's a bit odd, don't you think?"

"Hhmm, well, I'm not making the connection, you need to help me out," Hart prompts.

Ortega sits forward to mirror Hart's position across the table. "Well, if Ellis is funding secret research into experimental physics, he and the mad Professor might have cooked up some form of new military technology. Why would John be kept in the dark? It's suspicious at least. So if Garfield sniffed that he was going to be investigated, this might spark some sort of reaction," Ortega is speculating, and needs Abe Hart to keep up.

"Reaction?" Hart asks. Hart is a bright cookie, but he wants Ortega to do the work here.

"Look, what would you do if your boss had just found out that you had gone behind his back and were funding some sort of secret research that could be significant in terms of military intelligence? You'd try and cover it up *before* any investigation took place. That's potentially why some of those folks have disappeared – he could have *made* them disappear," she offers.

Hart looks at Ortega with a degree of skepticism.

She continues, "It makes sense, Abe. There is something worthy of further investigation here, and my take is that we need to put a few of our best people on this. I'm just keeping you informed as to what is going on, and I don't want anyone to panic."

Hart sits back. He's thinking this through. It's the last thing that anyone needs right now; further twists and turns in the highly charged environment at the heart of American political life. His job has become incredibly difficult since Montgomery's death, and the idea that there is a bigger web of misdemeanors out there fills him with dread. But, he has to listen to Maria. Although she's not the easiest person to get along with, he can't ignore what she has found.

Decisions need to be made, and despite her assertions on this, he knows that she is really asking for his approval and professional support in carrying out a secret investigation into the President of the United States. It is an extremely grave action to take, and not to be done lightly. If it were to be made public without collating any substantive evidence, both of them would look stupid at best, and be sacked at worst. The latter being more likely given Garfield's demeanor.

Hart lowers his voice a touch. "OK, here's my advice. Get as much as you can on the research side – what it is that is going on there – and talk to the Professor. That's the key. If it's what you think it is, then we could have a big problem like you say. But it might be something else entirely more innocent. After all, John didn't know what it was, he just wanted to find out, yes?" Ortega nods at Hart's prompt. He goes on, "And let's get a handle on Ellis' comms and absences. We need to know where he is if he's not here. Personally, I don't like the fact that you can't be more specific about that side. That's not good."

It's Ortega's turn to sit back. She is somewhat angered by Hart's criticism of her and her department's lack of information on Garfield, but decides not to react.

"Give me two days. Keep this to yourself for now, and I'll get in touch with findings," she says, in a matter-of-fact and business-like way. Hart nods, and they get up from the table. As they exit, Hart turns to her.

"Listen. These are crazy times. I can't remember things being any crazier. We have to keep our heads here. It's just too easy to see things that aren't there, and I want us both to still have jobs in six months' time. You feel the same?" he asks her.

Ortega looks at him square on. "Completely," she says, in a strong and positive tone. Although they have very different characters and approaches, they both know that this is the time for clarity and collaboration. That's why they are who they are.

—-

Camera twenty-three is inside the entrance hall to the living quarters of Ellis Garfield, President of the United States. The top of the head of the tall figure appears right in front of the camera, showing, for the first time, a thinning of the crown on Garfield's head. This is unusual, thinks George Beston, as it appears to be new. Himself thinning with classic, male-pattern baldness, Beston is only too familiar with other people's hairlines. And this is definitely new, because otherwise Garfield was always one of those men for whom, he had assumed, baldness would never be an issue. It was Montgomery's hair that had begun to go in the last couple of years.

Beston is intrigued, but lets it pass for the stress of the top and toughest job on the planet right now.

"Poor bastard," he mutters, and picks up the other half of his favorite deli sandwich.

Garfield disappears into his living quarters where, thankfully, security cameras cannot witness every single hair on his head. Back from another in a series of interviews with the nation's press, and subsequently a live television address, Garfield is shattered. After a quick shower, he lays down on the large king-sized bed and begins to doze off. His wife and kids have gone, and he has some much-needed time to reflect on how things are going. He is in the middle of a maelstrom; he knows that much. But it will only be through resilience and determination that he will win through. Despite certain obstacles around him, he begins to smile as he understands what he has to do.

After a short while, he gets up and goes through to the study, closing the door behind him. He sits down at his desk, and logs in to the computer, checking internal memos and news-feeds as they come through from CNN and Bloomberg. The noise of news reporters' voices fills the room, and to anyone outside listening, he would be presumed attentive and working. Garfield uses this time to super-position to his nearby special unit headquarters and catch up with agents Malic and Faye, the two inner-circle special forces men paid handsomely to support and protect him, believing that they are the chosen ones; only those who the Vice-President, now President, and ex-commanding officer in the field, trusts implicitly. It is blind faith, and Garfield's authority is unquestioned.

"You have the Professor?" Garfield asks of Malic.

"Yes, Sir. This way, Sir," Malic replies, ushering the President through a series of corridors until they come to a slate-grey reinforced steel door at the very end of the last corridor.

Walter Melrose is on the other side of the door, and is whimpering audibly.

"Well, well, what a pleasant surprise, Walter. How are you enjoying the 'hospitality'?" Garfield asks, as he and Malic enter the room to find the Professor huddled in a corner, clearly suffering. His wrists are bloodied and his bare feet look purple and bruised. He has been strung up with rope so that his body has been suspended from the ground, with his wrists taking most of his portly frame for a good hour or two. The purple swelling of his feet is where much of the blood in his body has migrated in this suspension. The pain is still visible on the Professor's face, and he can't bear to look round, even though he recognizes Garfield's voice.

"Now, Walter, I have to say that I am *very* disappointed. Very disappointed *indeed*. My friends here tell me that you have been keeping things from me. That many of your research findings have been folded away in secret little cubby-holes in your house. That you have found out much more than you have deemed me worthy of knowing. No?"

The Professor remains scrunched up in a ball, unresponsive. Garfield kneels down so as to be at Melrose's head-height.

"Very disappointed *indeed*," Garfield repeats. "If you cast your mind back, Professor, we had a deal. And in that deal, I managed to secure you substantial investment into your research, not to mention many opportunities to become a little bit famous and to mix with the stars. All I asked was for absolute candor, absolute openness with your results. Now it turns out that there are many things you have found which may be very important to me, and yet you have not thought it necessary to tell me about. So...my question to you is...'why'? Why have you kept these things from me, what is it you have found that you are so afraid that I might find enlightening?"

The Professor is still trembling, and shoots Garfield a hesitant glance. Even though he is in pain, the realisation that it is his long-standing funding partner, and test subject, that has been responsible for prosecuting such denigrating treatment on a man of his standing makes him deeply resentful. He looks away in disgust.

"What's the matter, Walter. Cat got your tongue? I can arrange for that to be permanent if you like? All you have to do is remain silent to my next question and I will ask my friend Pratin here to perform an emergency glosectomy. I take it you are familiar with such an operation?"

The Professor's eyes dart to Pratin Malic, who takes out a large knife, of the Bowie variety much-loved in the wilds in America. Panic is written across Melrose's face. He is one step away from being butchered and realistically has no options.

"OK, OK," he says, "For God's sake, Ellis." He doesn't finish this sentence, instead appealing to what little civility Garfield has left in him.
Garfield turns to Malic. "Get him clean and take him to the interview room."

About half an hour later a bedraggled-looking Walter Melrose is sat in a plain plastic chair facing another plain plastic chair in a completely white-washed room. Like something out of an Orwellian nightmare.
Garfield lights up a cigarette. The smell is pungent, but somehow manages to break the monotony of the stale smell of cheap paint.

"You know, I really would not have thought it would come to this. You, there. Me, here. Like this. Pretty messed up, huh? You see, the way I have it from my men here is that there is a whole lotta 'stuff' that you somehow were arrogant enough to decide I wasn't ready to know. Well, I read some of that stuff, Walter. And I don't like it. I don't like what you have done. Now, you are going to tell me what I need to know – right here, right now – or I will not hesitate to have you terminated. That means 'No more Walter Melrose'. You got that?"

Melrose is staring at Garfield. He'd only begun to see this side of Garfield at the diner a couple of days back. Now it looks like Garfield is really on his case, and doesn't seem to be bluffing. Melrose isn't a tough guy. He's an academic. He believes in knowing the truth about things. And he absolutely believes that it is true that Garfield will kill him unless he gets what he wants.

"Now there are two ways we can do this," continues Garfield, "I can ask you an endless series of questions based on some of the documents that you hid away in your little cubby holes at home, or you can start from the beginning and tell me what all this stuff is about and why you have kept it all to yourself? Which is it going to be?"

Melrose, forehead sweaty and nervously playing with his fingers, takes a deep breath, and decides that the only thing to do is give Garfield what he wants. In the back of his mind, he still fears for his life because something has happened to Garfield from which there is no turning back. He even *looks* different, although he can't quite pin down in what way.

"I'm sorry, Ellis. I really am. I made a mistake. I know that," Melrose starts, and Garfield nods in mock-approval as he takes a puff on his Camel Light. "It's just that I wasn't sure what I was looking at when I got some of the results and, well, I didn't want to jump to any conclusions, or give you any false dawns with any of this. That's the truth." The professor is speaking too quickly and nervously and Garfield stops him in his tracks by putting up his hand to silence him.

In a low and menacing tone, Garfield says "Walter. I'm not interested. I'm not interested in emotions or whining or what you thought was best. Look at me. I want to know what you have found, and the implications of what you have found for me, and for military intelligence. Do I make myself clear?"

Melrose nods, and continues, this time more slowly and in a more measured tone.

"About six months ago one of my students came to me with some results from her investigations into single-celled organisms – amoebas – and, well, I was amazed. She hadn't realised it, but the implications of those results were that not only was it possible for living creatures to act in the same way as groups of super-positioned particles, but that all subsequent cell duplication produced similarly-endowed cells," Melrose stops as he realises that Garfield is struggling with the content.

On the beckoning gesture from Garfield to explain more clearly, Melrose continues. "Well...this means...this *potentially* means that in fact large-objects with capacity to super-position may be far more plausible that we had ever thought. That, in effect, if gamete cells, or stem cells – in other words cells that can self-replicate and morph into different types of other cell necessary for a living organism to function – have the capacity in themselves to be split and super-position, then all offspring of those cells also – *potentially* – have that property. It's staggering."

Garfield's face remains still. Melrose is looking at him for a comment, or reflection, or just an acknowledgement, but he seems to be far away in thought. In this moment, Melrose begins to realise that Ellis Garfield is in fact beginning to take on certain features of his predecessor, John Montgomery. He doesn't have much time to dwell on it, though. Garfield's delay was merely him getting the bit between his teeth.

"Why do you keep saying 'potentially', Walter? Does this mean that it isn't automatic that everyone is able to do this?" he asks.

"It's not that it is automatic, no. In fact, I think it will still be, statistically, uncommon. What I am saying is that it is *more* likely that *some* people have this ability. That's because the original cells – the formation cells at the beginning of an organism's life – must have this capacity in the *first* place. And evidence so far is that this is not common. Well, I mean, you are the only test subject in the entire world, so that shows you how common it is," Melrose explains.

"Wait a second. So why would you keep this to yourself ? What would make you keep this from me?"

Melrose's face turns white. He knew this would come. He can't form any words. "I...I..." he stutters.

"Come on man! Godammit, Walter, you better open up or I promise I will get Malic here to do that for you!" And on that exclamation, Malic makes a move toward the Professor.

Melrose lets out a stifled moan, fearing the pain and violence that would be brought down on him by the ominous figure of Pratin Malic. "No!" he shouts. Malic smiles, mocking Melrose with a fake blow to the head with his large fist. Melrose is looking past Malic toward Garfield, who slants his head to indicate to Malic to stand down for now.

"I'm warning you, Walter, my patience is wearing thin. You have one minute to explain what is going on, or I'm going through that door. Pratin will be very happy when that happens."

Melrose nods furiously, and shakily continues. "I didn't tell you because my investigations into your own cell makeup revealed...um...revealed some...anomalies."

Garfield suddenly stands up and shouts "Enough!" Melrose is startled, as is Malic.

"Pratin, leave us, please," Garfield orders Malic, who looks confused; this wasn't part of the kind of drill he was used to with captives and suspects, so he gives Garfield a look which indicates that he requires confirmation before actually carrying out Garfield's order. Garfield gives him a very demonstrable nod to reinforce the fact that he wishes to be left alone with Melrose.

Malic is clearly disappointed. He is a thug at heart, and relishes the prospect of scaring and hurting whimpering cowards who are too clever for their own good. But he leaves, deferring as always to his superior officer.

In a hushed tone belying extreme frustration, Garfield spits in Melrose's ear, "Now then. Exactly what sort of *anomalies* are you talking about, *Walter*?"

Melrose's speech is peppered and faltering. "I...I couldn't identify, uh, some of the cells that were there. Uh, as I began to look at the physiological rather than just the physical, I...I realised that I had missed, uh, some key aspects about you by ignoring what biology and chemistry you have."

Garfield stares at him, his teeth gritted and bared. He is looking extremely threatening right now, as if he is just about to unleash untethered anger on the timid academic.

"What I mean is, I hadn't realised that your physiology is so different to what we might consider 'normal'."

There is a long pause. Garfield paces around the room while the Professor's eyes track him nervously.

"And who else have you consulted on this?" he prompts the Professor.
"No-one. I swear, Ellis. Absolutely no-one. I mean, I didn't even tell you because I have no idea what to make of it, or where it might take us in terms of the future!" Melrose pleads.

Garfield eventually comes to rest. He brings his face directly in front of Melrose's, his piercing eyes looking deep behind the Professor's and into his frightened mind. He pities him, someone so clever, yet so weak. Yet so dangerous. Maybe the surprise is more that it took the old man so long to understand that Garfield was so very different. That he didn't get ill. That he rarely slept. That his medical records had disappeared more than once. Of course, now that some form of penny had dropped, Garfield needed to know just how much the old man knew.

"You've been playing me, Walter. I see that now. So, go on. What is so very different then? What are your conclusions?" he asks.
Melrose knows that the answer to this could cost him his life. It's a tricky one. "Well, I can only say that you are perhaps the next stage in evolution of the human race, Ellis. I mean, your biochemistry and cell structures are like nothing I've ever seen before, and I'm guessing that you must have known from a little boy that you were different from other kids, no?" Melrose's tone is steadier now, and he hopes to regain some semblance of camaraderie with his long-standing funder. "What I mean to say is, you are clearly stronger than most other people, and I would imagine that your abilities in terms of super-positioning must mean that you have evolved beyond where normal human beings have evolved. So, you are like a 'super' human if I were to guess at a label."

Garfield paces around the room again. He is pensive, and reflecting on the Professor's proclamation of his super-humanness. That he is human, but better than most humans. This sits well with him. He was anxious about the Professor's conclusions. Still is. But somehow, if Walter Melrose is telling him the truth as far as he knows it, then this is a relief.

"Malic!" Garfield shouts. Pratin Malic rushes in. "Take the Professor back to his room. Make sure he is fed and watered," he orders, and Malic nods. Walter Melrose is dragged out of the white-washed interrogation room back to the relative comfort of his detention cell.

Garfield returns to the main attic room in the large warehouse in the middle of an industrial estate which acts as the meeting place and main control centre for his secret special ops unit. There are a bunch of folders and separate papers, all taken from Walter Melrose's house by his men. He needs to get back to the White House, but his eye is caught by one folder in particular, marked 'M.I. Classified'. He knows that M.I. is Military Intelligence. Opening it, there seems to be very few papers in it. The two at the top are turning yellow they are so old. The dates go back more than twenty years. They look particularly uninteresting and he is about to close the folder when part of a name jumps out of the page at him. It is unusual only in the fact that it reads 'JU'. The rest of the name is hidden. He shifts the paper on top a little and reveals the full name. 'JUMEAU'. 'Well, well', he says to himself, and picks up the paper, which can be no more than a bundle of about twenty or so pages. It is a paper that is attributed solely to Christophe Jumeau, cited only as a military physicist at Arlington laboratories. The title of the paper is in capital letters: 'LOCATING THE SOURCE: ENTANGLED OBJECTS.'
Garfield's ability to speed-read has been honed over many years, and he spends a few minutes with the paper, deciding to return to a couple of key paragraphs. The first thing that catches his eye is a section dealing with the results of work with living cells. It reads:
'Following re-experimentation to verify effects, it is possible to say with 95% probability that the test entangled pair, subsequently separated and unable to communicate using known methods, exhibit behavior manifest of a single particle. That is, an entangled pair

exhibit behavior which suggests influence from an originating source, split into two or more 'images' of itself, even though the plurality of images may present different appearances to the observer in terms of spin, state or reaction to environment.'

He re-reads the phrase '...suggests influence from an originating source.'

The other part of the paper that takes his eye is the final paragraph of the 'discussion' section. It reads:

'In conclusion, we can postulate that a possible *outcome* of the status of entanglement of particles is the phenomenon of reverse super-positioning. That is, the communication channel that forms the bridge between entangled particles can not only lead to super-positioning, but so too the converse possibility of return-to-source positioning. That is, two particles could use the delimitation of the time dimension associated with a spacetime independent transport mechanism, or 'worm-hole', to reunite.'

The word 'reunite' resounds around his head, and he flips back to the title page again. 'Christophe Jumeau', he thinks. The father of Catherine Jumeau, the girl who he saw in the Oldsmobile on the freeway. The girl who saw him super-positioning on the television. The girl whose father is now potentially more important to him than Walter Melrose. For the first time in many months, a broad smile comes to Garfield's face. He is putting it all together in his head; this may mean everything to him. But the smile doesn't last for long. He needs to get back to his real life as President.

—-

There is a large painting of George Washington behind Phil Kirkland. His office is the biggest outside the Presidential suite, even though he shares it with Mitch Nicolescu. The pair are acknowledged to be the best intelligence and security men in the entire country, and it's because of this that they are both also reeling from the breach in security around the President that must have taken place on the day of his assassination. The whole episode has undermined their own personal standing and authority and each is anxious to right whatever went wrong in whatever way they possibly can. So it is with some enthusiasm that Kirkland is hosting Maria Ortega and Abe Hart, two of America's most senior politicians right here in his own office.

"Thanks for seeing us, Phil. I realise how busy you are right now," Hart says.

"No problem, Abe. What can I do for you?" Kirkland responds, sitting up in his chair.

Maria Ortega sits forward. "Phil, this is level six security clearance, straight from Ava Redmond at Intelligence HQ."

She hands Kirkland a memo marked 'L6: Circulation Zero', the 'zero' relating to the prohibition of circulation beyond the list given. Ortega has asked Colonel Redmond, the feisty chief of CIA special operations and the most senior woman in the entire U.S. intelligence community, for a special missive to White House security which bypasses the President himself. It is a very short memo, the allowable circulation of which lists only Ortega, Hart, Kirkland and Nicolescu. It reads:

'Classified. #203147

Permission sought and given to begin 24/7 covert surveillance on E.G. relating to activity and behavior. Details to be transmitted by M.O. Report cycle: 12 hours, subject to findings, direct M.O. - A.R.
→ paper copy to shredder.

Signed: Col. Ava Redmond, Director – Special Operations, NSA/CIA/National Intelligence, Langley.'

Redmond's elaborate and unmistakably unique signature is written in dark purple fountain pen, as always. The fact that she has become involved indicates to Kirkland the gravity of the situation. Before becoming chief of special operations, Redmond had a successful career as a criminal lawyer and even made the front cover of both Vogue and Life magazines. She was at the heart of several high-profile investigations into corruption and fraud within the military, and was single-handedly responsible for nailing Nathaniel Blau, the extreme right-wing Republican candidate for the Senate who had plotted to assassinate his young Democrat challenger that was gaining ground in the contest for Texas. Her reputation is unparalleled, and Phil knows she would not be involved in this unless there was good reason. This offers him a ray of light; that his bosses believe that there may be an inside conspiracy going on. It could potentially relieve the pressure on himself and Nicolescu, even rescue their reputations if it turns out that they could not have done anything to prevent any of the events over the last week.

Phil Kirkland does not bat an eyelid at the memo, instead letting it sink in slowly. Ortega and Hart are looking at him for a reaction, unsure of where Kirkland might stand on this. He could find it difficult to reconcile loyalty to his President with the implications of the memo, but in effect they needn't have worried.

"OK. I guess we need to work out the details then," he says.

And with this, Ortega does most of the talking. She lays out what the suspicions are, and in particular advises that Walter Melrose and his PhD students are all missing, and that they need to be found. Kirkland confirms the requests and offers assurances that this will be done without Garfield's knowledge.

Before they leave, Kirkland asks Ortega what she and Hart suspect is going on.

"Well, look at it this way, Phil, Ellis Garfield isn't helping himself right now. If we don't get a clear picture within twelve hours, we'll need to take more overt action, more as a precaution that nothing else happens that shouldn't", Hart says.

Kirkland nods, and, on their departure, calls Mitch Nicolescu to come in for an 'additional shift.'

"What's the deal, Phil?" Nicolescu asks as he gets into the office, somewhat out of breath and looking anxiously at his colleague. He knows that an additional shift means that something serious is afoot. And on top of everything else that has happened recently, his immediate thoughts are negative.

"Take it easy, Mitch. Read this," Kirkland says as he passes the memo to Nicolescu. After reading it, Nicolescu's expression changes.

"Jesus. Redmond, eh? What the hell is going on?" he asks.

"Mitch, we got a live one here. My take on this is that Ortega, Hart and most of the spooks think that Garfield is central to Montgomery's assassination. At least, that's what I understand from all this. It's all to do with this Melrose character. Garfield and Melrose have been funding research which obviously has military and intelligence chiefs worried. I reckon they've built something big, something that the Jedi would use, if you get me."

"Uh-huh. And they were keeping it for themselves? Why would they do that?" Nicolescu asks.

"That's one of the things we've got to find out. But let your mind go for a minute. Let's go beyond the simple theory that Garfield just couldn't see himself ever fulfilling his ambition to be President of the United States and wanted rid of Montgomery. I just don't think that works. So, say Melrose, with Garfield's support, has a military weapon that could change the course of any war, any battle, any armed encounter. It's like the new nuclear bomb. Everyone in the world will want it, and the U.S. can control its distribution. But Garfield gets greedy, or Montgomery wants to keep it under wraps, or...well, there are a hundred reasons those two might have fallen out about all of this. It wouldn't take a huge leap of the imagination to get to Garfield seeing Montgomery as a block to all his plans and aspirations."

Nicolescu leans back in his chair, pensive and intense. "You know, Phil, I always knew that something like this would happen. I mean, I'm just surprised that it hasn't happened before now."

"How's that?" Kirkland asks, thinking that his colleague may have some insight beyond his own.

"Well, we both know that some of the research that those military scientists have been involved in is wacky enough. Heck, you and I have seen some of that shit. It was only a matter of time until the *next* breakthrough. The *game-changer*. Maybe that's what we've got here. And if that's so, then individuals become less important than the technology. It's almost as if nothing will stop new technology emerging. It's how it's deployed that matters."

Kirkland is struck by his counterpart's insight. If Garfield is just an agent of technology then of course anything that Montgomery did to stop its emergence and utilization would simply get in the way. But to Kirkland, it's not as straightforward as that. Most people see Garfield as a weak character in political and personal terms, and certainly out of his depth as the new President. It's all around the White House, and beyond. Is this really the same person that could have plotted to kill John Montgomery? Is this the same person who could potentially be so power-mad as to wish to control key military technology for his own professional gain? It wasn't likely, he thought. There had to be another angle.

"Listen, we have authorization to use whatever methods we wish under the terms of the Redmond memo. My gut tells me that there is a personal angle on all of this. Garfield himself is worth some very close scrutiny. I suggest we split so that you get the lowdown on Melrose and his students, and asap. I'll take a good look at Garfield here. OK?"

"Sure, Phil. Suits me. I want to find out what the hell this technology can do!" Nicolescu replies.

Phil Kirkland goes over to the shredder, and feeds in memo 203147. The machine is security grade, and the paper is not only shredded into the finest strips possible, but also output to different trays, then pulped with the addition of a jet of water. The chances of anyone being able to re-assemble the memo is less than one millionth of one percent. It strikes Kirkland that they still use paper, so many years after everyone predicted its demise.

—-

When Ellis Garfield gets back to the White House, tiredness overwhelms him. For some reason the super-positioning to the warehouse, where his secret ops unit is based, has taken a tremendous amount out of him. So much so, that he has to let his aides know that he can't make the scheduled evening dinner presentation. Flopping down on the bed, he longs for sleep, yet it won't come. It seems that most of his synapses are firing all at once, relentlessly punishing him for the intricacies and deviations that sum up his life.

Piecing some key facts together, a picture begins to emerge in his mind. That picture is of him, reunited with his entangled partner, in a place that is home. His home. It's a beautiful scene; vivid colors in the air, a gentle breeze washing over him, and those just like him who are congregating to provide a big welcome. It is at once inspiring and invigorating, and relieves his weary body of the lethargy that has invaded it. He gets up from the bed, and begins to pace around the room, his thoughts unravelling with every step.

Garfield believes that Christophe Jumeau clearly understands the bigger picture when it comes to being in two places at once. Critical to this is the knowledge that he, Garfield, is most likely entangled. But with whom? He must try and find out; it's the missing link that could get him back to where he came from: the source.

Jumeau's paper implied that if the entangled could reunite then it might be a way for him to escape his inexorable entrapment here. He knows that things are wrong, and that people will be questioning his performance, character, and motivations. He can sense that there is a net closing in around him, and that there isn't much time to be able to run out from underneath it. He can also sense something strange within him. As he watched John Montgomery die, he felt the same sense of gravitational imbalance that he did in Antarctica when he lost time. When he had the *encounter*. People talk about the soul. Its essence, its meaning. But he also knows it has physical mass. On both occasions when someone has died before him, Garfield has gained mass. That mass, he now believes, is mass associated with the release of a human soul at the point of death. And if Garfield is super-positioning at the same point in space-time as his victim, it would appear that, with the change in the environmental conditions around him, it is *he* who absorbs that mass by default. As a result, Ellis Garfield is probably hosting more than one soul.

He has always struggled with his own character and personality. What exactly are those? They can change, sure. But many aspects are more constant and predictable. That's what makes us familiar to others beyond just the way we look. But since Montgomery's death, he has been in a fight with Montgomery internally. It's as if Montgomery is still struggling to be seen, heard, felt. But instead of diminishing in intensity, the fight is getting tougher. On several occasions, Garfield has felt terrible remorse and a sense of wrong-doing has been welling up in him. He has felt guilt about abandoning his wife and children. A sense of duty to the American nation. But it's not him. It's Montgomery. It's *his* influence. And it has to stop. Otherwise he will go mad. There isn't enough room in this body for another person.

And the Jumeaus. What is the connection between Christophe Jumeau's work and his daughter's abilities? He needs to talk to Christophe about his work. And why would Christophe's daughter be dangerous? He casts his mind back to when the vehicles passed on the freeway. He saw her and the detective there. He had assumed that it is she and she alone that was able to super-position too. And now, with Walter Melrose's revelation that perhaps other humans are able to super-position, perhaps that is not true. It would seem that the Detective *too* has the ability, making the pair a formidable force. And with this thought, Garfield's mood changes. The net feels even closer.

He contacts Pratin Malic without further hesitation.

"What's happening with the Jumeau girl?" he asks.

"Sir, she has disappeared, Sir."

"What?"

"We tracked her down to a motel right here in Washington, Sir. Only after she ditched the car and took a hire car across town. She had gone by the time we got there. No trace, and looked like she left in a hurry, Sir," Malic reports.

Garfield thinks for a second before responding. "OK, tell your guys to stay there. I think she may still be in the area. What about the cop?"

"OK, Sir. Uh, the cop hasn't been seen since we saw him on the freeway a couple of days back. We have run taps and checks everywhere, but so far nothing. He wasn't with the girl at the motel."

Garfield pauses for a second. "OK, listen, I need you to get the number of Christophe Jumeau, the father. Contact him, tell him his daughter has been kidnapped for a reward and that you'll agree to a meeting to discuss the return of his beloved Catherine. Any police and she is disposed of. Await my instructions."

After Malic confirms, the two end the call.

—-

A couple of hours later Christophe Jumeau is speeding down the freeway. He has a rendezvous with the kidnappers of his daughter, and he couldn't even tell his wife where he was going. Everything seems to be confusing him, but he uses the time on the long straight road to collect his thoughts. The next few hours could be the most important of his daughter's life, and every move he makes could be critical.

Catherine is alive and well. Point one. She might not be. Point two. She was with Gill. Point three. She might not be any more.

Point four. He is meeting with people he doesn't know. Point five. Actually he might know them. Point six. And at that point, he stops making points. "Shit", he says to himself through the sound of the engine and his favorite music mix given to him by his daughter, which is playing an old Stan Getz tune called 'Dreams'. Getz' lazy sax is interrupted by George Mraz' bass solo which simultaneously interrupts Christophe's confused thinking. He calms down and begins to relax into the inevitability ahead; that he will have to play it by ear. This is something that doesn't come naturally to the Professor. But, needs must.

He pulls into the same diner where Walter Melrose and Steve Nelson met just days before. A hooded and huddled character over in the corner gestures to join him, which he does. The large frame of Jumeau hardly fits in the small plastic chair, and he looks and feels uncomfortable. He notices that the man sitting opposite him is not only wearing heavily tinted spectacles and a trucker's hat covering most of his head so that it is impossible to tell what kind of hair he might have under there, but is also sporting a beard, which, if Jumeau is not mistaken, is not real. Rather than kick up a fuss about this, he decides merely to observe.

"So, you're late," says the obscure figure opposite.

"Sorry, it was just a traffic thing and I didn't want to get stopped for speeding," Jumeau says.

Steve Nelson, aka Ellis Garfield, nods. "Do you know why you are here?" he asks Christophe.

"Well, I would imagine because you want money?" Jumeau says, but even then his gut tells him this isn't the reason.

"Hhmm. Not too bright for a clever man," says Garfield, continuing "but I will give you the benefit of the doubt. You know your daughter is missing I presume?" Jumeau nods. "Well, if you want to see her again, I suggest you co-operate fully. That's the only ground-rule. You got that?" Garfield says.

"Yes. But how do I know you have Catherine? I need to know that she is safe and not going to be harmed. I'm sure you must understand that," Jumeau resiliently replies.

"I wouldn't be here on a bluff, Professor. That's not my style," Garfield responds in a calm but reprimanding tone, to which Jumeau has no option but to comply.

"OK, but did she say anything to you before you came to meet me? I mean, did she say anything about me and her mother, any message? Her mother is ill with worry and she needs some assurance that Catherine is at least being treated well..." Jumeau asks.

"Look, the only thing she did say was that you were the best dad in the world and that you'd do anything to get her back. That's true, isn't it?" Garfield whispers from under the false moustache and beard that hide his facial movements and make it difficult for Jumeau to get a handle on the character of the man behind them. But the words reveal that he is lying. And this disconcerts Catherine's father. He is a shrewd man, and knows his daughter very well. She would never say something like that if she was being held captive. It would be the opposite; she would play down the relationship and not offer any succour to her captors at all.

"What is it you want then?" he asks the mysterious bearded figure.

"I need your brains," Garfield tells him.

"What?" the Professor exclaims, loud enough to let the next two booths know that they are there.

Garfield holds up his hand to stop Jumeau saying any more at that volume. In that moment, Jumeau gets more of an impression of the man. The hand is fine, with long fingers, and has seen some hard work in its time, but not for some while. The man is tall, long-limbed, and somewhat gaunt, he decides. Not in good shape. And perhaps under a lot of stress. It detracts from his threatening demeanor, and evens up the balance somehow between the two men.

"Keep your voice down. I need your knowledge on aspects of super-positioning," Garfield leaves his words hanging in the air for Jumeau to absorb in his own time. Jumeau at first looks puzzled, then, desperately trying to figure out what is going on, is interrupted by Garfield's explanation.

"Professor, your daughter is in danger, be clear about that. She needs your help, and she needs it quickly. For her to be returned safely I am going to need to tap into your knowledge. Do you understand?"

The Professor nods, still working in the background to put together what might be going on.

Garfield leans forward slightly as he gets to the main point of why he is here, in this place. "You wrote a paper over twenty years ago on entanglement and super-positioning. In it, you postulate that if two entangled objects can communicate, then they may reunite as well as use an open channel for such things as super-positioning, yes?"

Jumeau pauses, looking surprised at the nature of the question."I wouldn't characterize it quite like that, but broadly speaking, that's about it," the Professor replies.

Garfield gets excited, and his voice becomes more animated, giving away another clue as to his identity. "What I need to know is this: if one entangled object were to be trapped in a particular state following super-positioning, could that object open a communication channel with its partner to reunite? Do you understand?" Garfield asks. There is anxiety in his voice which urges a positive response. It's the only response really, but Jumeau's scientific mind can't make it that easy.

"You mean 'would a particle trapped in one state because it had been observed to be so, then be able to instigate further communication with its entangled partner?' Possibly, yes," the Professor offers.

Garfield takes this in, but it's not what he is getting at. "Listen, what I am asking you is this: you suggest in your paper that reverse super-positioning may be possible. If an object is entangled but trapped in a particular state, or reality, can it reunite with its entangled partner again? Can it super-position back to where its entangled partner is? What would be necessary for that to happen?...How would..." Garfield's voice is so full of tension that he sounds like he might burst.

Jumeau has to interrupt. "Whoa! I have to stop you there. This sounds like it is extremely important to you. Let's just take it one step at a time, yes?" to which Garfield nods. The power shift is tangible. Clearly Jumeau has something that this man wants, and it is nothing to do with money. Jumeau realises that the man opposite is vulnerable, and probably doesn't even have Catherine in his possession. But he also realises that he knows a lot about *him*. Things are still very unclear, but he must assert some control, and find out why this fellow is so intent on finding out about his past work.

"If I understand you, what you are saying is that there is an object which is entangled. Point one. Point two, that object has super-positioned but been observed, so therefore trapped in a particular state. Point three, that object has lost contact with its entangled partner but in some fashion requires communication with that partner in order to, point four, reunite with it, or at least escape its own entrapment. That it?" Jumeau asks.

Garfield nods.

"Well," the Professor continues, "any particle can theoretically super-position, and that includes a case where it was observed in a particular state. There needs to be some stimulus that would cause it to split and super-position. If the particle is entangled I would imagine that that stimulus – perhaps a reunion, yes - most likely would have to be instigated by some initiating communication between the two. But it would probably be outwith the control of the trapped entity, if that is what you mean," Jumeau states.

Garfield is intent and looking deep into Jumeau at this point. It is quite disconcerting. There is a pregnant pause which seems to go on for too long while Garfield seems to be searching for connections.

"Go on..." Garfield prompts.
"Go on...to what?" Jumeau asks.

Garfield is annoyed that Jumeau can't understand where this has come from, but this is the nature of the cat-and-mouse discussion. How much should he disclose? How much *can* he disclose? The answer is 'everything he needs to', and for this he needs guidance from the more knowledgeable Jumeau.

"Go on to tell me about this 'stimulus'. I mean, what would that *be*? How could I...could we instigate such an event? How could you make this happen? Quickly," Garfield asks.

It's Jumeau's turn to pause. The discussion is one of the strangest he has had for a long time, even by the standards of quantum physics and its associated weirdness. He takes a sip of his coffee, and winces. It's terrible coffee, but somehow has the effect of snapping his thoughts into place.

"You know, I don't know who you are. And maybe I don't care. But right now, you have come to me asking me for my knowledge and insight, and you have offered nothing in return. You say you have my daughter, but frankly I don't believe you. My suspicion is that you are a phoney, someone who is in trouble and is just fishing in the dark. So, unless you can offer me anything in return, I'm afraid this conversation is over. Goodbye," Christophe Jumeau states calmly and assuredly, before getting up and leaving.

In the car park, Jumeau is getting into his car when he feels a presence behind him. It's the tall figure of his daughter's supposed kidnapper. Jumeau is startled, and steps back, expecting some form of violent approach by his assailant. His instant assessment of the risk is that it might be possible to deal with the man, if he doesn't have the unfair advantage of a weapon, because although he is as tall, he is slighter. He automatically stiffens and prepares for fight.

"Wait!" says Garfield. "Calm down. I am not going to harm you," he says, "I just want to talk to you. Please. I know where you daughter is."

Jumeau looks at him in surprise for a second, before gesturing to join him in the car. He realises that this is a lost soul, full of contradictions, and realistically in need of some help. The desperation to find his daughter, and his compassion, kick in.

The two men are sat in Jumeau's car. Jumeau creates a silence, waiting for his anonymous passenger to speak. Before that happens, Christophe is about to get a shock. Ellis Garfield moves his hand to his face and strips off the false beard. He removes his heavy glasses, and then his cap, before turning to look at the Professor. Christophe Jumeau cannot speak. His pupils dilate so much they turn black, and everything seems to fall into them, including the illuminated vision in front of him.

He is looking at John Montgomery.

"Wha'?" Jumeau exclaims, frozen in position with his hands on the steering wheel.

"Calm down, Professor. I know it's a shock," Garfield says. He doesn't realise that he has the look of John Montgomery. As he speaks, so too the Professor sees Ellis Garfield. It looks like Ellis

Garfield as well. Jumeau can't quite take in what is going on, but it's enough to keep him rooted to his seat and require explanation.

Garfield offers it, at last. "Look, I need your help. You have two choices. You can leave now and never know what has happened to your daughter, or help me find her. And yes, I need to change things. I need to tell you what I am about, and why I need your help. But you have to take a chance, Professor. You have to roll the dice with me. I think I may be the only person who can save your daughter."

The tension subsides somewhat. Garfield. Of course, it's Garfield. It looks like a mix of Montgomery and Garfield but he recognizes that it is Ellis Garfield, current President of the United States. And this adds so much weight to unfolding events. Even to a Canadian like Jumeau, being sat right next to the President of the United States is an overwhelming experience. As much due to that as anything else, he decides to go along with things.

The turmoil inside Ellis Garfield is now at unmanageable levels. Montgomery's soul is obviously such a strong presence, full of integrity and the fight for good in the world, that it is fighting against the evil in Ellis Garfield. Whatever mass that Garfield attracted during the slaying of his President weighs heavy within him, and is emerging in a new openness and desperation. Christophe Jumeau senses that Garfield is such a contradiction that he may at any point regress and become threatening, or worse a block to getting Catherine back. Jumeau has to play this man very carefully, while keeping his eye on the prize; his daughter, wherever she is.

On the way back to Mansfield airport, Massachusetts, the two discuss what Garfield knows and what he needs to help Catherine. It is revelatory. For some reason Ellis Garfield has confided in Christophe Jumeau, possibly more than anyone else in his entire life, and as a result Jumeau decides without hesitation to help him out of his current predicament. For Garfield's predicament is, as a matter of fact, *his* predicament. Perhaps more profoundly, this whole situation is rekindling in Jumeau the hunger to discover more; about Garfield and his entanglement, and beyond. For he is undoubtedly entangled, at many levels. As he looks up at the stars on this clear night, Christophe Jumeau thinks long and hard about such matters. And about matter itself.

It's about half an hour later when Jumeau opens his mouth to speak.

"So, what I realise now, after all these years, is that my theoretical ramblings back then are actually being proven true. Well, well. I mean, I knew in my bones that the nature of reality is such that the size of an object is not the limiting factor in negotiating spacetime movement. What is it like when you do that?"

Garfield shrugs. "Listen, you just do it. Don't ask me how."

Jumeau thinks Garfield is hiding something, but the tone of Garfield's voice suggests that digging any further here might not reveal anything juicy. He continues with his line from a different angle. "OK, let's assume that my daughter and Detective Gill have both travelled – super-positioned – back to the point at which Montgomery is assassinated. In that reality, what are you suggesting we do to get them back?" he asks.

"The only way to get trapped in a particular place is if you are observed. Someone observed them, or they observed each other, or something. Heck, maybe Montgomery observed them", Garfield suggests, but Jumeau isn't buying it.

"OK, they were observed and are now in that reality until they can super-position their way out, right?" says Jumeau, Garfield nodding. "So," the Professor continues, "my assumption is that if you can locate yourself back to before that - in other words before the President's murder - then you can avoid both the assassination and Catherine and Gill being observed".

"That's it. Now you're getting it," says Garfield excitedly. "But the deal is that they must help me escape this reality. They....you...must help me to find my other half, otherwise I will undo everything. I have the power to make sure Montgomery never sees the light of day again," he threatens.

"But you have Montgomery inside you now. You are fighting with him, I can see that. Your life would be forever tormented by the battle between your, and Montgomery's, soul. Do you want that?" Jumeau asks him.

Garfield is holding back. Jumeau knows it, but can't pinpoint what is going on in Garfield's mind. After a long pause, Garfield speaks.

"I'd rather not have to do that, but I may have no other option. If I feel at any point that the plan is to trap me, or make it impossible for me to get out, I will carry out my threat. And I will regain my strength and come back stronger."

Jumeau doesn't know what Garfield means here. Is it an idle threat? If he were to be observed back in that reality, after making sure that Gill and Catherine could super-position back to this reality, then he would still be at large to kill the President. This is troubling. The President of the United States right now, in this reality - Ellis Garfield - has admitted to the Professor that he accidentally killed the President of the United States then - John Montgomery - and that he can undo that if he can travel back to a point in space-time before then. Of course, Jumeau does not believe it was an accident, but goes along with the story. It makes more sense to placate this troubled soul, his own goal only to ensure the safety of his daughter, who is clearly trapped and in danger, even if she is with Gill.

"OK. Listen, we need to be clear on the details of this, otherwise things may go badly wrong. You should know this. I am trying to get my daughter back, and as you say you are the one hope I have of making this so. I will try and help as much as I can to undo what has been done and which is wrong, but I can't support anything that will be detrimental either to my daughter or others. I am not like you, Garfield," he says in response.

"No, you are most definitely not like me, Professor," Garfield says with a wry look on his face.

"Look, you have Melrose, right? I mean, why couldn't you get all this from him. Why come to me?" Jumeau interrupts his own thinking with an aside that strikes him as something odd about Garfield, who, after all, Christophe Jumeau knew was funding Walter Melrose and had his own suspicions that this was not for entirely altruistic motives.

Garfield's contempt of Melrose comes spitting out. "That man is a fake, an idiot dressed up as a scientist. He knows less than his students, for goodness sake! But Melrose's worst feature is his plagiarism and lack of original thinking. He played a silly game. A game that he could only lose. The reason I knew I needed to speak to you is simple; while he accepted money and awards for years, with my help I should add, he hid really important advances in the field at the same time. Some of those documents are yours, do you realise that?"

Jumeau is taken aback. Quite how far his old colleague Walter Melrose had gone to make sure he got the lion's share of fame and fortune is not that surprising, but it is distasteful, and Jumeau reflects on what would have happened if either he or Melrose had walked different paths. But there is little time for conjecture or sentiment.

It's the Professor's turn to offer some insight. "He never realised the importance of entanglement, or what it means. 'Particles don't discriminate. They are the purest form of matter', that's what I used to tell him, but he never got it. But it's ironic that he has kept his own breakthrough – a *real* breakthrough if what you are telling me is correct – from being published. If entanglement can be replicated from a source pair of particles within gametes or, say, stem cells, then that suggests that entanglement could be much more prevalent than we ever imagined. And if all of the particles in a large object are entangled then that would also explain why an entire human being can super-position after all. Heck, the human race could eventually use individual worm-holes to locate to another part of the Universe where there are more bountiful resources. It could give us hope of a better existence and survival beyond any catastrophic events that may befall Earth." Jumeau is letting himself get carried away, but Garfield is mute, refusing to allow himself to get drawn into this discussion, and for very good reasons.
"That is the stuff of fantasy..." Garfield blurts out.

Given the nature of their conversation to date, and the revelations Garfield has made, Jumeau reckons it is an extremely odd thing to remark at this stage. The pair go silent for a minute or two. It is uneasy. It is filled by Elton John's vocal on 'Rocket Man'.

"Shit," says Jumeau.
"What?" replies Garfield.
"It could mean that the amount of entanglement in the Universe increases to a point where the Universe *itself* is entangled. That's mind-blowing; I can't even begin to..." Jumeau is interrupted by Garfield, who is clearly not interested in such musings. He needs to focus on the immediate task.

"Now listen up. I know this stuff is what you *do*, yes, but you can't go all blurry-eyed like this. I need you to focus, goddammit. Otherwise we have a problem. Do you want us to have a problem?" Garfield asks in a sinister tone.

"No. Absolutely, you're right of course. I just got carried away, is all..."

The pair reach the airport, and take a privately marked plane down to Washington Dulles. A black pickup collects them and takes them to Garfield's special ops unit. In the vehicle, Jumeau turns to Garfield and asks, "Who *do* you think your entangled partner is?" Garfield does not respond.

———-

"So, that's what Unitron does, huh?" asks Christophe Jumeau. He is in a large ante-room at Garfield's special ops location outside Washington, with Walter Melrose. The two haven't seen each other for some time, and it is Ellis Garfield that has brought them together in the name of science, and of course his own desperate need to escape imprisonment.

Melrose has just explained to Christophe Jumeau, on Garfield's instruction, exactly what he has discovered during his secret work under the auspices of Unitron, Melrose's brand name and front for most of his secretive research, funded initially by the State but more recently given millions of dollars in boosted revenues by Garfield personally. Melrose's revelation about the biochemistry and physiology behind the replication of the property of entanglement at cellular level has so many implications that the two men spend some time speculating on its meaning. For a short time, their checkered history and major differences are put to one side in the pursuit of knowledge.

"The only reason I couldn't go public with any of the physiology aspects is that, if I did, I'd have to reveal the whole history, including exposing Garfield as the test subject. He'd never let me do that. The next hurdle would be to get someone to verify it. It could make me the laughing stock of the whole scientific community, it's that fantastic. No-one is ready for these results. No-one would believe the inter-connectedness of everything that I have been researching," Melrose says.

"For once I think we agree. I felt the same way about twenty years ago. You know that Garfield has read my paper on reverse super-positioning?" Jumeau enquires of his one-time collaborator on military intelligence research.

"Hhmm. Yes. In fact, he's read just about everything I didn't want him to read," Melrose muses.

"It's too late to worry, Walter, everything is now out, and our job is to work with the incredible truth that is in front of us." Christophe Jumeau pauses for reflection before continuing. "Are you ready to do this?" he asks.

Melrose takes a deep breath, sucking in as much air as he can as if he is just about to attempt a long swim underwater to freedom, which may end up in him drowning, or escaping. One of the two. He lets the air out as he speaks. "I have no choice. Neither do you."

"Yes, but we may as well do it as best we can, otherwise we could all lose, and lose heavily," Jumeau replies, and Melrose nods in resigned agreement.

Melrose lurches over to the table and gingerly takes a seat, still feeling sore from the rough treatment he has endured over the last few hours. "Just one thing, Christophe. Have you always known that your daughter has special abilities?"

The question hangs in the air like a bad smell, before Jumeau simply says "What would you have done, Walter?" Melrose doesn't respond. He is a father too, and he guesses that Christophe would have been happy if Catherine had never discovered those abilities.

A little later Garfield enters, clearly in a bit of a rush.

"I need to know that this will work," he says once he has grabbed some air. "Give me the risks as well as the process."

Christophe glances at Walter Melrose, who indicates his comfort with Jumeau taking the lead. "OK, here's what we think from what we know so far. Bear in mind that we're obviously crystal-ball gazing to a certain extent...." he says, looking toward Garfield but quickly realising this is not what Garfield wants to hear. "Well, anyway, common sense would tend us toward saying that if you could find your location prior to the President's assassination, then all you need to do is make sure you are not with the President at the time that would have been the moment of his demise, if you know what I mean." Jumeau doesn't want to spell out the word 'murder' or 'assassination' and both Melrose and Garfield get this. It is still an uncomfortable moment though. "Now, here is the tricky bit. In this reality, where the President is fine, there would be no need for Gill or Catherine to locate there to prevent something that didn't happen, so, rather counter-intuitively we need you to locate *twice.*"

Garfield looks puzzled. "And why is that?" he asks.

"Because you need to find Gill and my daughter, that's why. They are your key to freedom. They are trapped back there somewhere. Most likely because Gill went back, got trapped somehow, and Catherine followed him when he didn't return. Do you understand? We know that Gill travelled back on his own – this makes sense as he was probably trying to protect Catherine. Besides, your men were following them and told you that Gill wasn't with her. Our guess is that Catherine super-positioned back precisely because something went wrong. We can only assume that Gill missed the timing and was unable to prevent you...prevent the President's death."

Garfield is beginning to get it. Melrose takes up the story.

"There are no certainties here, Ellis. The truth is we don't know if they are OK; we can only guess what might have happened. Ideally, your first stop is probably best to be a few hours after the time that you were with the President. That way, you will be able to find Gill at least, and most likely Catherine if they managed to find each other. Now, this is the most important thing for you to remember. You *must* be able to communicate with Gill and Catherine to the point where they know that they can resolve everything by all three of you super-positioning at once. This is going to be very difficult, and you may encounter things that you couldn't have predicted, so you'll have to be on your toes. You will need to wait on them, and my best guess is that they will try and lead you in to their own worm-hole. If you can get a vision of that – we think most probably the metaphor is a field of some description – then go towards it and, well, I guess that's where we say 'over to you', because, frankly, we have no idea what happens beyond that point. Our *hope* is that from there, you can do two things. First, you locate back to the day of the assassination and ensure the President is safe at the exact point of his death, and secondly, somehow work with Gill and Catherine to help you find your entangled partner."

Garfield looks pensive, his eyes darting from side to side as he fights to understand the intricacies of what he has to accomplish in order to achieve his primary goal.

"But what about *me*? The me back there. What happens if I see *me*?" he asks.

Melrose looks worried. "You *must not* encounter yourself back there. To do so would lead to unpredictable results."

"Like?" Garfield wants Melrose to be specific.

"Well, for example, it could be that both instances of you collapse into one on observing or identifying one another. That could be fusion or fission of particles for example. It's not clear exactly what might happen in such a situation, so you really should avoid that if you can," Melrose states, sounding much more anxious now.

"It's like that, huh?" Garfield mutters, clearly perturbed. "And if I do pull this off? You are saying that the here and now will be as if nothing happened?"

Christophe Jumeau senses Garfield's growing anxiety, and decides to step in. He walks over to Garfield and looks him straight in the eye.

"You realise we are dealing with some pretty heavy stuff here, I know. With past, present and future. It's a bit of a mind-rush. Well, it is for me. I have always dealt with the theory of such things, and hardly ever the practice. It's amazing to think that you have the capacity to do this kind of thing. And if you're right about my daughter, it makes me anxious, sure. So I share your sense of caution, and the need to know certain things. The way I see it is that the future is being made all the time. We are making it right now. But the future is co-creating the past too. Right now there are many paths available to us. In one past I might act by destroying a life, for example."

Jumeau sees the glare in Garfield's eyes, but carries on before he has a chance to react.

"If we could go back and change things so that such a life was preserved, then the amendment to history would have consequences for our *now*. So that might mean that the here and now is the same, or it could mean that it is quite different. That's what's unpredictable – the fact that between that change to history and now, there are many other possible pathways to be explored."

Melrose and Garfield are transfixed on Jumeau's account, highly speculative as it may be. After a pause for a deep breath, Jumeau continues.

"My best guess, for what it's worth, is that the further back in time one travels to change a major event like someone's death, the more profound the impact will be, because so many possibilities arising from that one change have time to effect other changes and so on. A bit like a three-D domino toppling where one train of dominoes might affect another, and another, and so on ad infinitum. But we are keeping to recent history here, and in a relatively well-defined spatial area. There is less time for the here and now to be affected very greatly, I would imagine, if we are only looking at a matter of days between Montgomery's death and today."

Walter Melrose begins to nod his head. He sees the logic Christophe is applying, and how it is calming Garfield who nods too, before frowning. He has spotted another problem.

"And what about the other two – I mean, how the hell am I going to avoid observing them, or them observing me and everything just collapsing?" Garfield enquires.
Jumeau gets in quickly. "Listen, I have been thinking about this. It's related to this thing about the TV address. The reason that no-one could trap you is because no-one was actually there dualling or measuring your behaviour in that location. If you can all communicate with each other, either by biocell or computer, you should be able to do it. But, as the Professor says, once you get to that worm-hole together, who knows what will happen."

Garfield reflects on Jumeau's words. Jumeau considers his next statement very carefully.

"Mr. Garfield, if I may..." he says. Garfield looks over at the large-framed Jumeau in anticipation.

"You are a father, yes?" Jumeau asks. Garfield hesitates for a moment, before nodding very slowly.

"I need you to understand that my child is out there. Will you promise that you won't jeopardize my daughter's life. Will you make me that promise? It means everything to me, Sir."

Garfield turns to the two men who are looking expectantly at the tall figure holding the key to a brighter future for them both. Walter Melrose and Christophe Jumeau watch in amazement as the face of John Montgomery begins to emerge through Garfield's jagged features.

"I understand, Professor. I will do what I can. It's all I can offer." Even the voice sounds like John Montgomery.

The two older men smile instinctively, for they both understand that John Montgomery is still alive in some form, talking to them through Garfield. It is a sign of hope. Yet before they can bask in that warmth, the features shift and return to that of Garfield. And with it, the face of the two academics also darken, as if eclipsed by the President's shadow.

Garfield turns away and walks towards the door. As he reaches for the handle, he turns back. "Just one thing - my entangled partner. How will I know?"

"Oh, I think you will *know*," says Jumeau assuredly.

Garfield looks pensive and tries to find some words of expression, but nothing comes. Perhaps there is too much going on in his mind. Garfield is momentarily lost, and his distant sparkling eyes focus on Jumeau's kindly face. It is only in the pause that Christophe, following many hours of deliberation on this, offers some parting words.

"I don't think you are a bad person, Mr Garfield. I think I know that you have struggled for a long time here on Earth, and that this is perhaps not the place for you. We are a funny lot. We hold dear certain values and principles some of the time, and yet at other times we break all our own rules and destroy what we should cherish. It must be confusing for you, and I dare say some of what you have seen here is truly corrupting. We still have much to learn. As it is here on Earth, if your partner is looking for you at the same time as you are looking for them, that will be of enormous help. I can only hope that when you reunite with your partner and perhaps get the chance to go home, you take the best of what you have seen here, and not the worst."

Walter Melrose is fixated on Jumeau, his old foe. He drags his stare away and looks across to Garfield who manages a hesitant smile. After a slight nod, he departs without a sound.

* * * *

CHAPTER 10: TRANSFORMATIONS

'I have to move', Catherine signals to Gill.

She is in severe discomfort on the hard metal floor of the high-security van. Gill nods in acknowledgement. He's using the time during the journey to try and figure out their best course of action, his biggest worry that both of them have lost the capacity to dual.

Catherine moves gingerly, trying to keep her head down to avoid being seen through the rear window. As she reaches out to stabilize her path by pushing on the left-hand wall of the van, the front wheel of the vehicle hits a pothole in the road causing the driver to swerve to avoid a collision with a passing car. Catherine loses her balance and is bumped from one wall to the other before grabbing desperately for Gill's outstretched hand.

He grasps her at the wrist. The sheer strength of his grip saves Catherine from being thrown around any more and getting hurt. And in that moment of touch, so too there is a glimmer of hope. The moment stretches somewhat, and although a pale shadow of their initial contact, nevertheless there is something there. In that instant, both sense that the connection is not lost; that although they are trapped in this nightmare world, their entanglement remains.

A further violent shudder of the van breaks the moment and sends Catherine hurtling away. She grabs for a handle up high on the rear corner of the compartment. As this is her only connection to the frame of the van, and her only way to prevent herself being tossed around like a rag doll, she cannot control the twisting movement that follows, and is squashed momentarily against the back rear window of the van as the driver regains control.

In that second, her long flowing hair and obvious femininity are revealed to the driver and passenger in the convoy vehicle behind. Both men look first in disbelief at the image they witness, and then

look to each other for some form of acknowledgement that
something is wrong.

"Did you see that?" the driver asks in a somewhat shrill voice
for a trained security man, his incredulity getting the better of him.

"Yeh, that's not right. Tell them to pull over," says Tomas
Schecter. He is as surprised as his colleague in the van, but has
quickly calculated that this is his chance to seize an early
opportunity to dispose of his target. The alternative is to wait until
the Air Force base, as planned. But that represents a potentially
riskier environment, and hazardous escape route. This way, he can
probably ensure the disposal of the target and fewer counter-threats
from the convoy personnel.

Just outside Morningside, and within five minutes of Andrews
Air Force base, the three vehicles in the convoy pull over to the hard
shoulder and come to a halt. To passing motorists the convoy
remains still, without movement. But inside there is a flurry of
activity among the security guards. Devi and Paul are in the lead
armored car. Larry and Rob are in the main van. Vinnie and Tomas
are in the rear van. Walkie talkies are sounding off without cessation.

The front doors to the lead car open and two uniformed security
officers - Devi and Paul, part of the crack team given the task of
ensuring delivery of the most wanted man in America to the nearby
airport - run over to the front of the van carrying Gill and Catherine,
who are waiting nervously in the back. Gill is shackled. Catherine,
while hurt by being thrown against the walls and doors, is free to
move.

"What's the problem, Larry?" Devi asks of his colleague in the
front of the main van.

"Looks like Vinnie back there saw another person in the cell.
You want to check that out? We'll cover."

There is no window from the driver's cabin to the back where
the security compartment is located, because too many visuals were
known to affect the security personnel which could lead to them
opening the doors of the compartment in error. The CCTV camera is
pointing to the rear right corner, with no-one there. Larry nods, and

he and his driver, Rob, exit the main van to go round the back to open the doors.

As they get to the rear of the van and open the doors, two shots fire in quick succession. Larry and Rob drop to the ground instantly with fatal bullet-wounds to the back of the head, losing consciousness instantly as their cerebral cortexes are torn apart from the inside. The convulsion that follows is the body's natural reaction to intense trauma. To the untrained eye it looks like the men are still alive and struggling to survive, but in fact they have no chance. They are already dead.

Two further shots follow shortly after. Two seconds later, a further shot rings out. Within a few seconds, five men are down.

The first four shots have been fired by Tomas Schecter. The third and fourth hit Devi and Paul from the front car as they come running around to the back to check what is happening with Larry and Rob.

At this point, Catherine and Gill are completely trapped in the back of the van. Catherine shouts "Gill!" as she sees the doors open and the figure of Schecter silhouetted against the bright sunshine. She instinctively knows he has come for them and scrambles to try and get over to close the door. If they die here they die forever.

Gill is trying to shift his position to see what is happening, when Thomas Schecter aims the guiding laser beam directly at Gill's forehead and prepares to pull the trigger. As his finger squeezes towards the point of no return, the fifth shot rings out.

It is the fifth shot in the sequence that will change the course of history.

Tomas Schecter looks down to Devi Rashan. He is dying of a gunshot wound to the neck, and blood is seeping out all around him. With intense pain etched across his face, he eventually drops his stare at Schecter. At which point, Tomas Schecter, hired to kill Denton Gill, falls to his knees. He has been shot in the chest. A single bullet has ruptured the main aorta in his heart, and although it is still beating and pumping blood around his body, it is also leaking and slowing down. The lack of blood pressure in his system forces the squat, powerful man to kneel, as if in worship to his slayer. As his system struggles insanely to cope with the inner trauma of a bullet to the heart, consciousness fades, his world becoming blurred and all of his professional focus descending into a desperate fight just to stay alive. But it's futile. He has been downed by Officer

Rashan, who was able to get off one shot before being incapacitated fully by the process of his own demise.

Catherine and Gill have witnessed most of this, sitting petrified and helpless in the back of the armored van. In the haze of the few seconds that it has taken for rapid-fire events to occur, one or two cars have slowed down near them, then sped up, presumably fearing that they may be subject to gunfire, or possible hijacking.

Besides that, things seem to have stabilized. Gill looks over to Catherine, quickly assessing that, although terribly shaken, she is OK. There is a pause. It is the pause that exists because neither knows if there are more people at the scene. It is only the paradoxically calming sound of the traffic on the freeway and the lack of anything else, that makes them think that they are now alone.

"Get me out of these things!" he shouts, deliberately forcing her to snap out of any shock with which she might be struggling. She responds first with a quizzical look, as if she can't quite bring herself to acknowledge what has happened, and then, with a widening of her pupils, a firm response.

"OK, wait here," she says, as she jumps down and surveys the scene. It is truly shocking, and makes her stop in hesitation.

"Go on, find the keys, Catherine. Stay focused," Gill instructs, this time in a more measured way. She turns to look at him. It is obvious that she is battling her own trauma, never having seen anything like this before in her life.

"Catherine! We have to get away from here!" Gill shouts.

Her reaction is critical – she responds to Gill's voice as if it is the only thing that cuts through all the sound of traffic and her own screaming inside. Moving over to Rashan, she takes the ring of keys attached to his belt and throws them into Gill. As Gill desperately tries to find the right key, Catherine reflects on the deaths of all these men, and the fact that she and Gill are directly responsible. They clearly need to undo this awful mess. Her spirits sink as she contemplates how badly wrong her super-positioning to find Gill has gone. Self-loathing washes over her like a heavy wave of opiate, slowing her right down and producing in her a catatonic aspect. She is transfixed by Rashan's face, a handsome man, cut down in his prime. Her lament is for his family, and she wonders about them, as she does about her own. She is so far from her mom and dad right now that all she would really like to do is regress back to the womb, warm and insulated from the realities of the world and the need to deal with the millions of possibilities it offers, good and bad.

After a seeming eternity, she manages to free Gill.

Now hands-free, he jumps down from the back of the security van and walks over to Schecter's body. The marksman's frame is small and compact. He would be unnoticeable in many situations, which presumably has many advantages. Catherine shouts something, which is enough to break his momentary fascination with Schecter, allowing his police brain to kick into action. He searches the hitman's body for anything that might give him and Catherine information as to Garfield's whereabouts. Gill is about to give up after finding nothing, when, about ten yards away, light bouncing off a metallic object strikes him in the eye. Raising a hand to shield the glare, he moves round to the back of the rear-most vehicle in the convoy. He is now in clear view of passing traffic, and feels exposed. He quickly grabs the device and runs back to Catherine. The pair are now acutely aware of time, which seems to have returned to some form of normality, and in a shared sense of panic run round to the front car of the convoy. The engine is still running, and after helping Catherine into the car, Gill puts his foot down on the gas and speeds off onto the freeway. It has been barely a minute since the convoy came to a halt.

"Oh Gill, what have we done?" asks Catherine, trembling and still in shock.

Gill is trying to think through the situation while surveying front and back on the freeway for any chasing vehicles – it would surely be no time at all before a major alert is raised and every route will be swarming with police and special service operations personnel.

"Listen to me," says Gill, rather anxiously, "things are bad, I know, but we have to focus. You got that?" Catherine is looking down at her hands. Gill is too busy thinking to try another time. "That guy wasn't part of the security services taking me over to the airport. My guess is that he was hired by Garfield to take me out."

Gill turns to Catherine and focuses on her face for the first time since the panic set in during the shootings. "The only way out of this situation is to find Garfield and get him to call off the dogs. Have a look at this guy's phone and see if there are any numbers there," he prompts her.

"OK," says Catherine, opening up the phone and beginning to navigate the menu system, "but what good is that going to do? I mean, if he's going to kill us, he's going to kill us, right?"

"Calm down. He wants to kill *me*. He most likely doesn't know that you are here. He wants to get rid of me because he knows that I arrived at the scene of the assassination and he thinks that I saw him kill the President. If he suspects that I have anything on him then he is still in danger of being caught. And of course forensics won't turn up anything on me. He knows that too," Gill remarks.

"So what *did* you see when you dualled to the Capitol building? Was it Garfield?" Catherine asks.

"I can't be certain, but it *felt* like it was him. He observed me before I could really get a handle on what it was that happened. But I did see a gun, and my gut feel is that there are probably some subtle forensics that I could get him with," Gill replies.

"But you can't go back. We're both trapped here, and we can't *dual*. So whatever we do has to be in the here and now," she reminds him.

"I know," Gill reflects. "What's on that phone?" he asks.

Catherine fumbles through the menu system on the rather unremarkable phone she is holding. "There's only one number here!" she exclaims.

Gill looks across at her. "Really?" he asks. Catherine nods, before giving him the phone. Gill takes the next exit off the freeway and pulls into a diner along a wide boulevard. He needs to turn around in any case, so turning off the freeway is a good idea, as well as providing a way to avoid being followed.

As he comes to a stop, the pair exit the car and walk across to the modest diner. Gill checks the number on the phone. It reads simply 'Steve'. The are two missed calls from 'Steve' in the last few minutes. Gill has no idea who this is, but guesses that it can only be Garfield.

—-

Five minutes earlier, Ellis Garfield was following the convoy along the freeway. Having super-positioned back to try and find Gill and Catherine, it was relatively easy to find out where they were, given the high profile nature of the security operation around Gill, the prime suspect in the assassination of President Montgomery. In his usual disguise, and under the name of Steve Nelson, he is planning to make contact with Gill at the airport ahead. He will need to reveal himself as the President and ask the security guards to stand down to allow him to talk to the suspect. Even then, he'll have to ensure that he doesn't come face-to-face with Detective Gill in case he is observed and trapped. It's a lousy plan, full of risk, but there is no alternative he believes at this late stage.

Several hours ago Tomas Schecter received an order to eliminate Gill when they reach the airport. It came from his other self of course, in this reality. The imminent hit on Gill is a complication he is going to have to deal with immediately.

A rush of adrenaline pumps into his stomach as he watches the three-vehicle convoy pull over onto the hard shoulder some way ahead. 'Ho hum' he hears himself saying. This is unplanned. In the space of time it takes him to reach the scene, he can see sparks fly and hear the shots ringing out. He pulls in behind the last car just in time to see Tomas Schecter falling to his knees. He opens his window and peers out his to see how bad it is. Out of the corner of his eye he sees two people inside the secure cell of the second van, and senses instantly it is Jumeau and Gill. He can't get close to Schecter without being seen, so he throws the cell phone as near to him as he can in the hope that Gill will find it. As part of his plan to communicate with Gill he has bought two new cell phones. It's not a good throw, and it lands a few feet away. He hesitates. He cannot risk being observed super-positioning. The mission will fail in such a circumstance. The decision is made and he speeds off trying to avoid looking directly at the scene, or anyone there.

He pulls over about a mile further up the freeway and keeps a sharp lookout for Gill and Catherine, guessing that they will use one of the convoy vehicles to make their escape. He gets one of the pair of phones out, and goes to the phonebook. There is one number in it.

—-

"What am I looking at here?" Ava Redmond is sitting behind her desk. Ortega, Hart, Nicolescu and Kirkland are sat round her desk. Phil Kirkland is presenting initial findings from the first twelve hours of surveillance commissioned by the Chief of Intelligence. Projected on a drop-down white canvas screen on one wall is a series of portrait photographs of Ellis Garfield's face from different events over the last few weeks lined up chronologically left to right. Some are clearer than others, but the progression is the aspect that Kirkland wants to bring to people's attention.

"OK, everyone, I'd like you to look at the dates on each of these photographs, then the facial details. These are all of Ellis Garfield, March last year through to the latest photograph, taken yesterday."

Each of the group takes a little time on Kirkland's cue to scrutinize the photos and the dates. There is a noticeable silence, before Redmond breaks this to check what is being offered.

"Is this a test of observation, Phil? I don't know about anyone else, but that last one doesn't look like the same person. I'd say that last one is a photo of John Montgomery, right?" Redmond asks.

"No, Ava. It can't be, it was taken yesterday. That's my point. We have something exceptionally strange going on here. Garfield is not only taking on the facial features of John, but even his skin is darker, and I have noticed his walk is different too. On a couple of long shots on White House CCTV, one of the security guards mentioned off-hand that Garfield was now walking with that quasi-limp that John has...*had*. I reviewed the tape and he's right."

"It's uncanny," interjects Maria Ortega, genuinely bemused by the revelation, "but what does it mean? Is Ellis Garfield turning into John Montgomery? Is that it?"

"Or Mr Montgomery is still alive in Ellis Garfield?" Nicolescu offers.

Abe Hart, tired of the conjecture, pitches in. "Folks. Why are we speculating on this? We can all see that something exceptional is taking place in the President, and that it's not normal. In fact, it's just bizarre. We aren't going to solve anything here. We need to stop pussyfooting around and get him tested. Heck, get him a full medical and see what the hell is going on. No choice in the matter. Put him under arrest if need be."

Ava Redmond gets up and paces around the room. "What else?" she asks directly to Kirkland, who shuffles through a small folder to consult his notes.

"OK, three things. First, two absences from his quarters in the last two days. One where he locked himself in his study for two hours. Didn't respond to calls until security were on the point of forcing entry. Nothing on his computer though. He wasn't active on that the whole time he was in there. That's the odd thing. Our hypothesis was that he was in contact with others using the Internet or internal pass-coded comms. But that's not it. It doesn't make sense. We still don't know what he is actually doing in there. We even tested for traces of drugs, things like that. Nothing." Kirkland allows a little space for anyone to chip in, but no-one has anything to offer, so he presses on.

"Secondly, we looked at the research side. This relationship with the eminent Professor Melrose. We've checked with his department up at Harvard, and not only has the Professor not checked in for a couple of days, but he has three PhD students, all missing. The staff are very worried. Mentioned that a Detective Gill from the local police department had visited the Professor when a couple of the students had first been reported missing. I've put people on this, and I'd like to make it priority," Kirkland says.

"Why so absolute on this, Phil? There are thousands of missing persons across the country at any one time - what's the hypothesis here?" asks Redmond.

"Well, it's the connection to the President, Ma'am. It is well-known that Melrose has received generous funding from the State Department to conduct leading-edge research into new technologies around physics and the nature of reality. We also know that some of this is military-grade. In other words, some of the developments may be game-changing in nature. We know that Montgomery was on the verge of ordering an inquiry into some of that research – my guess being that this was because he suspected Garfield of hiding some of Melrose's findings from both the research community and the military itself. We currently don't know why this would be."

"What's the nature of this technology, Phil?" asks Ortega.

Kirkland glances over at his colleague. "Mitch, do you want to take this one?" Nicolescu nods.

"OK, so I've looked at this from a worst-case scenario to be on the safe side, and I guess I can offer a certain amount of reassurance

in the first instance before we all get really hot under the collar."
Nicolescu initiates his briefing with a note on context, and it serves
to calm the group to an extent.

"Most importantly, I don't believe that any of the technology –
which is based around 'cloaking' of objects so that they cannot be
seen, and the possibility of remotely placing surveillance devices
wherever we like in the world – is operational in the field. I am
talking about, literally, sending physical bugging devices behind
enemy lines to check on what they are doing, building, planning etc,
without the need for local agents or in fact any secret bases. This has
not been deployed anywhere as far as we know. The trajectory for
deployment is probably two to three years. The details of the
research itself is obviously highly classified".

"You mean it's in our possession and no-one else's?" asks Abe
Hart.

"This may be a problem. Walter Melrose is missing. Not only
that, but his housekeeper reported a break-in the other night. Seems
like someone was looking for more information about the research –
maybe some papers he had at his home," Nicolescu adds.

"So, did they get anything? Do we know that?" asks Ortega this
time.

"It's unclear. They could have come up empty-handed or
discovered some further papers. We just don't know, as the Professor
isn't here to tell us," Nicolescu replies.

Ava Redmond interjects. She has heard enough to know that
there is a serious problem but needs to pull things together. "So what
is your conclusion, gentlemen? What are we looking at here?" she
asks.

There is a pause while Nicolescu prompts Kirkland to take up
the response.

"OK. Remember we have to look at things worst-case and work
backwards, right?" Kirkland states. The group nod in agreement. He
walks across to the images on the wall and peers at Ellis Garfield's
latest photograph, a dead-ringer for John Montgomery. He takes a
deep breath and exhales hard.

"Keep your minds open here – we need to think tangentially,"
he warns. "I believe we are dealing with someone who has
developed certain...capabilities. Capabilities that we might find

strange. I am not even sure if they are under control. But whatever the case, they need to be investigated fully."

Maria Ortega and Abe Hart are looking at Kirkland sceptically, while Ava Redmond, having access to the entire history of weird and wonderful, including paranormal and suspected extra-terrestrial encounters, is rather more sanguine. She would really like Kirkland, who she has known for years and considers a friend as well as one of the best security people in the country, to hurry-the-fuck-up and stop making a song and dance of it.

Kirkland, in the absence of any interjection, carries on, knowing that they all want him to explain what he means. "I spent a lot of time mulling over all the connections here. Melrose's research, Garfield's disappearances, his adoption of the features of John Montgomery, and of course Montgomery's assassination. The assassination that has no clues. No trail. No evidence. No suspect or suspects. The strangest crime I have have ever encountered..." he trails off, leaving the rest to ponder this for a moment. It serves to tee-up the conclusion he has arrived at.

"We have to conclude two things in all this. The first is that Garfield has some form of capacity to do something akin to astral projection. You know this term?" he asks, and everyone nods. "But it's more than this. My take on things is that he is somehow able to jump around from place to place without us knowing. I don't know how exactly he can do this, but I have an idea that it came about during his term of duty in Antarctica some years ago. That's when everything seems to have changed with him. If you watch the CCTV tapes of him alone, there are times when he just goes into some sort of trance. Or at least, gets himself into a position where he doesn't seem to move for long periods. Now, most humans will fidget. If you ran a time-lapse camera on anyone sitting in a chair, they will shift around very visibly. When you do that with Garfield, he doesn't move at all. During these times, I think he is able to locate himself somewhere else. In fact, I think the technology that Walter Melrose has developed can not only allow surveillance devices to travel huge distances instantly in order to provide intelligence to us from afar, but – and this is a stretch, I know – I believe Melrose worked with Garfield on something bigger than that."

Redmond looks searchingly into Kirkland's eyes. She knows him well enough to know that he wouldn't come out with this stuff unless he had good reason.

"You're saying that Ellis Garfield and Walter Melrose colluded to build Garfield some sort of machine that allows him to travel through space instantly. And that this has been used to do what? What do you suspect Garfield is doing with this, and how does this relate to Montgomery?" Redmond quizzes him.

"I'm not so sure it's even a machine, Ma'am. Well, I said that there were two things. The other is that I think that he might have used his ability – however he does it - to get into the washroom at the Capitol Building," Kirkland speculates.

Abe Hart butts in. "You've gone this far, Phil, you may as well go the whole hog. Are you going to tell us that Garfield killed Montgomery? That's what's next, right?"

"It's one possibility. If you accept that Garfield has some form of capacity for instant projection of himself to anywhere he wants, it might be that he isn't that good at it and he jumped into the John with President Montgomery by accident, but I'd be surprised. What's less certain is whether or not he meant to kill him. It could have been that he just wanted to scare Montgomery away from starting an investigation into what he and Melrose were up to and things went terribly wrong. We may never know this unless we can indict him and try him with evidence from Melrose."

"I don't get it," says Maria Ortega, struggling with some of the concepts involved here. "How did he come to get this kind of power? What happened to him? Has he always been like that and, if so, why wouldn't we have picked this up from his army or medical records?"

Kirkland comes back quickly. "I interviewed Julie Garfield yesterday evening. Turns out that something happened to him when he was down in Antarctica. She began to see big changes in her husband but didn't report it as she feared it would affect his career. She would have most likely put this down to post-traumatic stress – most wives do. Her take on it is that his whole character changed; he seemed so determined to gain power and influence beyond what he had ever desired as a younger man. He was like a different person after that tour."

"Has she ever reported him, uh, doing this double-act thing where he jumps around?" Ortega follows up.

"No, that's the thing. He turned from being a family guy to a kind of recluse – seeming to need a lot of space to himself. Again, she just put it down to trauma."

"But wouldn't he just disappear if he 'jumped' some place else? I mean, we'd see him disappear, right?" Ortega fathoms, trying to get her head around the mechanics of the thing.

Redmond chips in. "Not necessarily, I've heard about this. I think it's termed super-positioning, right?"

Kirkland and Nicolescu both look over to Redmond, impressed by her quick take-up, and nod in unison. Redmond smiles. It is a light moment in an otherwise tense and challenging environment. She carries on, buoyed up by the fact that she is as knowledgeable about the scientific aspects of this as anyone else in the room. "It's a known fact in physics that things can actually be in two places at once. The key is that this happens when we are not looking. If we try and measure the location of one of the instances of the thing that is super-positioned, then the whole thing collapses back to the original reality. Right?" One or two nods ensue round the room. "Well, that's probably why Garfield might appear to be in his study but is actually somewhere else."

"Hold up, just one second," says Abe Hart. "Are we actually saying that the President of the United States can be in two places at the one time, assassinated John Montgomery, has got rid of Melrose and his crew, and is now concocting some fiendish plot to...well, to do what? It's all sounding a bit ridiculous to me. It's just too fantastic, isn't it?"

Ava Redmond has been the Head of Intelligence for a while now, and has found her feet in the job. As part of her remit, she regularly has to absorb reports on surveillance and counter-intelligence. Most are unremarkable to someone in her position, who is time-served in the intelligence field and has seen many strange phenomena. It is from this privileged position that she can provide a more open reception for seemingly far-fetched theories. In this case, Kirkland's somewhat sketchy conclusions lack the sort of rigor that she would normally expect before deciding to act on things. On this occasion she knows that something needs to be done. She just isn't sure at this point what that should be. And there is something missing in Phil's argument.

"OK, folks. Now listen up, I want everyone to keep their minds receptive to this. I have seen some research and intelligence which would support the idea that the deployment of instant space-travel technology is not as far off as we may think. In fact, it surprises me that this stuff is not in operation by now, given the plausibility of the science." Her voice is calm, and strong. The rest of the group are happy to take her lead. She turns to Kirkland, giving Nicolescu and Ortega brief glances to include them in the line of questioning.

"We have motive; the discovery of the research. We have means; Garfield's super-positioning – however he does that. We have supporting evidence; Melrose and his staff's disappearance and our own surveillance records. But there's something missing; where is all this leading? Where is it going to end?" she asks.

Kirkland and Nicolescu breathe in. It is Maria Ortega who offers insight. She has been in listening mode for most of the discussion, but is about to offer a critical piece of the jigsaw.

"That's why Garfield is all over the place...." she mutters.
"What's that?" Abe Hart asks her.
"That's why Garfield is such a mess and can't function. He has been infected somehow by Montgomery. Something has happened to him when Montgomery died, and it is killing him. What would happen if, while super-positioning, you killed someone. The energy of that person whose life you stole would be in that space. It wouldn't be impossible that somehow Garfield attracted that energy and it stuck to him. Like glue. We all know how strong a character John was. And he was a *good* man, for all his faults. What if a bit of Montgomery lives on in Ellis? What if Ellis is coming apart because he can't live with it?" Ortega offers. It is highly unusual for Maria Ortega to think other than along logical lines. But in a way, she is being as logical as the situation demands.

There is creative tension in the room. The group are so far behind the actuality of what is going on, and not surprisingly so. Their minds have been trained in a certain way. To deal with due process, logical entailment, and swift reaction to immediate and urgent situations. This radical thinking session is in full swing and the group are exploring areas that otherwise would perhaps act as fanciful topics at a wild, drug-fuelled party, rather than at the heart of security services for the United States of America. Kirkland looks once more at the photos on the wall. The reality that Ortega has just painted washes over him like a breaker at the beach. He feels refreshed by it. His biggest fear for today was that Redmond and Hart would ridicule him for lurid and fantasy-driven conjecture. In fact, his left-field thinking has catalyzed a chain-reaction of thought that might just offer a way forward.

"The thing is. He is looking more like John each day. If you could project forward to the next series of photographs, you'd see him *turn into* John. He would *be* John. What does that mean?" he asks.

The group is silent. Kirkland seems to have delivered a curveball.

After a long pause, Abe Hart asks Kirkland, "What would you do if you were him?"

"Well, I guess I'd try and stop it," Kirkland answers.

"How, though?" Hart continues his line.

Kirkland hesitates. "I'd try and reverse things. I'd try to go back and make amends."

"You mean 'ask for forgiveness'?" Kirkland says.

"More like actually put the clock back," Nicolescu says, and he leans forward to look at Ava Redmond. She isn't quite getting where Nicolescu is going, and so raises her eyebrows in invitation to Mitch Nicolescu to follow through in his thinking. "You know, Ma'am, we have only been talking about the space dimension, but we all know that the time dimension exists too. You must have some reports on the possibility of time-travel. Heck, the world has been fascinated by it for hundreds of years. Could Mister Garfield perhaps jump around in time as well as in space?"

Redmond's piercing green eyes fix on Nicolescu, as she says, "Good point, Mitch. Carry on..." in a forthright and encouraging way. There has been a plethora of research on time travel and it has become a primary feature of many research projects of late. Mitch Nicolescu isn't an expert on such things, but accepts the prompt to go for it.

"Well, it's the clearing up business. I mean, if it was me, and Montgomery was just driving me crazy, I'd try and undo the whole lot. I mean, the *whole* lot – all the bad stuff. Try and re-create a world where everything wasn't truly...messed up," he explains, judging that the expletive he was going to use was better left out.

Everyone gets it. It's a strange atmosphere now. To reach this point seems to have taken its toll on people. The key question remains; 'where do we go from here?'

Redmond has to be as decisive as possible. There is little time to lose, she assesses, given the volatile nature of Garfield, and the evidence that is before her.

"OK folks, I think I've heard enough. Phil, Mitch, we need to bring Garfield in. I want him placed under house arrest within the next hour. Make sure it is all done properly. If you need to, get my secretary to process the necessary paperwork and I'll sign off as soon as. And give some thought to ways in which we can trace his movements – how we can tell if he's doing his *thing*. Rope in whoever you need to do that from the scientific community. There must be other people who know about this kind of stuff apart from Melrose. Maria, Abe, I need you to put together the possible indictment terms, and a line of questioning to get two things sorted. One, we need a positive statement as to his whereabouts at the time of Montgomery's murder; check out who was with him around that time, before and after, and get statements as to his demeanor, behavior, actions, that kind of thing. Two, get me the head of forensics who looked at that scene. I simply can't believe that there is *nothing* there. If someone else was in that room with John then there must be traces of that person there. Some sort of DNA imprint or something. Don't take no for an answer – those guys need to think outside the box too."

Redmond pauses to take stock, looking up at the picture of John Montgomery.

"Everybody. Last thing," she says. "This is still at circulation zero. Use your staff carefully, keep the function of the exercise as close to your chest as you possibly can. And no press. If anyone lets any of this slip, I'll haul your ass over so many hot coals you won't be able to sit down for a month. Got that?"

Hart and Ortega seem a bit bemused at Redmond's command of the situation, but remain silent. Kirkland nods. Nicolescu blurts out

"Sir" at the same time, apparently to Redmond. He flushes slightly at his automatic response which reveals the regard in which he sees Redmond, and quickly exits the room. Everyone now knows what they are doing, and everyone is struggling to come to terms with why they are doing it.

——-

Ava Redmond is on the phone to Julie Garfield. The President's wife is happy to speak to her. She is worried about her husband and he hasn't called her in the last twenty-four hours.

"Hello Ava. How are you?" Julie enquires. The two know each other from various business and social events, and get on reasonably well. Ava recognizes some of the suffering Julie is going through, and, apart from her current task to get information from her, genuinely wants to wish her well and reassure her about developments. But she can't.

"I'm good, Julie, just fine. Listen I called for a quick chat about Ellis. I'll get straight to the point; we think that he's struggling and seems to be shirking engagements required in conducting Presidential affairs. We really need to understand how to help him the best we can. I hope I'm not being too forward in all of this, Julie. I wouldn't have intruded on you and the kids like this if the level of concern weren't significant."

Redmond sets the tone of the discussion up front.

"I see. Well, thanks for that Ava. I appreciate your candor. Truth be told I don't know what has happened to Ellis. We just don't see much of him these days and I feel I can't really take much more," she replies.

Ava Redmond is concerned. It's worse than she thought. Julie Garfield sounds depressed.

"Julie, do you want to come down here? It might be nicer for you and the kids to come down and we'll sort some down time for you and Ellis. How about that?" she asks.

"Yes, I guess. Although it won't make any difference I don't think. He's just unable to focus on his family and I can't see that changing."

'Listen Julie, there is something that we're looking at here which we think might be significant in Ellis' lack of focus. I know that you've said in the past that Ellis seemed to go through some major changes after returning from his last duty in Antarctica. Can I ask you what, in your mind, you think happened to him there? It might be important in trying to help him."

Julie Garfield doesn't hesitate. She has kept so much to herself for the sake of her husband's career over the years, and it has ripped her apart, ruining her relationship with Ellis and his relationship with the kids, which seems non-existent most of the time.

"Oh Ava, I can't begin to tell you where things have changed so much. I don't know what happened to him, but it felt like I just got a shell of a man back after that tour. I didn't see him for months when he was at the field hospital. He has never told me what happened but you can be sure that it was something really life-changing. He has never been the same since. Like I lost the man I knew and loved somewhere in that cold place," Julie says.

"I'm so sorry, Julie," Redmond responds, offering a warm tone as some form of comfort. "Come down here, Julie. I think he may need you. Listen, one last thing..."

"Yes?" Julie Garfield says, fully engaged with Redmond at a woman-to-woman level as much as anything else.

"Have you noticed any physical changes in Ellis either since Antarctica, or even just it the last few days?"

There is a slight pause. It seems awkward. Redmond is about to offer a get-out for Julie Garfield when there is a slight cough at the other end of the line. It happens again, and Redmond asks what the matter is.

"It's...well, it's just that he isn't interested in me any more. Hasn't been since back then," Julie reveals. Redmond offers her condolences and asks if there is anything else.

"That isn't enough? My God, Ava, it has been years. He has no interest whatsoever. Here he is, a fit and healthy man with lots of life in him, just not sexually motivated at all. It never used to be like that."

After the two close off the call, Redmond puts in a request for copies of Garfield's medical records. She needs to pinpoint what the 'event' was in Antarctica. What happened down there? Another request to military intelligence, this time for anything on Ellis Garfield's military record that was reported during his final tour there. Only one; Garfield was on perimeter duty at one of the mountain camps but went missing after failing to respond to a routine check-in call. He had been registered AWOL for six days but following several different searches, was found by a fellow officer only two hundred meters from the perimeter. The reporting officer is listed as Grant Naseborough, a medic serving in Garfield's outfit. The classified report includes some photographs of Garfield's body and face which are described as having 'chemical burns'. Redmond looks more closely at Garfield's face. It looks a little like Garfield but the scalp and face are entirely hairless and the skin tone is an absolutely uniform, milky-white shade. Garfield's standard issue military picture is included for comparison. Garfield's features are bold, with quite a healthy complexion, and he has a cropped, crew-cut hair. The contrast is sharp.

Redmond looks again at the photograph of Garfield post-event. The eyes are haunted, looking directly at the camera with a mix of fear and panic. It is a disturbing image. Redmond stares at it for over a minute, trying to reconcile many things in her mind, not least of which is that she is looking at the current President of the United States of America.

The next step is to get hold of Naseborough. He is now based down in Texas. After a few minutes, a call comes through to Redmond's office.

"Sergeant Naseborough speaking, Ma'am".

"Hello, Sergeant. Thank you for taking the time to talk with me. I understand you have been given instructions that this conversation has been authorized by our commanding officer and that you are now under a de-classification order?" Redmond enquires.

"Yes, that is correct, Ma'am," Naseborough confirms.

"In that case, Sergeant, let's make a start. I want to focus on two very specific things relating to the time following your discovery of

Officer Garfield the night in question. You understand what I am referring to?"

"Yes, Ma'am."

"OK, good. Now, you reported that you found Officer Garfield some days after the first report of his disappearance. Can you describe to me how you found him?"

"Uh, Ma'am, well, I remember being so happy to find him; we all thought that he'd never be found. Well, at least not alive. I recollect that it was his uniform I caught sight of first. When I approached him, he was clearly very different to the way I remembered him. I mean, Officer Garfield was hardly recognizable. At first I thought it was just his skin that looked strange. When we returned to the barracks, we got him out of his clothes and could see that his entire body had changed. We...uh that is, me and the other medics there, figured it must have been a chemical of some sort that he had been exposed to because it sure wasn't the cold that did that. I thought I had said that in the report," Naseborough replies.

"Actually, Sergeant, you say, and I quote directly again, 'Officer Garfield's facial features have been affected, and up to the time of this report, very slow progress has been made in regaining normal function'. Can you elucidate?"

"As I recall, Ma'am, it was only after some weeks later after a spell in the field hospital that Officer Garfield's normal features returned," Naseborough adds without giving any more detail.

"I see," says Redmond, "and may I ask what tests you conducted to find out what chemicals he had been exposed to?"

"Well, we had very limited resources out there, Ma'am. I think Officer Garfield himself was insistent that he be treated in the field. He didn't want anyone to see him, particularly his family, until he was better. So we only conducted basic tests, and I think there is a section in the report dealing with that. I know we didn't find anything else to report, Ma'am."

"Yes, in fact the whole thing seems very strange, Sergeant. One final question; what did Officer Garfield tell you had happened?"

There is a pause at the other end of the line.

"Sergeant?" Redmond pushes.

"Uh, Ma'am, Officer Garfield didn't actually regain any memory for some weeks. I mean, just after we found him we had to tell him his rank, the mission he was on, that he had family and friends back home and so on. Although he eventually got better, as I recall he was never able to offer an account of the incident itself. I thought that was in the report."

"No, it's not, Sergeant. Are you telling me that Garfield has never explained the incident from his point of view? That no-one actually has any clue what happened out there? I mean, is there not even a hypothesis as to what happened?"

"With respect, Ma'am, that's not something I can help you with. I just happened to be the guy who found him. I can only tell you that I have never seen anything like that. I felt really sorry for Officer Garfield – the look on him. You could see it in his eyes. It was as if he had seen something terrible and couldn't engage with reality for a while. Having said that, it doesn't seem to have done him that much harm judging by his current success," Naseborough tells Redmond. It's the latter part of the Sergeant's statement that has Redmond perplexed.

"Alright, Sergeant, that will be all for now. Thank you for your time," she says, and hangs up.

Redmond sits back in her chair and turns to stare out of the window. For a few minutes she mulls over her discussions that day. She toys with the idea of putting in a visit to Garfield herself, fascinated to get his own account of what happened. Her suspicions about Garfield now go far beyond his capacity to super-position, whether aided by machines or not, and as those thoughts take hold, Ava Redmond involuntarily shivers.

—-

The number for 'Steve' is highlighted in the phonebook of the biocell Gill has in his hand. It is highlighted because it is the only entry. Catherine is looking at him in anticipation. In this reality and in their current predicament, communication with 'Steve' is all they've got.

In the far corner of the diner, away from any prying ears, the tension is palpable. "Here goes," Gill says.

Catherine smiles at him and places her hand on his forearm. There is a moment of incredible warmth between them. Gill senses too that Catherine's touch has become more intense. She seems the stronger of the two right now. He is about to hit the dial button, when the phone vibrates. Gill drops it on the floor, muttering 'shit' to himself. For a second they both think they have inadvertently lost a call. Then a ring tone begins to emerge, getting louder each time. It is the menacing opening to 'Phat Planet' by Leftfield. The pair give each other a hesitant look. Catherine shrugs her shoulder as if to say 'don't ask me'. In that moment Gill picks it up and answers.

"Hello," he says.

"This must be Detective Gill. Do you know who I am?" comes the voice.

Gill decides not to play around. There is no time. "Yes," he replies.

"Good. We don't have much time," Garfield states.

Gill pauses for a second. It is Garfield's use of 'we' that surprises him. He switches to speakerphone so that Catherine can hear too. "What do you mean?" Gill asks.

"Long story, Detective. Suffice it to say that you will need to trust me if you want to get out of your current predicament. Can you do that?"

"I don't see why I should. You are responsible for at least one death, possibly more. I don't think trust comes into this," Gill says in a somewhat defiant tone.

"Listen to me," Garfield commands, "you are both way out of your depth here, in this place."

There is a slight pause on the line. Gill and Catherine are looking at the phone which is on the seat between them.

"You are being traced right now. The car you are in will be located by satellite mapping within minutes and the police and security services will hunt you down and take you out without hesitation. You are the most wanted pair in the history of the United States since Bonnie and Clyde. I don't think you're in a position to debate the matter, Detective Gill. You have no choice but to accept my advice," Garfield summarizes the position without emotion.

It's a hard bargaining position, and Gill knows that he and Catherine are in great danger. The one thing he will not contemplate is being put back in solitary confinement and separated from the outside world without being able to dual. They are in a corner, and Garfield is their only contact. He decides to find out what Garfield is offering.

"OK, Garfield. But you are contacting me because you want something, right? If I can help, I will." Gill's sense of negotiation and his stubbornness to concede the desperation that he feels strikes a chord somewhere within Garfield. More precisely, within John Montgomery, within Ellis Garfield.

Garfield is struggling with the need to repair. To repair the damage that he has wrought on the United States, on John Montgomery and the people around him. The strength of John Montgomery was something he hadn't accounted for in all his plans. As he hesitates on the end of the line, he knows he is playing a game against a formidable opponent. He must persuade Detective Gill to do what he wants while helping him and the girl to get back to their own world. The driver is his own salvation and a chance to return home. So desperate is he to rid himself of the human condition, the influence and infection of John Montgomery that he will do anything to get what he needs. Right now, with Montgomery dead, his soul inside Garfield, things are deteriorating by the second.

"You are right, of course. I do need something from you. My idea is that we can all help each other. I know the girl is with you. She is very talented, Detective Gill. You should be congratulated on your good taste. My belief is that the three of us can all win out of this situation if we can put our differences to one side and work together for just a few minutes," Garfield says.

Gill and Catherine throw each other a glance, and Catherine smiles a little smile. She was panicking at Gill's aggressive positioning, but is relieved that it seems to have paid off. Gill is about to respond, when Garfield follows up.

"I wonder if you two might like to consult before you decide whether this is acceptable to you? I know Miss Jumeau is with you. You can call me back on this number," he says.

This is the first time that Catherine has heard Garfield mention her name, and it causes her heart to skip a beat. A rush of adrenaline goes right through her, and she swallows hard. Gill considers Garfield's offer for a second. "Thank you, Mr Garfield. I will call you right back."

With that, the two leave the diner.

Back at the car, Catherine turns to Gill. "That man really frightens me, Gill, but we need to do this." Gill nods. She is right.

She looks like she has something else to say, so he prompts her for her thinking. She puts the window down and looks up at the sky. The sound of traffic going by and the warm air coming into the car creates a bit of space for her thoughts to escape. "I think he is struggling, Gill. I had to think hard about this, but when we saw him in the pickup truck the other day I thought I saw something very strange."

Gill looks at her with a skeptical frown, as if to say 'yeh, that *was* very strange, so what's new'. She sees this, but has a point to make. "No, I mean I saw something else. I saw John Montgomery again. I believe Montgomery is trying to get out of Garfield, or at least is dictating what Garfield has to do."

"You mean we are dealing with Montgomery as well as Garfield? Well, it's possible. If Garfield murdered him, then maybe part of Montgomery got inside Garfield and is struggling to get out. I would, if I were Montgomery. But how can we tell who is saying what? And how do we help Montgomery?" Gill asks.

"It doesn't matter, Gill, we just need to listen to what he has to say. My guess is that he has a plan," she responds.

Gill picks up the phone and calls Garfield back and asks him what he has in mind.

Garfield has a warmer tone in his voice. "I'm glad you called back, Detective. Thank you. I don't think I should go into too much detail, mainly due to time constraints – you have thirty minutes maximum before you will be apprehended – but let me paint a picture for you. I don't believe I am the evil man you think I am. I know I have done wrong. You have presumably worked that out by now. I am guessing it was you, Detective, that somehow found out that I was responsible for Montgomery's death. My guess is that you can super-position and that you witnessed the event in some fashion. I understand that you, Miss Jumeau, also have this ability. Strange, you know. For years I had assumed that I was one of one. That it was just me who could do this, here on Earth. And in a strange way it is invigorating and encouraging to me that some of you can also perform this function. Whatever the bigger picture is, perhaps I will never know. But I do know this; if you wish to return to a world in which John Montgomery is alive and you are able to live your lives out in freedom, the collaboration among us must be unwavering in order to accomplish this. That much you have to understand."

Catherine and Gill are on speakerphone, and for the first time Catherine decides to speak.

"Mr Garfield. It's Catherine Jumeau." Catherine's statement of the obvious creates an unexpected silence for a few seconds. She follows up quickly to avoid any interruption. "I know you have many issues that you'd like to address. I...we know about you and John Montgomery, and what you have been doing with Walter Melrose. Please tell me that Walter, Wendy and Malcolm are OK. I need to know that you haven't harmed them before we go on with this."

Catherine's tangential question is unexpected, but understandable. Her primary concern for her friends and colleagues is paramount in the negotiation. If he confirms their safety, then she will be willing to help the man she most fears to get what he wants. Gill, a more skeptical sort, assumes that Garfield will say whatever he needs to say to get them to do what he wants.

"They are all fine, Miss Jumeau. They have been kindly working with me to make sure we have a plan. Your father has been very helpful too," Garfield says.
"My father?" Catherine exclaims.

"Yes, he has kindly offered his support to try and get us back on track. He and Walter are working together on the mechanics and process we need to get things back to normal."

Catherine looks across to Gill and shakes her head. Gill puts the speakerphone on mute for a second.

"Your father?" he asks

"That can't be! He would never help Garfield if he knew what he had done. And he would never work with Walter; he has said many times that he wouldn't work with him again. I don't believe him, Gill."

Gill looks down at the phone, Garfield on the other end. He sweeps his hair back, and lets out a long sigh. "You know, right now, it doesn't matter if we believe him, Catherine. We have to go along with this – you said so yourself. If we part company now, we are dead in the water. Can we just listen a bit more to what he has to say?"

Before Catherine has the chance to respond, Garfield's voice comes over the phone. "Are you still there?" he asks.

Gill switches off the mute function. "Yes, we are still here," he says, just to keep some form of momentum. Catherine stares at him with a frown. "What did you have in mind?" Gill prompts Garfield.

"It's not so complicated," Garfield says, "If, as I surmise, all of us can super-position, then my belief is that we can use our combined abilities to travel back to before the President was murdered and make sure that he is safe. Even though it is dangerous to intrude on alternative realities, time seems to be the directional element. Just as all parts of a hologram reflect the whole, so too a change in a part *affects* the whole. If we can undo the change that brought about John Montgomery's death, so too we can make the whole *whole again*. Presumably this is something you want as well as me."

Gill is struggling to come to terms with the fact that Garfield seems to have had such a profound change of heart. Yet Catherine's thoughts ring in his head. There are times when Garfield even sounds like Montgomery, whose accent was distinctly different from Garfield's.

Garfield explains his plan to them. The three are going to try and get to a place where they are in proximity, but not within sight of each other. On Garfield's phone call, they will dual and travel back to a pre-determined time before the President's assassination, taking great care to locate to different places inside the Capitol building to avoid observing each other. Garfield will ensure that the other instance of him, the one who murders the President, is, in that reality, prevented from carrying out the assassination. If the two Garfields meet, there may be unpredictable effects, but Garfield says he will handle this.

Either Gill or Catherine will get to the main chamber of the Senate, and on Montgomery's entrance and delivery of his speech on Defense, will have proof positive that Garfield has kept his word. If Montgomery is alive, Garfield will no longer have the burden of Montgomery on his conscience. By which Gill takes it that Montgomery's soul can return to where it belongs.

Garfield makes it seem pretty straightforward. They go back, change history, and provided everyone is happy, they go their separate ways. Except that Garfield has another condition.

"Now, once this is done, I have completed my end of the bargain. In return, I will ask for your help. You have both been lucky enough to find each other – I presume that's why you are together? Well, I'm sure you can appreciate that I need to find my own partner. I feel certain that I can have a more useful future if I am not alone. Do you understand?"

Gill and Catherine instinctively understand. Of course they do. They have reunited and are desperate to get on with their lives together. Gill thinks of Beth too. Maybe his sister has been lucky enough to find her universal partner and is happy somewhere out there. Or maybe not, but the more he thinks about it, the more he realises how important it is for everyone to at least have the chance to meet their soulmate, their one true partner in the Universe. Sentiment is welling up within him. He is emotionally and physically exhausted, and wants to get back to reality. And Catherine can hear him thinking that. Her sensitivity and capacity seem to be growing; she is becoming very strong. Stronger than Gill right now. Although she senses something isn't quite right about Garfield's focus on his entangled partner, she knows that he has got this idea from her father and his work. This makes her believe that Garfield was, in fact, telling the truth about having her father alongside Walter, Wendy and Malcolm. She is in a spin, trying to understand what Garfield really wants. It's almost too much for her. She sees in Gill the recognition that Garfield should have his chance, as he has had. But how on earth can she and Gill help Garfield to find his twin? Her approach ends up being much more measured.

"Look, assuming your plan works, how on earth do you think we can help you find your entangled partner? Even if we wanted to help you, how do you suggest we do that?" she asks.

Garfield's answer surprises even Catherine. "I talked to your father and Walter about that. They believe that you two, if it is true that you are entangled and existent in the same spacetime location, will have a special type of communication channel when you super-position. One possibility is that this type of *uniting* super-positioning will attract others towards it. Have either of you seen or heard others when you super-position? If you have, they have found your channel, a bit like tuning into a radio station, I imagine, except that you only broadcast very infrequently and it may be that many cannot receive or are too slow to tune in before you break the channel. My suggestion is that I try to tune in. It is potentially a way for me to find my salvation, and come to terms with my demons. It is my only hope, and you would be doing justice a great favor by allowing me the opportunity to rehabilitate and live a better life."

Catherine is quick to interject. She knows that her father is an exceptionally good person, and one who believes in the sense of justice. From her initial skepticism about Garfield's motives, it is almost as if she can hear her dad speaking through Garfield. It is her turn to feel the emotion, and together with her growing confidence in her abilities and strength, she is taking the lead.

"I hear what you are saying, Mr Garfield. I think we can try to help you. Let's make the arrangements and begin. We will call you back in five minutes," she suggests.

As Gill hangs up, Catherine immediately leans over to him and grabs his arm. The sense of power in her grip surges through Gill, who looks down, then back up to be caught square by her piercing and pleading green eyes.

"Gill, I am worried. How can we agree to this when you have lost the ability to dual? We can't say 'yes' to something we can't do," she says.

Gill looks down again at his arm. Out of the corner of his eye, he sees the traffic moving by. It seems slow. A woman is walking across the car park with a pram. As she passes, Gill notices that she is walking very slowly – almost in slow motion. He senses Catherine has retained some capacity to dual. Inside, he knows that Catherine is somehow key to all of this. How can that be if they are trapped?

"I may have lost the ability, but I don't think you have. Look outside," Gill says.

Catherine sees how things have slowed around them. Things are becoming clearer. Somewhere inside her she is regaining some ability to dual. She knows this. But she needs Gill to be there with her.

"You may have to help me," Gill continues, "maybe give me some of your good stuff." He smiles at her. It's no time for kidding around, but she likes his idea.

"I'll see what I can do, Mister," she says as she releases her grip. "Let's get out of here – there's a little hotel just back there."

The pair drive at speed back to the hotel on Hicks. Inside room thirty-seven it is extremely bright, the sun blazing through the full-length sliding windows. Catherine opens one half to allow a gentle breeze in. A low drone of distant traffic from the freeway is comforting in its consistency. Any sudden change to that sound will make them nervous for sure. She closes the long curtains to block out the sun, plunging the room into darkness while Gill goes to the bathroom to splash some water on his face.

Gill is patting his face dry with a towel. "What if he's double-crossing? I mean, this might just be a twisted plot where we are taken out of the equation. You realise that it's possible we are just patsies here?" he says, offering a line of cynicism which he thinks is long overdue.

He doesn't trust Garfield as far as he could throw him, and now Garfield, someone who he has never even met in person, has offered contrition and, at least ostensibly, a practical solution to overcome all their current predicaments. It just doesn't seem right. The only thing that mitigates that thought is the belief that Christophe Jumeau might be directing some of Garfield's energies in the right direction. But why? Jumeau senior must know something that he and Catherine don't know.

"I know what you are thinking," Catherine says.
"You do?" Gill responds, with a wry smile.
"My father has put things together and decided that this is the best way to do things. I know it. And you can sense that I will be able to dual. That's important, right? I mean, even if I have to go alone, I can still come back. What I don't know is why Garfield needs so desperately to find his entangled partner," she says.
"His half-freak, you mean. Can't imagine who might be entangled with *that*. I'm not exactly enthralled at the prospect," Gill says, ignoring any question about Catherine going it alone.
"Listen, we know what my father is saying is right though. You and I have both heard and seen other people at the clearing, yes?" says Catherine.
"Yes, well, I mean *I* have. When did you see or hear others there? This is news to me," Gill asks.
Catherine hesitates slightly before adding "Well, I'm pretty sure I saw a woman there the last time, just before I saw your watch and knew which path to take to come and find you."
Gill stares at Catherine in disbelief. "What woman? Who was that?" They both know Catherine's answer, but before Gill gets too worked up, Catherine approaches him and strokes his head. As she peers into his eyes, she realises how little time they have been able to have to themselves. To enjoy themselves free from any shackles or restraints. She stands on her toes and kisses him gently on the lips. Gill is cast into a warm ocean with waves of delight washing over him gently as he sinks under and opens his eyes. Catherine is swimming around him effortlessly, like a seal would ease their way in any direction despite the weight and pressure of the water around

them. Catherine is joined by Beth. They both circle around him, smiling. It is a vision he would like to linger. As he smiles and opens his eyes, their lips part and Catherine takes her hand away from his hair. As she does that, the slow fluttering of the curtains in the breeze begins to speed up. Somehow, Catherine is signalling to him that she can navigate these waters, and that he needs to go with her.

Gill prepares to call Ellis Garfield, and begin the combined attempt to dual back to before President Montgomery was assassinated. A three-pronged plan to minimize any risk of failure takes shape. Immediately after the call, Catherine tells Gill to take his clothes off.

"Hey, is this really the time for this?" Gill asks. Catherine can't quite make out if he is kidding around, and smiles hesitantly.

"Mister, if you are going to dual with me, we are going to have get close up and personal. I can feel myself getting pretty strong and if you are going to have some of that, then we need as much bodily contact as possible. But grab our clothes - we'll need to dress when we get there…" And with that, Catherine starts to undress.

Gill pauses and they both take a second to look at each other. He is struck by how much Catherine has changed. She has embraced her abilities and seems to be learning so quickly that she will be so much more capable than him in the future. As a pair, she may be the one who teaches him some new things about the Universe after all. He likes this. She is radiant, giving off an incredible aura which energizes him from head to foot. They are down to their underwear, and he approaches her, stroking her hair back behind her ears. His first touch charges the atmosphere and everything around them begins to blur and fade away. He kisses her neck, and she rolls her head back as his body presses up against her tightly. Her long arms wrap naturally around him and he moves his legs so that their thighs interlock and there is maximum skin-to-skin contact. If they didn't have a date with the President of the United States of America, they would surely rip the rest of their clothes off and make passionate love long into the night.

As they feel themselves about to dual, Catherine looks deep into Gill's oceanic eyes and says "Come with me", without moving her lips.

———

"What's up, George?" Al Mason asks George Beston in the security room at the White House. He has been invited in to the main security and surveillance room by Beston, as he is a bit concerned about some CCTV footage.

"Well, I just wanted to let you know that it looks like the President is doing one of his catatonia specials, Sir. He's been there for the best part of two hours, just staring blankly out of the window. This camera is one we had fitted specially – let's us see into his own quarters. It was requested by Maria Ortega herself."

Al Mason peers up at the small image. It's a picture of the back of a chair. There appears to be someone in it by virtue of a pair of shoes that you can see on the floor in front of it, as if someone is slouched in the chair, reclining and looking out the main window.

"OK. Well, it's his time, I guess. Not much we can do except keep an eye on things," Mason acknowledges.

As Mason gets up to leave, Phil Kirkland comes into the control room.

"Al, you got a minute?"
"Sure, Phil, what's up?"
"Al, I need you and your men to gather in Briefing Room B in five minutes," Kirkland states.
"Sure thing, Phil. Anything serious?" Mason asks.
"You could say that," Kirkland replies.

Ten minutes later, George Beston is instructed by Mason, in a chain of missives straight from Ava Redmond, to enter the President's quarters and quietly invite Ellis Garfield to accompany him and his men to the security block at the back of the building.

As the men enter the quarters and approach the high-backed chair so cherished by Presidents past and present, Mason politely addresses the President.

"Excuse me, Mr. President, I have a level six order here from the Secretary for Defense and Director Redmond at Intelligence HQ pertaining to your current security status. I would respectfully request your presence in Briefing Room B, and your full co-operation in such matters."

There is no reply.

Mason nods to one of his men to approach the chair. The officer swivels the chair around to reveal that it is empty. The pair of shoes on the ground are unfilled, and a robe is spread across the back of the chair giving the impression that a body was occupying it.

Mason looks around. "Johnson, Willis; check the rest of the quarters. You two, come with me." Mason and the two remaining security men quickly dart over to the West Wing and check in with Phil Kirkland. Together, they check the entire White House for the President, before emerging back in the main lobby. Kirkland is stony-faced. The President is nowhere to be found.

"What the sweet Mona Lisa is going on? Where the *hell* is he?" he asks, rhetorically.

At this point, the overweight George Beston comes running down the main east corridor. "Sir!" he is shouting. As he reaches Kirkland and his men, he is out of breath and rather red in the face. He has spent so many years sitting looking at CCTV that he is extremely out-of-shape.

"What is it, man?" Kirkland asks.

After a couple of extra breaths, Beston blurts out "It's the CCTV, Sir. I got everyone to look back over the last few hours footage. There's a fleeting image of an unidentified figure in the President's quarters – it's a male, about six-two and wearing a big jacket and trucker's cap. Looks like the same person got into a black pickup which was just out at the back gates. The men down there say that he had a security pass under the name 'Nelson'. It's legit – an employee named 'Steve Nelson' is listed as one of the catering staff."

"Willis, get an all-points out to local police for Nelson – get every available man on it. Dan, Oscar – come with me," Kirkland orders, trying to control the onset of panic. What next? Now the President is missing!

A call comes through to Maria Ortega with the news.

"Jesus," she exclaims. "Get onto Julie Garfield – check if he is hiding up there or has confided in her where he is going. He may have had a breakdown or maybe worse. If he's not up there, I want intelligent guesses as to where he is. Oh, and get a team onto his quarters. I want that place turned upside down for any clues. Get back to me every twenty minutes as per protocol. And *no statements. No press. Nothing!*"

Ava Redmond gets the news while driving home. She does a U-turn and, for the first time in her role as Chief of Intelligence, uses a red flashing light on the roof of her car to speed through traffic across town to get to the White House.

* * * *

CHAPTER 11: SHATTERED DREAMS

"'Nuveau'."

"'Nuveau'?"

"Yes, that's the word he kept saying, over and over, when I first found him. My commanding officer has shown me the CRUSE report to check the detail as you requested, but there is nothing about that in there."

It's Sergeant Naseborough.

"OK, Sergeant, this may be significant. Thanks for coming back to me – appreciate it," Ava Redmond says, and hangs up. She has just arrived at the White House to meet with Maria Ortega and Abe Hart, but taken a priority call in the main lobby as she waits.

A little while later she is rifling through the only folder on her desk, marked 'INTELL. CLASSIFIED: EXT/M.I. 2000-2020'. The folder contains several reports from the Centre for Research into Unexplained Significant Events, or CRUSE as it is known. CRUSE is a little-known unit consisting of fewer than twenty paid employees which is jointly sponsored by the NSA - the National Security Agency - and the military. Its mission is the collection, analysis and reporting of unexplained phenomena throughout the U.S. and the wider world. Unlike certain phantom organizations brought to life in coiffured TV shows, CRUSE is anything but glamorous. It applies highly sophisticated mathematical modelling and social profiling techniques to propose rigorous 'real-world' explanations for mysterious events with global security implications; events that might otherwise be labelled in some category such as 'paranormal' or 'supernatural'.

As Redmond reads through the file, her suspicions are confirmed. The chief signatory of the report is Robertson Davis over at CRUSE. 'Robbie' is an enigmatic character who always looks as if he just got out of bed. The paradox being that he never sleeps. He's well-respected in security circles, though, and so Redmond braces herself for a potentially tricky conversation.

"Robbie, how are you and the guys over there?" she opens.

"Ava, what a pleasant surprise. We're all good. All good. Busy. What's on your mind?" Robbie replies.

"Can you look up file EX:7198 for me. I need to ask you a couple of things about that one."

"Sure, just give me a second here while I get to my slate, it's just over in the corner there." After a couple of muffled sounds, Robbie is back. "OK, shoot."

"Just two things really. The first is that, on page nine of the Description, I notice that you didn't find any evidence of chemical burns and that the condition of Officer Garfield's skin was not identifiable as consistent with any known effect from recorded exposures tested by the military either here or anywhere else. My question is therefore why you never requisitioned Garfield in for complete testing – you know, the whole works. In a case like this it must be practice for you guys to require more analysis surely?"

"Let me see. Ah, yes, OK. Well, we did actually seek medical records from both the field hospital and his base medics over at Coulson. Now, I seem to have put a little note in somewhere about that. Let me see. Yes, page fourteen under 'Update'. I remark there that the field hospital records were missing on withdrawal of Garfield's unit, although the military base records from some months later all checked out. He had bloods and a couple of scans on his return. Everything looked normal at that point, so I guess everyone took that to mean he had recovered fully."

Redmond checks the reference. "Yes, I see that. So the skin condition resulting from his encounter is unexplained, in your view?"

"Well, I guess it is, yes. The odd thing was that his uniform was intact. There was no chemical present or any damage from chemicals on that, just a little blood. But, realistically, it could have been a nervous reaction. A bit like sudden hair loss – you know when people lose their hair overnight due to the rapid onset of a nervous reaction. That is a definite possibility," Davis says, pausing slightly before adding, "Are you looking at this as a class five?"

Class five cases are paranormal phenomena; the ones that cannot be explained, at least within known science. With all that Redmond knows now, she is convinced it is.

"Most likely, Robbie. You've seen the photographs, and we have some follow up on this case. You will understand why it is especially sensitive right now."

"Sure do. I was wondering if anyone would ever pick up on this, you know. I mean, I must admit I didn't know what to make of those images. But without any evidence from the medics or, for example, of DNA mutation, we can't do anything. Even though it's a while back, and we concluded that there was nothing really to conclude, it *is* the President we're talking about here," he replies.

"Yeh, well, here's the thing, Robbie, I don't know how you could write this one off in the first place. I mean there are things missing from the report apart from just the simplest of medical information. I spoke with the officer who found Garfield some time after he was reported missing, and, apart from the fact that he was practically unrecognizable, he was repeating a word over and over. He was saying 'Nuveau'. Does this mean anything to you?"

"Like, as in 'new' in French you mean? Well I don't remember seeing anything about that, and I don't know why it wouldn't be in there, Ava. Must have been an oversight. It's the first I have heard of it, but, you know, on its own that wouldn't make me believe that this is class five. Where are you going with this? That Garfield was abducted by little green men, then dropped back at the base camp after having alien injections?" Davis comes back, sounding somewhat skeptical; it is both in his nature and his job description to be so.

The last part of Davis' remarks gives Redmond some food for thought. She closes off the conversation with Davis and turns to look out of her window. 'Alien injections', she thinks. Then calls in Maria Ortega and Abe Hart.

As all three settle in their chairs to discuss the disappearance of President Garfield, Redmond offers the others a radical analysis of the reality of the current situation.

"How did we ever come to be in this position?" Hart asks, looking anxious and beginning to shift around in his chair.

"Abe, it's not the time for that. We can do all the soul-searching later. What we need is to focus on what we have to do right now," Ortega says with some degree of calm. She is right, of course.

"My guess is that we should stop trying to find him," Redmond interjects.

"What?" Hart exclaims.

"Let's try and find Melrose. If we find Melrose, then we'll find Garfield. Have we got anything – *anything* – on things like phones, cars, sightings?" Redmond asks.

"Not a..." Ortega says before her phone rings out loudly. Her ringtone is 'We Got Latin Soul' by Mongo Santamaria, an upbeat salsa tune with brass stabs and a seriously infectious rhythm. It's totally incongruous with the current mood, and causes her a little embarrassment as she fumbles in her jacket pocket to answer it.

"Hang on..." she tells the others. Redmond and Hart throw each other a glance in wonderment. This had better be a good interruption.

They needn't have feared. Ortega receives a report that a call into Melrose's mobile has eventually been traced by a Lieutenant Young up in Boston. Young's call to security services was precipitated by an alert put in by Detective Grady Jones from the South Boston police department. He reported that Detective Denton Gill, Professor Walter Melrose and Miss Catherine Jumeau were all reported as missing some days ago. Not only that, but Young and the Mayor of Boston had received warnings from Katie Melrose, the Professor's ex-wife, that he had not been contactable in several days. Government security service agents now have a location. Melrose may, or may not, be with the phone, but it's a start.

"You would think that information might flow just a little faster these days," says Abe Hart as the three disperse and Redmond and Ortega speed over to the west side of Washington behind two other cars, flashing lights and sirens helping to get them through heavy traffic that little bit faster.

—-

At Garfield's secret hideout on the west side, Pratin Malic is doing press-ups. He grabs little spaces of time during the day for various little intense workout activities. He has reached forty-eight, but is interrupted by Daniel Faye, the other agent guarding the captives Wendy Xiu, Malcolm Baines, Walter Melrose and Christophe Jumeau.

"We got a problem," reports Faye, a squat, muscular man with a shaved head and a myriad of tattoos on his arms and around his neck. If nothing else, he would be easy to pick out in an identity parade. The legacy of tattoos is something he doesn't particularly like, and certainly isn't good for his supposed low-key profile. Damaged by military and mercenary service in several wars, and extreme in his hatred of the soft Left, the man despises most Americans for adhering to liberal values. Faye and Malic have a long history of working together, Malic being Faye's superior officer from their time in the army, and now where Malic goes for privately-paid security work, Faye follows. Where Malic is brutal, Faye is psychotic. Where Malic has the lead, Faye should not be let off the lead. For when he is, he is like a wild animal. He would gladly slaughter all of the captives and then sit down to devour a large T-bone steak.

Malic raises his head and his eyebrows, asking Faye to enlighten him.

"Caballos has just called. White House security have reported Garfield missing and are heading in this direction."

"Fuck." Malic exclaims. "How can that happen when you got all the mobile devices turned off, everything locked down?"

"I don't know...Sir. There must be another device somewhere. You want me to find it or make them tell me where it is?" Faye responds.

"It's too late for that, Danny. We're going to have to get out of here. Get all of them in to the back of the van downstairs. And *don't* harm any of them. We need them as collateral. Understood?"

"Sir!" Faye belts out. He is excited. Excited that he is going to see some action. This is what he trains to do. There is nothing worse than being trained to do something and then not getting the chance to actually do it.

Xiu and Baines are brought out to the van outside the back entrance to the main warehouse complex in the industrial park.

Wendy and Malcolm look disheveled and pale. They wince as the sun hits them square in the face as they are led out, still handcuffed, and put into the back of the unmarked white Chevrolet. A few minutes later, the back doors to the van are opened again, and Wendy Xiu breaks down in floods of tears as she sees her Professor again for the first time in days. But her relief is momentary; right now two guns are trained on them so they don't bother with the pleasantries of formal greetings, and judging by the state of the Professor, he is not in a position to help. The other older man is Catherine's father, but they can't fathom why he is here.

The feeling of helplessness pervades. Trying to run at this stage is a death sentence, and each one of the four captives has an innate sense of this truth. One move in the wrong direction might just trigger the wrath of their captors.

Pratin Malic moves to close the door, when he hears Faye cock his semi-automatic weapon. He swivels round very quickly for a big man. Faye nods over to his right. There is a plume of dust about five hundred yards down the main track up to the park. It's enough to make both men very nervous.

"Get down. Get down from the van. Now!" Malic shouts.

All four hurry to get down from the van, fearing the worst. The panic in the voices of their captors automatically sends the adrenaline rushing into their systems and their hearts racing out of control. Malcolm trips as he gets down and Faye is over him like a shot.

"Get up, you sorry motherfucker. Now! I swear to God I'll blow your fuckin' head off if you don't," he shouts as he presses the barrel of his gun against Baines' temple. Baines begins to cry and struggles to his feet, which proves difficult with his hands cuffed behind his back. Wendy, Walter and Christophe are being guided back to the warehouse by Malic, such is the desperation to secure their position before the oncoming convoy arrives. As they scuttle away from the van, the sound of engines and the rumble of several vehicles gets much louder and the convoy comes into sight. Looking back, Walter Melrose sees Faye leaning over Malcolm in an extremely menacing pose. Melrose catches Faye's eye, bloodshot red, and manic, and in that moment fears for Malcolm's life. As Malcolm screams, a flurry of automatic fire rings out followed by two loud single shots and all hell is let loose. Wendy Xiu, Christophe Jumeau and Pratin Malic hunker down and scurry through huge hangar-like doors and back into the warehouse. As they look back, Christophe sees Walter Melrose fall to the ground as if he has lost his footing. Wendy is distraught, shouting 'Mal! Mal!', but she is being dragged inside by Malic who is using his gun to push her and Jumeau up the stairs back to the ops unit.

Upstairs, in the end room, the time around Ellis Garfield slows right down, just as it does for Gill and Catherine when they dual. As the value of time approaches zero, many things can happen in the same timeslice that normal folks would see go by in a blur. This is the fascination with time; that it can be slow or fast depending on what is happening. And for Ellis Garfield, in this moment as the security services close in on his hideout and Malic, Xiu and Jumeau rush up the stairs, he is super-positioning back to the Capitol building as it was a week ago.

—-

"Mr. President", says the on-duty guard outside washroom two in the east quadrant of the Capitol building. John Montgomery is approaching. He nods at the uniformed officer, who opens the door for him.

As he walks into the washroom, the President registers he is alone and takes a photograph of his family from his wallet and smiles. After a little moment reflecting on his good fortune, he walks across to the far cubicle and closes the door behind him. Despite the morale boost, he is quite nervous. He is about to give a major speech which is not going to be received well by many in the chamber. Reaching into his inside jacket pocket he brings out an oblong postcard. It's white, and written on one side is a list of the main prompts. As a man who prides himself on delivering speeches without the need for a script, he is now beginning to doubt whether his stubborn adherence to his own rule is, on this occasion, a good idea. As he goes over the prompts, muttering each bullet-pointed phrase to himself, a slight breeze comes from under the cubicle door.

At first, Denton Gill thinks he has misjudged his dual. 'Shit', he thinks. He's standing, semi-naked, opposite the main mirror in the sizeably plush washroom. He can feel the breeze around him gently fade away and as he begins to look around, he sees one cubicle door is closed. As he slowly hunkers down, he can see a pair of shiny black shoes and takes this to signify that John Montgomery is behind the door. He can hear him muttering something, but can't make out exactly what. It brings a smile to his face; he knows Montgomery is alive and as long as he can ensure that whatever version of Garfield turns up doesn't harm the President then the moment of assassination will pass, and history will be changed. Gill decides to wait for the flush before making any sudden move. He hears Montgomery blow his nose and clear his throat. Shortly after, the flush comes and Gill tip-toes quickly across to the other end cubicle, slipping on his short and trousers while standing on the seat and making himself as flat as possible against the wall so as not to be visible from the main washroom itself. The cubicles are generously proportioned, which is useful given Gill's large frame. He has a look at the clock high up on the far wall and sees it is about a minute before the reported time of death.

Outside the Capitol Building on New Jersey Avenue, Ellis Garfield, sporting a plain leather bomber jacket and long-peaked baseball cap slanted downwards to cover his face, looks like a normal sort of guy going back to his car. If CCTV coverage were to be scrutinized over various streets around the Capitol building over a half-hour period before the assassination of the President, they would see Garfield's lean figure wandering in and out of the various car parks in the area. He is trying to track down the tungsten metallic Dodge Challenger Hector Caballos dropped off on the morning of the fateful day. Inside it, there is a gun for Garfield. It's the one he uses to kill the President. But, like Catherine and Gill, Garfield is struggling too. He can't find the car. His paces become shorter and faster as his anxiety levels increase.

Catherine too is in some disarray. Having emerged from the Ladies washroom in the lobby, avoiding the security check at the main doors. she is desperately trying to get into the main chamber. There are seemingly hundreds of reporters, photographers, police, security personnel, waiters and reception staff, as well as the politicians themselves. The situation is chaotic, and she immediately wonders how any security operation can be in any way effective in such circumstances. There are just so many people. While this is helpful at one level in that she can blend in even though she has no official position there, it also means that it will be incredibly difficult to track down Ellis Garfield in the chamber. Her role is to get in there and get close enough to observe him dualling. That way, he will be trapped and unable to dual over to the washroom and carry out the assassination. But at this rate, she won't even get in the chamber doors.

As John Montgomery emerges from the cubicle in the washroom, he walks over towards the mirror and bends over to splash some water on his face. As he does so, Gill peers though the slit in the door frame and immediately wishes he hadn't. Torpor and sloth begin to wash over him as he feels incredibly heavy. On top of the tiredness that comes with repeated dualling, this is debilitating. Montgomery remains motionless at a right angle, bent over the washbasin. Realising that he may not get to the Vice President if and when he arrives to kill Montgomery, Gill's face strains as he tries with all his might to push against the sticky goo that is rooting him to the spot.

The three dualists – Gill, Catherine and Garfield – have misjudged the amount of time they were going to need to avoid the assassination. Each believes that if they are struggling, then at least the others will have a good chance of success. But this is the flaw. Their three-pronged plan to minimize any risk of failing to stop the assassination is going badly wrong for all three. Time, their fickle friend, may just act against them.

Vice President Ellis Garfield is contemplating his own image in the mirror. His angular features are striking, but quite asymmetrical. So his mirror image looks somewhat strange to him. Somehow much harder, more sinister. It's a momentary lapse in his concentration as he waits for his colleague, the President, to grab for the hand towel and dry his face. He wants to see the fear and submission in Montgomery's eyes when he confronts him; the man's penance for threatening to thwart his attempts to push science forward so that it can help him in his urgent quest to return home. But he is pressed for time, and Montgomery seems to be taking too long at the washbasin.
As the nervous signal from his brain travels down his arm to initiate the motion to reach for his gun inside his jacket, so too a reactive reciprocal travels back to tell his brain to prevent its movement. As he tries to deal with the ambiguity, so too his heart

misses a beat in realisation that something is wrong. He feels rooted to the spot. Just like Gill. There are just a few feet between Gill and Garfield. As both men are dualling in this confined space, the side-effect is similar to when Gill and Catherine are in the clearing. Both men are aware of the extra presence in the room, and Gill in particular is extremely concerned not to be observed by Garfield. The consequences of observation are too grave. As long as this version of Garfield, the Vice President several days previously, does not actually lay eyes on Gill and therefore verify his presence in this reality, he will be free to dual further. But, as a last resort, if the other two were to fail in their efforts to stop the killing, then Gill would have to risk being trapped in order to save the President's life.

Outside, there is a growing buzz of excitement in the main chamber of the Senate House as the last few senators take their seats. The low rumble of myriad conversations has been replaced by shouts across the hall from the reporters and staff, all trying to be heard above the crowd. Catherine is jostled as she pushes forward behind an enormous woman who is a private aide to one of the senators.

"Do you mind?" says the woman, indignantly. Catherine is taking advantage of the woman's size as an offensive centre and is slipstreaming behind her to gain yardage.

"No," says Catherine, as she tries to see round the woman to where the Vice President is likely to be seated. She can't spot him. She's going to have to get much closer. She looks at the huge clock on the wall behind the main lectern. It's only thirty seconds or so until the assassination. She is struggling against the panic that wants to control her. Tailing off and swerving left, she manages to get a couple of yards forward into one of the main aisles. Looking up at the rostrum, there is no sign of Ellis Garfield. This could be good or bad. Her only task is to find him and observe him. A muffled announcement is coming from the floor. It's Senator Abrim from South Dakota, the Speaker, calling for order. The moment is drawing close, and once again the adrenaline rushing through her body makes Catherine's eyes widen and her face to go unusually pale.

"Excuse me. Thanks. Excuse me. Thanks. Excuse Me..." she manages to get past three more people before beginning to emerge into a little opening where there is just enough space for a normal-sized human. Most of the people around her have body mass indexes over thirty and are in need of some serious dietary rehab. As she wrestles free from the last remaining obstacle between her and a clear view of the rostrum and surrounding Senator benches, she begins to scan around, trying to be as quick as she can. First time round: nothing. Second time round: nothing. 'What?' she thinks as she rolls her eyes upwards and takes a deep breath.

"Too quick. Too quick." she says out loud.
"Pardon me?" a large red-faced man asks her as he turns around and his double-chin gets caught on his shirt collar, preventing a full swivel action. Catherine is too busy. She looks at the clock again. It's ten seconds until the moment of death.

—-

Outside in the New Jersey Street car park, President Ellis Garfield is scanning for color. The tungsten hue of the Dodge was selected precisely because it would merge into the background. Useful at the time. Useless right now. He is panicking, because this is the last car park he has tried, and if the car isn't there, something is *very* wrong. Over in bay twelve he spots the sporty grill of a Challenger. A rush of excitement flows through him, and he begins to run over to the car. If he can get to the gun before the other instance of himself super-positions to collect it, then the gun won't be there as expected and the attempt at assassination will be foiled. He knows that if his other self turns up then anything might happen in the same spacetime location. This is terrifying him right now, and he picks up the pace to get to the car more quickly. As he approaches he notices that the car is empty. This is what he had hoped for. Inside his jacket he has a pair of gloves and a small metal chain. He puts on the gloves, wraps the chain around his right fist, and smashes the driver's window, clearing away some fragments before reaching in and opening the door. The alarm is going off, and there is precious little time before the assassination is due to take place. As he gets in, he checks the glove compartment. There is nothing there. He checks the rear seat. Then the boot. Nothing. All the time the alarm is going off. As he starts to panic and move away from the car he realises that he is too late. His other self has already collected the gun.

"Shit!" he shouts out loud, before scurrying off on foot and out through an exit onto the side road.

In the washroom, both Gill and Garfield are struggling desperately to escape the immense gravity rooting their new-found mass to the spot. Gill gives every sinew of effort until he manages to lean forward and create enough downward pull from his position a couple of feet up on the toilet seat to begin to fall. The momentum is carrying him down, and forward. As he does so, Garfield, some feet away and facing the mirror, is trying to move his hand to his jacket pocket. He musters an almighty focus of energy, raising his arm slightly against the downward force. In this environment it is so much more difficult than letting something fall of its own accord, but his efforts are rewarded and he gradually manages to get his hand to hip height, then upwards to reach inside his jacket pocket.

Gill's drop from the cubicle seat takes him to the ground, and his gathering momentum makes him land awkwardly and have to roll on the floor in slow motion. The slow speed breaks the landing somewhat and as he begins to lose control he realises that he may end up too close to Garfield or even right under him so that he is instantly observed. He glances across to see Garfield's shape from the rear with a hand going into his pocket. Montgomery is now beginning to look around. Somehow Gill and Garfield's huge efforts to overcome their constraints have made time around them slowly begin to return to normal.

Gill knows that merely trapping Garfield by observing him may not be enough to prevent the assassination, but he can at least attempt to grab the pistol emerging from Garfield's jacket. Montgomery has swivelled a half-turn to look directly at Garfield, and is struck dumb by his presence in front of him. As Garfield's gun comes out at chest height and trains on the President, Montgomery begins to flinch, and in so doing moves his head so that Garfield can see straight ahead in the mirror once more.

Gill's heart pumps so hard he cannot breathe. A profoundly chilling white light radiates so brilliantly that he naturally squints at the brightness before focusing in.

Garfield's flickering eyes come to a grinding halt as he stares in disbelief through the looking glass. Standing behind him is a beautiful woman with the most alluring pearlescent green eyes he has ever seen. She is staring back at him in silence, simultaneously puzzled and frightened. So confused is Garfield with this vision, that he hesitates for a second. And in that second, Gill's eyes, as they accustom themselves to the glare of the light, come to rest on a most unusual sight.

Gill is seeing double. He is looking at the face of John Montgomery in the mirror.

And despite the most disturbing imagery around him where eyes are deceived by distractions and ghouls, Gill's instinct pulls his attention to the outstretched arm of who he still believes to be Garfield as it descends and points at Montgomery's chest.

He must prevent the trigger being pulled, and desperately throws himself forward to try and knock the gun from Garfield's hand. As he teeters on one foot and falls, Gill's brain freeze-frames subsequent movement into time-slices. Gill sees his President's crouching stance, then the barrel of Garfield's gun come to rest just under Montgomery's jacket and into his chest. Garfield's gloved finger begins to squeeze the trigger.

And in that particular slice, Gill senses the fear from Garfield as the assassin becomes aware of the falling man beside him witnessing his crime. And as suddenly, the black and white chess pattern of the wall behind Garfield comes into view. As he continues his fall, Gill sees Garfield vanish before his eyes. He waits for the shot to come, but it doesn't. As he hits the ground, he sees the President, face still moist from freshening up and looking traumatized by what has just happened, push his hands into the space Garfield has just occupied. John Montgomery is in shock, and in that moment, perhaps as a reflex to protect himself, faints in front of Gill.

—-

Catherine's hard stare on Garfield has trapped him in his seat. After searching and scanning the entire complement of Senators and aides sat in the chamber, she finally found Garfield over on the right-hand side next to Walt Reinesberg, Democratic Senator for Michigan. He wasn't even in his own seat, having had to scurry back to the chamber after giving last minute support to the President in the ante-room behind the main lectern area. As she approached, her great advantage was that Garfield did not know who she was. Even from a distance, she could sense there was someone dualling in the large amphitheater. As she focused in during those last few seconds on the face of Ellis Garfield, there was a momentary recognition from Garfield that his assassination attempt had failed. She could see it on his face before she ducked down to avoid being seen by him.

Gill, although delighted that the President is alive, must make sure he gets out of the washroom. Incredibly tired and sapped of energy, he can only manage to locate to the Ladies down the corridor, such is his current weakness. As he emerges from there, he gets a strange look from one of the Press crew walking down the hall. He smiles at her, before remarking that only the President is allowed to use the Men's room right now. She doesn't understand him, but smiles back anyway.

Catherine manages to leave the Capitol building by following a large official and pretending to be with him. She makes her way to the main street and the nearest café. Gill arrives in the building's public foyer a few moments later, looking pale and in some pain. A security guard approaches him.

"Everything OK, Sir?" he asks.

"Oh, yes, Officer, just eaten something bad. I think. I just need to get home," he replies. There are only moments before the security operation will be automatically tightened when the President is found unconscious in the washroom, and he knows they have to leave immediately.

"OK, well, you sure don't look right. Good luck with that, Sir," he says, as he steps back to his allotted position.

Limping around outside the Capitol complex, having realised that he hurt his ankle in the fall from the toilet seat back in the washroom, Gill needs to get to a safe place to try and dual again. But he needs time to recover too. He decides to take a taxi back to the Holly Hotel. It is a risky strategy but on balance one that is necessary right now.

He figures that Vice-President Garfield will have a gun on him and this will be a black mark against him if, as is likely, he will have to pass through automatic security checks on the way out of the Senate building. Granted, it will not have been fired, but it is an insurance policy against Garfield trying anything silly in future. Even if he were to try and hide it, he is still likely to have fingerprints on it.

Back at the hotel he orders a coffee and takes it upstairs to his room. The coffee is awful. But it has caffeine. He makes a call to 'Steve' to tell him to begin dualling, and to tune in to Gill and Catherine's frequency.

Gill then musters all his strength to attempt to dual. He draws the curtains and sits in one of the soft pseudo-leather chairs in the room, and closes his eyes. And waits.

Catherine needs Gill to come if they are to help Garfield. It is only by opening the unique channel she and Gill combine to create that Garfield can try and reunite with his entangled partner. The conditions are calm at the clearing. She is beginning to feel heavy as mass from all around begins to attract and weigh her down. Gill must come soon or she will have to leave before she gets stuck.

Gill is a strong man, and one who has much experience of the demands of dualling. But even he is struggling. His energy levels seem to have drained away. He and Garfield dualling in the same spacetime location has had a profound effect on him, as if Garfield has sapped *his* ability to dual. Or Garfield's strange, face-changing mirror image has. That seemed to be when he had the most intense sensation of weakness. Further dualling will almost certainly affect him if Garfield is there.

In the distance, Gill hears a police siren. And then a voice. A voice calling to him.

—

Above Catherine in the clearing, the skies are dark grey and lightning flashes begin to appear in the distance. Rain starts to fall. With only few experiences of dualling, she doesn't know if this is to be expected or not. But it doesn't help ease her movement. As she tries to see Gill's face in her mind, a girl's voice calls out.

'Gill!' the voice calls softly as it reverberates throughout the sky. There are several echoes as the hushed tones of the girl's voice float away with the gathering wind.

Gill hears Beth's voice outside on the street, just above the sound of the sirens. He takes a sudden breath, and whispers 'Beth' to himself. His sister is around. She is calling. An instantaneous rush of energy flows through Gill from the tips of his toes upwards. His body becomes charged and stiffens in his seat. For a few moments all bodily systems slow and stabilize until there is barely any movement in Gill at all. He feels the rush of wind against his hands at first, then his face, and then the moisture of rain against his temples as he begins to rush through the reeds in the cornfield. Looking up, he can see the blackening sky and shooting bolts of lightning striking the ground up ahead. He has never seen the field like this. Whipping across it at huge speeds, his sister's voice resounds in his head as she tells him 'I am near'. The warm and familiar tone reassures, and he knows, although he may never see Beth in this place, she is nevertheless there. As he emerges at the clearing, his heart jumps as he anticipates what is to come.

His arrival helps Catherine, who has been struggling under the huge mass that has built up around her. His momentum and renewed faith in his sister's safety bolster his strength, and he and Catherine work together to move to the other side of the clearing where pathways will be revealed. There they will wait for Ellis Garfield.

The sense of anticipation is heavy in the air; so too is the smell of fear and the black rain that is falling like tiny bombs of oil out of the heavens. There is conflict all around them, their sacred place disturbed by dark forces that appear to encircle them. Gill is protective of his space, of Catherine, and of Beth. They will need to be strong in the coming moments.

Catherine's hand reaches out to Gill. As the two touch, and they reach the far side of the clearing, there is just one pathway visible. From above them, an almighty sonic boom bangs hard on their ears causing them to flinch and they can hear what sound like footsteps advancing. Louder and louder they become until suddenly falling silent, to be trailed by the brooding rumble of faraway thunder. The pounding rain ceases. Emerging from the reeds, Catherine sees the shimmering milky skin of a tall, smooth-bodied creature that appears to hover at the entrance to the pathway. Valves on the body open and close gently, revealing a clear interior. There are no recognizable legs as such; instead two nodules expelling air downwards allow the body to float about three feet in the air, giving the impression of height. The head seems to be separate from the body somehow. There is just one, intensely bright white eye, and an mouth which is opening and closing in time with the other valves in the body. Just visible through the milky white torso is the outline of a heart, pumping softly. The remarkable physiology is completed by what looks like a single horizontal limb about half way up the main torso just underneath the heart. It appears to be vestigial.

Catherine is transfixed, not knowing how to react or why this particular creature is here. As she turns to see what Gill is thinking, she sees recognition on his face.

"Gill?" she says. Gill somehow recognises this as the same being in the mirror in the washroom back in Washington.

"It's Garfield," Gill tells her. She looks back at the creature, and then back at Gill.

"Isn't it?" Gill asks the creature, which angles slightly to the right, then to the left in a motion akin to a skittle that is hit but then rights itself. The entire body flushes orange for an extremely short time, and returns to milky white. Gill wonders if the alien being in front of them will be able to converse, in this place. Suddenly, the orifice used for breathing forms the shape of a human mouth. It's very convincing, but makes the sight they are encountering stranger and more disconcerting, like some hideous human mutation.

Suddenly a voice. "Neu", the voice says, then corrects itself, "No," it says. There is a pause. It seems to go on forever. Gill is now transfixed too. He and Catherine are communicating with an extra-terrestrial, and the sense of awe is overpowering.

"Nuvo…" the creature says, "…Nuvo".

Catherine's voice is more than a bit shaky as she attempts to engage in dialogue.

"Nuvo, I hope we can help you to find what you want. You seek your entangled partner, who is out there somewhere…" she says as she looks up at the dark skies above them.

The creature seems to lift upwards slightly as Catherine looks up. The moment is broken by Gill.

"Where is Garfield?" asks Gill. And after a good few seconds go by with nothing to fill them, Nuvo flushes bright blue for a fraction of a second, then again, and back to milky white. What follows next makes Catherine whimper and Gill swallow hard. The alien body begins to distend at the bottom, and forms two legs. The horizontal limb across the front of the body comes out, splits into two and rejoins the body as two arms. The valves disappear and the torso takes on the shape and hue akin to that of a human male. On the head, eyes, ears, a nose and a mouth form out of the flexible and rubbery skin and take on the shape and characteristics of Ellis Garfield's face. Finally, hair forms on the head and chest, arms, legs and pubic area. Ellis Garfield is, to all intents and purposes, alive and naked as the day he was born on Earth. And standing in front of them. It is an incredible transformation, and truly spectacular in its splendor. Both Catherine and Gill are struck by the sophistication of the creature's physiological prowess.

Ellis Garfield begins to speak.

"My name is Nuvo. I am from a galaxy not too far from here. I borrowed Ellis Garfield's body when I arrived here by mistake some years ago. What you see is just an illusion. Some people on my planet have an ability to travel through space and time, and I am one of them. Except I am not an expert. No-one is. I made a serious error in judgment when I was trying to get better at this...ability, and I jumped too far. I landed here and had to survive. My only goal is to get back to my home by any means possible."

Gill is on one tack. Catherine on another. Gill fires first.

"Is Garfield still alive? Can you return him safely to us?" he asks.
Nuvo, in the form of Garfield, bows his head and then shakes from side to side. A tear runs down Garfield's cheek.

"Are there more of you here, or is it just you?" Catherine asks.
"Me," says Nuvo.

There is a pause as Garfield takes a little time to compose himself.

"You are a corrupt people. But so are we," he says.
"What's it like back home, Nuvo?" asks Catherine, sensing the grief this creature feels for losing contact with his kind. She is beginning to feel sympathy, despite the wrong-doing he has perpetrated since arriving here.

"Not like here. We build soft things, you build hard things," he says.

"But you breathe air, right?" says Gill. Nuvo looks at him. His question seems clearly misplaced, and his self-awareness at this makes him divert away from Nuvo. He begins to feel heavy again, and as he looks over towards Catherine, the wave in her hair from the breeze around them is beginning to slow down. The atmosphere is becoming difficult and he senses that if they are going to help Nuvo then they are going to have to do it now.

"Do you see other people here, Nuvo"? Catherine enquires.

"Yes, there are a few," he replies.

"Do you see a another girl – another human girl here," she asks, wondering if Nuvo can see Gill's sister.

Gill was about to prompt them to move on, but he stops with his mouth half-open. There is little time left to avoid being stuck again in the clearing, and he looks across to Nuvo, in the shape of Ellis Garfield, who looks at Catherine, and smiles. Before he gets the chance to reply, however, a second sonic boom blasts at deafening volume and pitch behind Garfield. The sound wave blasts across the field, momentarily flattening some of the reeds and revealing a vast plain of earth as far as the eye can see. There is a dark figure in the distance, just visible above the cowering reeds. There is a central beating heart that is unimaginably dark. The darkest, blackest heart. The image is burnt onto Catherine and Gill's retinas before the reeds reform, shooting upwards to hide the whereabouts of the sinister apparition far off in the field. Instinctively they are both terrified, feeling an icy chill splinter down through their spines before shooting back up and cracking them on the head. There is sheer physical pain running the entire length of their bodies. This is not right. Not here.

The sound of the beating echoes in the distance and bounces around the sky above them. Like the low grating grind of metal as an old goods train slowly approaches the station, the lethargic triplet heartbeat pounds louder and louder. Chrohm-cho-chohm. Chrohm-cho-chohm. Chrohm-cho-chohm. The low frequencies rumble the ground below the trio in the clearing. Something stirs in Garfield, and Catherine and Gill watch as he transmutates back to the alien Nuvo.

A flush of dark charcoal begins to pulse on and off against the milky white smooth skin of Nuvo, in time with the beat. Chrohm-cho-chohm. Chrohm-cho-chohm. Chrohm-cho-chohm. It is getting louder still, ever closer. As the grinding rhythm begins to change to include a high-pitched screech of searing metallic friction, Catherine and Gill's heads are filled with flying shards of sound that seem to rip the very fabric of their minds apart. Chrohm-cho-chohm. Chrohm-cho-chohm. Chrohm-cho-chohm. As they flinch and try to cover their ears to stop their drums from bursting, the vibrations become increasingly violent, almost as if the earth below them were being dented by the heavy footfall of a hundred thousand angry warriors marching in unison towards them, fixing them in their sights, and lowering their spears ready to destroy every ounce of life that exists in their path.

As the ground shakes, Gill and Catherine have to hold each other to balance and avoid falling over. As they do so, the sound becomes unbearable. Chrohm-cho-chohm. Chrohm-cho-chohm. Chrohm-cho-chohm. As the decibels of sound reach inside both of them to the core and threaten the life inside, they struggle to keep watching what is going on. They both cower down and hold each other as a huge wave of burbling, menacing sound swells up and grows to a swirling cacophony. At the very peak of this wave, Catherine and Gill can no longer support themselves and fall to the ground, clutching each other tightly. All they can see is a swathe of dark cloud above them that begins to circle around and around like a Tornado. The burbling, the incessant screeching of the triple beat and the vibrations beneath them surely signal their imminent death. They cannot survive beyond this onslaught. As they hold each other and look upwards towards heaven, suddenly the cloudswirl breaks apart in two and speeds off to each horizon left and right, revealing a clear dark sky that seems to oscillate like a wobble board. The cacophonous chrohm-cho-chohm, chrohm-cho-chohm, chrohm-cho-chohm of the beat morphs into a steady series of thunder claps, one after the other, faster and faster, like a drum roll heralding the entrance of something wondrous and heavenly. The sky above them cracks first once, then like shattered glass, and through these cracks is injected a stream of stars that begin to fill the space. As they arrive, each one begins to circle around an area devoid of light. The blackest hole. And as they begin to swirl around the hole ever faster, so too the roll of thunder becomes a series of resounding crashes, followed by the heavy boom like a beater hitting against the skin of a massive bass drum. As the swirl surrounds the beating black hole and forms a magnificent aura around it, suddenly a huge crash of thunder breaks through all other sound and is accompanied by a blinding flash of lightning that rips the hole above them in two across its diameter from top to bottom. Through the crack, a single shimmering spotlight strikes the ground at the clearing, impossibly bright and revealing Catherine and Gill in high resolution, exposing their vulnerable forms to the Gods.

As the pair look away from the light, and back towards Nuvo, blinking and flushing a rainbow of new colors they have never seen before, there is an explosion of light behind him and he is engulfed by a swirling plume of blinding white mist, like a giant gas claw tightening its grip around him. For a moment there is a look of absolute terror in the white eye of Nuvo, and his body-flushes stop dead. The mouth area begins to form into a large 'O' shape which covers much of of his head and simulates an extreme look of shock, and through this orifice a jet of brilliant purple light first escapes, then stops and begins to float slowly upwards, dissipating and morphing into the shape of a human form. It somehow seems familiar, but no sooner has it completed its formation as it is stretched into a thin vertical stream of more concentrated, intense radiance before shooting upwards at tremendous speed and disappearing through the crack in the black hole dominating the sky.

And then, through the purple haze, Catherine and Gill hear a piercing whine. An unnatural and disturbing cry is the only thing to escape from Nuvo as the sinister black form from the reeds snatches the alien back into the reeds at breakneck speed, his horizontal arm flying out towards them as if to call to them for help. But it is useless. As the reeds begin to spring back, Nuvo's white form becomes a minute speck in the distance before disappearing altogether. The pathway momentarily closes, before opening again, this time beating with the bang of the unremitting drum that berates the ear.

Gill feels a force coming between him and Catherine. His grip tightens on her and she throws him a look of sheer panic. They are aware of a presence creeping towards them. Instinctively, Gill moves to protect Catherine, fearing the worst; that some other force has come for them. Come for *her*. The oppression of the repeating booms all around them and a disorienting shimmering of light dancing on their eyes hamper Gill's ability to hear and see Catherine beside him. He thinks he can feel Catherine begin to convulse and immediately tries to get closer to control that, but the force splitting them is too great.

It is Gill who is convulsing. Sensing this, Catherine tries to turn towards him to see if she can hug him and bring it under control but the immense repulsion that comes between them forces her to roll the other way leaving a shimmering beam of light that now rests solely on Gill. It is Gill that is twitching all ways in the light, unable to control his body, open his eyes or turn his head towards his lovely Catherine. His body begins to rise up, the space underneath him totally black, as if the beam of light is picking him up. As Catherine witnesses this, the dread that fills her entire being chokes her vocal chords as she tries to scream. Nothing comes. 'Gill!!' she is shouting silently. 'Gill!! Gill!!' she tries to force her mind to connect with his mind, frantically trying to make contact to break the spell he is under and bring him back down to earth.

As he floats steadily upwards, body twisting and flinching as it floats away from Catherine, she screams insanely at Gill. 'Mister!! You get BACK here!!' she cries, as the frenzy of the drums marches ever onwards, louder and louder. Boom! Boom! Boom! Boom! There is no let up, and Catherine's screams seem to be deflected away from Gill's twisted torso.

Gill has lost all control of his motor functions. He is under the influence of a dark force that has not shown itself in the clearing, but is controlling everything around him. Inside, he is a seething mass of rage and torment as he feels himself losing Catherine and being manipulated so easily. His Samson-like strength and powerful abilities seemingly meaningless here, in this hallowed spot he so lovingly associates with Catherine and Beth. This is *their* spot. This is *their* place. Distant cries in his head sound like Catherine. It's his lifeline. He tries to find some space in his mind to focus on her beautiful face, her engaging smile and her marvellous eyes. The eyes that invite him to her world, her desire to be part of him and for their love to flourish until the end of time. As he thinks of the moment they came together for the first time, his heart skips a beat, and from afar Catherine can see his mouth open.

This time Catherine screams using her mind and her voice. The scream rings out around the clearing. "Gill!! Come back!!" she cries, her voice faltering as it struggles to be heard over the booming drums and rumbling thunder all around them. She sees Gill's body begin to angle upwards so that he is upright in the beam of light now. His entire body is encompassed in a cylindrical spotlight, like some superstar on the biggest stage in the world. It is an eerie sight. Catherine is trembling, sobbing helplessly as she sees her love, her only love, in front of her and looking straight at her.

"Gill," she lets out, quietly and through her tears. "Gill."

As Gill looks out at Catherine, he sees what he desires so overwhelmingly, so deeply, that the hurt shoots pain through him like a hot knife cutting butter. And with this he lets out a cry of his own.

"Aaaaagghhhhh!!" he exhales from inside the beam. And again. And again.

Catherine, seeing Gill is fighting, picks herself up, now freer to move outside the beam itself, but still immensely heavy and burdened with the gravity of the predicament. As she stretches every muscle, every sinew to reach out toward Gill and get him out of the light, an ominous sound of rustling comes from her right. It is the amplified rasp of ears of corn scraping against each other as a body carves its way through towards the clearing. Boom! Boom! Boom! Boom! come the footsteps behind, seemingly unburdened by the weight of the skies that press down on Catherine.

Where the solitary pathway opens to the clearing, a slow creeping red mist begins to seep out. Performing an eerie dance, it seems attracted to the light holding Gill. As it moves towards him, for a fleeting moment a finger juts out from this gas and comes right over to Catherine, stopping directly in front of her face. The gas forms the shape of a face. It is that of Ellis Garfield. And then it is that of Nuvo. And then it is that of another. Another like Nuvo, yet with a flaming red eye that shoots rays of daggers towards Catherine that penetrate her very soul and sear it dry with a branding iron.

"No!" she bursts out, as the finger retracts and the vortex of red gas shoots over to Gill. The beam of light turns red and begins to move towards the far side of the clearing. In this moment, Catherine feels like dying. She is losing Gill.

"Beth!" she cries. And again. "Beth!" And again. "Help us!" she wails at the top of her voice.

Out of the sky, a single star drops like a stone to the ground beyond Gill. Straight down, and instant. As it strikes the ground, the entire cacophony of sound that has been tormenting Gill and Catherine throughout, ceases. The only sound remaining is a low hum resounding around the skies.

The hue of radiating light from the star begins to puff up following its landing. As this billows out towards Gill and meets the fearsome red sword of light pinning him down, the interaction disrupts the beam. Catherine senses it is Beth. She has heard her cries. The disturbance in the waveforms diffracts the light and splays it at the bottom so that it forms a skirt around and underneath Gill, who is still suspended in mid-air.

Gill too senses Beth's presence. He is desperately trying to free himself. As his feet begin to feel free beneath him, he uses all his energy and willpower to create an upward wave of mobility to extricate himself from the light. As the external cloud of spreading light hits the boundary of the beam holding him, the hum all around them intensifies, and Gill feels himself being sucked down and into a chute. Although it seems there are only a few feet to the ground beneath him, he enters the chute and looks down at this feet to be confronted with a fractious array of dancing kaleidoscopic light. It is too much for his eyes to take and the nausea induced causes him to reel from side to side. He is about to die, he thinks. But he won't accept that. Desperately trying to hang on to an image in his mind to block out the overpowering shards of light stabbing his eyes, he remembers Beth's face.

She comes to him then. She is above him as they hurtle through the chute. He opens his eyes, and Beth is there. Amidst the chaos around him, Gill manages to see his sister for the first time in years. This, in itself, is a moment of living; a life-affirming vision. She smiles at him, and tells him to hold on.

From where Catherine is, she can see Gill begin to move slowly out of the light at an angle, prone as if being stretchered out of an ambulance. The low-pitch of humming begins to cause vibrations in the air to distort her view, but she can see that Gill's mouth and eyes have closed. Although she senses that Beth is here, she can't be sure where she is or what she is doing. Mustering some strength to move over to where Gill's body is being manoeuvred, tears running down her cheeks and oblivious to her own vulnerability, she reaches out for Gill's hand. Breaking the beam of light in the process burns her arm and she retracts, only to try again. The searing pain on her skin makes her scream, but she tugs at Gill's muscular arm as she tries to haul him back down to get away from the light beam.

As Gill looks at Beth, he can sense she is in pain too. Her comforting thoughts bely her struggle with the dark force that is approaching. Gill looks at her in silence. The enormity of the struggle between her and the force that holds him is evident in her, but she smiles as she helps bring him down to the terrain below. The ground feels closer as he thinks he can hear Catherine shout, but he can't hear what. And as the kaleidoscope outside begins to slow and come to a halt, he feels that the end might be in sight. Beth reaches in and closes his eyes, and he feels her leave him. She has done whatever she could do to help.

"Look at me! Gill!" Catherine is shouting at Gill, whose body is now hovering over at the far side of the clearing next to the darkened pathway. Catherine has hung on to his arm, trying to get him down, while being dragged across with him in the process. The beam of light that has brought him to the very edge of the clearing is now so weak and spread out that it collapses from above and, like a huge wave crashing down on top of them, the light soaks them both before spreading out all around them. Gill gets hit first and he crashes to the ground in a heap, with Catherine absorbing less of the impact but pressed down while the light dims and dissipates across the clearing.

As Gill gets up, he is disheveled, bruised, and blinking furiously to check for Catherine. They are both alive. They are both here. Above them, the flashes of lightning are less frequent, and now silent.

Moment by moment, sounds fade into the distance, and the entire field turns silent.

It is a beautiful silence. As Gill begins to focus on Catherine, she catches his eye. In the moment that follows, Gill is the happiest he has ever been. Catherine has helped him through the biggest ordeal of his life and somehow managed to involve Beth in this too. His gratitude, his admiration, his love, are radiating out to her in their special place. They are a perfect pair. Their duality is surely the most fantastic of couplings in the history of the Universe. And with this, he smiles his charming smile at her, and knows that her heart belongs to him.

Catherine feels two heartbeats inside her as she adores Gill. She smiles radiantly at him. And for the first time, Gill sends Catherine a thought.

'I love you' he says, with all his heart.

—-

Boom!
The silence is broken by a thunderous and plundering quake of the earth below them. Behind Gill the grating rustle of reeds slices through the darkness and out into the clearing, echoing around them, building to a crescendo. Before either can assimilate what is happening, the noise becomes unbearable and as they both flinch with the pain, an intensely dark red light bursts through the pathway entrance and Gill is engulfed by a glimmering speckled mist. As Catherine recoils and peers over towards the pathway entrance, she sees Gill's face through the haze. He is looking right into her eyes, and in him she sees the sudden realisation that he is in danger. As she desperately attempts to take the few steps to reach him, her body is weakened by the repulsive force of the thickening cloud around him. Her nightmare vision intensifies as the mist turns to black fog and wraps itself around Gill, swirling violently.

"No!" she screams. "No!"

But her cries of anguish become disembodied and futile chants of despair as a sickening nausea invades her.

And then it happens; behind Gill is a shadow. A black form, a negative of Nuvo who has come for him. The beautiful man that Catherine has come to love so profoundly in the last few days on Earth, vanishes suddenly into the black, his body becoming a tiny dot in the distance in a fraction of a second. As the speck of light that is Gill dims to black, the entrance to the pathway begins to close.

Catherine digs deep to force an almighty effort to follow him, but as she strains and stretches to clamber the few paces to the entrance, the gap shuts tight and the reeds spring up behind it. As she looks left and right for further pathways, there is only a uniform array of yellow in front of her.

The echoes of the rustling reeds float away into the far distance, and absolute silence returns.

Catherine is all alone. For a moment she believes it is a dream. That she will wake up and be beside Gill. That this has never happened. That this *couldn't* happen. She waits for some time; waiting for Gill to emerge through the reeds and back out into the clearing. But as she begins to feel heavy again, so too does her heart, and she breaks down, sobbing inconsolably.

——

As police and armed security services surround the warehouse outside Washington where Garfield's henchman Pratin Malic is holding Christophe Jumeau and Wendy Xiu hostage, Malic shouts to his boss through the door to the end room of the complex.

"Sir!", he yells with some urgency in his voice. "Sir! Are you in there, Sir?"

There is no response. His gun is still trained on Wendy Xiu and Christophe Jumeau, but it's beginning to waver, and they are suitably petrified at the prospect of a sudden over-reaction from the nervous and cornered thug.

"Don't move!" he tells them, with a manic look in his eye. They are absolutely still.

Malic knocks on the door. Nothing. And again. Nothing. Increasingly frustrated, he turns away from Christophe Jumeau and Wendy Xiu and enters the room. Garfield's chair is empty. The shock in Malic is evident; as it dawns on him that his superior officer has gone AWOL and that he is the only member of the crew holed up and under siege, his only bargaining chip will be the two hostages. He quickly turns back towards the door. But Christophe and Wendy are already running towards the stairs. As Malic scrambles out of Garfield's room, he manages to fire off a couple of shots which narrowly miss the Professor as he protects Wendy, his large frame shielding her from any fire.

As he gives chase, Malic diverts for a second into the main control room and picks up the master remote control, quickly keying in the passcode. His presence of mind and absolute adherence to protocols would be, in any other setting, admirable. As he rushes out and into the main corridor, he hears the sound of footsteps on metal. It is the iron staircase outside the main door that leads down to the huge hangar space below. The two hostages are escaping. He runs furiously to the end of the corridor and bursts out the front door. As he does so he sees Jumeau and Xiu nearing the bottom of the stairs. As he takes aim to fire directly into Christophe Jumeau's back, he is hit with the massive force of a 0.5 calibre bullet fired from the far side of the warehouse. It hits him square in the chest, and is followed by a 0.22 calibre bullet from a shorter-range pistol. The second bullet hits him in just below the knee, splitting the bone and causing him to buckle. As he goes down, Malic hits his head against the back rail of the iron stairhead and falls back against the main door to Garfield's hideout. As he takes his last few breaths, Malic hits the activating button on the remote, and an explosion is heard from inside the complex behind him. A massive orange plume of fire bursts out of the two long windows facing out into the warehouse space. Glass flies everywhere, and the intense heat of the explosion fans out high into the hangar. Christophe Jumeau and Wendy Xiu are cowering at the bottom of the stairs and are only saved from serious injury by being directly underneath and therefore avoiding the glass shards that splinter out across the main warehouse space.

Soon after, as the police help Wendy Xiu to a police patrol car, she looks around. There is no sign of Walter.

"Wendy?" It's Malcolm Baines. He has survived. Next to him, Daniel Faye lies with a gunshot wound straight though his temple, and several more dotted around his body. It looks like he was hit just before he was going to kill Malcolm.

"Mal!" Wendy cries as she rushes over to hug him so tightly he can't move his arms.

"Ouch", he says as she batters into his bruised ribs where Faye hit him with the butt of his gun, but still manages a smile.

Maria Ortega and Ava Redmond, who have arrived in a standard issue black Passat, rush across to accompany patrolmen and agents into the burnt-out office complex above the warehouse. A few minutes later they emerge looking serious. There is no sign of either Garfield or Melrose anywhere.

—-

Back at the police station, Christophe Jumeau is about to leave after several hours of questioning by senior police officers, Ava Redmond and Maria Ortega.

"We'll be in touch, Professor. And certainly do let us know if you hear from Professor Melrose. Our assumption at this stage must that he and Mr. Garfield are still out there somewhere," Ortega says.

"Yes, I'm sure they are out there. Somewhere," Jumeau responds with a look of resignation. "And my daughter and Detective Gill?" he enquires.

"We are looking into that, Sir. So far we have drawn a blank, but listen, on the flip-side there are no reports of anything else happening, so let's stay upbeat about this, and I'll give you a call when we get any news. How's that?" the duty Sergeant says in a chirpy manner designed to close off the conversation.

Ortega and Redmond throw each other a look, before Ava Redmond turns to Jumeau. "Professor, my advice is to listen to the radio for any news about the President, if you understand me?"

With a gentle smile, Christophe Jumeau takes his coat under his arm and heads outside into the late Spring sunshine.

Half an hour later, Christophe Jumeau is driving Wendy Xiu and Malcolm Baines back up to Boston. All three take turns every so often to call Catherine's cell phone. But each unanswered call makes them more anxious and knotted inside. Christophe has decided to keep much of the detail from the traumatized Xiu and Baines. They will need time to recover, he figures, and so, ironically, he gives them the same platitudes that he was given by the Sergeant back at the police station.

As time passes in the car, Christophe comes to the conclusion that Garfield's disappearance is, at one level, a good sign. It means that very possibly he has been able to return home. Jumeau realised of course that Garfield was at least part-alien. It all added up. But to what extent Gill and Catherine have been caught up in any spacetime travel is the more immediate unknown. Until he finds out Catherine is safe and well, he will remain fearful for her life. And in this moment he realises too that his fear for Catherine is automatically a fear for Gill, her partner.

On the radio, the news comes on. There is talk of the President's speech to the Senate on the issue of Defense, delayed due to security breaches reported last week. As the news bulletin comes to a close, 'Black and Gold' by Sam Sparro comes through the airwaves. Christophe Jumeau breathes deeply and allows himself a little grin. Not only is the news about the President what Redmond was referring to, but he remembers how much Catherine likes this song. Perhaps not a coincidence.

—-

There is a knock on the door of room twenty-three at the Parity Hotel on the outskirts of Washington. There is no reply. A louder knock this time.

"Service!" the voice shouts through the door.

Catherine stirs from a deep sleep. She comes to as the third knock on the door raps more insistently. She gets up and opens it only slightly. The maid outside is looking at her expectantly.

"Can you come back later, please?" Catherine asks, to which the maid nods shyly, assuming that the woman in twenty-three has been partying a bit too hard.

As Catherine flops back down on the bed, she looks at the clock. It is ten twenty-two in the morning. As if that mattered. Over on the table she can hear her phone vibrating against the glass surface. It eventually stops. As she floats back into semi-consciousness, lethargy and torpor taking hold, she relives the events at the clearing over and over in her head, eventually waking in a cold sweat. As she drags herself out of bed and across to take a shower, she can hear the phone vibrating again.

The warm droplets of water cascading down from the shower caress her body and form a protective cocoon from the outside world. She remains under there for half an hour, gradually sinking to the floor and curling up in a ball in the corner. Her tears are lost in the waterfall around her, but it feels like she is crying the waterfall all on her own. The hurt inside is so deep that it feels like she is being kicked, and her longing for Gill overpowers her whole being.

As she steps out of the shower and back into the hotel room, she looks at her phone. There are nine missed calls. From her mom and dad, from Wendy. She smiles. They are OK. A short while later she is outside Carlito's Car-Hire. As she walks down the street, her heart flutters as she reaches Gill's Oldsmobile. She gets in and breathes deeply. The smell of the old leather and air freshener sends a little rush of adrenaline through her, and she thinks of him as she starts the engine. She pulls out and onto the boulevard, stopping to fill the tank before taking the freeway north up through New York state and on to Boston towards Wendy and her parents, who are now back at their flat in Allston. As the miles drift by, Catherine turns on the stereo. It's Gill's favorite mix. Melody Gardot's poignant rendition of Bill Withers' song 'Ain't No Sunshine' is the first tune to come on. As tears form in her eyes as she listens to the words, the sun up above breaks through the cloud and shines directly down through the sunroof and onto Gill's sunglasses that are still lying on the tray under the stereo. As the rays of light flicker off the lenses and catch Catherine's eye, she reaches over and puts the glasses on. "Audrey", she mutters to herself, and a little smile takes her by surprise.

——-

In the canteen in the Heisenberg building at Harvard, Geoff Gregg, a young undergraduate studying quantum physics, sits down to watch the news during a short break from classes. The television is tuned to CNN, and Yusef Omar is reading the news.

"Good Afternoon, I'm Yusef Omar. The news this afternoon at three o'clock precisely. President John Montgomery today eventually delivered his long-awaited speech on Defense reform and funding at the Senate House in the Capitol Building. But only after what has been a series of delays. The speech, postponed from last week following a major security breach at the heart of government which warranted a thorough investigation of personnel and procedures at both the Capitol Building and the White House, was then *further* delayed by the disappearance of Vice President Ellis Garfield, reported yesterday by the Washington police.

In a related incident, the renowned professor of experimental physics at Harvard and long-time colleague and friend of Vice-President Garfield, Walter Melrose, has also been reported missing. Intense media speculation as to the whereabouts of both men has been circulating today as rumors abound that President Montgomery's office had intended to launch an investigation into Melrose's activities and state funding following the Defense speech today. Although no official statement has been made by the White House, Press Secretary Shammi Sarin told CNN that the President was, and I quote, 'very pleased with the response that the Senate offered to his proposals on Defense, and looks forward to receiving any news related to the on-going investigation into the disappearances of the Vice President and Professor Melrose'."

In the slight pause left after Omar's words ring out, the image switches to show a split screen with recent photographs of Garfield on the left and Melrose on the right. The picture of Garfield shows a man with a passing resemblance to John Montgomery, despite their different genetic backgrounds. Omar's voice comes in over the top of the picture as it switches to video footage of John Montgomery exiting the Senate House and talking to reporters.

"Despite concerns for the Vice President, President Montgomery seemed to remain upbeat as he left the Senate today. Our cameras were with him as he gave his thoughts on the day's business."

With this, the screen zooms in on John Montgomery who is talking to reporters. As he starts responding to questions, Gregg gets up and turns the volume down so that only the images remain. On the screen, there is a placeholder on the bottom left of the screen which says simply 'President John Montgomery' and on the bottom right is a clock, ticking away. Montgomery's face begins to fill the screen as the camera zooms in close. Geoff Gregg sits back down and takes a sip of his coffee, musing that all politicians seem much the same.

****

CHAPTER 12: AN END WITH A BEGINNING

Ryan Adams' words to 'Desire' float through Gill's car as if he is speaking directly to her. The penultimate song on Gill's mix on the stereo is as intense as Catherine can bear, and as the word 'Desire' resounds around her head, it proves too much and forces Catherine to shut off the music completely. She has no more tears left to shed, and the hollowness inside seems to be completed by the reminder that her one true romance has ended in separation.

As the Oldsmobile rumbles along the highway and reaches the edge of Boston, she gets a euphoric call from her father and they enthusiastically agree to meet at Catherine and Wendy's place.

"Dad!" she shouts as she runs up to Christophe Jumeau who is waiting just outside the record store underneath her apartment.

"Catherine," her father responds, holding out his arms as she approaches for a huge hug. They don't let each other go for a good thirty seconds, so delighted are they to see one another again. In the background, Josh, the record store owner, has put an old Gerardo Frisina track on the turntable.The wonderful breathy saxophone from 'Bluesanova' comes floating out into the street. It sounds like something Gill would play.

Eventually, Christophe suggests that they go up to the apartment and that he check the place out for her. The place seems to be just as Catherine remembers it, except the fridge magnet that warned her of Wendy's imminent danger, is nowhere to be seen.

"Bye, bye," she says.

Wendy has left Catherine a note to say she and Malcolm have gone to Malcolm's place, but will be in touch, so Catherine and

Christophe Jumeau make some tea and relax together in the large living room.

With great feeling, Catherine's father reflects on the last few days. "You realise, I didn't know whether I'd see you again. I had figured out most of what was going on, and just didn't know what you might have to do to work things out. I'm so relieved that you are OK, my dear Catherine. And your mother will be overjoyed when you come home."

Catherine smiles at her father. It seems like a lifetime ago that he turned up late at this very apartment and they went over to the Plaza hotel, and she reminisces that her father has visibly aged in those few days with all the worry and the ordeal he has gone through. As if to reassure him, she tells him that she'll travel with him back up to Montreal just as soon as she lets the police know that she is fine, and completes any questioning required. They talk for a few minutes about her experiences with Gill and the alien, her father becoming more intense and serious as she recounts events in the cornfield.

"Listen, some of what you've just told me makes me certain that we need some downtime to figure this thing out. Have you thought what you are going to tell the cops?" Jumeau senior asks.

"Oh, Dad, you know, I don't remember that much of what happened. Only that Gill and I went with Garfield to save Montgomery, and that somehow it worked," she replies.

"No, I don't mean that. I need hardly say this, honey, but no-one around here, including the authorities, know about your...your abilities. Do you see?" he says.

Catherine pauses. "How long have you known that I can do these things, Dad?' she asks him.

"I didn't," he states as he looks at Catherine, who appears skeptical. "Really. I didn't know. I mean, I didn't know that entanglement could be so pervasive. Even then, that entanglement is a property that can self-replicate doesn't mean people who are entangled *know* they are, or can super-position automatically. I guess because you were the experimenter, the scientist – the one outside the process – I always saw you as exempt from anything like that. I began to see things differently when you told me about what you saw in Garfield. Then Gill started asking me about entanglement and its connection to super-positioning. The fact that you were the only person who saw Garfield doing that made me think that such an observation would only have been possible if *you* had some kind of ability or insight yourself. But I was too afraid to open up that discussion." He gives Catherine a fatherly and concerned look.

"Dad, you don't need to worry about me. I have learnt a lot. I can control it. I guess when you said that abilities could be imprinted in stem-cells, I kind of thought you, or Mum..." she responds.

"I understand. I wish I knew how that stuff works, but I don't and I'm too old to bother. But seriously, honey, what about you - have you thought about what you are going to tell people?"

She takes a moment to herself, getting up and looking at the large Picasso on the wall before replying. "I don't know what I'd tell anyone. I wouldn't know where to start. All I want is to have Gill back. He is a good man, Dad, and I love him."

Christophe Jumeau smiles a relieved smile. "I know you do, my dear. But we must face facts. He is most likely with the aliens, or at least in some other alternative reality. We can spend some time together working out what to do, but right now it's probably best to keep things under your hat," he concludes, and throws his daughter a little knowing look which begs acknowledgement.

Catherine smiles an uncertain smile, and adds "I must go back to try and find him, Dad. You do realise this, don't you?"

"But not yet, honey. *Please*. We need to take a step back and think everything through. Knee-jerking won't help right now," he urges her.

With a heavy shrug of her shoulders, she enquires about her father's intentions. "And you? What about the ordeal you and the guys had to endure? Will you tell the police and the officials what Garfield was really trying to do?" she asks, looking at her weary and vulnerable father.

"I've already told them as much as they need to know. They won't be able to make anything better by knowing that Garfield was just a body housing an extra-terrestrial. If I were the alien, I would have done whatever I needed to try and get home too. It must have been an ordeal," he tells her.

Catherine remembers seeing the light emerge from Nuvo before he was snatched away, and sensing the release of a human being. "What about Montgomery, Dad? How did you know that he was

OK? How does the world know he is OK and not dead?" Catherine asks, struggling with the perception of time and how ordinary folks might deal with a change in history.

"It's strange. I mean, I heard on the radio today that Montgomery was giving his big Defense speech, and I knew right away that you and Gill had achieved what you wanted. I was incredibly happy because even though I remembered that Montgomery had been killed last week I knew you two changed history for the better. Then when I spoke to your mother, she didn't know what I was talking about. It's like that particular memory of Montgomery was just flushed away in her. Why I retained the memory, I don't know. Maybe it was to do with being so closely involved in events. I suspect only those who actually knew an alternative truth - that Garfield took John Montgomery's life - are the unique group who retain that memory and understand that a wrong has been righted. Those who had no information about Garfield's involvement, or the existence of Nuvo, will have their memories snapped at the point of Montgomery's survival. So, when, at the time of Montgomery's death a week ago, you changed history by preventing the malicious version of Garfield murdering Montgomery, so too the nation's collective memory acted as if nothing had happened, because actually it didn't in the end. No-one would feel any different, I think. I mean, you wouldn't be aware of the change because things would just be what they are - a natural 'truth' from the past like any other and you wouldn't give it a second thought."

"So all those people will just forget about the assassination? That sounds impossible; I mean, there was all the TV footage, the News, the papers?" Catherine puzzles.

"I don't think it works like that, Catherine. I'm not sure, because I haven't tested this yet, but I bet you won't find any newsreel or back papers that say anything about Montgomery's assassination, because when you changed history a week ago, everything from then on forms what we know and remember now. It's only a few of us who retain any information about that alternative reality, but even then I am not sure exactly why," the Professor states.

"Information cannot be destroyed," she mutters. Her father glances over at her and nods. She carries on, "I suppose it really depends on what you class as information," she says, just thinking out loud. "But it might be overwritten, or altered."

Her father rubs his eyes with his large fingers, seemingly to the point where there may be nothing left in the sockets. "Yes," he says softly. "Yes, that's it. It's like the hologram. If you change the source, then every fractured instance changes too. But we witnessed the source. Something about the reuniting of entangled pairs emulates the source, the original picture, the beginning. When you and Gill reunited, you brought particles together that came from a singularity – the source of information. So those who were explicitly active in the transformation of reality would see both the 'before' and 'after' versions."

Catherine seems to be engrossed in her own thinking. With a crease in her brow and a slight waver in her voice, she gets her thinking cap on. "It's not that it's emulated, Dad. Bringing entangled pairs together must create their own source. *Our* source. We can project the information from there outward, so that the ultimate reality becomes what we determine it to be," she concludes, and the two look at each other intently for a few seconds. The implications of what she has just said are profound. That the reuniting of particles - particles that originally split from each other at the horizon of a black hole or even further back to the beginning of the Universe - might allow for the reconfiguration of that very Universe; like starting a new instance. It's taking Christophe Jumeau's original postulation about the changing dimensions of time to the next level.

Catherine uses the natural pause in thought to go and refill her cup with hot water.As she comes back, she takes a different tack. "I guess I'm also thinking about all the implications if entanglement is possible at population level. We could witness a whole new breed of humans – the next evolutionary step. I know you must have thought this too. Don't we need to let the community know what we know?"

"Of course, but in time. Walter was too afraid to put his findings out into general circulation for fear of being ridiculed and losing his credibility and funding. If we just blurt out what we know without consideration for the implications – for you, us, for mankind - we will just be labeled as story-tellers at best - idiots at worst -and lose any chance to conduct credible research and pursue the truth scientifically. I think we are the foremost authorities on entanglement, super-positioning and spacetime travel, but we are probably the only ones who believe this right now," the Professor says.

"And all of Walter's most valuable research was lost in the fire at the warehouse?" she asks rhetorically. "Well, looks like it is down to us to conjure up some magic!" The unconvincing attempt at humor is lost on her father, who is now restless and gets up to join Catherine over at the window.

"It is astonishing, you know," he says as he scans the cityscape. "All this. Just one version of millions possible, changing with every action, every butterfly effect. And ugly. We are so ugly sometimes, Catherine. So much greed, so much crime. People stepping on other people to climb higher. Using all our resources too quickly. Maybe it needn't be like this. Potentially, out there, is another planet with air. With fertile land as far as the eye can see, and perhaps lots of room for humans to carve out a new life for themselves. Then again, it might be a terrible place, riddled with inequality, disease, famine, and crumbling under the weight of overpopulation. If I were your friend, 'Nuvo', I'd be reporting on what Earth is like to his people. And that might not be good for us if he thinks it is better here than it is there. Maybe we really have opened Pandora's box by letting others see into our world and by giving them a possible route to visit us."

Catherine stares at her father, letting his speculation settle for a moment. It scares her to think that she and Gill, by helping Nuvo to locate back to his own world, might have also opened up a causeway between there and here. A bridge that could be used to infiltrate our world. But of course that would presuppose that the aliens could dual. Certainly Nuvo could, yet he arrived here by error, regaining only a limited ability to dual locally on Earth. That suggests that his abilities were nascent. Yet the other dark presence in the cornfield... that force was strong. Whoever, *whatever*, that was, the menace there would surely stay with Catherine, haunting her.

"You think there could be some War Of The Worlds scenario here, Dad?" Catherine asks in a surprised tone.

"I don't know. You were the one in the line of fire with Gill before he was taken. What do you think?" he asks her.

"Well, it was Nuvo's shadow that dominated the entire area there. If that's Nuvo's entangled partner, then it scares me. It was an evil presence I know, and Gill was taken by it. I am so afraid for him. I think they may kill him and...." Catherine breaks down again, tears welling up in her eyes.

"Ssshhhh", Christophe Jumeau tells her as he puts his arms around her and holds her close. "It's alright, honey, we'll find him," he reassures. "Just promise me that you'll not do anything silly in the meantime, huh? No 'dualling' for now. Promise?"

He can feel Catherine agree. For now, she has talked enough, Christophe thinks. He holds her until her tears dry, then suggests she gets washed up and dressed as they are going out for dinner. Something, anything, to take her mind off Gill.

———

Maria Ortega, Abe Hart, Phil Kirkland and Mitch Nicolescu are in Briefing Room Two in the White House. There is little chat going on. Maria and Abe have grabbed some coffee and join the two security men around the large round mahogany table in the centre of the room. Phil and Mitch look on edge, as if they are about to undergo some sort of unwanted interrogation. Maria and Abe seem pensive, looking straight ahead at an empty chair as they cradle their coffee cups in their laps.

After a few minutes, the sharp, clicking sound of high heels reaches a crescendo outside the door, and Ava Redmond comes in and smiles at the group awaiting her.

"Gentlemen. Maria," she greets them. The group nod at different times to acknowledge the pleasantries are over.

"OK, we have a situation. A strange situation. And we need to resolve some outstanding issues, yes?" she says brightly, as if it is business-as-usual. But it is anything but.

Maria responds first. "Yes, everyone around this table is privy to some classified information, and my suggestion is that, first and foremost, we are clear on the level. In other words...." she says, as she turns to Mitch and Phil, "you two are clear that this is a level seven with no onward responsibility?" Kirkland and Nicolescu nod solemnly.

The level seven tag is the highest classification in government and military intelligence, and 'no onward responsibility' means that they are prohibited from discussing any aspect of the case with anyone else, not even the President of the United States or the Supreme Court. In other words, the level seven classification means that they take the information they have about the Garfield/Montgomery/Melrose situation to their graves. The reason Catherine and Gill are not mentioned in this discussion is largely down to Christophe Jumeau, and, before his disappearance, Walter Melrose. Neither man left much clue as to the significance of Catherine or Gill's involvement, and of course tracing Garfield's communications and whereabouts prior to his own disappearance will be practically impossible now that his complex has been burnt down and his remaining loyal agents are either dead or gone to ground.

There is another uneasy silence for a few seconds, before Abe Hart breaks into the vacuum with his thoughts.

"OK, listen, we all agree the classification. Ava, are we clear from any form of surveillance in here right now?" he asks. Redmond nods, throwing him a glance as if to say that this is a given in the current circumstances. Hart takes the cue to continue. "Right, whether we like it or not, we are the only ones who are aware of a change in circumstances in President Montgomery. I have checked before today's meeting, and there is no – repeat *no* – record of Montgomery's assassination anywhere. Not a trace. Now that is just bizarre, and frankly, it scares me. If it weren't for you guys reporting the same, I would be in an asylum right now."

"OK, Abe, calm down," Maria Ortega says. "Let's just think this through. According to Ava and our previous scenarios, we think it is possible that we all had some sort of collective hallucination about an alternative reality – a reality that was anything but real. It just didn't happen," she says.

"Except that Garfield and Melrose are now missing – how do you explain that?" asks Hart. "Is that part of what isn't real? I think that's pretty real to me."

"Abe, Maria. The situation at present is that we have President Montgomery back. The price seems to be that Ellis and Professor Melrose are no longer around. I think that's not such a bad deal," Redmond chips in.

"But you can't just shrug it off like that. This is the most significant paranormal event in the history of the United States and we are just going to file it away in one of your secret drawers? I don't think so," Hart responds defiantly.

"How do you know it is the most significant paranormal event in history?" Redmond challenges Hart, who looks blank for a moment, and then gives Redmond a quizzical look.

"You mean there are other events that are weirder than *this?* You gotta be kidding me – that's just ridiculous," Hart spits out.

Redmond doesn't answer directly, preferring instead to carry on with her thinking. "Look, it's almost as if the world doesn't remember anything about a week ago. That event – the assassination – has somehow been wiped from the collective memory. Maria, I think it's the other way around from your idea. I don't think any of us are hallucinating. We have the memory of what happened in the last week, and that somehow swapping Garfield for John was the price of getting John back. As soon as that swap happened, history was changed and everyone's memory became exactly what is should be – there was no assassination. We just lived in an alternative reality for a week – a vision of the future. A future none of us wanted. And guess what...it has been prevented, and we were all somehow part of that. That's why we have retained the memory when others haven't," she concludes.

"But why us?" Nicolescu suddenly pitches in. He is looking extremely worried.

Redmond gets up and clicks over to the French windows. She is silhouetted against the light and for a second looks like some sort of angel holding the key to salvation. "Why us, Mitch? I don't know. Because we happened to be the bit players supporting the main act. Because our jobs mean that we were always going to be the ones. Because we are the ones who worked out what was going on. Who knows? I wouldn't personalize it. It can only lead to dissonance in your head," she states.

Hart and Ortega look at each other and then back to Redmond. There is a sense of acknowledgement that, from a practical point of view – the point of view that allows people to get on with their lives and avoid descending into madness – everyone round the table needs to take a deep breath and stop over-analyzing the meaning of what has occurred.

Phil Kirkland, a seasoned veteran and long-time colleague of Nicolescu, breaks the silence following Redmond's reflections. "I think we have to think about the bigger picture here Mitch. Personally, I have no explanation as to why things happened the way they did, but I know I'm sure glad that John Montgomery is still our President. The bigger question is about Garfield and Melrose. Where are they now and could they be dangerous to the United States?" Kirkland's analysis is well-considered and relevant, and it stimulates Maria Ortega into some of her own speculation.

"You're right of course, Phil. We shouldn't be concentrating on Montgomery – he has no recollection of anything other than a hazy, stress-fuelled hallucination before he fainted in the washroom. But he remembers everything before, including questions being raised about Ellis and what he was up to with the Professor. No, this is about Garfield and Melrose. But you know, my take on this might give you some reassurance. I believe that Ellis and Melrose, even if they are holed up somewhere and nursing their wounds, will never be able to mount any sort of assault on the Presidency or anywhere else."

"And what makes you so sure, Maria?" Abe Hart asks.

Ortega puts her coffee cup on the table, and sits forward in her chair to get a little closer to Hart. "You know, Abe, the bottom line is that Ellis Garfield, and I suppose to a lesser extent Walter Melrose, is the most widely identified missing person on the planet right now. It's unprecedented that a Vice President of the United States just goes missing. Wherever he goes, he will be recognized. It will be impossible for him to escape that, and we'll find out where he is, without fail. Not only that, but if he tries his little trick of being in two places at once, he's *still* going to appear as Ellis Garfield. And, if Ava is right, anyone who witnesses him turning up somewhere unexpected will still report it, even challenge him right there and then," she states with convincing delivery.

"OK, but what about Melrose and his secret research. What about access to that and the possible implications?" Abe Hart comes back.

It's Redmond's turn to come in this time. "I think it's best if we shut that down short term. We might find something at the labs, but my suspicion is that we are not going to uncover anything significant. The information probably got lost with Melrose and the explosion at the warehouse. And if Melrose is still alive somewhere and trying to pursue his research, then we may just need to make sure we are ahead of him. We will obviously need to pursue this by making sure someone appropriate fills Melrose's shoes."

Ortega and Hart nod. Nicolescu does too, before adding "I think Garfield was probably sacrificed to let President Montgomery live..." he says, more to himself than anyone else. It causes a little stir in the group, but no-one takes on the possibility. It is pure conjecture at this point.

"So!" Ava Redmond exclaims, trying to find a way to wrap things up for now, "Under the class seven, nothing goes beyond here, and once I have documented the case and got a sign off – probably from you Maria – we are going to carry on with our jobs. We are going to do our jobs the best we can, as we have always done. And we are not going to have any more conversations about what might, or might not, have happened last week. Mitch, Phil - you need to operate the tightest security operation this country has ever seen around John Montgomery, you know that, right?"

Both men nod in agreement.

Redmond continues. "Maria, Abe, we will meet this evening to decide on any further security and intelligence protocols, and to discuss the implications of the re-appearance of either Garfield or Melrose. My department will, of course, continue to investigate our weird and wonderful world, like we do. Other than that, it is business as usual. We have important work to do, and people are relying on us to deliver. If anyone has, at any point, any urge to go running off and telling stories about alternative realities and people splitting into two to commit heinous crimes, you'll find no sympathy here, and probably end up in special care." Redmond's brash confidence and authoritative control of the situation is a role-playing coup. She has taken the part of leader, and used it effectively to give direction and focus back to colleagues in some disarray. At least for now.

———

Over the next few weeks, the national press continue to cover Montgomery's battle with both houses in the Capitol to drive through his reforms, and gradually Garfield's disappearance fades as new news takes its place. Walter Melrose's laboratories are searched from top to bottom and reveal little about the nature of the secretive research he and Garfield were undertaking. In his absence, the post of Head of Experimental Physics at the prestigious Heisenberg facilities becomes available. Christophe Jumeau considers applying, encouraged by colleagues, and most importantly his wife and daughter, who see it as a way to promote further legitimate research into large-object entanglement as well as what rightfully should be Jumeau's position – the foremost expert on advanced physics in the academic world.

A new Physics prize is announced internationally. It is the Schrödinger prize for outstanding contribution to the advancement of knowledge in the field of experimental physics. Wendy Xiu, Malcolm Baines and Catherine Jumeau all smile when they see the announcement in the papers.

Maria Ortega and Abe Hart keep their jobs, and flourish in the post-Garfield era, gaining in stature as the press begin to use Garfield as the absent whipping boy for some of the nation's woes as his dual-loyalties to Republican and Democrat parties become public and his involvement in secretive military research raises much speculation about his greed for power and the profits from sales of innovative technologies to the highest bidders. In a side-effect that could not have been foreseen, the top military brass have to confront a credibility gap as their generic reputation is impugned by a series of press investigations into the use of public funds for dubious and often arbitrary expenditure within army, navy and air forces. And in this, so John Montgomery gains a political edge over military chiefs and is both shrewd and disarming in his dealings with them.

Mitch Nicolescu and Phil Kirkland tighten security all around the White House and at the Capitol Building. Nicolescu has a brief period in counselling to cope with some of the 'pressures', using that time to explore his experiences in the confidentiality of secure and private sessions. Kirkland is the primary personal security contact for John Montgomery and has instigated a one-to-one communication system which Montgomery can use at any time to signal the need for intervention, with target response times less than five minutes anywhere in the United States.

Ava Redmond allocates a larger budget for CRUSE, the research outfit looking into the unexplained, and targets the increase specifically at an international search for reports of phenomena related to entanglement and super-positioning. She becomes aware of Catherine Jumeau's relation to Garfield through a more thorough investigation into the local police reports from Lieutenant Young at Boston Downtown precinct and an officer called Grady Jones who has filed a missing persons on the detective investigating the original Xiu and Baines disappearances. There is a file on her desk marked 'Jumeau/Gill' and underneath the title is a slider which, if pushed to the left, reveals the word 'CLOSED' and, to the right, 'OPEN'. The slider is to the right. Inside, clipped to the top of the sheet marked 'Case Overview' is a hand-written note written in Redmond's purple fountain pen, which says:

'Catherine Jumeau – call (Harvard main reception)'.

——

Sandra Chandry is on the front desk at the Downtown precinct in Boston. Outside, it is unusually warm. It is late August, early evening, Friday, and quiet. Chandry is reading a magazine. She looks up, believing that she has heard someone come through the door, but there is no-one there. She looks down again at her magazine. A second or two later, Lieutenant Young walks past and nods to her as he goes home early, hoping for a quiet weekend.

"Goodnight, Lieutenant," she says.

As the Lieutenant opens the front door, Sandra can hear a few words being exchanged before looking up to see a pretty young woman coming up the stairs, a little flushed. She is wearing a flowery skirt and a casual top which is stretched somewhat, revealing a slight distension of her stomach area. Chandry guesses that she is a few months pregnant.

"Yes, Miss?" she asks.

"Hi, my name's Catherine, I was here a few months ago with Detective Gill?" she says.

"Oh, yeh, I remember. I thought your face was familiar. What can I do for you, honey?" Sandra asks.

Gill has been missing for some months now, and this is the first time she has worked up the courage to revisit the station. "Well, I was just passing and I know it's a long shot, but I just wondered whether or not Detective Gill had any possessions which it might be OK for me to take as a memento?" she enquires.

"Aw, that's sweet. Is it his?" Chandry asks Catherine, looking down at Catherine's bump.

Catherine looks down, and runs her right hand over her stomach. "Oh! Oh yes, yes it is. That obvious, is it?"

Chandry has already developed a real soft spot for the young woman in front of her. As a single mother bringing up three children, she knows only too well what it's like to be alone without a partner. And in her own way she had been fond of Gill.

"Well...", Sandra says, trailing off and answering the original question, "The Feds came and took most of the stuff, but Gill's desk is much as he left it. And no-one else is big enough to sit in his chair, honey, so you go right ahead and have a look for yourself. There may be one or two bits and pieces there, and it might as well be you that gets a hold of them, for sure."

Catherine smiles. Officer Chandry is a kindly sort, if a bit stern in appearance, and she ushers Catherine through into the main office area. There are few people around, so Catherine walks purposefully over to Gill's shared desk and takes a seat. Only a few papers remain on his side of the desk. They turn out to be department memos that have just been piled there since Gill's desk became unused. There are three drawers underneath the right side of the desk unit, and she opens the top one. There is nothing in it. She opens the second. Nothing. And the third. Nothing. The drawers have obviously been cleared. Frustrated, she bangs the bottom drawer shut, and as she does so hears a 'clack' in one of them. Quickly, she opens first the top, then the middle. In the middle drawer, a key has appeared in the far left corner. It has white tape stuck to it, where it must have been affixed to the bottom of the drawer above. On the ring to which it is attached is a small grey plastic fob, unmarked.

She picks it up and looks at it. It's small, but sturdy. Looking around, there is no sign of any other compartment, but nevertheless she wanders around and over to some communal cupboards on the far side of the open office under the stairs. There are a couple of keyholes showing, but both cupboards are open. She tries the key in the hole just to see if one is meant for the other, but there is no fit.

One of the cleaners is coming down the stairs with some rags and a long brush.

"Excuse me."

"Yes?" says the cleaner.

"You wouldn't know where this key is for, would you? It's Detective Gill's and I'm his partner," Catherine asks.

"Let's have a look," the cleaner says, taking the key from Catherine and holding it up to the light. "Well, now, it's a small one, that. I think it must be for the lockers. They're through there, to the left as you go along the corridor."

"Thanks..." Catherine says as she immediately follows the pointed finger of the cleaner and hurries down towards the lockers.

As she enters the locker room, she realises she is alone. Looking along the rows of lockers she also realises that there is no number on the key. At the end of each row of lockers is a fob-detector, so she holds the key against the first one and it lights up the number twenty-two. She rushes over to number twenty-two and fumbles to get the key in the lock, excited and emotionally charged. This is Gill's locker, and she has the key. As she opens the locker, she gets a whiff of vanilla. Gill had put a jar of vanilla oil in there to keep it smelling nice. In the main compartment there is a dark grey, military-style overcoat and, below that, a basketball, a pair of basketball shoes and an umbrella. On the top shelf there is a dark blue basketball cap with the words 'Guard' on it, some CDs, a belt and a baton.

She goes through first the outside pockets of the coat. Nothing. Then the inner pockets. Nothing. Taking a deep breath, she decides that she is going to take the basketball cap for now and will come back for the rest. It is some form of keepsake. Something that she and her baby can always look at and conjure up Gill in an instant.

As she grabs for the cap, she can see a flash of white on the inside. She flips the cap over to reveal the inside lining. Just above the rim of the cap is a piece of paper jutting out. She sits down on the hard bench under the locker, removes the paper, unfolds it, and begins to read.

'Catherine, I hope you never get to read this. It's my note to you if I get lost somewhere along the way. By now, you will know what I do, and also why I do it. I will never rest until I find my sister, and until I have you completely. You will always be part of me, and I look forward to the day we can spend some more time together. All my love, G.'

A tear rolls down her cheek. For the first time in months of stoic appearances in front of the outside world, she gives in to sheer reminiscence and the memories he gave her, however short-lived.

She clutches the basketball cap to her chest. After some moments, Catherine decides to leave the police station, saying goodbye to Sandra Chandry on the way out. At the bottom of the stairs as she opens the door to the outside world, she looks back up at Sandra, who is smiling at her as she places Gill's basketball cap on her head. It's too big, and she looks a little silly. Sandra chuckles and they both smile at each other as Catherine wanders out onto the street outside.

As Catherine heads to the bus stop to get the bus back over to Allston and the flat that she and Wendy still share, she sees a sign outside Moynihan's Bar. It's advertising Gill's band, 'The Horizon'. They're playing inside, and she can hear saxophone. It's a version of Frisina's 'Bluesanova'. For a second she thinks it might be Gill. As she hurries into the bar and looks towards the stage, the band are in full swing, with a large figure with his back to the audience playing sax in front of the drummer.

"Gill!" she shouts though the music and the small crowd dancing to the bossa rhythm.

There is no response. As she peers through the red and purple lights coloring the stage, she sees that it is a tall black guy playing sax. As he turns around, he gives Catherine a friendly smile, not knowing why she is there or what her shouts are about. Her face shows her disappointment, and he loses interest, turning away to play to the band, wrapped up in the music.

Catherine turns and heads back to the main door. She would gladly down a beer or six right now if it were not for the new being that is growing inside and demanding so much of her.

As she waits for the bus, she looks up at the night sky. She can sense Gill. She knows he is out there, somewhere. She knows that her life is in limbo. That she must protect her child. Allow her child to develop. Gill's child. For he is inside her. He is all around her. And yet out of reach. All she wants is for Gill to return to her, to smile at her, to tell her that he is OK. To tell her that he loves her.

Stepping off the bus at Allston, it must be between eight and nine at night. The busker she remembers from the day the President was reported as assassinated is out on the street, this time playing

'Elizabeth, You Were Born To Play That Part' by Ryan Adams. It's beautifully sung, soulful, and poignant.

As she passes, he breaks into the instrumental coda. Instinctively, she grabs a five dollar bill and throws it into the young man's hat lying on the ground. Then hesitates, and puts another ten in.

"Gee, thanks!" he exclaims, clearly surprised and delighted with getting so much.

She throws him a big smile, and gently says "That's from the three of us."

# # #

ABOUT THE AUTHOR

Thank you for reading this book. I really hope you enjoyed it. I plan on continuing the saga if there is an appetite among my readers for more, so do please connect with me online if you like what you read.

Tipton Froy was born in Scotland quite a long time ago. He has studied natural sciences, sociology, psychology, music and languages, and traveled extensively. His writing reflects a quest to figure out the meaning of life.

Connect:
Mail: tipton.froy@gmail.com
Twitter: https://twitter.com/TiptonFroy
Smashwords: https://www.smashwords.com/profile/view/TiptonFroy
Amazon: http://www.amazon.com/dp/B088ZV4L33

www.ingramcontent.com/pod-product-compliance
Lightning Source LLC
Chambersburg PA
CBHW020225180626
46810CB00006B/2051